THE WORKS OF
CHARLES AND MARY LAMB

THE WORKS OF CHARLES AND MARY LAMB

Edited by E. V. Lucas

I. Miscellaneous Prose 1798-1834
II. Elia and the Last Essays of Elia
III. Books for Children
IV. Dramatic Specimens and the Garrick Plays
V. Poems and Plays
VI. and VII. Letters

The Life of Charles Lamb. By E. V. Lucas
Two Volumes. Demy 8vo.

[In Preparation

Charles Lamb. (aged 23)
From the drawing by Robert Hancock in 1798
now in the National Portrait Gallery.

THE WORKS OF
CHARLES AND MARY LAMB

EDITED BY

E. V. LUCAS

VOLUME V.

POEMS AND PLAYS

NEW YORK: G. P. PUTNAM'S SONS
LONDON: METHUEN & CO.
1903

PR4862
L7P

INTRODUCTION

THE earliest poem in this volume bears the date 1794, when Lamb was nineteen, the latest 1834, the year of his death; so that it covers an even longer period of his life than Vol. I.—the "Miscellaneous Prose." The chronological order which was strictly observed in that volume has been only partly observed in the following pages—since it seemed better to keep the plays together and to make a separate section of Lamb's epigrams. These, therefore, will be found to be outside the general scheme. Such of Lamb's later poems as he did not himself collect in volume form will also be found to be out of their chronological position, partly because it has seemed to me best to give prominence to those verses which Lamb himself reprinted, and partly because there is often no indication of the year in which the poem was written.

Another difficulty has been the frequency with which Lamb reprinted some of his earlier poetry. The text of many of his earliest and best poems was not fixed until 1818, twenty years or so after their composition. It had to be decided whether to print these poems in their true order as they were first published—in Coleridge's *Poems on Various Subjects*, 1796; in Charles Lloyd's *Poems on the Death of Priscilla Farmer*, 1796; in Coleridge's *Poems*, second edition, 1797; in *Blank Verse* by Charles Lloyd and Charles Lamb, 1798; and in *John Woodvil*, 1802—with all their early readings; or whether to disregard chronological sequence, and wait until the time of the *Works*—1818—had come, and print them all together then. I decided, in the interests of their biographical value, to print them in the order as they first appeared, particularly as Crabb Robinson tells us (*Diary*, second edition, II., 319) that Lamb once said of the arrangement of a poet's works: "There is only one good order— and that is the order in which they were written—that is, a history of the poet's mind." It then had to be decided whether to print them in their first shape, which, unless I repeated them later, would mean the relegation of Lamb's final text to the Notes, or to print them, at the expense of a slight infringement upon the chronological scheme, in their final 1818 state, and relegate all earlier readings to the Notes. After much deliberation I decided that to print them in their final 1818 state was best. I would therefore urge upon the reader of this volume the importance of taking, in the earlier pages at any rate, text and notes together.

In order, however, that the scheme of Lamb's 1818 edition of his *Works* might be preserved, I have indicated in the text the position in the *Works* occupied by all the poems that in the present volume have been printed earlier.

The chronological order, in so far as it has been followed, emphasises the dividing line between Lamb's poetry and his verse. As he grew older his poetry, for the most part, passed into his prose. His best and truest poems, with few exceptions, belong to the years before, say, 1805, when he was thirty. After this, following a long interval of silence, came the brief satirical outburst of 1812, in *The Examiner*, and the longer one, in 1820, in *The Champion*; then, after another interval, during which he was busy as Elia, came the period of album verses, which lasted to the end. The impulse to write personal prose, which was quickened in Lamb by the *London Magazine* in 1820, seems to have taken the place of his old ambition to be a poet. In his later and more mechanical period there were, however, occasional inspirations, as when he wrote the sonnet on "Work," in 1819; on "Leisure," in 1821; the lines in his own Album, in 1827, and, pre-eminently, the poem "On an Infant Dying as Soon as Born," in 1827. Lamb seems never quite to have satisfied himself that it was not in him to write successfully for the stage.

In addition to the poems by which Lamb is known this volume

INTRODUCTION

contains several others, for the most part album verses and acrostics, now printed for the first time, or for the first time collected together with Lamb's other work. For permission to use certain poems I am indebted to Mrs. Alfred Morrison, Miss Kendall and Mr. Augustus De Morgan. I have also to thank Mrs. Dykes Campbell and the editor of *The Athenæum* for the privilege of transferring the late Mr. Dykes Campbell's invaluable notes on *John Woodvil* to these pages.

In the autograph room of the British Museum is a manuscript (Add. MSS., 25,924) attributed to Lamb. It was bequeathed by Lamb's friend, P. G. Patmore, and was believed by him, as he explained in *My Friends and Acquaintances*, 1856, to be Lamb's work, in conjunction with the Sheridans, with whom, according to a letter from Mary Lamb to Sarah Stoddart, Lamb collaborated some time in the first decade of the last century. That collaboration, however, if it ever came to anything, was concerned, to use her own words, with a "speaking pantomime;" and this is comic opera pure and simple. Another alleged proof of Lamb's authorship lies in the Lamb-like character of the handwriting; but here again it is possible to differ from Patmore. As I do not share the view that Lamb was the author, and as the handwriting does not seem to me to be his, the play is omitted from this edition: it may be found by the curious in the late Mr. Charles Kent's Century edition of Lamb's writings. The catalogue of the autographs in the British Museum also attributes to Lamb a tragedy, signed John Patteshull, entitled "The Dissolution of the Roman Empire," but there seems to me no reason at all, beyond a superficial resemblance between the writing of Patteshull and Lamb, to permit this attribution to stand. The play is therefore omitted from this edition, nor has it been printed elsewhere.

This volume contains, with the exception of the verse for children, which will be found in Vol. III. of this edition, all the accessible poetical work of Charles and Mary Lamb that is known to exist. Two short poems, however (one of much charm), I have not been able to print, owing to the unwillingness of the owners of the Album in which they were written; and there are probably several other copies of album verses which have not yet seen the light. In the *London Magazine*, April, 1824, is a story entitled "The Bride of Modern Italy," which has for motto the following couplet :—

> My heart is fixt :
> This is the sixt.—*Elia*.

but the rest of what seems to be a pleasant catalogue is missing. In a letter to Coleridge, December 2, 1796, Lamb refers to a poem which has apparently perished, beginning, "Laugh, all that weep." In the Appendix to Vol. I. will be found a translation which Lamb possibly wrote of Gray's Alcaic ode "Oh tu, severi relligio loci." I have left in the Correspondence the rhyming letter to William Ayrton of May 17, 1817, and an epigram on "Cœlebs in Search of a Wife."

I have placed the dedication to Coleridge at the beginning of this volume, although it belongs properly only to those poems that are reprinted from the *Works* of 1818, the prose of which Lamb offered to Martin Burney. But it is too fine to be put among the Notes, and it may easily, by a pardonable stretch, be made to refer to the whole body of Lamb's poetical and dramatic work, although *Album Verses*, 1830, was dedicated separately to Edward Moxon.

The portrait which serves as frontispiece to this volume is from a drawing, preserved in the National Portrait Gallery, by Robert Hancock, made in 1798, when Lamb was twenty-three.

E. V. L.

May, 1903

CONTENTS

* The poems marked with one asterisk are now for the first time collected with Lamb's writings.

** The poems marked with two asterisks are now for the first time publicly identified as Lamb's.

	PAGE
Dedication	1
Poems in Coleridge's *Poems on Various Subjects*, 1796:—	
"As when a child..."	3
"Was it some sweet device..."	3
"Methinks how dainty sweet..."	4
"O! I could laugh..."	4
From Charles Lloyd's *Poems on the Death of Priscilla Farmer*, 1796:—	
The Grandame	5
Poems from Coleridge's *Poems*, 1797:—	
"When last I roved..."	7
"A timid grace..."	7
"If from my lips..."	8
"We were two pretty babes..."	8
Childhood	8
The Sabbath Bells	9
Fancy Employed on Divine Subjects	9
The Tomb of Douglas	9
To Charles Lloyd	11
A Vision of Repentance	12
Poems Written in the Years 1795-98, and not Reprinted by Lamb from Periodicals:—	
"The Lord of Life..."	14
To the Poet Cowper	14
Lines addressed to Sara and S. T. C.	15
Sonnet to a Friend	16
*To a Young Lady	16
Living Without God in the World	17
Poems from *Blank Verse*, by Charles Lloyd and Charles Lamb, 1798:—	
To Charles Lloyd	19
Written on the Day of My Aunt's Funeral	19
Written a Year After the Events	20

CONTENTS

	PAGE
Written Soon After the Preceding Poem	22
Written on Christmas Day, 1797	22
The Old Familiar Faces	23
Composed at Midnight	24

Poems at the End of *John Woodvil*, 1802 :—

Helen. By Mary Lamb	26
Ballad. From the German	27
Hypochondriacus	27
A Ballad Noting the Difference of Rich and Poor	28

Poems in Charles Lamb's *Works*, 1818, not Previously Printed in the Present Volume :—

Hester	30
Dialogue Between a Mother and Child. By Mary Lamb	31
A Farewell to Tobacco	32
To T. L. H.	35
Salome. By Mary Lamb	36
Lines Suggested by a Picture of Two Females by Lionardo da Vinci. By Mary Lamb	38
Lines on the Same Picture being Removed. By Mary Lamb	38
Lines on the Celebrated Picture by Lionardo da Vinci, called "The Virgin of the Rocks"	39
On the Same. By Mary Lamb	39
To Miss Kelly	40
On the Sight of Swans in Kensington Garden	40
The Family Name	41
To John Lamb, Esq.	41
To Martin Charles Burney, Esq.	42

Poems in *Album Verses*, 1830 :—

Album Verses :—

In the Album of a Clergyman's Lady	43
In the Autograph Book of Mrs. Sergeant W——	43
In the Album of Lucy Barton	44
In the Album of Miss ——	44
In the Album of a very Young Lady	45
In the Album of a French Teacher	45
In the Album of Miss Daubeny	46
In the Album of Mrs. Jane Towers	47
In My Own Album	47

Miscellaneous :—

Angel Help	48
The Christening	49
On an Infant Dying as Soon as Born	49
To Bernard Barton	51
The Young Catechist	52
She is Going	53
To a Young Friend	53
To the Same	54

CONTENTS

	PAGE
Sonnets:—	
Harmony in Unlikeness	54
Written at Cambridge	55
To a Celebrated Female Performer in the "Blind Boy"	55
Work	55
Leisure	56
To Samuel Rogers, Esq.	56
The Gipsy's Malison	57
Commendatory Verses:—	
To the Author of Poems Published under the Name of Barry Cornwall	57
To R. S. Knowles, Esq.	58
To the Editor of the *Every-Day Book*	58
Acrostics:—	
To Caroline Maria Applebee	59
To Cecilia Catherine Lawton	60
Acrostic, to a Lady who Desired Me to Write Her Epitaph	60
Another, to Her Youngest Daughter	61
Translations from the Latin of Vincent Bourne:—	
On a Sepulchral Statue of an Infant Sleeping	61
The Rival Bells	62
Epitaph on a Dog	62
The Ballad Singers	63
To David Cook	64
On a Deaf and Dumb Artist	65
Newton's Principia	66
The House-keeper	66
The Female Orators	67
Pindaric Ode to the Tread Mill	67
Going or Gone	70
Poems in *The Poetical Works of Charles Lamb*, 1836:—	
In the Album of Edith S——	73
To Dora W——.	73
In the Album of Rotha Q——	74
In the Album of Catherine Orkney	74
To T. Stothard, Esq.	75
To a Friend on His Marriage	75
The Self-Enchanted	76
To Louisa M——, whom I used to call "Monkey"	76
Cheap Gifts: a Sonnet	77
Free Thoughts on Several Eminent Composers	77
Miscellaneous Poems:—	
*Dramatic Fragment	79
*Epitaph on a Young Lady	80
The Ape	80
In tabulam eximii pictoris B. Haydoni	82

CONTENTS

	PAGE
Translation of Same	82
*Sonnet to Miss Burney	82
To My Friend the Indicator	83
*To Emma, Learning Latin, and Desponding	83
Lines Addressed to Lieut. R. W. H. Hardy, R.N.	84
*Lines for a Monument	84
To C. Aders, Esq.	85
Hercules Pacificatus	85
The Parting Speech of the Celestial Messenger to the Poet	88
Existence, Considered in Itself, no Blessing	89
*To Samuel Rogers, Esq.	90
To Clara N——	90
To Margaret W——	91

Additional Album Verses and Acrostics :—

What is an Album ?	92
The First Leaf of Spring	92
To Mrs. F——	93
To M. L—— F——	94
To Esther Field	94
To Mrs. Williams	94
To the Book	95
*To S. F.	96
To R. Q.	96
To S. L.	96
To M. L.	97
*An Acrostic Against Acrostics	97
On Being Asked to Write in Miss Westwood's Album	97
In Miss Westwood's Album. By Mary Lamb	98
*The Sisters	98
*To Sarah James of Beguildy	374

Eight Poems by Charles Lamb now Printed for the First Time :—

**Un Solitaire	99
**To S. T.	99
**To Mrs. Sarah Robinson	100
**To Sarah	100
**Acrostic	100
**To D. A.	101
**To Louisa Morgan	101
**Love Will Come	374

Political and Other Epigrams :—

To Sir James Mackintosh	102

Twelfth Night Characters :—

*Mr. A——	102
*Messrs. C——g and F——e	102

Epigrams :—

**"Princeps his rent . . ."	102
"Ye Politicians, tell me, pray . . ."	103

CONTENTS

	PAGE
The Triumph of the Whale	103
Sonnet. St. Crispin to Mr. Gifford	104
The Godlike	104
The Three Graves	105
Sonnet to Mathew Wood, Esq.	105
On a Projected Journey	106
On a Late Empiric of "Balmy" Memory	106
Song for the C———n	106
The Unbeloved	106
**On the Arrival in England of Lord Byron's Remains	107
Lines Suggested by a Sight of Waltham Cross	107
*For the *Table Book*	108
**The Royal Wonders	108
"Brevis Esse Laboro"	108
Suum Cuique	109
*On the *Literary Gazette*	109
*On the Fast-Day	109
Nonsense Verses	109
Satan in Search of a Wife	110
Part I.	111
Part II.	116
Prologues and Epilogues:—	
Epilogue to Godwin's Tragedy of "Antonio"	121
Prologue to Godwin's Tragedy of "Faulkener"	123
*Epilogue to Henry Siddons' Farce, "Time's a Tell-Tale"	123
Prologue to Coleridge's Tragedy of "Remorse"	125
*Epilogue to Kenney's Farce, "Debtor and Creditor"	126
Epilogue to an Amateur Performance of "Richard II."	128
*Prologue to Sheridan Knowles' Comedy, "The Wife"	129
Epilogue to Sheridan Knowles' Comedy, "The Wife"	130
John Woodvil	131
The Witch	177
Mr. H———	180
The Pawnbroker's Daughter	212
The Wife's Trial	243
NOTES	275
INDEX	377
INDEX OF FIRST LINES	385

ILLUSTRATIONS

Charles Lamb, aged 23 (after the drawing by Robert Hancock) . *Frontispiece*

ILLUSTRATIONS IN THE NOTES

Title-page of Coleridge's *Poems on Various Subjects*, 1796 .	To face page	276
Title-page of Lloyd's *Poems on the Death of Priscilla Farmer*, 1796	,, ,,	280
Title-page of Coleridge's *Poems*, 1797	,, ,,	282
Title-page of Lloyd and Lamb's *Blank Verse*, 1798 . . .	,, ,,	290
Title-page of Lamb's *John Woodvil*, 1802	,, ,,	294
Title-page of Lamb's *Works*, 1818	,, ,,	296
Hester Savory	,, ,,	298
Da Vinci's " Modestas et Vanitas "	,, ,,	300
Da Vinci's " The Virgin of the Rocks "	,, ,,	302
Title-page of Lamb's *Album Verses*, 1830	,, ,,	304
The picture sent by Lamb to Bernard Barton . . .	,, ,,	308
Haydon's " Christ's Entry into Jerusalem " . . .	,, ,,	324
Title-page of *Poetical Recreations of " The Champion,"* 1822 .	,, ,,	330
Title-page of Lamb's *Satan in Search of a Wife*, 1831 .	,, ,,	344
Frontispiece to *Satan in Search of a Wife* . . .	,, ,,	346
Illustration from Part I., *Satan in Search of a Wife* .	,, ,,	348
Frontispiece to Part II., *Satan in Search of a Wife* .	,, ,,	350
Illustration from Part II., *Satan in Search of a Wife* .	,, ,,	352
Tailpiece to *Satan in Search of a Wife*	,, ,,	354
The play-bill of " Mr. H."	,, ,,	368
Title-page of " Mr. H." (American Edition) . . .	,, ,,	370

DEDICATION

(1818)

TO S. T. COLERIDGE, ESQ.

MY DEAR COLERIDGE,
You will smile to see the slender labors of your friend designated by the title of *Works;* but such was the wish of the gentlemen who have kindly undertaken the trouble of collecting them, and from their judgment could be no appeal.

It would be a kind of disloyalty to offer to any one but yourself a volume containing the *early pieces,* which were first published among your poems, and were fairly derivatives from you and them. My friend Lloyd and myself came into our first battle (authorship is a sort of warfare) under cover of the greater Ajax. How this association, which shall always be a dear and proud recollection to me, came to be broken,—who snapped the three-fold cord,—whether yourself (but I know that was not the case) grew ashamed of your former companions,—or whether (which is by much the more probable) some ungracious bookseller was author of the separation, —I cannot tell;—but wanting the support of your friendly elm, (I speak for myself,) my vine has, since that time, put forth few or no fruits; the sap (if ever it had any) has become, in a manner, dried up and extinct; and you will find your old associate, in his second volume, dwindled into prose and *criticism.*

Am I right in assuming this as the cause? or is it that, as years come upon us, (except with some more healthy-happy spirits,) Life itself loses much of its Poetry for us? we transcribe but what we read in the great volume of Nature; and, as the characters grow dim, we turn off, and look another way. You yourself write no Christabels, nor Ancient Mariners, now.

Some of the Sonnets, which shall be carelessly turned over by the general reader, may happily awaken in you remembrances, which I should be sorry should be ever totally extinct—the memory

Of summer days and of delightful years—

DEDICATION

even so far back as to those old suppers at our old * * * * * * * * * * Inn,—when life was fresh, and topics exhaustless,—and you first kindled in me, if not the power, yet the love of poetry, and beauty, and kindliness.—

> What words have I heard
> Spoke at the Mermaid!

The world has given you many a shrewd nip and gird since that time, but either my eyes are grown dimmer, or my old friend is the *same*, who stood before me three and twenty years ago—his hair a little confessing the hand of time, but still shrouding the same capacious brain,—his heart not altered, scarcely where it "alteration finds."

One piece, Coleridge, I have ventured to publish in its original form, though I have heard you complain of a certain over-imitation of the antique in the style. If I could see any way of getting rid of the objection, without re-writing it entirely, I would make some sacrifices. But when I wrote John Woodvil, I never proposed to myself any distinct deviation from common English. I had been newly initiated in the writings of our elder dramatists; Beaumont and Fletcher, and Massinger, were then a *first love;* and from what I was so freshly conversant in, what wonder if my language imperceptibly took a tinge? The very *time*, which I have chosen for my story, that which immediately followed the Restoration, seemed to require, in an English play, that the English should be of rather an older cast, than that of the precise year in which it happened to be written. I wish it had not some faults, which I can less vindicate than the language.

I remain,
My dear Coleridge,
Your's,
With unabated esteem,
C. LAMB.

POEMS IN COLERIDGE'S *POEMS ON VARIOUS SUBJECTS*, 1796

(Written late in 1794. Text of 1797)

AS when a child on some long winter's night
 Affrighted clinging to its Grandam's knees
With eager wond'ring and perturb'd delight
Listens strange tales of fearful dark decrees
Mutter'd to wretch by necromantic spell;
Or of those hags, who at the witching time
Of murky midnight ride the air sublime,
And mingle foul embrace with fiends of Hell:
Cold Horror drinks its blood! Anon the tear
More gentle starts, to hear the Beldame tell
Of pretty babes, that lov'd each other dear,
Murder'd by cruel Uncle's mandate fell:
Ev'n such the shiv'ring joys thy tones impart,
Ev'n so thou, SIDDONS! meltest my sad heart!

(Probably 1795. Text of 1818)

Was it some sweet device of Faery
That mocked my steps with many a lonely glade,
And fancied wanderings with a fair-hair'd maid?
Have these things been? or what rare witchery,
Impregning with delights the charmed air,
Enlighted up the semblance of a smile
In those fine eyes? methought they spake the while
Soft soothing things, which might enforce despair
To drop the murdering knife, and let go by
His foul resolve. And does the lonely glade
Still court the foot-steps of the fair-hair'd maid?
Still in her locks the gales of summer sigh?
While I forlorn do wander reckless where,
And 'mid my wanderings meet no Anna there.

(Probably 1795.   *Text of* 1818)

Methinks how dainty sweet it were, reclin'd
Beneath the vast out-stretching branches high
Of some old wood, in careless sort to lie,
Nor of the busier scenes we left behind
Aught envying.   And, O Anna! mild-eyed maid!
Beloved! I were well content to play
With thy free tresses all a summer's day,
Losing the time beneath the greenwood shade.
Or we might sit and tell some tender tale
Of faithful vows repaid by cruel scorn,
A tale of true love, or of friend forgot;
And I would teach thee, lady, how to rail
In gentle sort, on those who practise not
Or love or pity, though of woman born.

(1794.   *Text of* 1818)

O! I could laugh to hear the midnight wind,
That, rushing on its way with careless sweep,
Scatters the ocean waves.   And I could weep
Like to a child.   For now to my raised mind
On wings of winds comes wild-eyed Phantasy,
And her rude visions give severe delight.
O winged bark! how swift along the night
Pass'd thy proud keel! nor shall I let go by
Lightly of that drear hour the memory,
When wet and chilly on thy deck I stood,
Unbonnetted, and gazed upon the flood,
Even till it seemed a pleasant thing to die,—
To be resolv'd into th' elemental wave,
Or take my portion with the winds that rave.

FROM CHARLES LLOYD'S *POEMS ON THE DEATH OF PRISCILLA FARMER*, 1796

THE GRANDAME

(Summer, 1796. *Text of* 1818)

      On the green hill top,
Hard by the house of prayer, a modest roof,
And not distinguish'd from its neighbour-barn,
Save by a slender-tapering length of spire,
The Grandame sleeps. A plain stone barely tells
The name and date to the chance passenger.
For lowly born was she, and long had eat,
Well-earned, the bread of service:—her's was else
A mounting spirit, one that entertained
Scorn of base action, deed dishonorable,
Or aught unseemly. I remember well
Her reverend image: I remember, too,
With what a zeal she served her master's house;
And how the prattling tongue of garrulous age
Delighted to recount the oft-told tale
Or anecdote domestic. Wise she was,
And wondrous skilled in genealogies,
And could in apt and voluble terms discourse
Of births, of titles, and alliances;
Of marriages, and intermarriages;
Relationship remote, or near of kin;
Of friends offended, family disgraced—
Maiden high-born, but wayward, disobeying
Parental strict injunction, and regardless
Of unmixed blood, and ancestry remote,
Stooping to wed with one of low degree.
But these are not thy praises; and I wrong
Thy honor'd memory, recording chiefly
Things light or trivial. Better 'twere to tell,
How with a nobler zeal, and warmer love,
She served her *heavenly master*. I have seen

That reverend form bent down with age and pain
And rankling malady.   Yet not for this
Ceased she to praise her maker, or withdrew
Her trust in him, her faith, and humble hope—
So meekly had she learn'd to bear her cross—
For she had studied patience in the school
Of Christ, much comfort she had thence derived,
And was a follower of the NAZARENE.

POEMS FROM COLERIDGE'S *POEMS*, 1797

(Summer, 1795.   Text of 1818)

WHEN last I roved these winding wood-walks green,
    Green winding walks, and shady pathways sweet,
Oft-times would Anna seek the silent scene,
Shrouding her beauties in the lone retreat.
No more I hear her footsteps in the shade:
Her image only in these pleasant ways
Meets me self-wandering, where in happier days
I held free converse with the fair-hair'd maid.
I passed the little cottage which she loved,
The cottage which did once my all contain;
It spake of days which ne'er must come again,
Spake to my heart, and much my heart was moved.
"Now fair befall thee, gentle maid!" said I,
And from the cottage turned me with a sigh.

(1795 or 1796.   Text of 1818)

A timid grace sits trembling in her eye,
As loth to meet the rudeness of men's sight,
Yet shedding a delicious lunar light,
That steeps in kind oblivious ecstasy
The care-crazed mind, like some still melody:
Speaking most plain the thoughts which do possess
Her gentle sprite: peace, and meek quietness,
And innocent loves, and maiden purity:
A look whereof might heal the cruel smart
Of changed friends, or fortune's wrongs unkind;
Might to sweet deeds of mercy move the heart
Of him who hates his brethren of mankind.
Turned are those lights from me, who fondly yet
Past joys, vain loves, and buried hopes regret.

POEMS FROM COLERIDGE'S *POEMS*, 1797

(End of 1795. Text of 1818)

If from my lips some angry accents fell,
Peevish complaint, or harsh reproof unkind,
'Twas but the error of a sickly mind
And troubled thoughts, clouding the purer well,
And waters clear, of Reason ; and for me
Let this my verse the poor atonement be—
My verse, which thou to praise wert ever inclined
Too highly, and with a partial eye to see
No blemish. Thou to me didst ever shew
Kindest affection ; and would oft-times lend
An ear to the desponding love-sick lay,
Weeping my sorrows with me, who repay
But ill the mighty debt of love I owe,
Mary, to thee, my sister and my friend.

(1795. Text of 1818)

We were two pretty babes, the youngest she,
The youngest, and the loveliest far, I ween,
And INNOCENCE her name. The time has been,
We two did love each other's company ;
Time was, we two had wept to have been apart.
But when by show of seeming good beguil'd,
I left the garb and manners of a child,
And my first love for man's society,
Defiling with the world my virgin heart—
My loved companion dropped a tear, and fled,
And hid in deepest shades her awful head.
Beloved, who shall tell me where thou art—
In what delicious Eden to be found—
That I may seek thee the wide world around ?

CHILDHOOD

(Summer, 1796. Text of 1818)

In my poor mind it is most sweet to muse
Upon the days gone by ; to act in thought
Past seasons o'er, and be again a child ;
To sit in fancy on the turf-clad slope,
Down which the child would roll ; to pluck gay flowers,
Make posies in the sun, which the child's hand,
(Childhood offended soon, soon reconciled,)
Would throw away, and strait take up again,
Then fling them to the winds, and o'er the lawn
Bound with so playful and so light a foot,
That the press'd daisy scarce declined her head.

THE SABBATH BELLS
(Summer, 1796. *Text of* 1818)

The cheerful sabbath bells, wherever heard,
Strike pleasant on the sense, most like the voice
Of one, who from the far-off hills proclaims
Tidings of good to Zion: chiefly when
Their piercing tones fall *sudden* on the ear
Of the contemplant, solitary man,
Whom thoughts abstruse or high have chanced to lure
Forth from the walks of men, revolving oft,
And oft again, hard matter, which eludes
And baffles his pursuit—thought-sick and tired
Of controversy, where no end appears,
No clue to his research, the lonely man
Half wishes for society again.
Him, thus engaged, the sabbath bells salute
Sudden! his heart awakes, his ears drink in
The cheering music; his relenting soul
Yearns after all the joys of social life,
And softens with the love of human kind.

FANCY EMPLOYED ON DIVINE SUBJECTS
(Summer, 1796. *Text of* 1818)

The truant Fancy was a wanderer ever,
A lone enthusiast maid. She loves to walk
In the bright visions of empyreal light,
By the green pastures, and the fragrant meads,
Where the perpetual flowers of Eden blow;
By chrystal streams, and by the living waters,
Along whose margin grows the wondrous tree
Whose leaves shall heal the nations; underneath
Whose holy shade a refuge shall be found
From pain and want, and all the ills that wait
On mortal life, from sin and death for ever.

THE TOMB OF DOUGLAS
See the Tragedy of that Name
(1796)

When her son, her Douglas died,
To the steep rock's fearful side
Fast the frantic Mother hied—

O'er her blooming warrior dead
Many a tear did Scotland shed,

And shrieks of long and loud lament
From her Grampian hills she sent.

Like one awakening from a trance,
She met the shock of [1] Lochlin's lance;
On her rude invader foe
Return'd an hundred fold the blow,
Drove the taunting spoiler home;
  Mournful thence she took her way
To do observance at the tomb
  Where the son of Douglas lay.

Round about the tomb did go
In solemn state and order slow,
Silent pace, and black attire,
Earl, or Knight, or good Esquire;
Whoe'er by deeds of valour done
In battle had high honours won;
Whoe'er in their pure veins could trace
The blood of Douglas' noble race.

With them the flower of minstrels came,
And to their cunning harps did frame
In doleful numbers piercing rhymes,
Such strains as in the older times
Had sooth'd the spirit of Fingal,
Echoing thro' his father's hall.

"Scottish maidens, drop a tear
O'er the beauteous Hero's bier!
Brave youth, and comely 'bove compare,
All golden shone his burnish'd hair;
Valour and smiling courtesy
Play'd in the sun-beams of his eye.
Clos'd are those eyes that shone so fair,
And stain'd with blood his yellow hair.
Scottish maidens, drop a tear
O'er the beauteous Hero's bier!"

"Not a tear, I charge you, shed
For the false Glenalvon dead;
Unpitied let Glenalvon lie,
Foul stain to arms and chivalry!"

"Behind his back the traitor came,
And Douglas died without his fame.

[1] Denmark.

Young light of Scotland early spent,
  Thy country thee shall long lament;
And oft to after-times shall tell,
  In Hope's sweet prime my Hero fell."

TO CHARLES LLOYD

An Unexpected Visitor

(*January*, 1797. *Text of* 1818)

Alone, obscure, without a friend,
  A cheerless, solitary thing,
Why seeks, my Lloyd, the stranger out?
  What offering can the stranger bring

Of social scenes, home-bred delights,
  That him in aught compensate may
For Stowey's pleasant winter nights,
  For loves and friendships far away?

In brief oblivion to forego
  Friends, such as thine, so justly dear,
And be awhile with me content
  To stay, a kindly loiterer, here:

For this a gleam of random joy
  Hath flush'd my unaccustom'd cheek;
And, with an o'er-charg'd bursting heart,
  I feel the thanks I cannot speak.

Oh! sweet are all the Muses' lays,
  And sweet the charm of matin bird;
'Twas long since these estranged ears
  The sweeter voice of friend had heard.

The voice hath spoke: the pleasant sounds
  In memory's ear in after time
Shall live, to sometimes rouse a tear,
  And sometimes prompt an honest rhyme.

For, when the transient charm is fled,
  And when the little week is o'er,
To cheerless, friendless, solitude
  When I return, as heretofore,

Long, long, within my aching heart
  The grateful sense shall cherish'd be;
I'll think less meanly of myself,
  That Lloyd will sometimes think on me.

A VISION OF REPENTANCE
(1796?   Text of 1818)

I saw a famous fountain, in my dream,
   Where shady path-ways to a valley led ;
A weeping willow lay upon that stream,
   And all around the fountain brink were spread
Wide branching trees, with dark green leaf rich clad,
Forming a doubtful twilight—desolate and sad.

The place was such, that whoso enter'd in
   Disrobed was of every earthly thought,
And straight became as one that knew not sin,
   Or to the world's first innocence was brought ;
Enseem'd it now, he stood on holy ground,
In sweet and tender melancholy wrapt around.

A most strange calm stole o'er my soothed sprite ;
   Long time I stood, and longer had I staid,
When, lo ! I saw, saw by the sweet moon-light,
   Which came in silence o'er that silent shade,
Where, near the fountain, SOMETHING like DESPAIR
Made, of that weeping willow, garlands for her hair.

And eke with painful fingers she inwove
   Many an uncouth stem of savage thorn—
"The willow garland, *that* was for her love,
   And *these* her bleeding temples would adorn."
With sighs her heart nigh burst, salt tears fast fell,
As mournfully she bended o'er that sacred well.

To whom when I addrest myself to speak,
   She lifted up her eyes, and nothing said ;
The delicate red came mantling o'er her cheek,
   And, gath'ring up her loose attire, she fled
To the dark covert of that woody shade,
And in her goings seem'd a timid gentle maid.

Revolving in my mind what this should mean,
   And why that lovely lady plained so ;
Perplex'd in thought at that mysterious scene,
   And doubting if 'twere best to stay or go,
I cast mine eyes in wistful gaze around,
When from the shades came slow a small and plaintive sound :

"PSYCHE am I, who love to dwell
In these brown shades, this woody dell,
Where never busy mortal came,
Till now, to pry upon my shame.

A VISION OF REPENTANCE

At thy feet what thou dost see
The waters of repentance be,
Which, night and day, I must augment
With tears, like a true penitent,

If haply so my day of grace
Be not yet past; and this lone place,
O'er-shadowy, dark, excludeth hence
All thoughts but grief and penitence."

"*Why dost thou weep, thou gentle maid!
And wherefore in this barren shade
Thy hidden thoughts with sorrow feed?
Can thing so fair repentance need?*"

"O! I have done a deed of shame,
And tainted is my virgin fame,
And stain'd the beauteous maiden white,
In which my bridal robes were dight."

"*And who the promised spouse, declare:
And what those bridal garments were.*"

"Severe and saintly righteousness
Compos'd the clear white bridal dress;
JESUS, the son of Heaven's high king,
Bought with his blood the marriage ring.

A wretched sinful creature, I
Deem'd lightly of that sacred tie,
Gave to a treacherous WORLD my heart,
And play'd the foolish wanton's part.

Soon to these murky shades I came,
To hide from the sun's light my shame.
And still I haunt this woody dell,
And bathe me in that healing well,
Whose waters clear have influence
From sin's foul stains the soul to cleanse;
And, night and day, I them augment
With tears, like a true penitent,
Until, due expiation made,
And fit atonement fully paid,
The lord and bridegroom me present,
Where in sweet strains of high consent,
God's throne before, the Seraphim
Shall chaunt the extatic marriage hymn."

"Now Christ restore thee soon"—I said,
And thenceforth all my dream was fled.

POEMS WRITTEN IN THE YEARS 1795-98, AND NOT REPRINTED BY LAMB FROM PERIODICALS

SONNET

(Summer, 1795)

THE Lord of Life shakes off his drowsihed,
    And 'gins to sprinkle on the earth below
Those rays that from his shaken locks do flow;
Meantime, by truant love of rambling led,
I turn my back on thy detested walls,
    Proud City! and thy sons I leave behind,
    A sordid, selfish, money-getting kind;
Brute things, who shut their ears when Freedom calls.

I pass not thee so lightly, well-known spire,
    That minded me of many a pleasure gone,
    Of merrier days, of love and Islington;
Kindling afresh the flames of past desire.
    And I shall muse on thee, slow journeying on
    To the green plains of pleasant Hertfordshire.

1795

TO THE POET COWPER

*On his Recovery from an Indisposition.
Written some Time Back*

(Summer, 1796)

Cowper, I thank my God, that thou art heal'd.
Thine was the sorest malady of all;
And I am sad to think that it should light
Upon the worthy head: but thou art heal'd,
And thou art yet, we trust, the destin'd man,
Born to re-animate the lyre, whose chords
Have slumber'd, and have idle lain so long;
To th' immortal sounding of whose strings

LINES

Did Milton frame the stately-paced verse;
Among whose wires with lighter finger playing
Our elder bard, Spencer, a gentler name,
The lady Muses' dearest darling child,
Enticed forth the deftest tunes yet heard
In hall or bower; taking the delicate ear
Of the brave Sidney, and the Maiden Queen.
Thou, then, take up the mighty epic strain,
Cowper, of England's bards the wisest and the best!

December 1, 1796

LINES

Addressed, from London, to Sara and S. T. C. at Bristol, in the Summer of 1796.

Was it so hard a thing? I did but ask
A fleeting holiday, a little week.

What, if the jaded steer, who, all day long,
Had borne the heat and burthen of the plough,
When ev'ning came, and her sweet cooling hour,
Should seek to wander in a neighbour copse,
Where greener herbage wav'd, or clearer streams
Invited him to slake his burning thirst?
The man were crabbed who should say him nay;
The man were churlish who should drive him thence.

A blessing light upon your worthy heads,
Ye hospitable pair! I may not come
To catch, on Clifden's heights, the summer gale;
I may not come to taste the Avon wave;
Or, with mine eye intent on Redcliffe tow'rs,
To muse in tears on that mysterious youth,
Cruelly slighted, who, in evil hour,
Shap'd his advent'rous course to London walls!

Complaint, be gone! and, ominous thoughts, away!
Take up, my Song, take up a merrier strain;
For yet again, and lo! from Avon's vales,
Another Minstrel[1] cometh. Youth endear'd,
God and good Angels guide thee on thy road,
And gentler fortunes 'wait the friends I love!

---

[1] "From vales where Avon winds, the Minstrel came."
        COLERIDGE'S *Monody on Chatterton.*

SONNET TO A FRIEND
(End of 1796)

Friend of my earliest years and childish days,
  My joys, my sorrows, thou with me hast shar'd
  Companion dear, and we alike have far'd
(Poor pilgrims we) thro' life's unequal ways.
It were unwisely done, should we refuse
  To cheer our path as featly as we may,
  Our lonely path to cheer, as trav'llers use,
  With merry song, quaint tale, or roundelay;
And we will sometimes talk past troubles o'er,
  Of mercies shewn, and all our sickness heal'd,
  And in his judgments God rememb'ring love;
And we will learn to praise God evermore,
  For those glad tidings of great joy reveal'd
  By that sooth Messenger sent from above.

TO A YOUNG LADY
(Early, 1797)

Hard is the heart that does not melt with ruth,
When care sits, cloudy, on the brow of youth;
When bitter griefs the female bosom swell,
And Beauty meditates a fond farewell
To her lov'd native land, prepar'd to roam,
And seek in climes afar the peace denied at home.
The Muse, with glance prophetic, sees her stand
(Forsaken, silent lady) on the strand
Of farthest India, sick'ning at the roar
Of each dull wave, slow dash'd upon the shore;
Sending, at intervals, an aching eye
O'er the wide waters, vainly, to espy
The long-expected bark, in which to find
Some tidings of a world she left behind.
At such a time shall start the gushing tear,
For scenes her childhood lov'd, now doubly dear.
At such a time shall frantic mem'ry wake
Pangs of remorse, for slighted England's sake;
And for the sake of many a tender tie
Of love, or friendship, pass'd too lightly by.
Unwept, unhonour'd, 'midst an alien race,
And the *cold* looks of many a *stranger* face,
How will her poor heart bleed, and chide the day,
That from her country took her far away.

LIVING WITHOUT GOD IN THE WORLD
(? 1798)

Mystery of God! thou brave and beauteous world,
Made fair with light and shade and stars and flowers,
Made fearful and august with woods and rocks,
Jagg'd precipice, black mountain, sea in storms,
Sun, over all, that no co-rival owns,
But thro' Heaven's pavement rides as in despite
Or mockery of the littleness of man!
I see a mighty arm, by man unseen,
Resistless, not to be controul'd, that guides,
In solitude of unshared energies,
All these thy ceaseless miracles, O world!
Arm of the world, I view thee, and I muse
On Man, who, trusting in his mortal strength,
Leans on a shadowy staff, a staff of dreams.
We consecrate our total hopes and fears
To idols, flesh and blood, our love, (heaven's due)
Our praise and admiration; praise bestowed
By man on man, and acts of worship done
To a kindred nature, certes do reflect
Some portion of the glory and rays oblique
Upon the politic worshipper,—so man
Extracts a pride from his humility.
Some braver spirits of the modern stamp
Affect a Godhead nearer: these talk loud
Of mind, and independent intellect,
Of energies omnipotent in man,
And man of his own fate artificer;
Yea of his own life Lord, and of the days
Of his abode on earth, when time shall be,
That life immortal shall become an art,
Or Death, by chymic practices deceived,
Forego the scent, which for six thousand years
Like a good hound he has followed, or at length
More manners learning, and a decent sense
And reverence of a philosophic world,
Relent, and leave to prey on carcasses.

But these are fancies of a few: the rest,
Atheists, or Deists only in the name,
By word or deed deny a God. They eat
Their daily bread, and draw the breath of heaven

VOL. V.—2

Without or thought or thanks; heaven's roof to them
Is but a painted ceiling hung with lamps,
No more, that lights them to their purposes.
They wander "loose about," they nothing see,
Themselves except, and creatures like themselves,
Short-liv'd, short-sighted, impotent to save.
So on their dissolute spirits, soon or late,
Destruction cometh "like an armed man,"
Or like a dream of murder in the night,
Withering their mortal faculties, and breaking
The bones of all their pride.

POEMS FROM *BLANK VERSE*, BY CHARLES LLOYD AND CHARLES LAMB. 1798

TO CHARLES LLOYD

A STRANGER, and alone, I past those scenes
    We past so late together; and my heart
Felt something like desertion, when I look'd
Around me, and the well-known voice of friend
Was absent, and the cordial look was there
No more to smile on me. I thought on Lloyd;
All he had been to me. And now I go
Again to mingle with a world impure,
With men who make a mock of holy things
Mistaken, and of man's best hope think scorn.
The world does much to warp the heart of man,
And I may sometimes join its ideot laugh.
Of this I now complain not. Deal with me,
Omniscient Father! as thou judgest best,
And in thy season *tender* thou my heart.
I pray not for myself; I pray for him
Whose soul is sore perplex'd: shine thou on him,
Father of Lights! and in the difficult paths
Make plain his way before him. His own thoughts
May he not think, his own ends not pursue;
So shall he best perform thy will on earth.
Greatest and Best, thy will be ever ours!

August, 1797.

WRITTEN ON THE DAY OF MY AUNT'S FUNERAL

Thou too art dead, ...! very kind
Hast thou been to me in my childish days,
Thou best good creature. I have not forgot
How thou didst love thy Charles, when he was yet

A prating schoolboy: I have not forgot
The busy joy on that important day,
When, child-like, the poor wanderer was content
To leave the bosom of parental love,
His childhood's play-place, and his early home,
For the rude fosterings of a stranger's hand,
Hard uncouth tasks, and school-boy's scanty fare.
How did thine eye peruse him round and round,
And hardly know him in his yellow coats,[1]
Red leathern belt, and gown of russet blue!
Farewell, good aunt!
Go thou, and occupy the same grave-bed
Where the dead mother lies.
Oh my dear mother, oh thou dear dead saint!
Where's now that placid face, where oft hath sat
A mother's smile, to think her son should thrive
In this bad world, when she was dead and gone;
And where a tear hath sat (take shame, O son!)
When that same child has prov'd himself unkind.
One parent yet is left—a wretched thing,
A sad survivor of his buried wife,
A palsy-smitten, childish, old, old man,
A semblance most forlorn of what he was,
A merry cheerful man. A merrier man,
A man more apt to frame matter for mirth,
Mad jokes, and anticks for a Christmas eve;
Making life social, and the laggard time
To move on nimbly, never yet did cheer
The little circle of domestic friends.

February, 1797.

WRITTEN A YEAR AFTER THE EVENTS

Alas! how am I chang'd! Where be the tears,
The sobs, and forc'd suspensions of the breath,
And all the dull desertions of the heart,
With which I hung o'er my dead mother's corse?
Where be the blest subsidings of the storm
Within, the sweet resignedness of hope
Drawn heavenward, and strength of filial love
In which I bow'd me to my father's will?
My God, and my Redeemer! keep not thou
My soul in brute and sensual thanklessness

[1] The dress of Christ's Hospital.

WRITTEN A YEAR AFTER THE EVENTS 21

Seal'd up; oblivious ever of that dear grace,
And health restor'd to my long-loved friend,
Long-lov'd, and worthy known. Thou didst not leave
Her soul in death! O leave not now, my Lord,
Thy servants in far worse, in spiritual death!
And darkness blacker than those feared shadows
Of the valley all must tread. Lend us thy balms,
Thou dear Physician of the sin-sick soul,
And heal our cleansed bosoms of the wounds
With which the world has pierc'd us thro' and thro'.
Give us new flesh, new birth. Elect of heav'n
May we become; in thine election sure
Contain'd, and to one purpose stedfast drawn,
Our soul's salvation!

      Thou, and I, dear friend,
With filial recognition sweet, shall know
One day the face of our dear mother in heaven;
And her remember'd looks of love shall greet
With looks of answering love; her placid smiles
Meet with a smile as placid, and her hand
With drops of fondness wet, nor fear repulse.
Be witness for me, Lord, I do not ask
Those days of vanity to return again
(Nor fitting me to ask, nor thee to give),
Vain loves and wanderings with a fair-hair'd maid,
Child of the dust as I am, who so long
My captive heart steep'd in idolatry
And creature-loves. Forgive me, O my Maker!
If in a mood of grief I sin almost
In sometimes brooding on the days long past,
And from the grave of time wishing them back,
Days of a mother's fondness to her child,
Her little one.

      O where be now those sports,
And infant play-games? where the joyous troops
Of children, and the haunts I did so love?
O my companions, O ye loved names
Of friend or playmate dear; gone are ye now;
Gone diverse ways; to honour and credit some,
And some, I fear, to ignominy and shame!
I only am left, with unavailing grief
To mourn one parent dead, and see one live
Of all life's joys bereft and desolate:
Am left with a few friends, and one, above

The rest, found faithful in a length of years,
Contented as I may, to bear me on
To the not unpeaceful evening of a day
Made black by morning storms!

September, 1797.

WRITTEN SOON AFTER THE PRECEDING POEM

Thou should'st have longer liv'd, and to the grave
Have peacefully gone down in full old age!
Thy children would have tended thy gray hairs.
We might have sat, as we have often done,
By our fireside, and talk'd whole nights away,
Old times, old friends, and old events recalling;
With many a circumstance, of trivial note,
To memory dear, and of importance grown.
How shall we tell them in a stranger's ear?
A wayward son ofttimes was I to thee;
And yet, in all our little bickerings,
Domestic jars, there was, I know not what,
Of tender feeling, that were ill exchang'd
For this world's chilling friendships, and their smiles
Familiar, whom the heart calls strangers still.
A heavy lot hath he, most wretched man!
Who lives the last of all his family.
He looks around him, and his eye discerns
The face of the stranger, and his heart is sick.
Man of the world, what canst thou do for him?
Wealth is a burden, which he could not bear;
Mirth a strange crime, the which he dares not act;
And wine no cordial, but a bitter cup.
For wounds like his Christ is the only cure,
And gospel promises are his by right,
For these were given to the poor in heart.
Go, preach thou to him of a world to come,
Where friends shall meet, and know each other's face.
Say less than this, and say it to the winds.

October, 1797.

WRITTEN ON CHRISTMAS DAY, 1797

I am a widow'd thing, now thou art gone!
Now thou art gone, my own familiar friend,
Companion, sister, help-mate, counsellor!

Alas! that honour'd mind, whose sweet reproof
And meekest wisdom in times past have smooth'd
The unfilial harshness of my foolish speech,
And made me loving to my parents old,
(Why is this so, ah God! why is this so?)
That honour'd mind become a fearful blank,
Her senses lock'd up, and herself kept out
From human sight or converse, while so many
Of the foolish sort are left to roam at large,
Doing all acts of folly, and sin, and shame?
Thy paths are mystery!
      Yet I will not think,
Sweet friend, but we shall one day meet, and live
In quietness, and die so, fearing God.
Or if *not*, and these false suggestions be
A fit of the weak nature, loth to part
With what it lov'd so long, and held so dear;
If thou art to be taken, and I left
(More sinning, yet unpunish'd, save in thee),
It is the will of God, and we are clay
In the potter's hands; and, at the worst, are made
From absolute nothing, vessels of disgrace,
Till, his most righteous purpose wrought in us,
Our purified spirits find their perfect rest.

THE OLD FAMILIAR FACES

(*January*, 1798. *Text of* 1818)

I have had playmates, I have had companions,
In my days of childhood, in my joyful school-days,
All, all are gone, the old familiar faces.

I have been laughing, I have been carousing,
Drinking late, sitting late, with my bosom cronies,
All, all are gone, the old familiar faces.

I loved a love once, fairest among women;
Closed are her doors on me, I must not see her—
All, all are gone, the old familiar faces.

I have a friend, a kinder friend has no man;
Like an ingrate, I left my friend abruptly;
Left him, to muse on the old familiar faces.

Ghost-like, I paced round the haunts of my childhood.
Earth seemed a desart I was bound to traverse,
Seeking to find the old familiar faces.

Friend of my bosom, thou more than a brother,
Why wert not thou born in my father's dwelling?
So might we talk of the old familiar faces—

How some they have died, and some they have left me,
And some are taken from me; all are departed;
All, all are gone, the old familiar faces.

COMPOSED AT MIDNIGHT

(1797? Text of 1818)

From broken visions of perturbed rest
I wake, and start, and fear to sleep again.
How total a privation of all sounds,
Sights, and familiar objects, man, bird, beast,
Herb, tree, or flower, and prodigal light of heaven.
'Twere some relief to catch the drowsy cry
Of the mechanic watchman, or the noise
Of revel reeling home from midnight cups.
Those are the moanings of the dying man,
Who lies in the upper chamber; restless moans,
And interrupted only by a cough
Consumptive, torturing the wasted lungs.
So in the bitterness of death he lies,
And waits in anguish for the morning's light.
What can that do for him, or what restore?
Short taste, faint sense, affecting notices,
And little images of pleasures past,
Of health, and active life—health not yet slain,
Nor the other grace of life, a good name, sold
For sin's black wages. On his tedious bed
He writhes, and turns him from the accusing light,
And finds no comfort in the sun, but says
"When night comes I shall get a little rest."
Some few groans more, death comes, and there an end.
'Tis darkness and conjecture all beyond;
Weak Nature fears, though Charity must hope,
And Fancy, most licentious on such themes
Where decent reverence well had kept her mute,
Hath o'er-stock'd hell with devils, and brought down,
By her enormous fablings and mad lies,
Discredit on the gospel's serious truths
And salutary fears. The man of parts,
Poet, or prose declaimer, on his couch
Lolling, like one indifferent, fabricates
A heaven of gold, where he, and such as he,

COMPOSED AT MIDNIGHT

Their heads encompassed with crowns, their heels
With fine wings garlanded, shall tread the stars
Beneath their feet, heaven's pavement, far removed
From damned spirits, and the torturing cries
Of men, his breth'ren, fashioned of the earth,
As he was, nourish'd with the self-same bread,
Belike his kindred or companions once—
Through everlasting ages now divorced,
In chains and savage torments to repent
Short years of folly on earth. Their groans unheard
In heav'n, the saint nor pity feels, nor care,
For those thus sentenced—pity might disturb
The delicate sense and most divine repose
Of spirits angelical. Blessed be God,
The measure of his judgments is not fixed
By man's erroneous standard. He discerns
No such inordinate difference and vast
Betwixt the sinner and the saint, to doom
Such disproportion'd fates. Compared with him,
No man on earth is holy called : they best
Stand in his sight approved, who at his feet
Their little crowns of virtue cast,-and yield
To him of his own works the praise, his due.

POEMS AT THE END OF *JOHN WOODVIL*, 1802

HELEN

By Mary Lamb

(Summer, 1800.   Text *of* 1818)

HIGH-BORN Helen, round your dwelling
    These twenty years I've paced in vain:
Haughty beauty, thy lover's duty
    Hath been to glory in his pain.

High-born Helen, plainly telling
    Stories of thy cold disdain;
I starve, I die, now you comply,
    And I no longer can complain.

These twenty years I've lived on tears,
    Dwelling for ever on a frown;
On sighs I've fed, your scorn my bread;
    I perish now you kind are grown.

Can I, who loved my beloved
    But for the scorn "was in her eye,"
Can I be moved for my beloved,
    When she "returns me sigh for sigh?"

In stately pride, by my bed-side,
    High-born Helen's portrait's hung;
Deaf to my praise, my mournful lays
    Are nightly to the portrait sung.

To that I weep, nor ever sleep,
    Complaining all night long to her—
Helen, grown old, no longer cold,
    Said, "you to all men I prefer."

BALLAD

From the German

(*Spring*, 1800.   Text of 1818)

The clouds are blackening, the storms threatening,
   And ever the forest maketh a moan :
Billows are breaking, the damsel's heart aching,
   Thus by herself she singeth alone,
     Weeping right plenteously.

"The world is empty, the heart is dead surely,
   In this world plainly all seemeth amiss:
To thy breast, holy one, take now thy little one,
   I have had earnest of all earth's bliss,
     Living right lovingly."

HYPOCHONDRIACUS

(*October*, 1800.   Text of 1818)

By myself walking,
To myself talking,
When as I ruminate
On my untoward fate,
Scarcely seem I
Alone sufficiently,
Black thoughts continually
Crowding my privacy ;
They come unbidden,
Like foes at a wedding,
Thrusting their faces
In better guests' places,
Peevish and malecontent,
Clownish, impertinent,
Dashing the merriment:
So in like fashions
Dim cogitations
Follow and haunt me,
Striving to daunt me,
In my heart festering,
In my ears whispering,
"Thy friends are treacherous,
"Thy foes are dangerous,
"Thy dreams ominous."

    Fierce Anthropophagi,
    Spectra, Diaboli,
    What scared St. Anthony,
    Hobgoblins, Lemures,
    Dreams of Antipodes,
    Night-riding Incubi
    Troubling the fantasy,
    All dire illusions
    Causing confusions;
    Figments heretical,
    Scruples fantastical,
    Doubts diabolical,
    Abaddon vexeth me,
    Mahu perplexeth me,
    Lucifer teareth me——

Jesu! Maria! liberate nos ab his diris tentationibus Inimici.

A BALLAD:

Noting the Difference of Rich and Poor, in the Ways of a Rich Noble's Palace and a Poor Workhouse

To the tune of the "*Old and Young Courtier*"

(*August*, 1800. *Text of* 1818)

In a costly palace Youth goes clad in gold;
In a wretched workhouse Age's limbs are cold:
There they sit, the old men by a shivering fire,
Still close and closer cowering, warmth is their desire.

In a costly palace, when the brave gallants dine,
They have store of good venison, with old canary wine,
With singing and music to heighten the cheer;
Coarse bits, with grudging, are the pauper's best fare.

In a costly palace Youth is still carest
By a train of attendants which laugh at my young **Lord's jest**;
In a wretched workhouse the contrary prevails:
Does Age begin to prattle?—no man heark'neth to his tales.

In a costly palace if the child with a pin
Do but chance to prick a finger, strait the doctor is called in;
In a wretched workhouse men are left to perish
For want of proper cordials, which their old age might cherish.

A BALLAD

In a costly palace Youth enjoys his lust;
In a wretched workhouse Age, in corners thrust,
Thinks upon the former days, when he was well to do,
Had children to stand by him, both friends and kinsmen too.

In a costly palace Youth his temples hides
With a new devised peruke that reaches to his sides;
In a wretched workhouse Age's crown is bare,
With a few thin locks just to fence out the cold air.

In peace, as in war, 'tis our young gallants' pride,
To walk, each one i' the streets, with a rapier by his side,
That none to do them injury may have pretence;
Wretched Age, in poverty, must brook offence.

POEMS IN CHARLES LAMB'S *WORKS*, 1818, NOT PREVIOUSLY PRINTED IN THE PRESENT VOLUME; TOGETHER WITH REFERENCES TO THOSE POEMS THAT HAVE BEEN PREVIOUSLY PRINTED

HESTER

(February, 1803)

WHEN maidens such as Hester die,
 Their place ye may not well supply,
Though ye among a thousand try,
  With vain endeavour.

A month or more hath she been dead,
Yet cannot I by force be led
To think upon the wormy bed,
  And her together.

A springy motion in her gait,
A rising step, did indicate
Of pride and joy no common rate,
  That flush'd her spirit.

I know not by what name beside
I shall it call :—if 'twas not pride,
It was a joy to that allied,
  She did inherit.

Her parents held the Quaker rule,
Which doth the human feeling cool,
But she was train'd in Nature's school,
  Nature had blest her.

A waking eye, a prying mind,
A heart that stirs, is hard to bind,
A hawk's keen sight ye cannot blind,
  Ye could not Hester.

My sprightly neighbour, gone before
To that unknown and silent shore,
Shall we not meet, as heretofore,
    Some summer morning,

When from thy cheerful eyes a ray
Hath struck a bliss upon the day,
A bliss that would not go away,
    A sweet fore-warning?

Here came "To Charles Lloyd." See page 11.
Here came "The Three Friends," followed by "To a River in which a Child was drowned," first printed in *Poetry for Children*, 1809. See vol. iii. of this edition, pages 362 and 382.
Here came "The Old Familiar Faces." See page 23.
Here came "Helen," by Mary Lamb. See page 26.
Here came "A Vision of Repentance." See page 12.

DIALOGUE BETWEEN A MOTHER AND CHILD

(By Mary Lamb. 1804)

Child
"O Lady, lay your costly robes aside,
No longer may you glory in your pride."

Mother
"Wherefore to-day art singing in mine ear
Sad songs, were made so long ago, my dear;
This day I am to be a bride, you know,
Why sing sad songs, were made so long ago?"

Child
"O, mother, lay your costly robes aside,
For you may never be another's bride.
That line I learn'd not in the old sad song."

Mother
"I pray thee, pretty one, now hold thy tongue,
Play with the bride-maids, and be glad, my boy,
For thou shalt be a second father's joy."

Child
"One father fondled me upon his knee.
One father is enough, alone, for me."

Here came " Queen Oriana's Dream," from *Poetry for Children.*
See vol. iii, page 423.

Here came " A Ballad Noting the Difference of Rich and Poor."
See page 28.

Here came " Hypochondriacus." See page 27.

A FAREWELL TO TOBACCO
(1805)

May the Babylonish curse
Strait confound my stammering verse,
If I can a passage see
In this word-perplexity,
Or a fit expression find,
Or a language to my mind,
(Still the phrase is wide or scant)
To take leave of thee, GREAT PLANT!
Or in any terms relate
Half my love, or half my hate:
For I hate, yet love, thee so,
That, whichever thing I shew,
The plain truth will seem to be
A constrain'd hyperbole,
And the passion to proceed
More from a mistress than a weed.

Sooty retainer to the vine,
Bacchus' black servant, negro fine;
Sorcerer, that mak'st us dote upon
Thy begrimed complexion,
And, for thy pernicious sake,
More and greater oaths to break
Than reclaimed lovers take
'Gainst women: thou thy siege dost lay
Much too in the female way,
While thou suck'st the lab'ring breath
Faster than kisses or than death.

Thou in such a cloud dost bind us,
That our worst foes cannot find us,
And ill fortune, that would thwart us,
Shoots at rovers, shooting at us;
While each man, thro' thy height'ning steam,
Does like a smoking Etna seem,
And all about us does express
(Fancy and wit in richest dress)
A Sicilian fruitfulness.

A FAREWELL TO TOBACCO

Thou through such a mist dost shew us,
That our best friends do not know us,
And, for those allowed features,
Due to reasonable creatures,
Liken'st us to fell Chimeras,
Monsters that, who see us, fear us;
Worse than Cerberus or Geryon,
Or, who first lov'd a cloud, Ixion.

Bacchus we know, and we allow
His tipsy rites. But what art thou,
That but by reflex can'st shew
What his deity can do,
As the false Egyptian spell
Aped the true Hebrew miracle?
Some few vapours thou may'st raise,
The weak brain may serve to amaze,
But to the reins and nobler heart
Can'st nor life nor heat impart.

Brother of Bacchus, later born,
The old world was sure forlorn,
Wanting thee, that aidest more
The god's victories than before
All his panthers, and the brawls
Of his piping Bacchanals.
These, as stale, we disallow,
Or judge of *thee* meant: only thou
His true Indian conquest art;
And, for ivy round his dart,
The reformed god now weaves
A finer thyrsus of thy leaves.

Scent to match thy rich perfume
Chemic art did ne'er presume
Through her quaint alembic strain,
None so sov'reign to the brain.
Nature, that did in thee excel,
Fram'd again no second smell.
Roses, violets, but toys
For the smaller sort of boys,
Or for greener damsels meant;
Thou art the only manly scent.

Stinking'st of the stinking kind,
Filth of the mouth and fog of the mind,

Africa, that brags her foyson,
Breeds no such prodigious poison,
Henbane, nightshade, both together,
Hemlock, aconite——
                    Nay, rather,
Plant divine, of rarest virtue;
Blisters on the tongue would hurt you.
'Twas but in a sort I blam'd thee;
None e'er prosper'd who defam'd thee;
Irony all, and feign'd abuse,
Such as perplext lovers use,
At a need, when, in despair
To paint forth their fairest fair,
Or in part but to express
That exceeding comeliness
Which their fancies doth so strike,
They borrow language of dislike;
And, instead of Dearest Miss,
Jewel, Honey, Sweetheart, Bliss,
And those forms of old admiring,
Call her Cockatrice and Siren,
Basilisk, and all that's evil,
Witch, Hyena, Mermaid, Devil,
Ethiop, Wench, and Blackamoor,
Monkey, Ape, and twenty more;
Friendly Trait'ress, loving Foe,—
Not that she is truly so,
But no other way they know
A contentment to express,
Borders so upon excess,
That they do not rightly wot
Whether it be pain or not.

Or, as men, constrain'd to part
With what's nearest to their heart,
While their sorrow's at the height,
Lose discrimination quite,
And their hasty wrath let fall,
To appease their frantic gall,
On the darling thing whatever
Whence they feel it death to sever,
Though it be, as they, perforce,
Guiltless of the sad divorce.

For I must (nor let it grieve thee,
Friendliest of plants, that I must) leave thee.

TO T. L. H.

For thy sake, Tobacco, I
Would do any thing but die,
And but seek to extend my days
Long enough to sing thy praise.
But, as she, who once hath been
A king's consort, is a queen
Ever after, nor will bate
Any tittle of her state,
Though a widow, or divorced,
So I, from thy converse forced,
The old name and style retain,
A right Katherine of Spain;
And a seat, too, 'mongst the joys
Of the blest Tobacco Boys;
Where, though I, by sour physician,
Am debarr'd the full fruition
Of thy favours, I may catch
Some collateral sweets, and snatch
Sidelong odours, that give life
Like glances from a neighbour's wife;
And still live in the by-places
And the suburbs of thy graces;
And in thy borders take delight,
An unconquer'd Canaanite.

TO T. L. H.
A Child
(1814)

Model of thy parent dear,
Serious infant worth a fear:
In thy unfaultering visage well
Picturing forth the son of Tell,
When on his forehead, firm and good,
Motionless mark, the apple stood;
Guileless traitor, rebel mild,
Convict unconscious, culprit-child!
Gates that close with iron roar
Have been to thee thy nursery door;
Chains that chink in cheerless cells
Have been thy rattles and thy bells;
Walls contrived for giant sin
Have hemmed thy faultless weakness in;
Near thy sinless bed black Guilt
Her discordant house hath built,

And filled it with her monstrous brood—
Sights, by thee not understood—
Sights of fear, and of distress,
That pass a harmless infant's guess!

But the clouds, that overcast
Thy young morning, may not last.
Soon shall arrive the rescuing hour,
That yields thee up to Nature's power.
Nature, that so late doth greet thee,
Shall in o'er-flowing measure meet thee.
She shall recompense with cost
For every lesson thou hast lost.
Then wandering up thy sire's lov'd hill,[1]
Thou shalt take thy airy fill
Of health and pastime. *Birds shall sing
For thy delight each May morning.*
'Mid new-yean'd lambkins thou shalt play,
Hardly less a lamb than they.
Then thy prison's lengthened bound
Shall be the horizon skirting round.
And, while thou fillest thy lap with flowers,
To make amends for wintery hours,
The breeze, the sunshine, and the place,
Shall from thy tender brow efface
Each vestige of untimely care,
That sour restraint had graven there;
And on thy every look impress
A more excelling childishness.

So shall be thy days beguil'd,
THORNTON HUNT, my favourite child.

Here came "Ballad from the German." See page 27.
Here came "David in the Cave of Adullam," by Mary Lamb, from *Poetry for Children.* See vol. iii., page 428.

SALOME

(*By Mary Lamb. Probably* 1808 *or* 1809)

Once on a charger there was laid,
And brought before a royal maid,
As price of attitude and grace,
A guiltless head, a holy face.

[1] Hampstead.

SALOME

It was on Herod's natal day,
Who o'er Judea's land held sway.
He married his own brother's wife,
Wicked Herodias. She the life
Of John the Baptist long had sought,
Because he openly had taught
That she a life unlawful led,
Having her husband's brother wed.

This was he, that saintly John,
Who in the wilderness alone
Abiding, did for clothing wear
A garment made of camel's hair;
Honey and locusts were his food,
And he was most severely good.
He preached penitence and tears,
And waking first the sinner's fears,
Prepared a path, made smooth a way,
For his diviner master's day.

Herod kept in princely state
His birth-day. On his throne he sate,
After the feast, beholding her
Who danced with grace peculiar;
Fair Salome, who did excel
All in that land for dancing well.
The feastful monarch's heart was fired,
And whatsoe'er thing she desired,
Though half his kingdom it should be,
He in his pleasure swore that he
Would give the graceful Salome.
The damsel was Herodias' daughter:
She to the queen hastes, and besought her
To teach her what great gift to name.
Instructed by Herodias, came
The damsel back; to Herod said,
"Give me John the Baptist's head;
"And in a charger let it be
"Hither straitway brought to me."
Herod her suit would fain deny,
But for his oath's sake must comply.

When painters would by art express
Beauty in unloveliness,
Thee, Herodias' daughter, thee,
They fittest subject take to be.

They give thy form and features grace;
But ever in thy beauteous face
They shew a steadfast cruel gaze,
An eye unpitying; and amaze
In all beholders deep they mark,
That thou betrayest not one spark
Of feeling for the ruthless deed,
That did thy praiseful dance succeed.
For on the head they make you look,
As if a sullen joy you took,
A cruel triumph, wicked pride,
That for your sport a saint had died.

LINES

Suggested by a Picture of Two Females by Lionardo da Vinci.

(*By Mary Lamb.* 1804)

The Lady Blanch, regardless of all her lovers' fears,
To the Urs'line convent hastens, and long the Abbess hears.
"O Blanch, my child, repent ye of the courtly life ye lead."
Blanch looked on a rose-bud and little seem'd to heed.
She looked on the rose-bud, she looked round, and thought
On all her heart had whisper'd, and all the Nun had taught.
"I am worshipped by lovers, and brightly shines my fame,
" All Christendom resoundeth the noble Blanch's name.
" Nor shall I quickly wither like the rose-bud from the tree,
" My queen-like graces shining when my beauty's gone from me.
" But when the sculptur'd marble is raised o'er my head,
" And the matchless Blanch lies lifeless among the noble dead,
" This saintly lady Abbess hath made me justly fear,
" It nothing will avail me that I were worshipp'd here."

LINES

On the Same Picture being Removed to make Place for a Portrait of a Lady by Titian.

(*By Mary Lamb.* 1805)

Who art thou, fair one, who usurp'st the place
Of Blanch, the lady of the matchless grace?
Come, fair and pretty, tell to me,
Who, in thy life-time, thou might'st be.
Thou pretty art and fair,
But with the lady Blanch thou never must compare.

No need for Blanch her history to tell;
Whoever saw her face, they there did read it well.
But when I look on thee, I only know
There lived a pretty maid some hundred years ago.

LINES

*On the Celebrated Picture by Lionardo da Vinci, called
The Virgin of the Rocks.*

(? 1805)

While young John runs to greet
The greater Infant's feet,
The Mother standing by, with trembling passion
Of devout admiration,
Beholds the engaging mystic play, and pretty adoration;
Nor knows as yet the full event
Of those so low beginnings,
From whence we date our winnings,
But wonders at the intent
Of those new rites, and what that strange child-worship meant.
But at her side
An angel doth abide,
With such a perfect joy
As no dim doubts alloy,
An intuition,
A glory, an amenity,
Passing the dark condition
Of blind humanity,
As if he surely knew
All the blest wonders should ensue,
Or he had lately left the upper sphere,
And had read all the sovran schemes and divine riddles there.

ON THE SAME

(*By Mary Lamb.* 1805)

Maternal lady with the virgin grace,
Heaven-born thy Jesus seemeth sure,
And of a virgin pure.
Lady most perfect, when thy sinless face
Men look upon, they wish to be
A Catholic, Madonna fair, to worship thee.

SONNETS

TO MISS KELLY

You are not, Kelly, of the common strain,
That stoop their pride and female honor down
To please that many-headed beast *the town*,
And vend their lavish smiles and tricks for gain;
By fortune thrown amid the actor's train,
You keep your native dignity of thought;
The plaudits that attend you come unsought,
As tributes due unto your natural vein.
Your tears have passion in them, and a grace
Of genuine freshness, which our hearts avow;
Your smiles are winds whose ways we cannot trace,
That vanish and return we know not how—
And please the better from a pensive face,
And thoughtful eye, and a reflecting brow.

ON THE SIGHT OF SWANS IN KENSINGTON GARDEN

Queen-bird that sittest on thy shining nest,
And thy young cygnets without sorrow hatchest,
And thou, thou other royal bird, that watchest
Lest the white mother wandering feet molest:
Shrined are your offspring in a chrystal cradle,
Brighter than Helen's ere she yet had burst
Her shelly prison. They shall be born at first
Strong, active, graceful, perfect, swan-like able
To tread the land or waters with security.
Unlike poor human births, conceived in sin,
In grief brought forth, both outwardly and in
Confessing weakness, error, and impurity.
Did heavenly creatures own succession's line,
The births of heaven like to your's would shine.

Here came " Was it some sweet device." See page 3.
Here came " Methinks how dainty sweet." See page 4.
Here came " When last I roved." See page 7.
Here came " A timid grace." See page 7.
Here came " If from my lips." See page 8.

THE FAMILY NAME

What reason first imposed thee, gentle name,
Name that my father bore, and his sire's sire,
Without reproach? we trace our stream no higher;
And I, a childless man, may end the same.
Perchance some shepherd on Lincolnian plains,
In manners guileless as his own sweet flocks,
Received thee first amid the merry mocks
And arch allusions of his fellow swains.
Perchance from Salem's holier fields returned,
With glory gotten on the heads abhorr'd
Of faithless Saracens, some martial lord
Took HIS meek title, in whose zeal he burn'd.
Whate'er the fount whence thy beginnings came,
No deed of mine shall shame thee, gentle name.

TO JOHN LAMB, ESQ.

Of the South-Sea-House

John, you were figuring in the gay career
Of blooming manhood with a young man's joy,
When I was yet a little peevish boy—
Though time has made the difference disappear
Betwixt our ages, which *then* seemed so great—
And still by rightful custom you retain
Much of the old authoritative strain,
And keep the elder brother up in state.
O! you do well in this. 'Tis man's worst deed
To let the "things that have been" run to waste,
And in the unmeaning present sink the past:
In whose dim glass even now I faintly read
Old buried forms, and faces long ago,
Which you, and I, and one more, only know.

Here came "O! I could laugh." See page 4.
Here came "We were two pretty babes." See page 8.
Here came, under the heading "Blank Verse," "Childhood," see page 8; "The Grandame," see page 5; "The Sabbath Bells," see page 9; "Fancy employed on Divine Subjects," see page 9; and "Composed at Midnight," see page 24.

TO MARTIN CHARLES BURNEY, ESQ.

(The Dedication to Vol. II. of Lamb's *Works*, 1818)

Forgive me, BURNEY, if to thee these late
And hasty products of a critic pen,
Thyself no common judge of books and men,
In feeling of thy worth I dedicate.
My *verse* was offered to an older friend;
The humbler *prose* has fallen to thy share:
Nor could I miss the occasion to declare,
What spoken in thy presence must offend—
That, set aside some few caprices wild,
Those humorous clouds that flit o'er brightest days,
In all my threadings of this worldly maze,
(And I have watched thee almost from a child),
Free from self-seeking, envy, low design,
I have not found a whiter soul than thine.

POEMS IN *ALBUM VERSES*, 1830

ALBUM VERSES

IN THE ALBUM OF A CLERGYMAN'S LADY

(? 1830)

AN Album is a Garden, not for show
    Planted, but use; where wholesome herbs should grow.
A Cabinet of curious porcelain, where
No fancy enters, but what's rich or rare.
A Chapel, where mere ornamental things
Are pure as crowns of saints, or angels' wings.
A List of living friends; aholier Room
For names of some since mouldering in the tomb,
Whose blooming memories life's cold laws survive;
And, dead elsewhere, they here yet speak, and live.
Such, and so tender, should an Album be;
And, Lady, such I wish this book to thee.

IN THE AUTOGRAPH BOOK OF MRS. SERGEANT W——

Had I a power, Lady, to my will,
You should not want Hand Writings. I would fill
Your leaves with Autographs—resplendent names
Of Knights and Squires of old, and courtly Dames,
Kings, Emperors, Popes. Next under these should stand
The hands of famous Lawyers—a grave band—
Who in their Courts of Law or Equity
Have best upheld Freedom and Property.
These should moot cases in your book, and vie
To show their reading and their Serjeantry.
But I have none of these; nor can I send
The notes by Bullen to her Tyrant penn'd
In her authentic hand; nor in soft hours
Lines writ by Rosamund in Clifford's bowers.
The lack of curious Signatures I moan,
And want the courage to subscribe my own.

IN THE ALBUM OF LUCY BARTON
(1824)

Little Book, surnamed of *white*,
Clean as yet, and fair to sight,
Keep thy attribution right.

Never disproportion'd scrawl;
Ugly blot, that's worse than all;
On thy maiden clearness fall!

In each letter, here design'd,
Let the reader emblem'd find
Neatness of the owner's mind.

Gilded margins count a sin,
Let thy leaves attraction win
By the golden rules within;

Sayings fetch'd from sages old;
Laws which Holy Writ unfold,
Worthy to be graved in gold:

Lighter fancies not excluding;
Blameless wit, with nothing rude in,
Sometimes mildly interluding

Amid strains of graver measure:
Virtue's self hath oft her pleasure
In sweet Muses' groves of leisure.

Riddles dark, perplexing sense;
Darker meanings of offence;
What but *shades*—be banished hence.

Whitest thoughts in whitest dress,
Candid meanings, best express
Mind of quiet Quakeress.

IN THE ALBUM OF MISS ——

I

Such goodness in your face doth shine,
With modest look, without design,
That I despair, poor pen of mine
    Can e'er express it.

To give it words I feebly try;
My spirits fail me to supply
Befitting language for 't, and I
    Can only bless it!

II

But stop, rash verse! and don't abuse
A bashful Maiden's ear with news
Of her own virtues. She'll refuse
    Praise sung so loudly.
Of that same goodness, you admire,
The best part is, she don't aspire
To praise—nor of herself desire
    To think too proudly.

IN THE ALBUM OF A VERY YOUNG LADY

(? 1830)

Joy to unknown Josepha who, I hear,
Of all good gifts, to Music most is given;
Science divine, which through the enraptured ear
Enchants the Soul, and lifts it nearer Heaven.
Parental smiles approvingly attend
Her pliant conduct of the trembling keys,
And listening strangers their glad suffrage lend.
Most musical is Nature. Birds—and Bees
At their sweet labour—sing. The moaning winds
Rehearse a *lesson* to attentive minds.
In louder tones "Deep unto Deep doth call;"
And there is Music in the Waterfall.

IN THE ALBUM OF A FRENCH TEACHER

(? 1829)

Implored for verse, I send you what I can;
But you are so exact a Frenchwoman,
As I am told, Jemima, that I fear
To wound with English your Parisian ear,
And think I do your choice collection wrong
With lines not written in the Frenchman's tongue.
Had I a knowledge equal to my will,
With airy *Chansons* I your leaves would fill;
With *Fabliaux*, that should emulate the vein
Of sprightly Gresset, or of La Fontaine;
Or *Scenes Comiques*, that should approach the air

Of your own favourite—renowned Moliere.
But at my suit the Muse of France looks sour,
And strikes me dumb! Yet, what is in my power
To testify respect for you, I pray,
Take in plain English—our rough Enfield way.

IN THE ALBUM OF MISS DAUBENY

I

Some poets by poetic law
Have Beauties praised, they never saw;
And sung of Kittys, and of Nancys,
Whose charms but lived in their own fancies.
So I, to keep my Muse a going,
That willingly would still be doing,
A Canzonet or two must try
In praise of—*pretty* Daubeny.

II

But whether she indeed be comely,
Or only very good and homely,
Of my own eyes I cannot say;
I trust to Emma Isola.
But sure I think her voice is tuneful,
As smoothest birds that sing in June full;
For else would strangely disagree
The *flowing* name of—Daubeny.

III

I hear that she a Book hath got—
As what young Damsel now hath not,
In which they scribble favorite fancies,
Copied from poems or romances?
And prettiest draughts, of her design,
About the curious Album shine;
And therefore she shall have for me
The style of—*tasteful* Daubeny.

IV

Thus far I have taken on believing;
But well I know without deceiving,
That in her heart she keeps alive still
Old school-day likings, which survive still
In spite of absence—worldly coldness—
And thereon can my Muse take boldness
To crown her other praises three
With praise of—*friendly* Daubeny.

IN THE ALBUM OF MRS. JANE TOWERS
(1828)

Lady Unknown, who crav'st from me Unknown
The trifle of a verse these leaves to grace,
How shall I find fit matter? with what face
Address a face that ne'er to me was shown?
Thy looks, tones, gesture, manners, and what not,
Conjecturing, I wander in the dark.
I know thee only Sister to Charles Clarke!
But at that name my cold Muse waxes hot,
And swears that thou art such a one as he,
Warm, laughter-loving, with a touch of madness,
Wild, glee-provoking, pouring oil of gladness
From frank heart without guile. And, if thou be
The pure reverse of this, and I mistake—
Demure one, I will like thee for his sake.

IN MY OWN ALBUM
(1827)

Fresh clad from heaven in robes of white,
A young probationer of light,
Thou wert my soul, an Album bright,

A spotless leaf; but thought, and care,
And friend and foe, in foul or fair,
Have "written strange defeatures" there;

And Time with heaviest hand of all,
Like that fierce writing on the wall,
Hath stamp'd sad dates—he can't recal;

And error gilding worst designs—
Like speckled snake that strays and shines—
Betrays his path by crooked lines;

And vice hath left his ugly blot;
And good resolves, a moment hot,
Fairly began—but finish'd not;

And fruitless, late remorse doth trace—
Like Hebrew lore a backward pace—
Her irrecoverable race.

Disjointed numbers; sense unknit;
Huge reams of folly, shreds of wit;
Compose the mingled mass of it.

My scalded eyes no longer brook
Upon this ink-blurr'd thing to look—
Go, shut the leaves, and clasp the book.

MISCELLANEOUS

ANGEL HELP[1]

(1827)

This rare tablet doth include
Poverty with Sanctitude.
Past midnight this poor Maid hath spun,
And yet the work is not half done,
Which must supply from earnings scant
A feeble bed-rid parent's want.
Her sleep-charged eyes exemption ask,
And Holy hands take up the task:
Unseen the rock and spindle ply,
And do her earthly drudgery.
Sleep, saintly poor one, sleep, sleep on;
And, waking, find thy labours done.
Perchance she knows it by her dreams;
Her eye hath caught the golden gleams,
Angelic presence testifying,
That round her every where are flying;
Ostents from which she may presume,
That much of Heaven is in the room.
Skirting her own bright hair they run,
And to the sunny add more sun:
Now on that aged face they fix,
Streaming from the Crucifix;
The flesh-clogg'd spirit disabusing,
Death-disarming sleeps infusing,
Prelibations, foretastes high,
And equal thoughts to live or die.
Gardener bright from Eden's bower,
Tend with care that lily flower;
To its leaves and root infuse
Heaven's sunshine, Heaven's dews.
'Tis a type, and 'tis a pledge,
Of a crowning privilege.

[1] Suggested by a drawing in the possession of Charles Aders, Esq., in which is represented the Legend of a poor female Saint; who, having spun past midnight, to maintain a bed-rid mother, has fallen asleep from fatigue, and Angels are finishing her work. In another part of the chamber, an Angel is tending a lily, the emblem of purity.

Careful as that lily flower,
This Maid must keep her precious dower
Live a sainted Maid, or die
Martyr to virginity.

THE CHRISTENING
(1829)

Array'd—a half-angelic sight—
In vests of pure Baptismal white,
The Mother to the Font doth bring
The little helpless nameless thing,
With hushes soft and mild caressing,
At once to get—a name and blessing.
Close by the Babe the Priest doth stand,
The Cleansing Water at his hand,
Which must assoil the soul within
From every stain of Adam's sin.
The Infant eyes the mystic scenes,
Nor knows what all this wonder means;
And now he smiles, as if to say
" I am a Christian made this day;"
Now frighted clings to Nurse's hold,
Shrinking from the water cold,
Whose virtues, rightly understood,
Are, as Bethesda's waters, good.
Strange words—The World, The Flesh, The Devil—
Poor Babe, what can it know of Evil?
But we must silently adore
Mysterious truths, and not explore.
Enough for him, in after-times,
When he shall read these artless rhymes,
If, looking back upon this day,
With quiet conscience, he can say
" I have in part redeem'd the pledge
Of my Baptismal privilege;
And more and more will strive to flee
All which my Sponsors kind did then renounce for me."

ON
AN INFANT DYING AS SOON AS BORN
(1827)

I saw where in the shroud did lurk
A curious frame of Nature's work.
A flow'ret crushed in the bud,

A nameless piece of Babyhood,
Was in a cradle-coffin lying;
Extinct, with scarce the sense of dying;
So soon to exchange the imprisoning womb
For darker closets of the tomb!
She did but ope an eye, and put
A clear beam forth, then strait up shut
For the long dark: ne'er more to see
Through glasses of mortality.
Riddle of destiny, who can show
What thy short visit meant, or know
What thy errand here below?
Shall we say, that Nature blind
Check'd her hand, and changed her mind,
Just when she had exactly wrought
A finish'd pattern without fault?
Could she flag, or could she tire,
Or lack'd she the Promethean fire
(With her nine moons' long workings sicken'd)
That should thy little limbs have quicken'd?
Limbs so firm, they seem'd to assure
Life of health, and days mature:
Woman's self in miniature!
Limbs so fair, they might supply
(Themselves now but cold imagery)
The sculptor to make Beauty by.
Or did the stern-eyed Fate descry,
That babe, or mother, one must die;
So in mercy left the stock,
And cut the branch; to save the shock
Of young years widow'd; and the pain,
When Single State comes back again
To the lone man who, 'reft of wife,
Thenceforward drags a maimed life?
The economy of Heaven is dark;
And wisest clerks have miss'd the mark,
Why Human Buds, like this, should fall,
More brief than fly ephemeral,
That has his day; while shrivel'd crones
Stiffen with age to stocks and stones;
And crabbed use the conscience sears
In sinners of an hundred years.
Mother's prattle, mother's kiss,
Baby fond, thou ne'er wilt miss.
Rites, which custom does impose,

Silver bells and baby clothes;
Coral redder than those lips,
Which pale death did late eclipse;
Music framed for infants' glee,
Whistle never tuned for thee;
Though thou want'st not, thou shalt have them,
Loving hearts were they which gave them.
Let not one be missing; nurse,
See them laid upon the hearse
Of infant slain by doom perverse.
Why should kings and nobles have
Pictured trophies to their grave;
And we, churls, to thee deny
Thy pretty toys with thee to lie,
A more harmless vanity?

TO BERNARD BARTON

With a Coloured Print[1]

(1827)

When last you left your Woodbridge pretty,
To stare at sights, and see the City,
If I your meaning understood,
You wish'd a Picture, cheap, but good;
The colouring? decent; clear, not muddy;
To suit a Poet's quiet study,
Where Books and Prints for delectation
Hang, rather than vain ostentation.
The subject? what I pleased, if comely;
But something scriptural and homely:
A sober Piece, not gay or wanton,
For winter fire-sides to descant on;
The theme so scrupulously handled,
A Quaker might look on unscandal'd;
Such as might satisfy Ann Knight,
And classic Mitford just not fright.
Just such a one I've found, and send it;
If liked, I give—if not, but lend it.
The moral? nothing can be sounder.
The fable? 'tis its own expounder—
A Mother teaching to her Chit
Some good book, and explaining it.

---

[1] From the venerable and ancient Manufactory of Carrington Bowles: some of my readers may recognise it.

He, silly urchin, tired of lesson,
His learning lays no mighty stress on,
But seems to hear not what he hears;
Thrusting his fingers in his ears,
Like Obstinate, that perverse funny one,
In honest parable of Bunyan.
His working Sister, more sedate,
Listens; but in a kind of state,
The painter meant for steadiness;
But has a tinge of sullenness;
And, at first sight, she seems to brook
As ill her needle, as he his book.
This is the Picture. For the Frame—
'Tis not ill-suited to the same;
Oak-carved, not gilt, for fear of falling;
Old-fashion'd; plain, yet not appalling;
And sober, as the Owner's Calling.

THE YOUNG CATECHIST[1]

(1827)

While this tawny Ethiop prayeth,
Painter, who is she that stayeth
By, with skin of whitest lustre,
Sunny locks, a shining cluster,
Saint-like seeming to direct him
To the Power that must protect him?
Is she of the Heaven-born Three,
Meek Hope, strong Faith, sweet Charity:
Or some Cherub?—
    They you mention
Far transcend my weak invention.
'Tis a simple Christian child,
Missionary young and mild,
From her stock of Scriptural knowledge,
Bible-taught without a college,
Which by reading she could gather,
Teaches him to say OUR FATHER
To the common Parent, who
Colour not respects, nor hue.
White and black in him have part,
Who looks not to the skin, but heart.

[1] A Picture by Henry Meyer, Esq.

SHE IS GOING

For their elder Sister's hair
Martha does a wreath prepare
Of bridal rose, ornate and gay:
To-morrow is the wedding day:
      She is going.

Mary, youngest of the three,
Laughing idler, full of glee,
Arm in arm does fondly chain her,
Thinking, poor trifler, to detain her—
      But she's going.

Vex not, maidens, nor regret
Thus to part with Margaret.
Charms like your's can never stay
Long within doors; and one day
      You'll be going.

TO A YOUNG FRIEND

On Her Twenty-First Birth-Day

Crown me a cheerful goblet, while I pray
A blessing on thy years, young Isola;
Young, but no more a child. How swift have flown
To me thy girlish times, a woman grown
Beneath my heedless eyes! in vain I rack
My fancy to believe the almanac,
That speaks thee Twenty-One. Thou should'st have still
Remain'd a child, and at thy sovereign will
Gambol'd about our house, as in times past.
Ungrateful Emma, to grow up so fast,
Hastening to leave thy friends!—for which intent,
Fond Runagate, be this thy punishment.
After some thirty years, spent in such bliss
As this earth can afford, where still we miss
Something of joy entire, may'st thou grow old
As we whom thou hast left! That wish was cold.
O far more ag'd and wrinkled, till folks say,
Looking upon thee reverend in decay,
"This Dame for length of days, and virtues rare,
With her respected Grandsire may compare."—

Grandchild of that respected Isola,
Thou should'st have had about thee on this day
Kind looks of Parents, to congratulate
Their Pride grown up to woman's grave estate.
But they have died, and left thee, to advance
Thy fortunes how thou may'st, and owe to chance
The friends which Nature grudg'd. And thou wilt find,
Or make such, Emma, if I am not blind
To thee and thy deservings. That last strain
Had too much sorrow in it. Fill again
Another cheerful goblet, while I say
" Health, and twice health, to our lost Isola."

TO THE SAME

External gifts of fortune, or of face,
Maiden, in truth, thou hast not much to show;
Much fairer damsels have I known, and know,
And richer may be found in every place.
In thy *mind* seek thy beauty, and thy wealth.
Sincereness lodgeth there, the soul's best health.
O guard that treasure above gold or pearl,
Laid up secure from moths and worldly stealth—
And take my benison, plain-hearted girl.

SONNETS

HARMONY IN UNLIKENESS

By Enfield lanes, and Winchmore's verdant hill,
Two lovely damsels cheer my lonely walk:
The fair Maria, as a vestal, still;
And Emma brown, exuberant in talk.
With soft and Lady speech the first applies
The mild correctives that to grace belong
To her redundant friend, who her defies
With jest, and mad discourse, and bursts of song.
O differing Pair, yet sweetly thus agreeing,
What music from your happy discord rises,
While your companion hearing each, and seeing,
Nor this, nor that, but both together, prizes;
This lesson teaching, which our souls may strike,
That harmonies may be in things unlike!

WRITTEN AT CAMBRIDGE
(*August* 15. 1819)

I was not train'd in Academic bowers,
And to those learned streams I nothing owe
Which copious from those twin fair founts do flow;
Mine have been any thing but studious hours.
Yet can I fancy, wandering 'mid thy towers,
Myself a nursling, Granta, of thy lap;
My brow seems tightening with the Doctor's cap,
And I walk *gowned*; feel unusual powers.
Strange forms of logic clothe my admiring speech,
Old Ramus' ghost is busy at my brain;
And my scull teems with notions infinite.
Be still, ye reeds of Camus, while I teach
Truths, which transcend the searching Schoolmen's vein,
And half had stagger'd that stout Stagirite!

TO A CELEBRATED FEMALE PERFORMER IN THE "BLIND BOY"
(1819)

Rare artist! who with half thy tools, or none,
Canst execute with ease thy curious art,
And press thy powerful'st meanings on the heart,
Unaided by the eye, expression's throne!
While each blind sense, intelligential grown
Beyond its sphere, performs the effect of sight:
Those orbs alone, wanting their proper might,
All motionless and silent seem to moan
The unseemly negligence of nature's hand,
That left them so forlorn. What praise is thine,
O mistress of the passions; artist fine!
Who dost our souls against our sense command,
Plucking the horror from a sightless face,
Lending to blank deformity a grace.

WORK
(1819)

Who first invented work, and bound the free
And holyday-rejoicing spirit down
To the ever-haunting importunity
Of business in the green fields, and the town—
To plough, loom, anvil, spade—and oh! most sad,
To that dry drudgery at the desk's dead wood?
Who but the Being unblest, alien from good,

Sabbathless Satan! he who his unglad
Task ever plies 'mid rotatory burnings,
That round and round incalculably reel—
For wrath divine hath made him like a wheel—
In that red realm from which are no returnings;
Where toiling, and turmoiling, ever and aye
He, and his thoughts, keep pensive working-day.

LEISURE
(1821)

They talk of time, and of time's galling yoke,
That like a mill-stone on man's mind doth press,
Which only works and business can redress:
Of divine Leisure such foul lies are spoke,
Wounding her fair gifts with calumnious stroke.
But might I, fed with silent meditation,
Assoiled live from that fiend Occupation—
Improbus Labor, which my spirits hath broke—
I'd drink of time's rich cup, and never surfeit:
Fling in more days than went to make the gem,
That crown'd the white top of Methusalem:
Yea on my weak neck take, and never forfeit,
Like Atlas bearing up the dainty sky,
The heaven-sweet burthen of eternity.

DEUS NOBIS HÆC OTIA FECIT.

TO SAMUEL ROGERS, ESQ.
(1829)

Rogers, of all the men that I have known
But slightly, who have died, your Brother's loss
Touch'd me most sensibly. There came across
My mind an image of the cordial tone
Of your fraternal meetings, where a guest
I more than once have sat; and grieve to think,
That of that threefold cord one precious link
By Death's rude hand is sever'd from the rest.
Of our old Gentry he appear'd a stem—
A Magistrate who, while the evil-doer
He kept in terror, could respect the Poor,
And not for every trifle harass them,
As some, divine and laic, too oft do.
This man's a private loss, and public too.

THE GIPSY'S MALISON

(1829)

"Suck, baby, suck, mother's love grows by giving,
Drain the sweet founts that only thrive by wasting;
Black manhood comes, when riotous guilty living
Hands thee the cup that shall be death in tasting.

Kiss, baby, kiss, mother's lips shine by kisses,
Choke the warm breath that else would fall in blessings;
Black manhood comes, when turbulent guilty blisses
Tend thee the kiss that poisons 'mid caressings.

Hang, baby, hang, mother's love loves such forces,
Strain the fond neck that bends still to thy clinging;
Black manhood comes, when violent lawless courses
Leave thee a spectacle in rude air swinging."

So sang a wither'd Beldam energetical,
And bann'd the ungiving door with lips prophetical.

COMMENDATORY VERSES

TO THE AUTHOR OF POEMS,

Published under the name of Barry Cornwall

(1820)

Let hate, or grosser heats, their foulness mask
Under the vizor of a borrowed name;
Let things eschew the light deserving blame:
No cause hast thou to blush for thy sweet task.
"Marcian Colonna" is a dainty book;
And thy "Sicilian Tale" may boldly pass;
Thy "Dream" 'bove all, in which, as in a glass,
On the great world's antique glories we may look.
No longer then, as "lowly substitute,
Factor, or Proctor, for another's gains,"
uffer the admiring world to be deceived;
Lest thou thyself, by self of fame bereaved,
Lament too late the lost prize of thy pains,
And heavenly tunes piped through an alien flute.

TO R [J.] S. KNOWLES, ESQ.

On his Tragedy of Virginius

(1820)

Twelve years ago I knew thee, Knowles, and then
Esteemed you a perfect specimen
Of those fine spirits warm-soul'd Ireland sends,
To teach us colder English how a friend's
Quick pulse should beat. I knew you brave, and plain,
Strong-sensed, rough-witted, above fear or gain;
But nothing further had the gift to espy.
Sudden you re-appear. With wonder I
Hear my old friend (turn'd Shakspeare) read a scene
Only to *his* inferior in the clean
Passes of pathos : with such fence-like art—
Ere we can see the steel, 'tis in our heart.
Almost without the aid language affords,
Your piece seems wrought. That huffing medium, *words*,
(Which in the modern Tamburlaines quite sway
Our shamed souls from their bias) in your play
We scarce attend to. Hastier passion draws
Our tears on credit : and we find the cause
Some two hours after, spelling o'er again
Those strange few words at ease, that wrought the pain.
Proceed, old friend ; and, as the year returns,
Still snatch some new old story from the urns
Of long-dead virtue. We, that knew before
Your worth, may admire, we cannot love you more.

TO THE EDITOR OF THE "EVERY-DAY BOOK"

(1825)

I like you, and your book, ingenuous Hone !
  In whose capacious all-embracing leaves
The very marrow of tradition's shown ;
  And all that history—much that fiction—weaves.

By every sort of taste your work is graced.
  Vast stores of modern anecdote we find,
With good old story quaintly interlaced—
  The theme as various as the reader's mind.

Rome's life-fraught legends you so truly paint—
  Yet kindly,—that the half-turn'd Catholic
Scarcely forbears to smile at his own saint,
  And cannot curse the candid heretic.

TO CAROLINE MARIA APPLEBEE

Rags, relics, witches, ghosts, fiends, crowd your page;
  Our fathers' mummeries we well-pleased behold,
And, proudly conscious of a purer age,
  Forgive some fopperies in the times of old.

Verse-honouring Phœbus, Father of bright *Days*,
  Must needs bestow on you both good and many,
Who, building trophies of his Children's praise,
  Run their rich Zodiac through, not missing any

Dan Phœbus loves your book—trust me, friend Hone—
  The title only errs, he bids me say:
For while such art, wit, reading, there are shown,
  He swears, 'tis not a work of *every day*.

ACROSTICS

TO CAROLINE MARIA APPLEBEE

An Acrostic

Caroline glides smooth in verse,
And is easy to rehearse;
Runs just like some crystal river
O'er its pebbly bed for ever.
Lines as harsh and quaint as mine
In their close at least will shine,
Nor from sweetness can decline,
Ending but with *Caroline*.

Maria asks a statelier pace—
"*Ave Maria*, full of grace!"
Romish rites before me rise,
Image-worship, sacrifice,
And well-meant but mistaken pieties.

Apple with *Bee* doth rougher run.
Paradise was lost by one;
Peace of mind would we regain,
Let us, like the other, strain
Every harmless faculty,
Bee-like at work in our degree,
Ever some sweet task designing,
Extracting still, and still refining.

TO CECILIA CATHERINE LAWTON

An Acrostic

Choral service, solemn chanting,
Echoing round cathedrals holy—
Can aught else on earth be wanting
In heav'n's bliss to plunge us wholly?
Let us great *Cecilia* honour
In the praise we give unto them,
And the merit be upon her.

Cold the heart that would undo them,
And the solemn organ banish
That this sainted Maid invented.
Holy thoughts too quickly vanish,
Ere the expression can be vented.
Raise the song to *Catherine*,
In her torments most divine!
Ne'er by Christians be forgot—
Envied be—this Martyr's lot.

Lawton, who these *names* combinest,
Aim to emulate their praises;
Women were they, yet divinest
Truths they taught; and story raises
O'er their mouldering bones a Tomb,
Not to die till Day of Doom.

ACROSTIC,

TO A LADY WHO DESIRED ME TO WRITE HER EPITAPH

(1830)

Grace Joanna here doth lie:
Reader, wonder not that I
Ante-date her hour of rest.
Can I thwart her wish exprest,
Ev'n unseemly though the laugh

Jesting with an Epitaph?
On her bones the turf lie lightly,
And her rise again be brightly!
No dark stain be found upon her—
No, there will not, on mine honour—
Answer that at least I can.

TO HER YOUNGEST DAUGHTER

Would that I, thrice happy man,
In as spotless garb might rise,
Light as she will climb the skies,
Leaving the dull earth behind,
In a car more swift than wind.
All her errors, all her failings,
(Many they were not) and ailings,
Sleep secure from Envy's railings.

ANOTHER,

TO HER YOUNGEST DAUGHTER

(1830)

Least Daughter, but not least beloved, of *Grace!*
O frown not on a stranger, who from place
Unknown and distant these few lines hath penn'd.
I but report what thy Instructress Friend
So oft hath told us of thy gentle heart.
A pupil most affectionate thou art,
Careful to learn what elder years impart.
Louisa—Clare—by which name shall I call thee?
A prettier pair of names sure ne'er was found,
Resembling thy own sweetness in sweet sound.
Ever calm peace and innocence befal thee!

TRANSLATIONS

From the Latin of Vincent Bourne

I

ON A SEPULCHRAL STATUE OF AN INFANT SLEEPING

Beautiful Infant, who dost keep
Thy posture here, and sleep'st a marble sleep,
May the repose unbroken be,
Which the fine Artist's hand hath lent to thee,
While thou enjoy'st along with it
That which no art, or craft, could ever hit,
Or counterfeit to mortal sense,
The heaven-infused sleep of Innocence!

II

THE RIVAL BELLS

A tuneful challenge rings from either side
Of Thames' fair banks. Thy twice six Bells, Saint **Bride**,
Peal swift and shrill; to which more slow reply
The deep-toned eight of Mary Overy.
Such harmony from the contention flows,
That the divided ear no preference knows;
Betwixt them both disparting Music's State,
While one exceeds in number, one in weight.

III

EPITAPH ON A DOG

(1820)

Poor Irus' faithful wolf-dog here I lie,
That wont to tend my old blind master's steps,
His guide and guard; nor, while my service lasted,
Had he occasion for that staff, with which
He now goes picking out his path in fear
Over the highways and crossings, but would plant
Safe in the conduct of my friendly string,
A firm foot forward still, till he had reach'd
His poor seat on some stone, nigh where the tide
Of passers-by in thickest confluence flow'd:
To whom with loud and passionate laments
From morn to eve his dark estate he wail'd.
Nor wail'd to all in vain: some here and there,
The well disposed and good, their pennies gave.
I meantime at his feet obsequious slept;
Not all-asleep in sleep, but heart and ear
Prick'd up at his least motion, to receive
At his kind hand my customary crumbs,
And common portion in his feast of scraps;
Or when night warn'd us homeward, tired and spent
With our long day, and tedious beggary.
These were my manners, this my way of life,
Till age and slow disease me overtook,
And sever'd from my sightless master's side.
But lest the grace of so good deeds should die,
Through tract of years in mute oblivion lost,
This slender tomb of turf hath Irus rear'd,
Cheap monument of no ungrudging hand,

And with short verse inscribed it, to attest,
In long and lasting union to attest,
The virtues of the Beggar and his Dog.

IV

THE BALLAD SINGERS

Where seven fair Streets to one tall Column[1] draw,
Two Nymphs have ta'en their stand, in hats of straw;
Their yellower necks huge beads of amber grace,
And by their trade they're of the Sirens' race:
With cloak loose-pinn'd on each, that has been red,
But long with dust and dirt discoloured
Belies its hue; in mud behind, before,
From heel to middle leg becrusted o'er.
One a small infant at the breast does bear;
And one in her right hand her tuneful ware,
Which she would vend. Their station scarce is taken,
When youths and maids flock round. His stall forsaken,
Forth comes a Son of Crispin, leathern-capt,
Prepared to buy a ballad, if one apt
To move his fancy offers. Crispin's sons
Have, from uncounted time, with ale and buns
Cherish'd the gift of *Song*, which sorrow quells;
And, working single in their low-rooft cells,
Oft cheat the tedium of a winter's night
With anthems warbled in the Muses' spight.
Who now hath caught the alarm? the Servant Maid
Hath heard a buzz at distance; and, afraid
To miss a note, with elbows red comes out.
Leaving his forge to cool, Pyracmon stout
Thrusts in his unwash'd visage. *He* stands by,
Who the hard trade of Porterage does ply
With stooping shoulders. What cares he? he sees
The assembled ring, nor heeds his tottering knees,
But pricks his ears up with the hopes of song.
So, while the Bard of Rhodope his wrong
Bewail'd to Proserpine on Thracian strings,
The tasks of gloomy Orcus lost their stings,
And stone-vext Sysiphus forgets his load.
Hither and thither from the sevenfold road
Some cart or waggon crosses, which divides
The close-wedged audience; but, as when the tides

[1] Seven Dials.

To ploughing ships give way, the ship being past,
They re-unite, so these unite as fast.
The older Songstress hitherto hath spent
Her elocution in the argument
Of their great Song in *prose;* to wit, the woes
Which Maiden true to faithless Sailor owes—
Ah! "*Wandering He!*"—which now in loftier *verse*
Pathetic they alternately rehearse.
All gaping wait the event. This Critic opes
His right ear to the strain. The other hopes
To catch it better with his left. Long trade
It were to tell, how the deluded Maid
A victim fell. And now right greedily
All hands are stretching forth the songs to buy,
That are so tragical; which She, and She,
Deals out, and *sings the while;* nor can there be
A breast so obdurate here, that will hold back
His contribution from the gentle rack
Of Music's pleasing torture. Irus' self,
The staff-propt Beggar, his thin-gotten pelf
Brings out from pouch, where squalid farthings rest,
And boldly claims his ballad with the best.
An old Dame only lingers. To her purse
The penny sticks. At length, with harmless curse,
"Give me," she cries. "I'll paste it on my wall,
While the wall lasts, to show what ills befal
Fond hearts seduced from Innocency's way;
How Maidens fall, and Mariners betray."

v

TO DAVID COOK,

Of the Parish of Saint Margaret's, Westminster, Watchman

For much good-natured verse received from thee,
A loving verse take in return from me.
"Good morrow to my masters," is your cry;
And to our David "twice as good," say I.
Not Peter's monitor, shrill chanticleer,
Crows the approach of dawn in notes more clear,
Or tells the hours more faithfully. While night
Fills half the world with shadows of affright,
You with your lantern, partner of your round,
Traverse the paths of Margaret's hallow'd bound.

The tales of ghosts which old wives' ears drink up,
The drunkard reeling home from tavern cup,
Nor prowling robber, your firm soul appal;
Arm'd with thy faithful staff thou slight'st them all.
But if the market gard'ner chance to pass,
Bringing to town his fruit, or early grass,
The gentle salesman you with candour greet,
And with reit'rated "good mornings" meet.
Announcing your approach by formal bell,
Of nightly weather you the changes tell;
Whether the Moon shines, or her head doth steep
In rain-portending clouds. When mortals sleep
In downy rest, you brave the snows and sleet
Of winter; and in alley, or in street,
Relieve your midnight progress with a verse.
What though fastidious Phœbus frown averse
On your didactic strain—indulgent Night
With caution hath seal'd up both ears of Spite,
And critics sleep while you in staves do sound
The praise of long-dead Saints, whose Days abound
In wintry months; but Crispin chief proclaim:
Who stirs not at that Prince of Coblers' name?
Profuse in loyalty some couplets shine,
And wish long days to all the Brunswick line!
To youths and virgins they chaste lessons read;
Teach wives and husbands how their lives to lead;
Maids to be cleanly, footmen free from vice;
How death at last all ranks doth equalise;
And, in conclusion, pray good years befal,
With store of wealth, your "worthy masters all."
For this and other tokens of good will,
On boxing day may store of shillings fill
Your Christmas purse; no householder give less,
When at each door your blameless suit you press:
And what you wish to us (it is but reason)
Receive in turn—the compliments o' th' season!

VI

ON A DEAF AND DUMB ARTIST[1]

And hath thy blameless life become
A prey to the devouring tomb?
A more mute silence hast thou known,
A deafness deeper than thine own,

[1] Benjamin Ferrers—died A.D. 1732.

While Time was? and no friendly Muse,
That mark'd thy life, and knows thy dues,
Repair with quickening verse the breach,
And write thee into light and speech?
The Power, that made the Tongue, restrain'd
Thy lips from lies, and speeches feign'd;
Who made the Hearing, without wrong
Did rescue thine from Siren's song.
He let thee *see* the ways of men,
Which thou with pencil, not with pen,
Careful Beholder, down did'st note,
And all their motley actions quote,
Thyself unstain'd the while. From look
Or gesture reading, more than *book*,
In letter'd pride thou took'st no part,
Contented with the Silent Art,
Thyself as silent. Might I be
As speechless, deaf, and good, as He!

VII

NEWTON'S PRINCIPIA

Great Newton's self, to whom the world's in debt,
Owed to School Mistress sage his Alphabet;
But quickly wiser than his Teacher grown,
Discover'd properties to her unknown;
Of A *plus* B, or *minus*, learn'd the use,
Known Quantities from unknown to educe;
And made—no doubt to that old dame's surprise—
The Christ-Cross-Row his Ladder to the skies.
Yet, whatsoe'er Geometricians say,
Her Lessons were his true Principia!

VIII

THE HOUSE-KEEPER

The frugal snail, with fore-cast of repose,
Carries his house with him, where'er he goes;
Peeps out—and if there comes a shower of rain,
Retreats to his small domicile amain.
Touch but a tip of him, a horn—'tis well—
He curls up in his sanctuary shell.
He's his own landlord, his own tenant; stay
Long as he will, he dreads no Quarter Day.

Himself he boards and lodges; both invites,
And feasts, himself; sleeps with himself o' nights.
He spares the upholsterer trouble to procure
Chattles; himself is his own furniture,
And his sole riches. Wheresoe'er he roam—
Knock when you will—he's sure to be at home.

IX

THE FEMALE ORATORS

Nigh London's famous Bridge, a Gate more famed
Stands, or once stood, from old Belinus named,
So judged Antiquity; and therein wrongs
A name, allusive strictly to *two Tongues*.[1]
Her School hard by the Goddess Rhetoric opes,
And *gratis* deals to Oyster-wives her Tropes.
With Nereid green, green Nereid disputes,
Replies, rejoins, confutes, and still confutes.
One her coarse sense by metaphors expounds,
And one in literalities abounds;
In mood and figure these keep up the din:
Words multiply, and every word tells in.
Her hundred throats here bawling Slander strains;
And unclothed Venus to her tongue gives reins
In terms, which Demosthenic force outgo,
And baldest jests of foul-mouth'd Cicero.
Right in the midst great Ate keeps her stand,
And from her sovereign station taints the land.
Hence Pulpits rail; grave Senates learn to jar;
Quacks scold; and Billinsgate infects the Bar.

PINDARIC ODE TO THE TREAD MILL

(1825)

I

Inspire my spirit, Spirit of De Foe,
That sang the Pillory,
In loftier strains to show
A more sublime Machine

[1] *Billingis* in the Latin.

Than that, where thou wert seen,
With neck out-stretcht and shoulders ill awry,
Courting coarse plaudits from vile crowds below—
A most unseemly show !

II

In such a place
Who could expose thy face,
Historiographer of deathless Crusoe !
That paint'st the strife
And all the naked ills of savage life,
Far above Rousseau ?
Rather myself had stood
In that ignoble wood,
Bare to the mob, on holyday or high day.
If nought else could atone
For waggish libel,
I swear on bible,
I would have spared him for thy sake alone,
Man Friday !

III

Our ancestors' were sour days,
Great Master of Romance !
A milder doom had fallen to thy chance
In our days :
Thy sole assignment
Some solitary confinement,
(Not worth thy care a carrot,)
Where in world-hidden cell
Thou thy own Crusoe might have acted well,
Only without the parrot ;
By sure experience taught to know,
Whether the qualms thou mak'st him feel were truly such
or no.

IV

But stay ! methinks in statelier measure—
A more companionable pleasure—
I see thy steps the mighty Tread Mill trace,
(The subject of my song
Delay'd however long,)
And some of thine own race,
To keep thee company, thou bring'st with thee along.

PINDARIC ODE TO THE TREAD MILL

There with thee go,
Link'd in like sentence,
With regulated pace and footing slow,
Each old acquaintance,
Rogue—harlot—thief—that live to future ages;
Through many a labour'd tome,
Rankly embalm'd in thy too natural pages.
Faith, friend De Foe, thou art quite at home!
Not one of thy great offspring thou dost lack,
From pirate Singleton to pilfering Jack.
Here Flandrian Moll her brazen incest brags;
Vice-stript Roxana, penitent in rags,
There points to Amy, treading equal chimes,
The faithful handmaid to her faithless crimes.

V

Incompetent my song to raise
To its just height thy praise,
Great Mill!
That by thy motion proper
(No thanks to wind, or sail, or working rill)
Grinding that stubborn corn, the Human will,
Turn'st out men's consciences,
That were begrimed before, as clean and sweet
As flour from purest wheat,
Into thy hopper.
All reformation short of thee but nonsense is,
Or human, or divine.

VI

Compared with thee,
What are the labours of that Jumping Sect,
Which feeble laws connive at rather than respect?
Thou dost not bump,
Or jump,
But *walk* men into virtue; betwixt crime
And slow repentance giving breathing time,
And leisure to be good;
Instructing with discretion demi-reps
How to direct their steps.

VII

Thou best Philosopher made out of wood!
Not that which framed the tub,
Where sate the Cynic cub,
With nothing in his bosom sympathetic;

But from those groves derived, I deem,
Where Plato nursed his dream
Of immortality;
Seeing that clearly
Thy system all is merely
Peripatetic.
Thou to thy pupils dost such lessons give
Of how to live
With temperance, sobriety, morality,
(A new art,)
That from thy school, by force of virtuous deeds,
Each Tyro now proceeds
A " Walking Stewart!"

EPICEDIUM
GOING OR GONE
(1827)

I

Fine merry franions,
Wanton companions,
My days are ev'n banyans
    With thinking upon ye;
How Death, that last stinger,
Finis-writer, end-bringer,
Has laid his chill finger,
    Or is laying on ye.

II

There's rich Kitty Wheatley,
With footing it featly
That took me completely,
    She sleeps in the Kirk House;
And poor Polly Perkin,
Whose Dad was still firking
The jolly ale firkin,
    She's gone to the Work-house;

III

Fine Gard'ner, Ben Carter
(In ten counties no smarter)
Has ta'en his departure
    For Proserpine's orchards;
And Lily, postillion,
With cheeks of vermilion,
Is one of a million
    That fill up the church-yards;

IV

And, lusty as Dido,
Fat Clemitson's widow
Flits now a small shadow
    By Stygian hid ford;
And good Master Clapton
Has thirty years nap't on
The ground he last hap't on,
    Intomb'd by fair Widford;

V

And gallant Tom Dockwra,
Of nature's finest crockery,
Now but thin air and mockery,
    Lurks by Avernus,
Whose honest grasp of hand
Still, while his life did stand,
At friend's or foe's command,
    Almost did burn us.

VI

Roger de Coverley
Not more good man than he;
Yet has he equally
    Push'd for Cocytus,
With drivelling Worral,
And wicked old Dorrell,
'Gainst whom I've a quarrel,
    Whose end might affright us!—

VII

Kindly hearts have I known;
Kindly hearts, they are flown;
Here and there if but one
    Linger yet uneffaced,
Imbecile tottering elves,
Soon to be wreck'd on shelves,
These scarce are half themselves,
    With age and care crazed.

VIII

But this day Fanny Hutton
Her last dress has put on;
Her fine lessons forgotten,
    She died, as the dunce died:

And prim Betsy Chambers,
Decay'd in her members,
No longer remembers
    Things, as she once did;

IX

And prudent Miss Wither
Not in jest now doth *wither*,
And soon must go—whither
    Nor I well, nor you know;
And flaunting Miss Waller,
That soon must befal her,
Whence none can recal her,
    Though proud once as Juno![1]

---

[1] Here came, in *Album Verses* 1830, "The Wife's Trial," for which see **page 243**, where it is placed with Lamb's other plays.

POEMS ADDED TO *ALBUM VERSES* IN THE 1836 EDITION OF LAMB'S *POETICAL WORKS*

IN THE ALBUM OF EDITH S[OUTHEY]

(1833)

IN Christian world MARY the garland wears!
  REBECCA sweetens on a Hebrew's ear;
Quakers for pure PRISCILLA are more clear;
And the light Gaul by amorous NINON swears.
Among the lesser lights how LUCY shines!
What air of fragrance ROSAMOND throws round!
How like a hymn doth sweet CECILIA sound!
Of MARTHAS, and of ABIGAILS, few lines
Have bragg'd in verse. Of coarsest household stuff
Should homely JOAN be fashioned. But can
You BARBARA resist, or MARIAN?
And is not CLARE for love excuse enough?
Yet, by my faith in numbers, I profess,
These all, than Saxon EDITH, please me less.

TO DORA W[ORDSWORTH],

On Being Asked by Her Father to Write in Her Album

An Album is a Banquet: from the store,
In his intelligential Orchard growing,
Your Sire might heap your board to overflowing;—
One shaking of the Tree—'twould ask no more
To set a Salad forth, more rich than that
Which Evelyn[1] in his princely cookery fancied:
Or that more rare, by Eve's neat hands enhanced,
Where, a pleased guest, the angelic Virtue sat.
But like the all-grasping Founder of the Feast,
Whom Nathan to the sinning king did tax,

[1] Acetaria, a Discourse of Sallets, by J. E., 1706.

From his less wealthy neighbours he exacts;
Spares his own flocks, and takes the poor man's beast.
Obedient to his bidding, lo, I am,
A zealous, meek, *contributory*

                        LAMB.

IN THE ALBUM OF ROTHA Q[UILLINAN]

A passing glance was all I caught of thee,
In my own Enfield haunts at random roving.
Old friends of ours were with thee, faces loving;
Time short: and salutations cursory,
Though deep, and hearty. The familiar Name
Of you, yet unfamiliar, raised in me
Thoughts—what the daughter of that Man should be,
Who call'd our Wordsworth friend. My thoughts did frame
A growing Maiden, who, from day to day
Advancing still in stature, and in grace,
Would all her lonely Father's griefs efface,
And his paternal cares with usury pay.
I still retain the phantom, as I can;
And call the gentle image—Quillinan.

IN THE ALBUM OF CATHERINE ORKNEY

    Canadia! boast no more the toils
    Of hunters for the furry spoils;
    Your whitest ermines are but foils
        To brighter Catherine Orkney.

    That such a flower should ever burst
    From climes with rigorous winter curst!—
    We bless you, that so kindly nurst
        This flower, this Catherine Orkney.

    We envy not your proud display
    Of lake—wood—vast Niagara:
    Your greatest pride we've borne away.
        How spared you Catherine Orkney?

    That Wolfe on Heights of Abraham fell,
    To your reproach no more we tell:
    Canadia, you repaid us well
        With rearing Catherine Orkney.

O Britain, guard with tenderest care
The charge allotted to your share :
You've scarce a native maid so fair,
 So good, as Catherine Orkney.

TO T. STOTHARD, ESQ.

On His Illustrations of the Poems of Mr. Rogers

(1833)

Consummate Artist, whose undying name
With classic Rogers shall go down to fame,
Be this thy crowning work! In my young days
How often have I with a child's fond gaze
Pored on the pictured wonders [1] thou hadst done :
Clarissa mournful, and prim Grandison!
All Fielding's, Smollett's heroes, rose to view ;
I saw, and I believed the phantoms true.
But, above all, that most romantic tale [2]
Did o'er my raw credulity prevail,
Where Glums and Gawries wear mysterious things,
That serve at once for jackets and for wings.
Age, that enfeebles other men's designs,
But heightens thine, and thy free draught refines.
In several ways distinct you make us feel—
Graceful as Raphael, as Watteau *genteel.*
Your lights and shades, as Titianesque, we praise ;
And warmly wish you Titian's length of days.

TO A FRIEND ON HIS MARRIAGE

(1833)

What makes a happy wedlock ? What has fate
Not given to thee in thy well-chosen mate ?
Good sense—good humour ;—these are trivial things,
Dear M——, that each trite encomiast sings.
But she hath these, and more. A mind exempt
From every low-bred passion, where contempt,
Nor envy, nor detraction, ever found
A harbour yet ; an understanding sound ;
Just views of right and wrong ; perception full
Of the deformed, and of the beautiful,
In life and manners ; wit above her sex,
Which, as a gem, her sprightly converse decks ;

---

[1] Illustrations of the British Novelists.   [2] Peter Wilkins.

Exuberant fancies, prodigal of mirth,
To gladden woodland walk, or winter hearth;
A noble nature, conqueror in the strife
Of conflict with a hard discouraging life,
Strengthening the veins of virtue, past the power
Of those whose days have been one silken hour,
Spoil'd fortune's pamper'd offspring; a keen sense
Alike of benefit, and of offence,
With reconcilement quick, that instant springs
From the charged heart with nimble angel wings;
While grateful feelings, like a signet sign'd
By a strong hand, seem burnt into her mind.
If these, dear friend, a dowry can confer
Richer than land, thou hast them all in her;
And beauty, which some hold the chiefest boon,
Is in thy bargain for a make-weight thrown.

THE SELF-ENCHANTED
(1833)

I had a sense in dreams of a beauty rare,
Whom Fate had spell-bound, and rooted there,
Stooping, like some enchanted theme,
Over the marge of that crystal stream,
Where the blooming Greek, to Echo blind,
With Self-love fond, had to waters pined.
Ages had waked, and ages slept,
And that bending posture still she kept:
For her eyes she may not turn away,
'Till a fairer object shall pass that way—
'Till an image more beauteous this world can show,
Than her own which she sees in the mirror below.
Pore on, fair Creature! for ever pore,
Nor dream to be disenchanted more;
For vain is expectance, and wish is vain,
'Till a new Narcissus can come again.

TO LOUISA M[ARTIN], WHOM I USED TO CALL "MONKEY"
(1831)

Louisa, serious grown and mild,
I knew you once a romping child,
Obstreperous much and very wild.
Then you would clamber up my knees,
And strive with every art to tease,

When every art of yours could please.
Those things would scarce be proper now.
But they are gone, I know not how,
And woman's written on your brow.
Time draws his finger o'er the scene;
But I cannot forget between
The Thing to me you once have been
Each sportive sally, wild escape,—
The scoff, the banter, and the jape,—
And antics of my gamesome Ape.

CHEAP GIFTS: A SONNET
(1834)

[In a leaf of a quarto edition of the 'Lives of the Saints, written in Spanish by the learned and reverend father, Alfonso Villegas, Divine, of the order of St. Dominick, set forth in English by John Heigham, Anno 1630,' bought at a Catholic book-shop in Duke Street, Lincoln's Inn Fields, I found, carefully inserted, a painted flower, seemingly coeval with the book itself; and did not, for some time, discover that it opened in the middle, and was the cover to a very humble draught of a St. Anne, with the Virgin and Child; doubtless the performance of some poor, but pious Catholic, whose meditations it assisted.]

O lift with reverent hand that tarnish'd flower,
That 'shrines beneath her modest canopy
Memorials dear to Romish piety;
Dim specks, rude shapes, of Saints! in fervent hour
The work perchance of some meek devotee,
Who, poor in worldly treasures to set forth
The sanctities she worshipped to their worth,
In this imperfect tracery might see
Hints, that all Heaven did to her sense reveal.
Cheap gifts best fit poor givers. We are told
Of the lone mite, the cup of water cold,
That in their way approved the offerer's zeal.
True love shows costliest, where the means are scant;
And, in her reckoning, they *abound*, who *want*.

FREE THOUGHTS ON SEVERAL EMINENT COMPOSERS
(1830)

Some cry up Haydn, some Mozart,
Just as the whim bites; for my part,
I do not care a farthing candle
For either of them, or for Handel.—
Cannot a man live free and easy,
Without admiring Pergolesi?

Or thro' the world with comfort go,
That never heard of Doctor Blow?
So help me heaven, I hardly have;
And yet I eat, and drink, and shave,
Like other people, if you watch it,
And know no more of stave or crotchet,
Than did the primitive Peruvians;
Or those old ante-queer-diluvians
That lived in the unwash'd world with Jubal,
Before that dirty blacksmith Tubal
By stroke on anvil, or by summ'at,
Found out, to his great surprise, the gamut.
I care no more for Cimarosa,
Than he did for Salvator Rosa,
Being no painter; and bad luck
Be mine, if I can bear that Gluck!
Old Tycho Brahe, and modern Herschel,
Had something in them; but who's Purcel?
The devil, with his foot so cloven,
For aught I care, may take Beethoven;
And, if the bargain does not suit,
I'll throw him Weber in to boot.
There's not the splitting of a splinter
To chuse 'twixt him last named, and Winter.
Of Doctor Pepusch old queen Dido
Knew just as much, God knows, as I do.
I would not go four miles to visit
Sebastian Bach (or Batch, which is it?);
No more I would for Bononcini.
As for Novello, or Rossini,
I shall not say a word to grieve 'em,
Because they're living; so I leave 'em.

MISCELLANEOUS POEMS, MANY OF WHICH WERE PRINTED IN PERIODICALS, BUT NOT COLLECTED BY LAMB

DRAMATIC FRAGMENT
(1798)

>   Fie upon't.
> All men are false, I think. The date of love
> Is out, expired, its stories all grown stale,
> O'er past, forgotten, like an antique tale
> Of Hero and Leander.
>   JOHN WOODVIL.

All are not false. I knew a youth who died
For grief, because his Love proved so,
And married with another.
I saw him on the wedding-day,
For he was present in the church that day,
In festive bravery deck'd,
As one that came to grace the ceremony.
I mark'd him when the ring was given,
His countenance never changed;
And when the priest pronounced the marriage blessing,
He put a silent prayer up for the bride,
For so his moving lip interpreted.
He came invited to the marriage feast
With the bride's friends,
And was the merriest of them all that day:
But they, who knew him best, called it feign'd mirth;
And others said,
He wore a smile like death upon his face.
His presence dash'd all the beholders' mirth,
And he went away in tears.

What followed then?

Oh! then
He did not, as neglected suitors use,
Affect a life of solitude in shades,
But lived,

In free discourse and sweet society,
Among his friends who knew his gentle nature best.
Yet ever when he smiled,
There was a mystery legible in his face,
That whoso saw him said he was a man
Not long for this world.——
And true it was, for even then
The silent love was feeding at his heart
Of which he died:
Nor ever spake word of reproach,
Only, he wish'd in death that his remains
Might find a poor grave in some spot, not far
From his mistress' family vault, "being the place
Where one day Anna should herself be laid."

EPITAPH ON A YOUNG LADY WHO LIVED NEGLECTED AND DIED OBSCURE

(? 1801)

UNDER this cold marble stone
    Lie the sad remains of one
Who, when alive, by few or none
Was lov'd, as lov'd she might have been,
If she prosp'rous days had seen,
Or had thriving been, I ween.
Only this cold funeral stone
Tells, she was beloved by one,
Who on the marble graves his moan.

THE APE

(1806)

An Ape is but a trivial beast,
    Men count it light and vain;
But I would let them have their thoughts,
    To have my Ape again.

To love a beast in any sort,
    Is no great sign of grace;
But I have loved a flouting Ape's
    'Bove any lady's face.

I have known the power of two fair eyes,
    In smile, or else in glance,
And how (for I a lover was)
    They make the spirits dance;

THE APE

But I would give two hundred smiles,
   Of them that fairest be,
For one look of my staring Ape,
   That used to stare on me.

This beast, this Ape, it had a face—
   If face it might be styl'd—
Sometimes it was a staring Ape,
   Sometimes a beauteous child—

A Negro flat—a Pagod squat,
   Cast in a Chinese mold—
And then it was a Cherub's face,
   Made of the beaten gold!

But TIME, that's meddling, meddling still
   And always altering things—
And, what's already at the best,
   To alteration brings—

That turns the sweetest buds to flowers,
   And chops and changes toys—
That breaks up dreams, and parts old friends,
   And still commutes our joys—

Has changed away my Ape at last
   And in its place convey'd,
Thinking therewith to cheat my sight,
   A fresh and blooming maid!

And fair to sight is she—and still
   Each day doth sightlier grow,
Upon the ruins of the Ape,
   My ancient play-fellow!

The tale of Sphinx, and Theban jests,
   I true in me perceive;
I suffer riddles; death from dark
   Enigmas I receive:

Whilst a hid being I pursue,
   That lurks in a new shape,
My darling in herself I miss—
   And, in my Ape, THE APE.

In tabulam eximii pictoris B. HAYDONI, *in quâ Solymœi, adveniente Domino, palmas in viâ prosternentes mirâ arte depinguntur*

(1820)

Quid vult iste equitans? et quid oclit ista virorum
Palmifera ingens turba, et vox tremebunda Hosanna,
Hosanna Christo semper semperque canamus.

Palma fuit *Senior* pictor celeberrimus olim;
Sed palmam cedat, modò si foret ille superstes,
Palma, Haydone, tibi: tu palmas omnibus aufers.

Palma negata macrum, donataque reddit opimum.
Si simul incipiat cum famâ increscere corpus,
Tu citò pinguesces, fies et, amicule, obesus.

Affectat lauros pictores atque poetæ
Sin laurum invideant (sed quis tibi?) laurigerentes,
Pro lauro palmâ viridante tempora cingas.

CARLAGNULUS.

Translation of the Latin Verses on Mr. Haydon's Picture

What rider's that? and who those myriads bringing
Him on his way with palms, Hosannas singing?
Hosanna to the *Christ,* HEAVEN—EARTH—should still be ringing.

In days of old, old Palma won renown:
But Palma's self must yield the painter's crown,
Haydon, to thee. Thy palm put every other down.

If Flaccus' sentence with the truth agree,
That "palms awarded make men plump to be,"
Friend Horace, Haydon soon in bulk shall match with thee.

Painters with poets for the laurel vie:
But should the laureat band thy claims deny,
Wear thou thy own green palm, Haydon, triumphantly.

SONNET

To Miss Burney, on her Character of Blanch in "Country Neighbours," a Tale

(1820)

Bright spirits have arisen to grace the BURNEY name,
   And some in letters, some in tasteful arts,
     In learning some have borne distinguished parts;
Or sought through science of sweet sounds their fame:

And foremost *she*, renowned for many a tale
    Of faithful love perplexed, and of that good
    Old man, who, as CAMILLA's guardian, stood
In obstinate virtue clad like coat of mail.
Nor dost thou, SARAH, with unequal pace
    Her steps pursue. The pure romantic vein
    No gentler creature ever knew to feign
Than thy fine Blanch, young with an elder grace,
    In all respects without rebuke or blame,
    Answering the antique freshness of her name.

TO MY FRIEND THE INDICATOR

(1820)

Your easy Essays indicate a flow,
Dear Friend, of brain which we may elsewhere seek;
And to their pages I, and hundreds, owe,
That Wednesday is the sweetest of the week.
Such observation, wit, and sense, are shewn,
We think the days of Bickerstaff returned;
And that a portion of that oil you own,
In his undying midnight lamp which burned.
I would not lightly bruise old Priscian's head,
Or wrong the rules of grammar understood;
But, with the leave of Priscian be it said,
The *Indicative* is your *Potential Mood*.
Wit, poet, prose-man, party-man, translator—
H[unt], your best title yet is INDICATOR.

TO EMMA, LEARNING LATIN, AND DESPONDING

(*By Mary Lamb.* ? 1829)

Droop not, dear Emma, dry those falling tears,
And call up smiles into thy pallid face,
Pallid and care-worn with thy arduous race:
In few brief months thou hast done the work of years.
To young beginnings natural are these fears.
A right good scholar shalt thou one day be,
And that no distant one; when even she,
Who now to thee a star far off appears,
That most rare Latinist, the Northern Maid—
The language-loving Sarah [1] of the Lake—

---

[1] Daughter of S. T. Coleridge, Esq.; an accomplished linguist in the Greek and Latin tongues, and translatress of a History of the Abipones. [Mary Lamb's note.]

Shall hail thee Sister Linguist. This will make
Thy friends, who now afford thee careful aid,
A recompense most rich for all their pains,
Counting thy acquisitions their best gains.

LINES

Addressed to Lieut. R. W. H. Hardy, R.N., on the Perusal of his Volume of Travels in the Interior of Mexico

'Tis pleasant, lolling in our elbow chair,
Secure at home, to read descriptions rare
Of venturous traveller in savage climes;
His hair-breadth 'scapes, toil, hunger—and sometimes
The merrier passages that, like a foil
To set off perils past, sweetened that toil,
And took the edge from danger; and I look
With such fear-mingled pleasure thro' thy book,
Adventurous Hardy! Thou a *diver*[1] art,
But of no common form; and for thy part
Of the adventure, hast brought home to the nation
Pearls of discovery—*jewels* of observation.

ENFIELD, *January*, 1830.

LINES

[*For a Monument Commemorating the Sudden Death by Drowning of a Family of Four Sons and Two Daughters*]

(1831)

Tears are for lighter griefs. Man weeps the doom,
That seals a single victim to the tomb.
But when Death riots—when, with whelming sway,
Destruction sweeps a family away;
When infancy and youth, a huddled mass,
All in an instant to oblivion pass,
And parents' hopes are crush'd; what lamentation
Can reach the depth of such a desolation?
Look upward, Feeble Ones! look up and trust,
That HE who lays their mortal frame in dust,
Still hath the immortal spirit in his keeping—
In Jesus' sight they are not dead but sleeping.

[1] Captain Hardy practised this art with considerable success. [Note in *Athenæum*.]

TO C. ADERS, ESQ.

On his Collection of Paintings by the old German Masters

(1831)

Friendliest of men, ADERS, I never come
Within the precincts of this sacred Room,
But I am struck with a religious fear,
Which says "Let no profane eye enter here."
With imagery from Heav'n the walls are clothed,
Making the things of Time seem vile and loathed.
Spare Saints, whose bodies seem sustain'd by Love,
With Martyrs old in meek procession move.
Here kneels a weeping Magdalen, less bright
To human sense for her blurr'd cheeks; in sight
Of eyes, new-touch'd by Heav'n, more winning fair
Than when her beauty was her only care.
A Hermit here strange mysteries doth unlock
In desart sole, his knees worn by the rock.
There Angel harps are sounding, while below
Palm-bearing Virgins in white order go.
Madonnas, varied with so chaste design,
While all are different, each seems genuine,
And hers the only Jesus: hard outline,
And rigid form, by DURER's hand subdued
To matchless grace, and sacro-sanctitude;
DURER, who makes thy slighted Germany
Vie with the praise of paint-proud Italy.

Whoever enter'st here, no more presume
To name a Parlour, or a Drawing Room;
But, bending lowly to each holy Story,
Make this thy Chapel, and thine Oratory.

HERCULES PACIFICATUS

A Tale from Suidas

(1831)

In days of yore, ere early Greece
Had dream'd of patrols or police,
A crew of rake-hells *in terrorem*
Spread wide, and carried all before 'em,
Rifled the poultry, and the women,
And held that all things were in common;
Till Jove's great Son the nuisance saw,
And did abate it by Club Law.

Yet not so clean he made his work,
But here and there a rogue would lurk
In caves and rocky fastnesses,
And shunn'd the strength of Hercules.

Of these, more desperate than others,
A pair of ragamuffin brothers
In secret ambuscade join'd forces,
To carry on unlawful courses.
These Robbers' names, enough to shake us,
Were, Strymon one, the other Cacus.
And, more the neighbourhood to bother,
A wicked dam they had for mother,
Who knew their craft, but not forbid it,
And whatsoe'er they nymm'd, she hid it;
Received them with delight and wonder,
When they brought home some 'special **plunder**;
Call'd them her darlings, and her white boys,
Her ducks, her dildings—all was right boys—
"Only," she said, "my lads, have care
Ye fall not into BLACK BACK's snare;
For, if he catch, he'll maul your *corpus*,
And clapper-claw you to some purpose."
She was in truth a kind of witch,
Had grown by fortune-telling rich;
To spells and conjurings did tackle her,
And read folks' dooms by light oracular;
In which she saw, as clear as daylight,
What mischief on her bairns would a-light;
Therefore she had a special loathing
For all that own'd that sable clothing.

Who can 'scape fate, when we're decreed to 't?
The graceless brethren paid small heed to 't.
A brace they were of sturdy fellows,
As we may say, that fear'd no colours,
And sneer'd with modern infidelity
At the old gipsy's fond credulity.
It proved all true tho', as she'd mumbled—
For on a day the varlets stumbled
On a green spot—*sit linguæ fides*—
'Tis Suidas tells it—where Alcides
Secure, as fearing no ill neighbour,
Lay fast asleep after a "Labour."
His trusty oaken plant was near—
The prowling rogues look round, and leer,

And each his wicked wits 'gan rub,
How to bear off the famous Club;
Thinking that they *sans* price or hire wou'd
Carry 't strait home, and chop for fire wood.
'Twould serve their old dame half a winter—
You stare? but 'faith it was no splinter;
I would not for much money 'spy
Such beam in any neighbour's eye,
The villains, these exploits not dull in,
Incontinently fell a pulling.
They found it heavy—no slight matter—
But tugg'd, and tugg'd it, till the clatter
'Woke Hercules, who in a trice
Whipt up the knaves, and with a splice,
He kept on purpose—which before
Had served for giants many a score—
To end of Club tied each rogue's head fast;
Strapping feet too, to keep them steadfast;
And pickaback them carries townwards,
Behind his brawny back head-downwards
(So foolish calf—for rhyme I bless X—
Comes *nolens volens* out of Essex);
Thinking to brain them with his *dextra*,
Or string them up upon the next tree.
That Club—so equal fates condemn—
They thought to catch, has now catch'd them.

Now Hercules, we may suppose,
Was no great dandy in his clothes;
Was seldom, save on Sundays, seen
In calimanco, or nankeen;
On anniversaries would try on
A jerkin spick-span new from lion;
Went bare for the most part, to be cool,
And save the time of his Groom of the Stole;
Besides, the smoke he had been in
In Stygian gulf, had dyed his skin
To a natural sable—a right hell-fit—
That seem'd to careless eyes black velvet.

The brethren from their station scurvy,
Where they hung dangling topsy turvy,
With horror view the black costume,
And each presumes his hour is come!
Then softly to themselves 'gan mutter
The warning words their dame did utter;

Yet not so softly, but with ease
Were overheard by Hercules.
Quoth Cacus—"This is he she spoke of,
Which we so often made a joke of."
"I see," said th' other, "thank our sin for 't,
'Tis BLACK BACK sure enough—we're in for 't."

His Godship who, for all his brag
Of roughness, was at heart a wag,
At his new name was tickled finely,
And fell a laughing most divinely.
Quoth he, "I'll tell this jest in heaven—
The musty rogues shall be forgiven."
So in a twinkling did uncase them,
On mother earth once more to place them—
The varlets, glad to be unhamper'd,
Made each a leg—then fairly scamper'd.

THE PARTING SPEECH OF THE CELESTIAL MESSENGER TO THE POET

From the Latin of Palingenius, in the Zodiacus Vitæ

(1832)

But now time warns (my mission at an end)
That to Jove's starry court I re-ascend;
From whose high battlements I take delight
To scan your earth, diminish'd to the sight,
Pendant, and round, and, as an apple, small;
Self-propt, self-balanced, and secure from fall
By her own weight: and how with liquid robe
Blue ocean girdles round her tiny globe,
While lesser Nereus, gliding like a snake,
Betwixt her hands his flexile course doth take,
Shrunk to a rivulet; and how the Po,
The mighty Ganges, Tanais, Ister, show
No bigger than a ditch which rains have swell'd.
Old Nilus' seven proud mouths I late beheld,
And mock'd the watery puddles. Hosts steel-clad
Ofttimes I thence behold; and how the sad
Peoples are punish'd by the fault of kings,
Which from the purple fiend Ambition springs.
Forgetful of mortality, they live
In hot strife for possessions fugitive,
At which the angels grieve. Sometimes I trace
Of fountains, rivers, seas, the change of place;

By ever-shifting course, and Time's unrest,
The vale exalted, and the mount deprest
To an inglorious valley; plough-shares going
Where tall trees rear'd their tops; and fresh trees growing
In antique pastures. Cities lose their site.
Old things wax new. O what a rare delight
To him, who from this vantage can survey
At once stern Afric, and soft Asia,
With Europe's cultured plains; and in their turns
Their scatter'd tribes: those whom the hot Crab burns,
The tawny Ethiops; Orient Indians;
Getulians; ever-wandering Scythians;
Swift Tartar hordes; Cilicians rapacious,
And Parthians with back-bended bow pugnacious;
Sabeans incense-bringing, men of Thrace,
Italian, Spaniard, Gaul, and that rough race
Of Britons, rigid as their native colds;
With all the rest the circling sun beholds!
But clouds, and elemental mists, deny
These visions blest to any fleshly eye.

EXISTENCE, CONSIDERED IN ITSELF, NO BLESSING

From the Latin of Palingenius

(1832)

The Poet, after a seeming approval of suicide, from a consideration of the cares and crimes of life, finally rejecting it, discusses the negative importance of existence, contemplated in itself, without reference to good or evil.

Of these sad truths consideration had—
Thou shalt not fear to quit this world so mad,
So wicked; but the tenet rather hold
Of wise Calanus, and his followers old,
Who with their own wills their own freedom wrought,
And by self-slaughter their dismissal sought
From this dark den of crime—this horrid lair
Of men, that savager than monsters are;
And scorning longer, in this tangled mesh
Of ills, to wait on perishable flesh,
Did with their desperate hands anticipate
The too, too slow relief of lingering fate.
And if religion did not stay thine hand,
And God, and Plato's wise behests, withstand,
I would in like case counsel thee to throw
This senseless burden off, of cares below.

Not wine, *as* wine, men choose, but as it came
From such or such a vintage : 'tis the same
With life, which simply must be understood
A black negation, if it be not good.
But if 'tis wretched all—as men decline
And loath the sour lees of corrupted wine—
'Tis so to be contemn'd. Merely TO BE
Is not a boon to seek, nor ill to flee,
Seeing that every vilest little Thing
Has it in common, from a gnat's small wing,
A creeping worm, down to the moveless stone,
And crumbling bark from trees. Unless TO BE,
And TO BE BLEST, be one, I do not see
In bare existence, *as* existence, aught
That's worthy to be loved, or to be sought.

TO SAMUEL ROGERS, ESQ.
On the New Edition of his " Pleasures of Memory "
(1833)

When thy gay book hath paid its proud devoirs,
Poetic friend, and fed with luxury
The eye of pampered aristocracy
In glittering drawing-rooms and gilt boudoirs,
O'erlaid with comments of pictorial art,
However rich and rare, yet nothing leaving
Of healthful action to the soul-conceiving
Of the true reader—yet a nobler part
Awaits thy work, already classic styled.
Cheap-clad, accessible, in homeliest show
The modest beauty through the land shall go
From year to year, and render life more mild ;
Refinement to the poor man's hearth shall give,
And in the moral heart of England live.

TO CLARA N[OVELLO]
(1834)

The Gods have made me most unmusical,
With feelings that respond not to the call
Of stringed harp, or voice—obtuse and mute
To hautboy, sackbut, dulcimer, and flute ;
King David's lyre, that made the madness flee
From Saul, had been but a jew's-harp to me :
Theorbos, violins, French horns, guitars,

TO MARGARET W——

Leave in my wounded ears inflicted scars;
I hate those trills, and shakes, and sounds that float
Upon the captive air; I know no note,
Nor ever shall, whatever folks may say,
Of the strange mysteries of *Sol* and *Fa*;
I sit at oratorios like a fish,
Incapable of sound, and only wish
The thing was over. Yet do I admire,
O tuneful daughter of a tuneful sire,
Thy painful labours in a science, which
To your deserts I pray may make you rich
As much as you are loved, and add a grace
To the most musical Novello race.
Women lead men by the nose, some cynics say;
You draw them by the ear—a delicater way.

TO MARGARET W——

Margaret, in happy hour
Christen'd from that humble flower
   Which we a daisy[1] call!
May thy pretty name-sake be
In all things a type of thee,
   And image thee in all.

Like *it* you show a modest face,
An unpretending native grace;—
   The tulip, and the pink,
The china and the damask rose,
And every flaunting flower that blows,
   In the comparing shrink.

Of lowly fields you think no scorn;
Yet gayest gardens would adorn,
   And grace, wherever set.
Home-seated in your lonely bower,
Or wedded—a transplanted flower—
   I bless you, Margaret!

EDMONTON, 8*th October*, 1834.

[1] Marguerite, in French, signifies a daisy. [Note in *Athenæum*.]

ADDITIONAL ALBUM VERSES AND ACROSTICS

WHAT IS AN ALBUM?

'TIS a Book kept by modern Young Ladies for show,
    Of which their plain grandmothers nothing did know.
'Tis a medley of scraps, fine verse, and fine prose,
And some things not very like either, God knows.
The soft First Effusions of Beaux and of Belles,
Of future LORD BYRONS, and sweet L. E. L.'s;
Where wise folk and simple both equally shine,
And you write your nonsense, that I may write mine.
Stick in a fine landscape, to make a display,
A flower-piece, a foreground, all tinted so gay,
As NATURE herself (could she see them) would strike
With envy, to think that she ne'er did the like:
And since some LAVATERS, with head-pieces comical,
Have pronounc'd people's hands to be physiognomical,
Be sure that you stuff it with AUTOGRAPHS plenty,
All framed to a pattern, so stiff, and so dainty.
They no more resemble folks' every-day writing,
Than lines penn'd with pains do extemp'rel enditing;
Or the natural countenance (pardon the stricture)
The faces we make when we sit for our picture.

Thus you have, dearest EMMA, an ALBUM complete—
Which may *you* live to finish, and *I* live to see it;
And since you began it for innocent ends,
May it swell, and grow bigger each day with new friends,
Who shall set down kind names, as a token and test,
As I my poor *autograph* sign with the rest.

THE FIRST LEAF OF SPRING

Written on the First Leaf of a Lady's Album

    Thou fragile, filmy, gossamery thing,
    First leaf of spring!
    At every lightest breath that quakest,
    And with a zephyr shakest;

TO MRS. F.

Scarce stout enough to hold thy slender form together,
In calmest halcyon weather;
Next sister to the web that spiders weave,
Poor flutterers to deceive
Into their treacherous silken bed:
O! how art thou sustained, how nourishèd!
All trivial as thou art,
Without dispute,
Thou play'st a mighty part;
And art the herald to a throng
Of buds, blooms, fruit,
That shall thy cracking branches sway,
While birds on every spray
Shall pay the copious fruitage with a sylvan song.
So 'tis with thee, whoe'er on thee shall look,
First leaf of this beginning modest book.
Slender thou art, God knowest,
And little grace bestowest,
But in thy train shall follow after,
Wit, wisdom, seriousness, in hand with laughter;
Provoking jests, restraining soberness,
In their appropriate dress;
And I shall joy to be outdone
By those who brighter trophies won;
Without a grief,
That I thy slender promise have begun,
First leaf.

1832.

TO MRS. F[IELD]

On Her Return from Gibraltar

Jane, you are welcome from the barren Rock,
And Calpe's sounding shores. Oh do not mock,
Now you have rais'd, our greetings; nor again
Ever revisit that dry nook of Spain.

Friends have you here, and friendships to command,
In merry England. Love this hearty land.
Ease, comfort, competence—of these possess'd,
Let prodigal adventurers seek the rest:
Dear England is *as you*,—a "*Field* the Lord hath blest."

TO M[ARY] L[OUISA] F[IELD]

(Expecting to See Her Again after a Long Interval)

How many wasting, many wasted years,
Have run their round, since I beheld your face!
In Memory's dim eye it yet appears
Crown'd, as it *then* seem'd, with a cheerful grace,
Young prattling maiden, on the Thames' fair side,
Enlivening pleasant Sunbury with your smiles.
Time may have changed you: coy reserve, or pride,
To sullen looks reduced those mirthful wiles.
I will not 'bate one inch on that clear brow,
But take of Time a rigorous account
When next I see you; and Maria now
Must *be* the thing she *was*. To what amount
These verses else?—All hollow and untrue—
This was not writ, these lines not meant, for *You*.

TO ESTHER FIELD

Esther, holy name and sweet,
Smoothly runs on even feet,
To the mild Acrostic bending;
Hebrew recollections blending.
Ever keep that Queen in view—
Royal namesake—bold and true!

Firm she stood in evil times,
In the face of Haman's crimes.
Ev'n as She, do Thou possess
Loftiest virtue in the dress
(Dear F.) of native loveliness.

[TO MRS. WILLIAMS]

(1830)

Go little Poem, and present
Respectful terms of compliment;
A gentle lady bids thee speak!
Courteous is *she*, tho' thou be weak—
Evoke from Heaven as thick as manna

Joy after joy on Grace Joanna:
On Fornham's Glebe and Pasture land
A blessing pray. Long, long may stand,

Not touched by Time, the Rectory blithe;
No grudging churl dispute his Tithe;
At Easter be the offerings due

With cheerful spirit paid; each pew
In decent order filled; no noise
Loud intervene to drown the voice,
Learning, or wisdom of the Teacher;
Impressive be the Sacred Preacher,
And strict his notes on holy page;
May young and old from age to age
Salute, and still point out, 'The good man's Parsonage!'

TO THE BOOK

Little Casket! Storehouse rare
Of rich conceits, to please the Fair!
Happiest he of mortal men,—
(I crown him monarch of the pen,)—
To whom Sophia deigns to give
The flattering prerogative
To inscribe his name in chief,
On thy first and maiden Leaf.
When thy pages shall be full
Of what brighter wits can cull
Of the Tender or Romantic,
Creeping Prose or Verse Gigantic,—
Which thy spaces so shall cram
That the Bee-like Epigram
(Which a two-fold tribute brings,
Honey gives at once, and stings,)
Hath not room left wherewithal
To infix its tiny scrawl;
Haply some more youthful swain,
Striving to describe his pain,
And the Damsel's ear to seize
With more expressive lays than these,
When he finds his own excluded
And these counterfeits intruded;
While, loitering in the Muse's bower,
He overstayed the eleventh hour,
Till the tables filled—shall fret,
Die, or sicken with regret
Or into a shadow pine:
While this triumphant verse of mine,

Like to some favoured stranger-guest,
Bidden to a good man's Feast
Shall sit—by merit less than fate—
In the upper Seat in State.

TO S[OPHIA] F[REND].

Acrostic

Solemn Legends we are told
Of bright female Names of old,
Phyllus fair, Laodameia,
Helen, but methinks Sophia
Is a name of better meaning
And a sort of Christian leaning.

For it *Wisdom* means, which passes
Rubies, pearls, or golden masses.
Ever try that Name to merit;
Never quit what you inherit,
Duly from your Father's spirit.

TO R[OTHA] Q[UILLINAN]

Acrostic

Rotha, how in numbers light,
Ought I to express thee?
Take my meaning in its flight—
Haste imports not always slight—
And believe, I bless thee.

TO S[ARAH] L[OCKE]

Acrostic

Shall I praise a face unseen,
And extol a fancied mien,
Rave on visionary charm,
And from shadows take alarm?
Hatred hates *without a cause;*

Love may love, with more applause,
Or, without a reason given,
Charmed be with unknown Heaven.
Keep the secrets, though, unmocked,
Ever in your bosom *Locke'd.*

IN MISS WESTWOOD'S ALBUM

TO M[ARY] L[OCKE]

Acrostic

Must I write with pen unwilling
And describe those graces killing
Rightly, which I never saw?
Yes—it is the Album's law.

Let me then Invention strain
On your excelling charms to feign—
Cold is Fiction? I *believe* it
Kindly, as I did receive it,
Even as J. F.'s tongue did weave it.

AN ACROSTIC AGAINST ACROSTICS

Envy not the wretched Poet
Doomed to pen these teasing strains,
Wit so cramped, ah, who can show it,
Are the trifles worth the pains.
Rhyme compared with this were easy,
Double Rhymes may not displease ye.

Homer, Horace sly and caustic,
Owed no fame to vile acrostic.
G's, I am sure, the Readers choked with,
Good men's names must not be joked with.

ON BEING ASKED TO WRITE IN MISS WESTWOOD'S ALBUM

My feeble Muse, that fain her best wou'd
Write, at command of Frances Westwood,
But feels her wits not in their best mood,
Fell lately on some idle fancies,
As she's much given to romances,
About this self-same style as Frances;
Which seems to be a name in common
Attributed to man or woman.
She thence contrived this flattering moral,
With which she hopes no soul will quarrel,
That she, whom this twin title decks,
Combines what's good in either sex;

Unites—how very rare the case is!—
Masculine sense to female graces;
And, quitting not her proper rank,
Is both in one—*Fanny*, and *frank*.

12th October, 1827.

[IN MISS WESTWOOD'S ALBUM]

By Mary Lamb

Small beauty to your Book my lines can lend,
Yet you shall have the best I can, sweet friend,
To serve for poor memorials 'gainst the day
That calls you from your Parent-roof away,
From the mild offices of Filial life
To the more serious duties of a Wife.
The World is opening to you—may you rest
With all your prospects realised, and blest!—
I, with the Elder Couple left behind,
On evenings chatting, oft shall call to mind
Those spirits of Youth, which Age so ill can miss,
And, wanting you, half grudge your S—n's bliss;
Till mirthful malice tempts us to exclaim
'Gainst the dear Thief, who robb'd you of your *Name*.

ENFIELD CHASE, 17th May, 1828.

THE SISTERS

On Emma's honest brow we read display'd
The constant virtues of the Nut Brown Maid;
Mellifluous sounds on Clara's tongue we hear,
Notes that once lured a Seraph from his sphere;
Cecilia's eyes such winning beauties crown
As without song might draw *her* Angel down.

SEVEN POEMS BY CHARLES LAMB NOW PRINTED FOR THE FIRST TIME

UN SOLITAIRE

A Drawing by E. I.

SOLITARY man, around thee
   Are the mountains: Peace hath found thee
Resting by that rippling tide;
All vain toys of life expelling,
Hermit-like, thou find'st a dwelling,
Lost 'mid foliage stretching wide.
Angels here alone may find thee,
Contemplation fast may bind thee.
Holier spot, or more fantastic,
Livelier scene of deep seclusion,
Armed by Nature 'gainst intrusion,
Never graced a seat Monastic.

TO S[ARAH] T[HOMAS]

An Acrostic

Sarah, blest wife of "Terah's faithful Son,"
After a race of years with goodness run,
Regardless heard the promised miracle,
And mocked the blessing as impossible.
How weak is Faith!—even He, the most sincere,

Thomas, to his meek Master not least dear,
Holy, and blameless, yet refused assent
Of full belief, until he could content
Mere human senses. In your piety,
As you are *one* in *name*, industriously
So copy them: but *shun* their weak part—*Incredulity.*

TO MRS. SARAH ROBINSON

Soul-breathing verse, thy gentlest guise put on
And greet the honor'd name of Robinson.
Rome in her throng'd and stranger-crowded streets,
And palaces, where pilgrim *pilgrim* meets,
Holds not, respected Sarah, one that can

Revered make the name of Englishman,
Or loved, more than thy Kinsman, dear to me
By many a friendly act.   His heart I see
In thee with answering courtesy renew'd.
Nor shall to thee my debt of gratitude
Soon fade, that didst receive with open hand
One that was come a stranger to thy land—
Now call[s] thee Friend.   Her thanks, and mine, command.

ENFIELD, 14*th March*, 1831.

TO SARAH [APSEY]

Acrostic

Sarah,—your other name I know not,
And fine encomiums I bestow not,
Regard me as an utter stranger,
A hair-brain'd, hasty, album-ranger,
Heaven shield you, Girl, from every danger!

ACROSTIC

Judgements are about us thoroughly;
O'er all Enfield hangs the Cholera,
Savage monster, none like him
Ever rack'd a human limb.
Pest, nor plague, nor fever yellow,
Has made patients more to bellow.

Vain his threatnings!   Asbury comes,
And defiance beats by drums;
Label, bottle, box, pill, potion,
Each enlists in the commotion.

And with Vials, like to those
Seen in Patmos,[1] charged with woes,
Breathing Wrath, he falls pell-mell
Upon the Foe, and pays him well.
Revenge!—he has made the monster sick,
Yea, Cholera vanish, choleric.

[1] *Vide* Revelations.

TO D[OROTHY] A[SBURY]
Acrostic

Divided praise, Lady, to you we owe,
Of all the health your husband doth bestow,
Respected wife of skilful Asbury!
Oracular foresight named thee Dorothy;
Tis a Greek word, and signifies God's Gift;
(How Learning helps poor Poets at a shift!)—
You are that gift. When, tired with human ails,

And tedious listening to the sick man's tales,
Sore spent, and fretted, he comes home at eve,
By mild medicaments you his toils deceive.
Under your soothing treatment he revives;
(Restorative is the smile of gentle wives):
You lengthen *his*, who lengthens *all our lives*.

TO LOUISA MORGAN

How blest is he who in his *age*, exempt
From fortune's frowns, and from the troublous strife
Of storms that harass still the private life,
"Below ambition, and above contempt,"
Hath gain'd a quiet harbour, where he may
Look back on shipwrecks past, without a sigh
For busier scenes, and hope's gay dreams gone by!
And such a nook of blessedness, they say,
Your Sire at length has found; while you, best Child,
Content in *his* contentment, acquiesce
In patient toils; and in a station less,
Than you might image, when your prospects smiled.
In your meek virtues there is found a calm,
That on his life's soft evening sheds a balm.[1]

---

[1] See also page 373 for two poems which came to hand too late to be included in their right place.

POLITICAL AND OTHER EPIGRAMS

TO SIR JAMES MACKINTOSH
(1801)

Though thou'rt like Judas, an apostate black,
  In the resemblance one thing thou dost lack:
When he had gotten his ill-purchased pelf,
He went away, and wisely hanged himself.
This thou may'st do at last; yet much I doubt,
If thou hast any *bowels* to gush out!

TWELFTH NIGHT
Characters That Might Have Been Drawn on the Above Evening
(1802)

MR. A[DDINGTON]

I put my night-cap on my head,
And went, as usual, to my bed;
And, most surprising to relate,
I woke—a Minister of State!

MESSRS. C[ANNIN]G AND F[RER]E

At Eton School brought up with dull boys,
We shone like *men* among the *school-boys*;
But since we in the world have been,
We are but *school-boys* among *men*.

EPIGRAMS
(1812)

I

Princeps his rent from tinneries draws,
  His best friends are refiners;—
What wonder then his other friends
  He leaves for under-*miners*.

(102)

THE TRIUMPH OF THE WHALE

II

Ye Politicians, tell me, pray,
Why thus with woe and care rent?
This is the worst that you can say,
Some wind has blown the *wig* away,
And left the *hair apparent*.

THE TRIUMPH OF THE WHALE

(1812)

Io! Pæan! Io! sing
To the finny people's King.
Not a mightier whale than this
In the vast Atlantic is;
Not a fatter fish than he
Flounders round the polar sea.
See his blubbers—at his gills
What a world of drink he swills,
From his trunk, as from a spout,
Which next moment he pours out.
Such his person—next declare,
Muse, who his companions are.—
Every fish of generous kind
Scuds aside, or slinks behind;
But about his presence keep
All the Monsters of the Deep;
Mermaids, with their tails and singing
His delighted fancy stinging;
Crooked Dolphins, they surround him,
Dog-like Seals, they fawn around him.
Following hard, the progress mark
Of the intolerant salt sea shark.
For his solace and relief,
Flat fish are his courtiers chief.
Last and lowest in his train,
Ink-fish (libellers of the main)
Their black liquor shed in spite:
(Such on earth the things *that write*.)
In his stomach, some do say,
No good thing can ever stay.
Had it been the fortune of it
To have swallowed that old Prophet,
Three days there he'd not have dwell'd,
But in one have been expell'd.

Hapless mariners are they,
Who beguil'd (as seamen say),
Deeming him some rock or island,
Footing sure, safe spot, and dry land,
Anchor in his scaly rind;
Soon the difference they find;
Sudden plumb, he sinks beneath them;
Does to ruthless seas bequeath them.

Name or title what has he?
Is he Regent of the Sea?
From this difficulty free us,
Buffon, Banks or sage Linnæus.
With his wondrous attributes
Say what appellation suits.
By his bulk, and by his size,
By his oily qualities,
This (or else my eyesight fails),
This should be the Prince of Whales.

SONNET

St. Crispin to Mr. Gifford
(1819)

All unadvised, and in an evil hour,
 Lured by aspiring thoughts, my son, you daft
 The lowly labours of the Gentle Craft
For learned toils, which blood and spirits sour.
All things, dear pledge, are not in all men's power;
 The wiser sort of shrub affects the ground;
 And sweet content of mind is oftener found
In cobbler's parlour, than in critic's bower.
The sorest work is what doth cross the grain;
 And better to this hour you had been plying
 The obsequious awl with well-waxed finger flying,
Than ceaseless thus to till a thankless vein;
 Still teazing Muses, which are still denying;
Making a stretching-leather of your brain.

THE GODLIKE
(1820)

In one great man we view with odds
A parallel to all the gods.
Great Jove, that shook heaven with his brow,
Could never match his princely bow.

In him a Bacchus we behold :
Like Bacchus, too, he ne'er grows old.
Like Phœbus next, a flaming lover ;
And then he's Mercury—all over.
A Vulcan, for domestic strife,
He lamely lives without his wife.
And sure—unless our wits be dull—
Minerva-like, when moon was full,
He issued from paternal skull.

THE THREE GRAVES
(1820)

Close by the ever-burning brimstone beds
Where Bedloe, Oates and Judas, hide their heads,
I saw great Satan like a Sexton stand
With his intolerable spade in hand,
Digging three graves. Of coffin shape they were,
For those who, coffinless, must enter there
With unblest rites. The shrouds were of that cloth
Which Clotho weaveth in her blackest wrath :
The dismal tinct oppress'd the eye, that dwelt
Upon it long, like darkness to be felt.
The pillows to these baleful beds were toads,
Large, living, livid, melancholy loads,
Whose softness shock'd. Worms of all monstrous size
Crawl'd round ; and one, upcoil'd, which never dies.
A doleful bell, inculcating despair,
Was always ringing in the heavy air.
And all about the detestable pit
Strange headless ghosts, and quarter'd forms, did flit ;
Rivers of blood, from living traitors spilt,
By treachery stung from poverty to guilt.
I ask'd the fiend, for whom these rites were meant ?
"These graves," quoth he, " when life's brief oil is spent,
When the dark night comes, and they're sinking bedwards,
—I mean for Castles, Oliver, and Edwards."

SONNET TO MATHEW WOOD, ESQ.
Alderman and M.P.
(1820)

Hold on thy course uncheck'd, heroic WOOD !
   Regardless what the player's son may prate,
    Saint Stephens' fool, the Zany of Debate—
Who nothing generous ever understood.

London's twice Prætor! scorn the fool-born jest—
    The stage's scum, and refuse of the players—
    Stale topics against Magistrates and Mayors—
City and Country both thy worth attest.
Bid him leave off his shallow Eton wit,
    More fit to sooth the superficial ear
    Of drunken PITT, and that pickpocket Peer,
When at their sottish orgies they did sit,
Hatching mad counsels from inflated vein,
Till England, and the nations, reeled with pain.

ON A PROJECTED JOURNEY
(1820)

To gratify his people's wish
    See G[eorg]e at length prepare—
He's setting out for Hanover—
    We've often wished him there.

ON A LATE EMPIRIC OF "BALMY" MEMORY
(1820)

His namesake, born of Jewish breeder,
Knew "from the Hyssop to the Cedar;"
But he, unlike the Jewish leader,
Scarce knew the Hyssop from the Cedar.

SONG FOR THE C[ORONATIO]N
Tune, "Roy's Wife of Aldivalloch"
(1820)

Roi's wife of Brunswick Oëls!
Roi's wife of Brunswick Oëls!
Wot you how she came to him,
While he supinely dreamt of no ills?
Vow! but she is a canty Queen,
And well can she scare each royal orgie.—
To us she ever must be dear,
Though she's for ever cut by Georgie.—
    Roi's wife, etc. *Da capo.*

THE UNBELOVED
(1820)

Not a woman, child, or man in
All this isle, that loves thee, C[anni]ng.
Fools, whom gentle manners sway,
May incline to C[astlerea]gh,

Princes, who old ladies love,
Of the Doctor may approve,
Chancery lads do not abhor
Their chatty, childish Chancellor.
In Liverpool some virtues strike,
And little Van's beneath dislike.
Tho, if I were to be dead for't,
I could never love thee, H[eadfor]t:
(Every man must have his way)
Other grey adulterers may.
But thou unamiable object,—
Dear to neither prince, nor subject;—
Veriest, meanest scab, for pelf
Fastning on the skin of Guelph,
Thou, thou must, surely, *loathe thyself.*

ON THE ARRIVAL IN ENGLAND OF LORD BYRON'S REMAINS

(1824)

Manners, they say, by climate alter not:
Who goes a drunkard will return a sot.
So lordly Juan, damn'd to lasting fame,
Went out a pickle, and came back the same.

LINES

Suggested by a Sight of Waltham Cross

(1827)

Time-mouldering CROSSES, gemm'd with imagery
   Of costliest work, and Gothic tracery,
Point still the spots, to hallow'd wedlock dear,
   Where rested on its solemn way the bier,
That bore the bones of Edward's Elinor
   To mix with Royal dust at Westminster.—
Far different rites did thee to dust consign,
   Duke Brunswick's daughter, Princely Caroline.
A hurrying funeral, and a banish'd grave,
   High-minded Wife! were all that thou could'st have.
Grieve not, great Ghost, nor count in death thy losses;
   Thou in thy life-time had'st thy share of *crosses.*

FOR THE "TABLE BOOK"
(1827)

Laura, too partial to her friends' enditing,
Requires from each a pattern of their *writing*.
A weightier trifle Laura might command;
For who to Laura would refuse his—*hand?*

THE ROYAL WONDERS
(1830)

Two miracles at once! Compell'd by fate,
His tarnish'd throne the Bourbon doth vacate;
While English William,—a diviner thing,—
Of his free pleasure hath put off *the king*.
The forms of distant old respect lets pass,
And melts his crown into the common mass.
Health to fair France, and fine regeneration!
But England's is the nobler abdication.

"BREVIS ESSE LABORO"
"ONE DIP"
(1830)

Much speech obscures the sense; the soul of wit
Is brevity: our tale one proof of it.
Poor Balbulus, a stammering invalid,
Consults the doctors, and by them is bid
To try sea-bathing, with this special heed,
"One Dip was all his malady did need;
More than that one his certain death would be."
Now who so nervous or so shook as he,
For Balbulus had never dipped before?
Two well-known dippers at the Broadstairs' shore,
Stout, sturdy churls, have stript him to the skin,
And naked, cold, and shivering plunge him in.
Soon he emerges, with scarce breath to say,
"I'm to be dip—dip—dipt——." "We know it," they
Reply; expostulation seemed in vain,
And over ears they souse him in again,
And up again he rises, his words trip,
And falter as before. Still "dip—dip—dip"—
And in again he goes with furious plunge,
Once more to rise; when, with a desperate lunge,
At length he bolts these words out, "Only once!"
The villains crave his pardon. Had the dunce
But aimed at these bare words the rogues had found him,
But striving to be prolix, they half drowned him.

SUUM CUIQUE
(1830)

Adsciscit sibi divitias et opes alienas
Fur, rapiens, spolians quod mihi, quodque tibi
Proprium erat, temnens haec verba, Meumque Tuumque ;
  Omne Suum est. Tandem cuique suum tribuit.
Dat laqueo collum : vestes, vah ! carnifici dat :
  Sese Diabolo ; sic bene, Cuique Suum.

[ON THE *LITERARY GAZETTE*]
(? 1831)

On English ground I calculated once
How many block-heads—taking dunce by dunce—
There are *four hundred* (if I don't forget)—
The Readers of the *Literary Gazette*.

ON THE FAST-DAY

To name a Day for general prayer and fast
  Is surely worse than of no sort of use ;
For you may see with grief, from first to last,
  On *fast*-days people of all ranks are *loose*.

NONSENSE VERSES

Lazy-bones, lazy-bones, wake up, and peep !
The cat's in the cupboard, your mother's asleep.
There you sit snoring, forgetting her ills ;
Who is to give her her Bolus and Pills ?
Twenty fine Angels must come into town,
All for to help you to make your new gown :
Dainty AERIAL Spinsters, and Singers ;
Aren't you ashamed to employ such white fingers ?
Delicate hands, unaccustom'd to reels,
To set 'em a working a poor body's wheels ?
Why they came down is to me all a riddle,
And left HALLELUJAH broke off in the middle :
Jove's Court, and the Presence angelical, cut—
To eke out the work of a lazy young slut.
Angel-duck, Angel-duck, winged, and silly,
Pouring a watering-pot over a lily,
Gardener gratuitous, careless of pelf,
Leave her to water her lily herself,
Or to neglect it to death if she chuse it :
Remember the loss is her own, if she lose it.

SATAN IN SEARCH OF A WIFE

WITH THE WHOLE PROCESS OF
HIS COURTSHIP AND MARRIAGE,
AND WHO DANCED AT THE WEDDING
BY
AN EYE WITNESS
(1831)

DEDICATION

TO delicate bosoms, that have sighed over the *Loves of the Angels*, this Poem is with tenderest regard consecrated. It can be no offence to you, dear Ladies, that the author has endeavoured to extend the dominion of your darling passion; to shew Love triumphant in places, to which his advent has been never yet suspected. If one Cecilia drew an Angel down, another may have leave to attract a Spirit upwards; which, I am sure, was the most desperate adventure of the two. Wonder not at the inferior condition of the agent; for, if King Cophetua wooed a Beggar Maid, a greater king need not scorn to confess the attractions of a fair Tailor's daughter. The more disproportionate the rank, the more signal is the glory of your sex. Like that of Hecate, a triple empire is now confessed your own. Nor Heaven, nor Earth, nor deepest tracts of Erebus, as Milton hath it, have power to resist your sway. I congratulate your last victory. You have fairly made an Honest Man of the Old One; and, if your conquest is late, the success must be salutary. The new Benedict has employment enough on his hands to desist from dabbling with the affairs of poor mortals; he may fairly leave human nature to herself; and we may sleep for one while at least secure from the attacks of this hitherto restless Old Bachelor. It remains to be seen, whether the world will be much benefited by the change in his condition.

PART THE FIRST

I

The Devil was sick and queasy of late,
  And his sleep and his appetite fail'd him ;
His ears they hung down, and his tail it was clapp'd
Between his poor hoofs, like a dog that's been rapp'd—
  None knew what the devil ail'd him.

II

He tumbled and toss'd on his mattress o' nights,
  That was fit for a fiend's disportal ;
For 'twas made of the finest of thistles and thorn,
Which Alecto herself had gather'd in scorn
  Of the best down beds that are mortal.

III

His giantly chest in earthquakes heaved,
  With groanings corresponding ;
And mincing and few were the words he spoke,
While a sigh, like some delicate whirlwind, broke
  From a heart that seem'd desponding.

IV

Now the Devil an Old Wife had for his Dam,
  I think none e'er was older :
Her years—old Parr's were nothing to them ;
And a chicken to her was Methusalem,
  You'd say, could you behold her.

V

She remember'd Chaos a little child,
  Strumming upon hand organs ;
At the birth of Old Night a gossip she sat,
The ancientest there, and was godmother at
  The christening of the Gorgons.

VI

Her bones peep'd through a rhinoceros' skin,
  Like a mummy's through its cerement ;
But she had a mother's heart, and guess'd
What pinch'd her son ; whom she thus address'd
  In terms that bespoke endearment.

VII

" What ails my Nicky, my darling Imp,
   My Lucifer bright, my Beelze?
My Pig, my Pug-with-a-curly-tail,
You are not well.   Can a mother fail
   To see *that* which all Hell see?"

VIII

" O Mother dear, I am dying, I fear;
   Prepare the yew, and the willow,
And the cypress black : for I get no ease
By day or by night for the cursed fleas,
   That skip about my pillow."

IX

" Your pillow is clean, and your pillow-beer,
   For I wash'd 'em in Styx last night, son,
And your blankets both, and dried them upon
The brimstony banks of Acheron—
   It is not the *fleas* that bite, son."

X

" O I perish of cold these bitter sharp nights,
   The damp like an ague ferrets ;
The ice and the frost hath shot into the bone ;
And I care not greatly to sleep alone
   O' nights—for the fear of Spirits."

XI

" The weather is warm, my own sweet boy,
   And the nights are close and stifling ;
And for fearing of Spirits, you cowardly Elf—
Have you quite forgot you're a Spirit yourself?
   Come, come, I see you are trifling.

XII

I wish my Nicky is not in love "——
   " O mother, you have nick't it "——
And he turn'd his head aside with a blush—
Not red hot pokers, or crimson plush,
   Could half so deep have prick'd it.

SATAN IN SEARCH OF A WIFE

XIII

"These twenty thousand good years or more,"
  Quoth he, " on this burning shingle
I have led a lonesome Bachelor's life,
Nor known the comfort of babe or wife—
  'Tis a long time to live single."

XIV

Quoth she, "If a wife is all you want,
  I shall quickly dance at your wedding.
I am dry nurse, you know, to the Female Ghosts"—
And she call'd up her charge, and they came in hosts
  To do the old Beldam's bidding:

XV

All who in their lives had been servants of sin—
  Adulteress, Wench, Virago—
And Murd'resses old that had pointed the knife
Against a husband's or father's life,
  Each one a She Iago.

XVI

First Jezebel came—no need of paint,
  Or dressing, to make her charming;
For the blood of the old prophetical race
Had heighten'd the natural flush of her face
  To a pitch 'bove rouge or carmine.

XVII

Semiramis there low tendered herself,
  With all Babel for a dowry:
With Helen, the flower and the bane of Greece—
And bloody Medea next offer'd her fleece,
  That was of Hell the Houri.

XVIII

Clytemnestra, with Joan of Naples, put in;
  Cleopatra, by Anthony quicken'd;
Jocasta, that married where she should not,
Came hand in hand with the Daughters of Lot;
  Till the Devil was fairly sicken'd.

XIX

For the Devil himself, a dev'l as he is,
    Disapproves unequal matches.
" O Mother," he cried, " dispatch them hence !
No Spirit—I speak it without offence—
    Shall have me in her hatches."

XX

With a wave of her wand they all were gone !
    And now came out the slaughter:
" 'Tis none of these that can serve my turn ;
For a wife of flesh and blood I burn—
    I'm in love with a Taylor's Daughter.

XXI

Tis she must heal the wounds that she made,
    'Tis she must be my physician.
O parent mild, stand not my foe "—
For his mother had whisper'd something low
    About " matching beneath his condition."—

XXII

" And then we must get paternal consent,
    Or an unblest match may vex ye "—
" Her father is dead ; I fetched him away.
In the midst of his goose, last Michaelmas day—
    He died of an apoplexy.

XXIII

His daughter is fair, and an only heir—
    With her I long to tether—
He has left her his *hell*, and all that he had ;
The estates are contiguous, and I shall be mad'
    'Till we lay our two Hells together."

XXIV

" But how do you know the fair maid's mind ? "—
    Quoth he, " Her loss was but recent ;
And I could not speak *my* mind you know,
Just when I was fetching her father below—
    It would have been hardly decent.

XXV

But a leer from her eye, where Cupids lie,
    Of love gave proof apparent;
And, from something she dropp'd, I shrewdly ween'd,
In her heart she judged, that a *living Fiend*
    Was better than a *dead Parent*.

XXVI

But the time is short; and suitors may come,
    While I stand here reporting;
Then make your son a bit of a Beau,
And give me your blessing, before I go
    To the other world a courting."

XXVII

" But what will you do with your horns, my son?
    And that tail—fair maids will mock it—"
" My tail I will dock—and as for the horn,
Like husbands above I think no scorn
    To carry it in my pocket."

XXVIII

" But what will you do with your feet, my son? "
    " Here are stockings fairly woven:
My hoofs I will hide in silken hose;
And cinnamon-sweet are my pettitoes—
    Because, you know, they are *cloven*."

XXIX

" Then take a blessing, my darling Son,"
    Quoth she, and kiss'd him civil—
Then his neckcloth she tied; and when he was drest
From top to toe in his Sunday's best,
    He appear'd a comely devil.

XXX

So his leave he took:—but how he fared
    In his courtship—barring failures—
In a Second Part you shall read it soon,
In a bran new song, to be sung to the tune
    Of the " Devil among the Tailors."

THE SECOND PART
CONTAINING
THE COURTSHIP, AND THE WEDDING

I

Who is She that by night from her balcony looks
    On a garden, where cabbage is springing?
'Tis the Tailor's fair Lass, that we told of above;
She muses by moonlight on her True Love;
    So sharp is Cupid's stinging.

II

She has caught a glimpse of the Prince of the Air
    In his Luciferian splendour,
And away with her coyness and maiden reserve!—
For none but the Devil her turn will serve,
    Her sorrows else will end her.

III

She saw when he fetch'd her father away,
    And the sight no whit did shake her;
For the Devil may sure with his own make free—
And "it saves besides," quoth merrily she,
    "The expence of an Undertaker.—

IV

Then come, my Satan, my darling Sin,
    Return to my arms, my Hell Beau;
My Prince of Darkness, my crow-black Dove"—
And she scarce had spoke, when her own True Love
    Was kneeling at her elbow!

V

But she wist not at first that this was He,
    That had raised such a boiling passion;
For his old costume he had laid aside,
And was come to court a mortal bride
    In a coat-and-waistcoat fashion.

VI

She miss'd his large horns, and she miss'd his fair tail,
    That had hung so retrospective;
And his raven plumes, and some other marks
Regarding his feet, that had left their sparks
    In a mind but too susceptive:

VII

And she held in scorn that a mortal born
  Should the Prince of Spirits rival,
To clamber at midnight her garden fence—
For she knew not else by what pretence
  To account for his arrival.

VIII

" What thief art thou," quoth she, " in the dark
  That stumblest here presumptuous?
Some Irish Adventurer I take you to be—
A Foreigner, from your garb I see,
  Which besides is not over sumptuous."

IX

Then Satan, awhile dissembling his rank,
  A piece of amorous fun tries:
Quoth he, " I'm a Netherlander born;
Fair Virgin, receive not my suit with scorn;
  I'm a Prince in the Low Countries—

X

Though I travel *incog*. From the Land of Fog
  And Mist I am come to proffer
My crown and my sceptre to lay at your feet;
It is not every day in the week you may meet,
  Fair Maid, with a Prince's offer."

XI

" Your crown and your sceptre I like full well,
  They tempt a poor maiden's pride, Sir;
But your lands and possessions—excuse if I'm rude—
Are too far in a Northerly latitude
  For me to become your Bride, Sir.

XII

In that aguish clime I should catch my death,
  Being but a raw new comer "—
Quoth he, " We have plenty of fuel stout;
And the fires, which I kindle, never go out
  By winter, nor yet by summer.

XIII

I am Prince of Hell, and Lord Paramount
    Over Monarchs there abiding.
My Groom of the Stables is Nimrod old ;
And Nebuchadnazor my stirrups must hold,
    When I go out a riding.

XIV

To spare your blushes, and maiden fears,
    I resorted to these inventions—
But, Imposture, begone ; and avaunt, Disguise ! "—
And the Devil began to swell and rise
    To his own diabolic dimensions.

XV

Twin horns from his forehead shot up to the moon,
    Like a branching stag in Arden ;
Dusk wings through his shoulders with eagle's strength
Push'd out ; and his train lay floundering in length
    An acre beyond the garden.—

XVI

To tender hearts I have framed my lay—
    Judge ye, all love-sick Maidens,
When the virgin saw in the soft moonlight,
In his proper proportions, her own true knight,
    If she needed long persuadings.

XVII

Yet a maidenly modesty kept her back,
    As her sex's art had taught her :
For " the biggest Fortunes," quoth she, " in the land—
Are not worthy "—then blush'd—" of your Highness's hand—
    Much less a poor Taylor's daughter.

XVIII

There's the two Miss Crockfords are single still,
    For whom great suitors hunger ;
And their Father's hell is much larger than mine "—
Quoth the Devil, " I've no such ambitious design,
    For their Dad is an old Fishmonger ;

XIX

And I cannot endure the smell of fish—
　　I have taken an anti-bias
To their livers, especially since the day
That the Angel smoked my cousin away
　　From the chaste spouse of Tobias.

XX

Had my amorous kinsman much longer staid,
　　The perfume would have seal'd his obit;
For he had a nicer nose than the wench,
Who cared not a pin for the smother and stench,
　　In the arms of the Son of Tobit."

XXI

"I have read it," quoth she, "in Apocryphal Writ"—
　　And the Devil stoop'd down, and kiss'd her;
Not Jove himself, when he courted in flame,
On Semele's lips, the love-scorch'd Dame,
　　Impress'd such a burning blister.

XXII

The fire through her bones and her vitals shot—
　　"O, I yield, my winsome marrow—
I am thine for life"—and black thunders roll'd—
And she sank in his arms through the garden mould,
　　With the speed of a red-hot arrow.

XXIII

Merrily, merrily, ring the bells
　　From each Pandemonian steeple;
For the Devil hath gotten his beautiful Bride,
And a Wedding Dinner he will provide,
　　To feast all kinds of people.

XXIV

Fat bulls of Basan are roasted whole,
　　Of the breed that ran at David;
With the flesh of goats, on the sinister side,
That shall stand apart, when the world is tried;
　　Fit meat for souls unsaved!

XXV

The fowl from the spit were the Harpies' brood,
   Which the bard sang near Cremona,
With a garnish of bats in their leathern wings imp't;
And the fish was—two delicate slices crimp't,
   Of the whale that swallow'd Jonah.

XXVI

Then the goblets were crown'd, and a health went round
   To the Bride, in a wine like scarlet;
No earthly vintage so deeply paints,
For 'twas dash'd with a tinge from the blood of the Saints
   By the Babylonian Harlot.

XXVII

No Hebe fair stood Cup Bearer there,
   The guests were their own skinkers;
But Bishop Judas first blest the can,
Who is of all Hell Metropolitan,
   And kiss'd it to all the drinkers.

XXVIII

The feast being ended, to dancing they went,
   To a music that did produce a
Most dissonant sound, while a hellish glee
Was sung in parts by the Furies Three;
   And the Devil took out Medusa.

XXIX

But the best of the sport was to hear his old Dam,
   Set up her shrill forlorn pipe—
How the wither'd Beldam hobbled about,
And put the rest of the company out—
   For she needs must try a horn-pipe.

XXX

But the heat, and the press, and the noise, and the din,
   Were so great, that, howe'er unwilling,
Our Reporter no longer was able to stay,
But came in his own defence away,
   And left the Bride quadrilling.

PROLOGUES AND EPILOGUES

EPILOGUE TO GODWIN'S TRAGEDY OF "ANTONIO"
(1800)

LADIES, ye've seen how Guzman's consort died,
    Poor victim of a Spaniard brother's pride,
When Spanish honour through the world was blown,
And Spanish beauty for the best was known.[1]
In that romantic, unenlighten'd time,
A *breach of promise*[2] was a sort of crime—
Which of you handsome English ladies here,
But deem the penance bloody and severe?
A whimsical old Saragossa[3] fashion,
That a dead father's dying inclination,
Should *live* to thwart a living daughter's passion,[4]
Unjustly on the sex *we*[5] men exclaim,
Rail at *your*[6] vices,—and commit the same;—
Man is a promise-breaker from the womb,
And goes a promise-breaker to the tomb—
What need we instance here the lover's vow,
The sick man's purpose, or the great man's bow?[7]
The truth by few examples best is shown—
Instead of many which are better known,
Take poor Jack Incident, that's dead and gone.
Jack, of dramatic genius justly vain,
Purchased a renter's share at Drury-lane;
A prudent man in every other matter,
Known at his club-room for an honest hatter;
Humane and courteous, led a civil life,
And has been seldom known to beat his wife;
But Jack is now grown quite another man,
Frequents the green-room, knows the plot and plan
    Of each new piece,

---

[1] Four *easy* lines.   [2] For which the *heroine died*.
[3] In *Spain*!!   [4] Two *neat* lines.   [5] Or *you*.
[6] Or *our*, as *they* have altered it.   [7] Antithesis!!

And has been seen to talk with Sheridan!
In at the play-house just at six he pops,
And never quits it till the curtain drops,
Is never absent on the *author's night,*
Knows actresses and actors too—by sight ;
So humble, that with Suett he'll confer,
Or take a pipe with plain Jack Bannister ;
Nay, with an author has been known so free,
He once suggested a catastrophe—
In short, John dabbled till his head was turn'd :
His wife remonstrated, his neighbours mourn'd,
His customers were dropping off apace,
And Jack's affairs began to wear a piteous face.
  One night his wife began a curtain lecture ;
'My dearest Johnny, husband, spouse, protector,
Take pity on your helpless babes and me,
Save us from ruin, you from bankruptcy—
Look to your business, leave these cursed plays,
And try again your old industrious ways.'
  Jack, who was always scared at the Gazette,
And had some bits of scull uninjured yet,
Promised amendment, vow'd his wife spake reason,
' He would not see another play that season—'
  Three stubborn fortnights Jack his promise kept,
Was late and early in his shop, eat, slept,
And walk'd and talk'd, like ordinary men ;
No *wit,* but John the hatter once again—
Visits his club : when lo ! one *fatal night*
His wife with horror view'd the well-known sight—
John's *hat, wig, snuff-box*—well she knew his tricks—
And Jack decamping at the hour of six.
Just at the counter's edge a playbill lay,
Announcing that ' Pizarro' was the play—
'O Johnny, Johnny, this is your old doing.'
Quoth Jack, ' Why what the devil storm's a-brewing ?
About a harmless play why all this fright ?
I'll go and see it, if it's but for spite—
Zounds, woman ! Nelson's [8] to be there to-night.'

[8] "A good clap-trap. Nelson has exhibited two or three times at both theatres—and advertised himself."

PROLOGUE TO GODWIN'S TRAGEDY OF "FAULKENER"
(1807)

An author who has given you all delight,
Furnish'd the tale our stage presents to-night.
Some of our earliest tears He taught to steal
Down our young cheeks, and forc'd us first to feel.
To solitary shores whole years confin'd,
Who has not read how pensive *Crusoe* pin'd?
Who, now grown old, that did not once admire
His goat, his parrot, his uncouth attire,
The stick, due-notch'd, that told each tedious day
That in the lonely island wore away?
Who has not shudder'd, where he stands aghast
At sight of human footsteps in the waste?
Or joy'd not, when his trembling hands unbind
Thee, *Friday*, gentlest of the savage kind?
  The genius who conceiv'd that magic tale
  Was skill'd by native pathos to prevail.
His stories, though rough-drawn, and fram'd in haste,
Had that which pleas'd our homely grandsires' taste.
  His was a various pen, that freely rov'd
  Into all subjects, was in most approv'd.
Whate'er the theme, his ready Muse obey'd—
Love, courtship, politics, religion, trade—
Gifted alike to shine in every sphere,
Nov'list, historian, poet, pamphleteer.
  In some blest interval of party-strife,
  He drew a striking sketch from private life,
Whose moving scenes of intricate distress
We try to-night in a dramatic dress:
A real story of domestic woe,
That asks no aid from music, verse, or show,
But trusts to truth, to nature, and *Defoe*.

EPILOGUE TO HENRY SIDDONS' FARCE, "TIME'S A TELL-TALE"
(1807)

Bound for the port of matrimonial bliss,
Ere I hoist sail, I hold it not amiss,
(Since prosp'rous ends ask prudent introductions)
To take a slight peep at my written instructions.

There's nothing like determining in time
All questions marital or maritime.

In all seas, straits, gulphs, ports, havens, lands, creeks.
Oh! Here it begins.
    "Season, spring, wind standing at point Desire—
    "The good ship Matrimony—Commander. Blandford, Esq.

Art. I.
    " The captain that has the command of her,
    " Or in his absence, the acting officer,
    " To see her planks are sound, her timbers tight."—
That acting officer I don't relish quite,
No, as I hope to tack another verse on,
I'll do those duties in my proper person.

Art. II.
    " All mutinies to be suppress'd at first."
That's a good caution to prevent the worst.

Art. III.
    " That she be properly victual'd, mann'd and stor'd,
    " To see no foreigners are got aboard."
That's rather difficult. Do what we can,
A vessel sometimes may mistake her man.
The safest way in such a parlous doubt,
Is steady watch and keep a sharp look out.

Art. IV.
    " Whereas their Lords Commissioners (the church)
    " Do strictly authorise the right of search:
    " As always practis'd—you're to understand
    " By these what articles are contraband;
    " Guns, mortars, pistols, halberts, swords, pikes, lances,
    " Ball, powder, shot, and the appurtenances.
    " Videlicet—whatever can be sent
    " To give the enemy encouragement.
    " Ogles are small shot (so the instruction runs),
    " Touches hand grenades, and squeezes rifle guns."

Art. V.
    " That no free-bottom'd neutral waiting maid
    " Presume to exercise the carrying trade:
    " The prohibition here contained extends
    " To all commerce cover'd by the name of Friends.
    " Heaven speed the good ship well "—and so it ends.
Oh with such wholesome jealousies as these
May Albion cherish his old spouse the seas;
Keep over her a husband's firm command,
Not with too rigid nor too lax a hand.

Be gently patient to her swells and throws
When big with safeties to himself she goes;
Nor while she clips him in a fast embrace,
Stand for some female frowns upon her face.
But tell the rival world—and tell in Thunder,
Whom Nature joined, none ere shall put asunder.

PROLOGUE TO COLERIDGE'S TRAGEDY OF "REMORSE"
(1813)

There are, I am told, who sharply criticise
Our modern theatres' unwieldy size.
We players shall scarce plead guilty to that charge,
Who think a house can never be too large:
Griev'd when a rant, that's worth a nation's ear,
Shakes some prescrib'd Lyceum's petty sphere;
And pleased to mark the grin from space to space
Spread epidemic o'er a town's broad face.—
O might old Betterton or Booth return
To view our structures from their silent urn,
Could Quin come stalking from Elysian glades,
Or Garrick get a day-rule from the shades—
Where now, perhaps, in mirth which Spirits approve,
He imitates the ways of men above,
And apes the actions of our upper coast,
As in his days of flesh he play'd the ghost:—
How might they bless our ampler scope to please,
And hate their own old shrunk up audiences.—
Their houses yet were palaces to those,
Which Ben and Fletcher for their triumphs chose.
Shakspeare, who wish'd a kingdom for a stage,
Like giant pent in disproportion'd cage,
Mourn'd his contracted strengths and crippled rage.
He who could tame his vast ambition down
To please some scatter'd gleanings of a town,
And, if some hundred auditors supplied
Their meagre meed of claps, was satisfied,
How had he felt, when that dread curse of Lear's
Had burst tremendous on a thousand ears,
While deep-struck wonder from applauding bands
Return'd the tribute of as many hands!
Rude were his guests; he never made his bow
To such an audience as salutes us now.
He lack'd the balm of labor, female praise.
Few Ladies in his time frequented plays,

Or came to see a youth with aukward art
And shrill sharp pipe burlesque the woman's part.
The very use, since so essential grown,
Of painted scenes, was to his stage unknown.
The air-blest castle, round whose wholesome crest,
The martlet, guest of summer, chose her nest—
The forest walks of Arden's fair domain,
Where Jaques fed his solitary vein.
No pencil's aid as yet had dared supply,
Seen only by the intellectual eye.
Those scenic helps, denied to Shakspeare's page,
Our Author owes to a more liberal age.
Nor pomp nor circumstance are wanting here;
'Tis for himself alone that he must fear.
Yet shall remembrance cherish the just pride,
That (be the laurel granted or denied)
He first essay'd in this distinguish'd fane,
Severer muses and a tragic strain.

EPILOGUE TO KENNEY'S FARCE, "DEBTOR AND CREDITOR"

(1814)

Spoken by Mr. Liston and Mr. Emery in character

Gosling. False world——
Sampson. You're bit, Sir.
Gosling. Boor! what's that to you?
With Love's soft sorrows what hast thou to do?
'Tis *here* for consolation I must look.
(*Takes out his pocket book*).
Sampson. Nay, Sir, don't put us down in your black book.
Gosling. All Helicon is here.
Sampson. All Hell.
Gosling. You Clod!
Did'st never hear of the Pierian God,
And the Nine Virgins on the Sacred Hill?
Sampson. Nine Virgins!—Sure!
Gosling. I have them all at will.
Sampson. If Miss fight shy, then——
Gosling. And my suit decline.
Sampson. You'll make a dash at them.
Gosling. I'll tip all nine.
Sampson. What, wed 'em, Sir?
Gosling. O, no—that thought I banish.
I woo—not wed; they never bring the Spanish.
Their favours I pursue, and court the bays.

EPILOGUE TO "DEBTOR AND CREDITOR."

Sampson. Mayhap, you're one of them that write the plays?
Gosling. Bumpkin!
Sampson. I'm told the public's well-nigh crammed
With such like stuff.
Gosling. The public may be damned.
Sampson. They ha'nt damned you? (*inquisitively*).
Gosling. This fellow's wond'rous shrewd!
I'd tell him if I thought he'd not be rude.
Once in my greener years, I wrote a piece.
Sampson. Aye, so did I—at school like——
Gosling. Booby, cease!
I mean a Play.
Sampson. Oh!
Gosling. And to crown my joys,
'Twas acted——
Sampson. Well, and how——
Gosling. It made a noise,
A kind of mingled—— (*as if musing*).
Sampson. Aye, describe it, try.
Gosling. Like—Were you ever in the pillory?
Sampson. No, Sir, I thank ye, no such kind of game.
Gosling. Bate but the eggs, and it was much the same.
Shouts, clamours, laughs, and a peculiar sound,
Like, like——
Sampson. Like geese, I warrant, in a pound.
I like this mainly!
Gosling. Some began to cough,
Some cried——
Sampson. Go on——
Gosling. A few—and some—"Go off!"
I can't suppress it. Gods! I hear it now;
It was in fact a most confounded row.
Dire was the din, as when some storm confounds
Earth, sea, and sky, with all terrific sounds.
Not hungry lions send forth notes more strange,
Not bulls and bears, that have been hoaxed on 'Change.
Sampson. Exeter 'Change you mean—I've seen they bears.
Gosling. The beasts I mean are far less tame than theirs.
Change Alley Bruins, nattier though their dress,
Might at Polito's study politesse.
Brief let me be. My gentle Sampson, pray,
Fight Larry Whack, but never write a play.
Sampson. I won't, Sir: and these christian souls petition,
To spare all wretched folks in such condition.

EPILOGUE TO AN AMATEUR PERFORMANCE OF "RICHARD II."

(1824)

Of all that act, the hardest task is theirs,
Who, bred no Players, play at being Players;
Copy the shrug—in Kemble once approved;—
Mere mimics' mimics—nature twice removed.
Shades of a shadow! who but must have seen
The stage-struck hero, in some swelling scene
Aspiring to be Lear—stumble on Kean?
The admired actor's faults our steps betray,—
No less his very beauties lead astray!

In "sad civility" once Garrick sate
To see a Play, mangled in form and state;
Plebeian Shakspeare must the words supply,—
The actors all were Fools—of Quality.
The scenes—the dresses—were above rebuke;—
Scarce a Performer there below a Duke.
He sate, and mused how in his Shakspeare's mind
The idea of old Nobility enshrined
Should thence a grace and a refinement have
Which passed these living Nobles to conceive,—
Who with such apish, base gesticulation,
Remnants of starts, and dregs of playhouse passion,
So foul belied their great forefathers' fashion!
He saw—and true Nobility confessed
Less in the high-born blood, than lowly poet's breast.

If Lords enacting Lords sometimes may fail,
What gentle plea, Spectators, can avail
For wight of low degree who dares to stir
The long-raked ashes of old Lancaster,
And on his nothing-martial front to set
Of warlike Gaunt the lofty burgonet?
For who shall that Plantagenet display,
Majestical in sickness and decay?
Or paint the shower of passions fierce and thick
On Richard's head—that Royal Splenetic?

Your pardon, not your plaudits, then we claim
If we've come short, where Garrick had been tame!

PROLOGUE TO SHERIDAN KNOWLES' COMEDY, "THE WIFE"

(1833)

Untoward fate no luckless wight invades
More sorely than the Man who drives *two trades;*
Like Esop's bat, between two natures placed,
Scowl'd at by *mice,* among the *birds* disgraced.
Our author thus, of two-fold fame exactor,
Is doubly scouted,—both as Bard, and Actor!
Wanting in haste a Prologue, he applied
To three poetic friends; was thrice denied.
Each glared on him with supercilious glance,
As on a Poor Relation met by chance;
And one was heard, with more repulsive air,
To mutter "Vagabond," "Rogue," "Strolling Player!"
A poet once, he found—and look'd aghast—
By turning actor, he had lost his *caste.*
The verse patch'd up at length—with like ill fortune
His friends behind the scenes he did importune
To speak his lines. He found them all fight shy,
Nodding their heads in cool civility.
"There service in the Drama was enough,
The poet might recite the poet's stuff!"
The rogues—they like him hugely—but it stung 'em,
Somehow—to think a Bard had got among 'em.
Their mind made up—no earthly pleading shook it,
In pure compassion 'till I undertook it.
Disown'd by Poets, and by Actors too,
Dear Patrons of both arts, he turns to you!
If in your hearts some tender feelings dwell
From sweet Virginia, or heroic Tell:
If in the scenes which follow you can trace
What once has pleased you—an unbidden grace—
A touch of nature's work—an awkward start
Or ebullition of an Irish heart—
Cry, clap, commend it! If you like them not,
Your former favours cannot be forgot.
Condemn them—damn them—hiss them, if you will—
Their author is your grateful servant still!

EPILOGUE TO SHERIDAN KNOWLES' COMEDY "THE WIFE"

(1833)

When first our Bard his simple will express'd,
That I should in his Heroine's robes be dress'd,
My fears were with my vanity at strife,
How I could act that untried part—a " Wife."
But Fancy to the Grison hills me drew,
Where Mariana like a wild flower grew,
Nursing her garden-kindred: so far I
Liked her condition, willing to comply
With that sweet single life: when, with a cranch,
Down came that thundering, crashing avalanche,
Startling my mountain-project! "Take this spade,"
Said Fancy then; "dig low, adventurous Maid,
For hidden wealth." I did: and, Ladies, lo!
Was e'er romantic female's fortune so,
To dig a life-warm lover from the—snow?

A Wife and Princess see me next, beset
With subtle toils, in an Italian net;
While knavish Courtiers, stung with rage or fear,
Distill'd lip-poison in a husband's ear.
I ponder'd on the boiling Southern vein;
Racks, cords, stilettos, rush'd upon my brain!
By poor, good, weak Antonio, too disowned—
I dream'd each night, I should be Desdemona'd:
And, being in Mantua, thought upon the shop,
Whence fair Verona's youth his breath did stop:
And what if Leonardo, in foul scorn,
Some lean Apothecary should suborn
To take my hated life? A "tortoise" hung
Before my eyes, and in my ears scaled "alligators" rung.
But *my* Othello, to his vows more zealous—
Twenty Iagos could not make *him* jealous!

New raised to reputation, and to life—
At your commands behold me, without strife,
Well-pleased, and ready to repeat—" The Wife."

JOHN WOODVIL

A Tragedy

(1798-1802. *Text of* 1818)

CHARACTERS

Sir Walter Woodvil.
John. \
Simon. / *his sons.*
Lovel. \
Gray. / *pretended friends of John.*
Sandford. Sir Walter's old steward.
Margaret. Orphan ward of Sir Walter.
Four Gentlemen. John's riotous companions.
Servants.

Scene — *for the most part at Sir Walter's mansion in* Devonshire; *at other times in the forest of* Sherwood.

Time — *soon after the* Restoration.

ACT THE FIRST

Scene.—*A Servants' Apartment in Woodvil Hall.*
Servants drinking—*Time, the morning.*

A Song by Daniel
"*When the King enjoys his own again.*"

PETER

A delicate song. Where did'st learn it, fellow?

DANIEL

Even there, where thou learnest thy oaths and thy politics—at our master's table.—Where else should a serving-man pick up his poor accomplishments?

(131)

MARTIN

Well spoken, Daniel.   O rare Daniel!—his oaths and his politics! excellent!

FRANCIS

And where did'st pick up thy knavery, Daniel?

PETER

That came to him by inheritance. His family have supplied the shire of Devon, time out of mind, with good thieves and bad serving-men. All of his race have come into the world without their conscience.

MARTIN

Good thieves, and bad serving-men! Better and better. I marvel what Daniel hath got to say in reply.

DANIEL

I marvel more when thou wilt say any thing to the purpose, thou shallow serving-man, whose swiftest conceit carries thee no higher than to apprehend with difficulty the stale jests of us thy compeers. When was't ever known to club thy own particular jest among us?

MARTIN

Most unkind Daniel, to speak such biting things of me!

FRANCIS

See—if he hath not brought tears into the poor fellow's eyes with the saltness of his rebuke.

DANIEL

No offence, brother Martin—I meant none. 'Tis true, Heaven gives gifts, and with-holds them. It has been pleased to bestow upon me a nimble invention to the manufacture of a jest; and upon thee, Martin, an indifferent bad capacity to understand my meaning.

MARTIN

Is that all?   I am content.   Here's my hand.

FRANCIS

Well, I like a little innocent mirth myself, but never could endure bawdry.

DANIEL

Quot homines tot sententiæ.

MARTIN
And what is that?

DANIEL
'Tis Greek, and argues difference of opinion.

MARTIN
I hope there is none between us.

DANIEL
Here's to thee, brother Martin. (*Drinks.*)

MARTIN
And to thee, Daniel. (*Drinks.*)

FRANCIS
And to thee, Peter. (*Drinks.*)

PETER
Thank you, Francis. And here's to thee. (*Drinks.*)

MARTIN
I shall be fuddled anon.

DANIEL
And drunkenness I hold to be a very despicable vice.

ALL
O! a shocking vice. (*They drink round.*)

PETER
In as much as it taketh away the understanding.

DANIEL
And makes the eyes red.

PETER
And the tongue to stammer.

DANIEL
And to blab out secrets.
(*During this conversation they continue drinking.*)

PETER
Some men do not know an enemy from a friend when they are drunk.

DANIEL
Certainly sobriety is the health of the soul.

MARTIN
Now I know I am going to be drunk.

DANIEL
How can'st tell, dry-bones?

MARTIN
Because I begin to be melancholy. That's always a sign.

FRANCIS
Take care of Martin, he'll topple off his seat else.

(Martin drops asleep.)

PETER
Times are greatly altered, since young master took upon himself the government of this household.

ALL
Greatly altered.

FRANCIS
I think every thing be altered for the better since His Majesty's blessed restoration.

PETER
In Sir Walter's days there was no encouragement given to good house-keeping.

ALL
None.

DANIEL
For instance, no possibility of getting drunk before two in the afternoon.

PETER
Every man his allowance of ale at breakfast—his quart!

ALL
A quart!! *(In derision.)*

DANIEL
Nothing left to our own sweet discretions.

PETER
Whereby it may appear, we were treated more like beasts than what we were—discreet and reasonable serving-men.

ALL
Like beasts.

MARTIN
(*Opening his eyes.*) Like beasts.

DANIEL
To sleep, wag-tail!

FRANCIS
I marvel all this while where the old gentleman has found means to secrete himself. It seems no man has heard of him since the day of the King's return. Can any tell why our young master, being favoured by the court, should not have interest to procure his father's pardon?

DANIEL
Marry, I think 'tis the obstinacy of the old Knight, that will not be beholden to the court for his safety.

MARTIN
Now that is wilful.

FRANCIS
But can any tell me the place of his concealment?

PETER
That cannot I; but I have my conjectures.

DANIEL
Two hundred pounds, as I hear, to the man that shall apprehend him.

FRANCIS
Well, I have my suspicions.

PETER
And so have I.

MARTIN
And I can keep a secret.

FRANCIS
(*To Peter.*) Warwickshire you mean. (*Aside.*)

PETER
Perhaps not.

FRANCIS
Nearer perhaps.

PETER
I say nothing.

DANIEL

I hope there is none in this company would be mean enough to betray him.

ALL

O Lord, surely not. (*They drink to Sir Walter's safety.*)

FRANCIS

I have often wondered how our master came to be excepted by name in the late Act of Oblivion.

DANIEL

Shall I tell the reason?

ALL

Aye, do.

DANIEL

'Tis thought he is no great friend to the present happy establishment.

ALL

O! monstrous!

PETER

Fellow servants, a thought strikes me.—Do we, or do we not, come under the penalties of the treason-act, by reason of our being privy to this man's concealment.

ALL

Truly a sad consideration.

To them enters Sandford suddenly.

SANDFORD

You well-fed and unprofitable grooms,
Maintained for state, not use;
You lazy feasters at another's cost,
That eat like maggots into an estate,
And do as little work,
Being indeed but foul excrescences,
And no just parts in a well-order'd family;
You base and rascal imitators,
Who act up to the height your master's vices,
But cannot read his virtues in your bond:
Which of you, as I enter'd, spake of betraying?
Was it you, or you, or, thin-face, was it you?

MARTIN

Whom does he call thin-face?

SANDFORD

No prating, loon, but tell me who he was,
That I may brain the villain with my staff,
That seeks Sir Walter's life?
You miserable men,
With minds more slavish than your slave's estate,
Have you that noble bounty so forgot,
Which took you from the looms, and from the ploughs,
Which better had ye follow'd, fed ye, cloth'd ye,
And entertain'd ye in a worthy service,
Where your best wages was the world's repute,
That thus ye seek his life, by whom ye live?
Have you forgot too,
How often in old times
Your drunken mirths have stunn'd day's sober ears,
Carousing full cups to Sir Walter's health?—
Whom now ye would betray, but that he lies
Out of the reach of your poor treacheries.
This learn from me,
Our master's secret sleeps with trustier tongues,
Than will unlock themselves to carls like you.
Go, get you gone, you knaves. Who stirs? this staff
Shall teach you better manners else.

ALL

Well, we are going.

SANDFORD

And quickly too, ye had better, for I see
Young mistress Margaret coming this way.

(Exeunt all but Sandford.)

Enter Margaret, as in a fright, pursued by a Gentleman, who, seeing Sandford, retires muttering a curse.

Sandford. Margaret.

SANDFORD

Good-morrow to my fair mistress. 'Twas a chance
I saw you, lady, so intent was I
On chiding hence these graceless serving-men,
Who cannot break their fast at morning meals
Without debauch and mis-timed riotings.

This house hath been a scene of nothing else
But atheist riot and profane excess,
Since my old master quitted all his rights here.

MARGARET

Each day I endure fresh insult from the scorn
Of Woodvil's friends, the uncivil jests,
And free discourses, of the dissolute men,
That haunt this mansion, making me their mirth.

SANDFORD

Does my young master know of these affronts?

MARGARET

I cannot tell. Perhaps he has not been told.
Perhaps he might have seen them if he would.
I have known him more quick-sighted. Let that pass.
All things seem chang'd, I think. I had a friend,
(I can't but weep to think him alter'd too,)
These things are best forgotten; but I knew
A man, a young man, young, and full of honor,
That would have pick'd a quarrel for a straw,
And fought it out to the extremity,
E'en with the dearest friend he had alive,
On but a bare surmise, a possibility,
That Margaret had suffer'd an affront.
Some are too tame, that were too splenetic once.

SANDFORD

'Twere best he should be *told* of these affronts.

MARGARET

I am the daughter of his father's friend,
Sir Walter's orphan-ward.
I am not his servant maid, that I should wait
The opportunity of a gracious hearing,
Enquire the times and seasons when to put
My peevish prayer up at young Woodvil's feet,
And sue to him for slow redress, who was
Himself a suitor late to Margaret.
I am somewhat proud: and Woodvil taught me pride.
I was his favourite once, his playfellow in infancy,
And joyful mistress of his youth.
None once so pleasant in his eyes as Margaret.
His conscience, his religion, Margaret was,
His dear heart's confessor, a heart within that heart,

And all dear things summ'd up in her alone.
As Margaret smil'd or frown'd John liv'd or died:
His dress, speech, gesture, studies, friendships, all
Being fashion'd to her liking.
His flatteries taught me first this self-esteem,
His flatteries and caresses, while he loved.
The world esteem'd her happy, who had won
His heart, who won all hearts;
And ladies envied me the love of Woodvil.

SANDFORD

He doth affect the courtier's life too much,
Whose art is to forget,
And that has wrought this seeming change in him,
That was by nature noble.
'Tis these court-plagues, that swarm about our house,
Have done the mischief, making his fancy giddy
With images of state, preferment, place,
Tainting his generous spirits with ambition.

MARGARET

I know not how it is;
A cold protector is John grown to me.
The mistress, and presumptive wife, of Woodvil
Can never stoop so low to supplicate
A man, her equal, to redress those wrongs,
Which he was bound first to prevent;
But which his own neglects have sanction'd rather,
Both sanction'd and provok'd: a mark'd neglect,
And strangeness fast'ning bitter on his love,
His love which long has been upon the wane.
For me, I am determined what to do:
To leave this house this night, and lukewarm John,
And trust for food to the earth and Providence.

SANDFORD

O lady, have a care
Of these indefinite and spleen-bred resolves.
You know not half the dangers that attend
Upon a life of wand'ring, which your thoughts now,
Feeling the swellings of a lofty anger,
To your abused fancy, as 'tis likely,
Portray without its terrors, painting *lies*
And representments of fallacious liberty—
You know not what it is to leave the roof that shelters you.

MARGARET

I have thought on every possible event,
The dangers and discouragements you speak of,
Even till my woman's heart hath ceas'd to fear them,
And cowardice grows enamour'd of rare accidents.
Nor am I so unfurnish'd, as you think,
Of practicable schemes.

SANDFORD

Now God forbid ; think twice of this, dear lady.

MARGARET

I pray you spare me, Mr. Sandford,
And once for all believe, nothing can shake my purpose.

SANDFORD

But what course have you thought on ?

MARGARET

To seek Sir Walter in the forest of Sherwood.
I have letters from young Simon,
Acquainting me with all the circumstances
Of their concealment, place, and manner of life,
And the merry hours they spend in the green haunts
Of Sherwood, nigh which place they have ta'en a house
In the town of Nottingham, and pass for foreigners,
Wearing the dress of Frenchmen.—
All which I have perus'd with so attent
And child-like longings, that to my doting ears
Two sounds now seem like one,
One meaning in two words, Sherwood and Liberty.
And, gentle Mr. Sandford,
'Tis you that must provide now
The means of my departure, which for safety
Must be in boy's apparel.

SANDFORD

Since you will have it so
(My careful age trembles at all may happen)
I will engage to furnish you.
I have the keys of the wardrobe, and can fit you
With garments to your size.
I know a suit
Of lively Lincoln Green, that shall much grace you
In the wear, being glossy fresh, and worn but seldom.
Young Stephen Woodvil wore them, while he lived.

I have the keys of all this house and passages,
And ere day-break will rise and let you forth.
What things soe'er you have need of I can furnish you;
And will provide a horse and trusty guide,
To bear you on your way to Nottingham.

MARGARET

That once this day and night were fairly past!
For then I'll bid this house and love farewell;
Farewell, sweet Devon; farewell, lukewarm John;
For with the morning's light will Margaret be gone.
Thanks, courteous Mr. Sandford.—

(*Exeunt divers ways.*)

ACT THE SECOND

Scene.—*An Apartment in Woodvil Hall.*

John Woodvil—alone.

(*Reading Parts of a Letter.*)

"When Love grows cold, and indifference has usurped upon old Esteem, it is no marvel if the world begin to account *that* dependence, which hitherto has been esteemed honorable shelter. The course I have taken (in leaving this house, not easily wrought thereunto,) seemed to me best for the once-for-all releasing of yourself (who in times past have deserved well of me) from the now daily, and not-to-be-endured, tribute of forced love, and ill-dissembled reluctance of affection. MARGARET."

Gone! gone! my girl? so hasty, Margaret!
And never a kiss at parting? shallow loves,
And likings of a ten days' growth, use courtesies,
And shew red eyes at parting. Who bids "farewell"
In the same tone he cries "God speed you, Sir?"
Or tells of joyful victories at sea,
Where he hath ventures? does not rather muffle
His organs to emit a leaden sound,
To suit the melancholy dull "farewell,"
Which they in Heaven not use?—
So peevish, Margaret?
But 'tis the common error of your sex,
When our idolatry slackens, or grows less,

(As who of woman born can keep his faculty
Of Admiration, being a decaying faculty,
For ever strain'd to the pitch? or can at pleasure
Make it renewable, as some appetites are,
As, namely, Hunger, Thirst?—) this being the case,
They tax us with neglect, and love grown cold,
Coin plainings of the perfidy of men,
Which into maxims pass, and apothegms
To be retailed in ballads.—
                              I know them all.
They are jealous, when our larger hearts receive
More guests than one. (Love in a woman's heart
Being all in one.) For me, I am sure I have room here
For more disturbers of my sleep than one.
Love shall have part, but Love shall not have all.
Ambition, Pleasure, Vanity, all by turns,
Shall lie in my bed, and keep me fresh and waking;
Yet Love not be excluded.—Foolish wench,
I could have lov'd her twenty years to come,
And still have kept my liking. But since 'tis so,
Why, fare thee well, old play-fellow! I'll try
To squeeze a tear for old acquaintance sake.
I shall not grudge so much.——

To him enters Lovel.

LOVEL

Bless us, Woodvil! what is the matter? I protest, man, I thought you had been weeping.

WOODVIL

Nothing is the matter, only the wench has forced some water into my eyes, which will quickly disband.

LOVEL

I cannot conceive you.

WOODVIL

Margaret is flown.

LOVEL

Upon what pretence?

WOODVIL

Neglect on my part: which it seems she has had the wit to discover, maugre all my pains to conceal it.

LOVEL

Then, you confess the charge?

WOODVIL
To say the truth, my love for her has of late stopt short on this side idolatry.

LOVEL
As all good Christians' should, I think.

WOODVIL
I am sure, I could have loved her still within the limits of warrantable love.

LOVEL
A kind of brotherly affection, I take it.

WOODVIL
We should have made excellent man and wife in time.

LOVEL
A good old couple, when the snows fell, to crowd about a sea-coal fire, and talk over old matters.

WOODVIL
While each should feel, what neither cared to acknowledge, that stories oft repeated may, at last, come to lose some of their grace by the repetition.

LOVEL
Which both of you may yet live long enough to discover. For, take my word for it, Margaret is a bird that will come back to you without a lure.

WOODVIL
Never, never, Lovel. Spite of my levity, with tears I confess it, she was a lady of most confirmed honour, of an unmatchable spirit, and determinate in all virtuous resolutions; not hasty to anticipate an affront, nor slow to feel, where just provocation was given.

LOVEL
What made you neglect her, then?

WOODVIL
Mere levity and youthfulness of blood, a malady incident to young men, physicians call it caprice. Nothing else. He, that slighted her, knew her value: and 'tis odds, but, for thy sake, Margaret, John will yet go to his grave a bachelor.

(*A noise heard, as of one drunk and singing.*)

LOVEL

Here comes one, that will quickly dissipate these humours.

(Enter one drunk.)

DRUNKEN MAN

Good-morrow to you, gentlemen. Mr. Lovel, I am your humble servant. Honest Jack Woodvil, I will get drunk with you to-morrow.

WOODVIL

And why to-morrow, honest Mr. Freeman?

DRUNKEN MAN

I scent a traitor in that question. A beastly question. Is it not his Majesty's birth-day? the day, of all days in the year, on which King Charles the second was graciously pleased to be born. (*Sings*) "Great pity 'tis such days as those should come but once a year."

LOVEL

Drunk in a morning! foh! how he stinks!

DRUNKEN MAN

And why not drunk in a morning? can'st tell, bully?

WOODVIL

Because, being the sweet and tender infancy of the day, methinks, it should ill endure such early blightings.

DRUNKEN MAN

I grant you, 'tis in some sort the youth and tender nonage of the day. Youth is bashful, and I give it a cup to encourage it. (*Sings*) "Ale that will make Grimalkin prate."—At noon I drink for thirst, at night for fellowship, but, above all, I love to usher in the bashful morning under the auspices of a freshening stoop of liquor. (*Sings*) "Ale in a Saxon rumkin then makes valour burgeon in tall men."—But, I crave pardon. I fear I keep that gentleman from serious thoughts. There be those that wait for me in the cellar.

WOODVIL

Who are they?

DRUNKEN MAN

Gentlemen, my good friends, Cleveland, Delaval, and Truby. I know by this time they are all clamorous for me. (*Exit, singing.*)

WOODVIL

This keeping of open house acquaints a man with strange companions.

(*Enter, at another door, Three calling for Harry Freeman.*)

Harry Freeman, Harry Freeman.
He is not here.   Let us go look for him.
Where is Freeman?
Where is Harry?
(*Exeunt the Three, calling for Freeman.*)

WOODVIL

Did you ever see such gentry? (*laughing*).   These are they that fatten on ale and tobacco in a morning, drink burnt brandy at noon to promote digestion, and piously conclude with quart bumpers after supper, to prove their loyalty.

LOVEL

Come, shall we adjourn to the Tennis Court?

WOODVIL

No, you shall go with me into the gallery, where I will shew you the *Vandyke* I have purchased.   "The late King taking leave of his children."

LOVEL

I will but adjust my dress, and attend you.
(*Exit Lovel.*)

JOHN WOODVIL (*alone*)

Now Universal England getteth drunk
For joy that Charles, her monarch, is restored:
And she, that sometime wore a saintly mask,
The stale-grown vizor from her face doth pluck,
And weareth now a suit of morris bells,
With which she jingling goes through all her towns and villages.
The baffled factions in their houses sculk:
The common-wealthsman, and state machinist,
The cropt fanatic, and fifth-monarchy-man,
Who heareth of these visionaries now?
They and their dreams have ended.   Fools do sing,
Where good men yield God thanks; but politic spirits,
Who live by observation, note these changes
Of the popular mind, and thereby serve their ends.
Then why not I?   What's Charles to me, or Oliver,

VOL. V.—10

But as my own advancement hangs on one of them?
I to myself am chief.——I know,
Some shallow mouths cry out, that I am smit
With the gauds and shew of state, the point of place,
And trick of precedence, the ducks, and nods,
Which weak minds pay to rank. 'Tis not to sit
In place of worship at the royal masques,
Their pastimes, plays, and Whitehall banquetings,
For none of these,
Nor yet to be seen whispering with some great one,
Do I affect the favours of the court.
I would be great, for greatness hath great *power*,
And that's the fruit I reach at.—
Great spirits ask great play-room. Who could sit,
With these prophetic swellings in my breast,
That prick and goad me on, and never cease,
To the fortunes something tells me I was born to?
Who, with such monitors within to stir him,
Would sit him down, with lazy arms across,
A unit, a thing without a name in the state,
A something to be govern'd, not to govern,
A fishing, hawking, hunting, country gentleman?
(*Exit.*)

Scene.—*Sherwood Forest.*

SIR WALTER WOODVIL. SIMON WOODVIL.
(*Disguised as Frenchmen.*)

SIR WALTER

How fares my boy, Simon, my youngest born,
My hope, my pride, young Woodvil, speak to me?
Some grief untold weighs heavy at thy heart:
I know it by thy alter'd cheer of late.
Thinkest, thy brother plays thy father false?
It is a mad and thriftless prodigal,
Grown proud upon the favours of the court;
Court manners, and court fashions, he affects,
And in the heat and uncheck'd blood of youth,
Harbours a company of riotous men,
All hot, and young, court-seekers, like himself,
Most skilful to devour a patrimony;
And these have eat into my old estates,
And these have drain'd thy father's cellars dry;

But these so common faults of youth not named,
(Things which themselves outgrow, left to themselves,)
I know no quality that stains his honor.
My life upon his faith and noble mind,
Son John could never play thy father false.

SIMON

I never thought but nobly of my brother,
Touching his honor and fidelity.
Still I could wish him charier of his person,
And of his time more frugal, than to spend
In riotous living, graceless society,
And mirth unpalatable, hours better employ'd
(With those persuasive graces nature lent him)
In fervent pleadings for a father's life.

SIR WALTER

I would not owe my life to a jealous court,
Whose shallow policy I know it is,
On some reluctant acts of prudent mercy,
(Not voluntary, but extorted by the times,
In the first tremblings of new-fixed power,
And recollection smarting from old wounds,)
On these to build a spurious popularity.
Unknowing what free grace or mercy mean,
They fear to punish, therefore do they pardon.
For this cause have I oft forbid my son,
By letters, overtures, open solicitings,
Or closet-tamperings, by gold or fee,
To beg or bargain with the court for my life.

SIMON

And John has ta'en you, father, at your word,
True to the letter of his paternal charge.

SIR WALTER

Well, my good cause, and my good conscience, boy,
Shall be for sons to me, if John prove false.
Men die but once, and the opportunity
Of a noble death is not an every-day fortune :
It is a gift which noble spirits pray for.

SIMON

I would not wrong my brother by surmise ;
I know him generous, full of gentle qualities,
Incapable of base compliances,

No prodigal in his nature, but affecting
This shew of bravery for ambitious ends.
He drinks, for 'tis the humour of the court,
And drink may one day wrest the secret from him,
And pluck you from your hiding place in the sequel.

SIR WALTER

Fair death shall be my doom, and foul life his.
Till when, we'll live as free in this green forest
As yonder deer, who roam unfearing treason;
Who seem the Aborigines of this place,
Or Sherwood theirs by tenure.

SIMON

'Tis said, that Robert Earl of Huntingdon,
Men call'd him Robin Hood, an outlaw bold,
With a merry crew of hunters here did haunt,
Not sparing the king's venison. May one believe
The antique tale?

SIR WALTER

There is much likelihood,
Such bandits did in England erst abound,
When polity was young. I have read of the pranks
Of that mad archer, and of the tax he levied
On travellers, whatever their degree,
Baron, or knight, whoever pass'd these woods,
Layman, or priest, not sparing the bishop's mitre
For spiritual regards; nay, once, 'tis said,
He robb'd the king himself.

SIMON

A perilous man.   (*Smiling*.)

SIR WALTER

How quietly we live here,
Unread in the world's business,
And take no note of all its slippery changes.
'Twere best we make a world among ourselves,
A little world,
Without the ills and falsehoods of the greater;
We two being all the inhabitants of ours,
And kings and subjects both in one.

SIMON

Only the dangerous errors, fond conceits,
Which make the business of that greater world,

Must have no place in ours :
As, namely, riches, honors, birth, place, courtesy,
Good fame and bad, rumours and popular noises,
Books, creeds, opinions, prejudices national,
Humours particular,
Soul-killing lies, and truths that work small good,
Feuds, factions, enmities, relationships,
Loves, hatreds, sympathies, antipathies,
And all the intricate stuff quarrels are made of.

(*Margaret enters in boy's apparel.*)

SIR WALTER
What pretty boy have we here?

MARGARET
Bon jour, messieurs. Ye have handsome English faces,
I should have ta'en you else for other two,
I came to seek in the forest.

SIR WALTER
Who are they?

MARGARET
A gallant brace of Frenchmen, curled monsieurs,
That, men say, haunt these woods, affecting privacy,
More than the manner of their countrymen.

SIMON
We have here a wonder.
The face is Margaret's face.

SIR WALTER
The face is Margaret's, but the dress the same
My Stephen sometimes wore.
(*To Margaret*)
Suppose us them; whom do men say we are?
Or know you what you seek?

MARGARET
A worthy pair of exiles,
Two whom the politics of state revenge,
In final issue of long civil broils,
Have houseless driven from your native France,
To wander idle in these English woods,
Where now ye live; most part

Thinking on home, and all the joys of France,
Where grows the purple vine.

SIR WALTER

These woods, young stranger,
And grassy pastures, which the slim deer loves,
Are they less beauteous than the land of France,
Where grows the purple vine?

MARGARET

I cannot tell.
To an indifferent eye both shew alike.
'Tis not the scene,
But all familiar objects in the scene,
Which now ye miss, that constitute a difference.
Ye had a country, exiles, ye have none now;
Friends had ye, and much wealth, ye now have nothing;
Our manners, laws, our customs, all are foreign to you,
I know ye loathe them, cannot learn them readily;
And there is reason, exiles, ye should love
Our English earth less than your land of France,
Where grows the purple vine; where all delights grow,
Old custom has made pleasant.

SIR WALTER

You, that are read
So deeply in our story, what are you?

MARGARET

A bare adventurer; in brief a woman,
That put strange garments on, and came thus far
To seek an ancient friend:
And having spent her stock of idle words,
And feeling some tears coming,
Hastes now to clasp Sir Walter Woodvil's knees,
And beg a boon for Margaret, his poor ward. (*Kneeling.*)

SIR WALTER

Not at my feet, Margaret, not at my feet.

MARGARET

Yes, till her suit is answer'd.

SIR WALTER

Name it.

MARGARET
A little boon, and yet so great a grace,
She fears to ask it.

SIR WALTER
Some riddle, Margaret?

MARGARET
No riddle, but a plain request.

SIR WALTER
Name it.

MARGARET
Free liberty of Sherwood,
And leave to take her lot with you in the forest.

SIR WALTER
A scant petition, Margaret, but take it,
Seal'd with an old man's tears.—
Rise, daughter of Sir Rowland.
          (*Addresses them both.*)
                O you most worthy,
You constant followers of a man proscribed,
Following poor misery in the throat of danger;
Fast servitors to craz'd and penniless poverty,
Serving poor poverty without hope of gain;
Kind children of a sire unfortunate;
Green clinging tendrils round a trunk decay'd,
Which needs must bring on you timeless decay;
Fair living forms to a dead carcase join'd;—
What shall I say?
Better the dead were gather'd to the dead,
Than death and life in disproportion meet.—
Go, seek your fortunes, children.—

SIMON
Why, whither should we go?

SIR WALTER
You to the Court, where now your brother John
Commits a rape on Fortune.

SIMON
Luck to John!
A light-heel'd strumpet, when the sport is done.

SIR WALTER
You to the sweet society of your equals,
Where the world's fashion smiles on youth and beauty.

MARGARET
Where young men's flatteries cozen young maids' beauty,
There pride oft gets the vantage hand of duty,
There sweet humility withers.

SIMON
Mistress Margaret,
How fared my brother John, when you left Devon?

MARGARET
John was well, Sir.

SIMON
'Tis now nine months almost,
Since I saw home. What new friends has John made?
Or keeps he his first love?—I did suspect
Some foul disloyalty. Now do I know,
John has prov'd false to her, for Margaret weeps.
It is a scurvy brother.

SIR WALTER
Fie upon it.
All men are false, I think. The date of love
Is out, expired, its stories all grown stale,
O'erpast, forgotten, like an antique tale
Of Hero and Leander.

SIMON
I have known some men that are too general-contemplative for the narrow passion. I am in some sort a *general* lover.

MARGARET
In the name of the boy God, who plays at hood-man-blind with the Muses, and cares not whom he catches: what is it *you* love?

SIMON
Simply, all things that live,
From the crook'd worm to man's imperial form,
And God-resembling likeness. The poor fly,
That makes short holyday in the sun beam,
And dies by some child's hand. The feeble bird
With little wings, yet greatly venturous
In the upper sky. The fish in th' other element,

That knows no touch of eloquence. What else?
Yon tall and elegant stag,
Who paints a dancing shadow of his horns
In the water, where he drinks.

MARGARET

I myself love all these things, yet so as with a difference:—for example, some animals better than others, some men rather than other men; the nightingale before the cuckoo, the swift and graceful palfrey before the slow and asinine mule. Your humour goes to confound all qualities.

What sports do you use in the forest?—

SIMON

Not many; some few, as thus:—
To see the sun to bed, and to arise,
Like some hot amourist with glowing eyes,
Bursting the lazy bands of sleep that bound him,
With all his fires and travelling glories round him.
Sometimes the moon on soft night clouds to rest,
Like beauty nestling in a young man's breast,
And all the winking stars, her handmaids, keep
Admiring silence, while those lovers sleep.
Sometimes outstretcht, in very idleness,
Nought doing, saying little, thinking less,
To view the leaves, thin dancers upon air,
Go eddying round; and small birds, how they fare,
When mother Autumn fills their beaks with corn,
Filch'd from the careless Amalthea's horn;
And how the woods berries and worms provide
Without their pains, when earth has nought beside
To answer their small wants.
To view the graceful deer come tripping by,
Then stop, and gaze, then turn, they know not why,
Like bashful younkers in society.
To mark the structure of a plant or tree,
And all fair things of earth, how fair they be.

MARGARET (*smiling*)

And, afterwards them paint in simile.

SIR WALTER

Mistress Margaret will have need of some refreshment. Please you, we have some poor viands within.

MARGARET

Indeed I stand in need of them.

SIR WALTER

Under the shade of a thick-spreading tree,
Upon the grass, no better carpeting,
We'll eat our noon-tide meal ; and, dinner done,
One of us shall repair to Nottingham,
To seek some safe night-lodging in the town,
Where you may sleep, while here with us you dwell,
By day, in the forest, expecting better times,
And gentler habitations, noble Margaret.

SIMON

Allons, young Frenchman—

MARGARET

Allons, Sir Englishman. The time has been,
I've studied love-lays in the English tongue,
And been enamour'd of rare poesy :
Which now I must unlearn. Henceforth,
Sweet mother-tongue, old English speech, adieu ;
For Margaret has got new name and language new.

(Exeunt.)

ACT THE THIRD

Scene.—*An Apartment of State in Woodvil Hall.—
Cavaliers drinking.*

JOHN WOODVIL, LOVEL, GRAY,
and four more.

JOHN

More mirth, I beseech you, gentlemen—
Mr. Gray, you are not merry.—

GRAY

More wine, say I, and mirth shall ensue in course. What! we have not yet above three half-pints a man to answer for. Brevity is the soul of drinking, as of wit. Despatch, I say. More wine.
(Fills.)

FIRST GENTLEMAN

I entreat you, let there be some order, some method, in our drinkings. I love to lose my reason with my eyes open, to commit the deed of drunkenness with forethought and deliberation. I love to feel the fumes of the liquor gathering here, like clouds.

SECOND GENTLEMAN

And I am for plunging into madness at once. Damn order, and method, and steps, and degrees, that he speaks of. Let confusion have her legitimate work.

LOVEL

I marvel why the poets, who, of all men, methinks, should possess the hottest livers, and most empyreal fancies, should affect to see such virtues in cold water.

GRAY

Virtue in cold water! ha! ha! ha!—

JOHN

Because your poet-born hath an internal wine, richer than lippara or canaries, yet uncrushed from any grapes of earth, unpressed in mortal wine-presses.

THIRD GENTLEMAN

What may be the name of this wine?

JOHN

It hath as many names as qualities. It is denominated indifferently, wit, conceit, invention, inspiration, but its most royal and comprehensive name is *fancy*.

THIRD GENTLEMAN

And where keeps he this sovereign liquor?

JOHN

Its cellars are in the brain, whence your true poet deriveth intoxication at will; while his animal spirits, catching a pride from the quality and neighbourhood of their noble relative, the brain, refuse to be sustained by wines and fermentations of earth.

THIRD GENTLEMAN

But is your poet-born always tipsy with this liquor?

JOHN

He hath his stoopings and reposes; but his proper element is the sky, and in the suburbs of the empyrean.

THIRD GENTLEMAN

Is your wine-intellectual so exquisite? henceforth, I, a man of plain conceit, will, in all humility, content my mind with canaries.

FOURTH GENTLEMAN

I am for a song or a catch. When will the catches come on, the sweet wicked catches?

JOHN

They cannot be introduced with propriety before midnight. Every man must commit his twenty bumpers first. We are not yet well roused. Frank Lovel, the glass stands with you.

LOVEL

Gentlemen, the Duke. (*Fills.*)

ALL

The Duke. (*They drink.*)

GRAY

Can any tell, why his Grace, being a Papist—

JOHN

Pshaw! we will have no questions of state now. Is not this his Majesty's birth-day?

GRAY

What follows?

JOHN

That every man should sing, and be joyful, and ask no questions.

SECOND GENTLEMAN

Damn politics, they spoil drinking.

THIRD GENTLEMAN

For certain, 'tis a blessed monarchy.

SECOND GENTLEMAN

The cursed fanatic days we have seen! The times have been when swearing was out of fashion.

THIRD GENTLEMAN

And drinking.

FIRST GENTLEMAN

And wenching.

GRAY

The cursed yeas and forsooths, which we have heard uttered, when a man could not rap out an innocent oath, but strait the air was thought to be infected.

LOVEL

'Twas a pleasant trick of the saint, which that trim puritan *Swear-not-at-all Smooth-speech* used, when his spouse chid him with an oath for committing with his servant-maid, to cause his house to be fumigated with burnt brandy, and ends of scripture, to disperse the devil's breath, as he termed it.

ALL

Ha! ha! ha!

GRAY

But 'twas pleasanter, when the other saint *Resist-the-devil-and-he-will-flee-from-thee Pure-man* was overtaken in the act, to plead an illusio visûs, and maintain his sanctity upon a supposed power in the adversary to counterfeit the shapes of things.

ALL

Ha! ha! ha!

JOHN

Another round, and then let every man devise what trick he can in his fancy, for the better manifesting our loyalty this day.

GRAY

Shall we hang a puritan?

JOHN

No, that has been done already in Coleman-Street.

SECOND GENTLEMAN

Or fire a conventicle?

JOHN

That is stale too.

THIRD GENTLEMAN

Or burn the assembly's catechism?

FOURTH GENTLEMAN

Or drink the king's health, every man standing upon his head naked?

JOHN (*to Lovel*)

We have here some pleasant madness.

THIRD GENTLEMAN

Who shall pledge me in a pint bumper, while we drink to the king upon our knees?

LOVEL

Why on our knees, Cavalier?

JOHN (*smiling*)

For more devotion, to be sure. (*To a servant.*) Sirrah, fetch the gilt goblets.

(*The goblets are brought. They drink the king's health, kneeling. A shout of general approbation following the first appearance of the goblets.*)

JOHN

We have here the unchecked virtues of the grape. How the vapours curl upwards! It were a life of gods to dwell in such an element: to see, and hear, and talk brave things. Now fie upon these casual potations. That a man's most exalted reason should depend upon the ignoble fermenting of a fruit, which sparrows pluck at as well as we!

GRAY (*aside to Lovel*)

Observe how he is ravished.

LOVEL

Vanity and gay thoughts of wine do meet in him and engender madness.

(*While the rest are engaged in a wild kind of talk, John advances to the front of the stage and soliloquizes.*)

JOHN

My spirits turn to fire, they mount so fast.
My joys are turbulent, my hopes shew like fruition.
These high and gusty relishes of life, sure,
Have no allayings of mortality in them.
I am too hot now and o'ercapable,
For the tedious processes, and creeping wisdom,
Of human acts, and enterprizes of a man.
I want some seasonings of adversity,
Some strokes of the old mortifier Calamity,
To take these swellings down, divines call vanity.

FIRST GENTLEMAN

Mr. Woodvil, Mr. Woodvil.

SECOND GENTLEMAN

Where is Woodvil?

GRAY

Let him alone. I have seen him in these lunes before. His abstractions must not taint the good mirth.

JOHN (*continuing to soliloquize*)
O for some friend now,
To conceal nothing from, to have no secrets.
How fine and noble a thing is confidence,
How reasonable too, and almost godlike!
Fast cement of fast friends, band of society,
Old natural go-between in the world's business,
Where civil life and order, wanting this cement,
Would presently rush back
Into the pristine state of singularity,
And each man stand alone.

(*A Servant enters.*)
Gentlemen, the fire-works are ready.

FIRST GENTLEMAN
What be they?

LOVEL
The work of London artists, which our host has provided in honour of this day.

SECOND GENTLEMAN
'Sdeath, who would part with his wine for a rocket?

LOVEL
Why truly, gentlemen, as our kind host has been at the pains to provide this spectacle, we can do no less than be present at it. It will not take up much time. Every man may return fresh and thirsting to his liquor.

THIRD GENTLEMAN
There is reason in what he says.

SECOND GENTLEMAN
Charge on then, bottle in hand. There's husbandry in that.

(*They go out, singing. Only Lovel remains, who observes Woodvil.*)

JOHN (*still talking to himself*)
This Lovel here's of a tough honesty,
Would put the rack to the proof. He is not of that sort,
Which haunt my house, snorting the liquors,
And when their wisdoms are afloat with wine,
Spend vows as fast as vapours, which go off

Even with the fumes, their fathers. He is one,
Whose sober morning actions
Shame not his o'ernight's promises;
Talks little, flatters less, and makes no promises;
Why this is he, whom the dark-wisdom'd fate
Might trust her counsels of predestination with,
And the world be no loser.
Why should I fear this man?
     (*Seeing Lovel.*)
 Where is the company gone?

LOVEL

To see the fire-works, where you will be expected to follow.
But I perceive you are better engaged.

JOHN

I have been meditating this half-hour
On all the properties of a brave friendship,
The mysteries that are in it, the noble uses,
Its limits withal, and its nice boundaries.
Exempli gratia, how far a man
May lawfully forswear himself for his friend;
What quantity of lies, some of them brave ones,
He may lawfully incur in a friend's behalf;
What oaths, blood-crimes, hereditary quarrels,
Night brawls, fierce words, and duels in the morning,
He need not stick at, to maintain his friend's honor, or his
 cause.

LOVEL

I think many men would die for their friends.

JOHN

Death! why 'tis nothing. We go to it for sport,
To gain a name, or purse, or please a sullen humour,
When one has worn his fortune's livery threadbare,
Or his spleen'd mistress frowns. Husbands will venture on it,
To cure the hot fits and cold shakings of jealousy.
A friend, sir, must do more.

LOVEL

Can he do more than die?

JOHN

To serve a friend this he may do. Pray mark me.
Having a law within (great spirits feel one)
He cannot, ought not to be bound by any

Positive laws or ord'nances extern,
But may reject all these : by the law of friendship
He may do so much, be they, indifferently,
Penn'd statutes, or the land's unwritten usages,
As public fame, civil compliances,
Misnamed honor, trust in matter of secrets,
All vows and promises, the feeble mind's religion,
(Binding our morning knowledge to approve
What last night's ignorance spake);
The ties of blood withal, and prejudice of kin.
Sir, these weak terrors
Must never shake me.   I know what belongs
To a worthy friendship.   Come, you shall have my
  confidence.

LOVEL

I hope you think me worthy.

JOHN

You will smile to hear now—
Sir Walter never has been out of the island.

LOVEL

You amaze me.

JOHN

That same report of his escape to France
Was a fine tale, forg'd by myself—
Ha! ha!
I knew it would stagger him.

LOVEL

Pray, give me leave.
Where has he dwelt, how liv'd, how lain conceal'd?
Sure I may ask so much.

JOHN

From place to place, dwelling in no place long,
My brother Simon still hath borne him company,
('Tis a brave youth, I envy him all his virtues.)
Disguis'd in foreign garb, they pass for Frenchmen,
Two Protestant exiles from the Limosin
Newly arriv'd.   Their dwelling's now at Nottingham,
Where no soul knows them.

LOVEL

Can you assign any reason, why a gentleman of Sir Walter's known prudence should expose his person so lightly?

JOHN

I believe, a certain fondness,
A child-like cleaving to the land that gave him birth,
Chains him like fate.

LOVEL

I have known some exiles thus
To linger out the term of the law's indulgence,
To the hazard of being known.

JOHN

You may suppose sometimes
They use the neighb'ring Sherwood for their sport,
Their exercise and freer recreation.—
I see you smile. Pray now, be careful.

LOVEL

I am no babbler, sir; you need not fear me.

JOHN

But some men have been known to talk in their sleep,
And tell fine tales that way.

LOVEL

I have heard so much. But, to say truth, I mostly sleep alone.

JOHN

Or drink, sir? do you never drink too freely?
Some men will drink, and tell you all their secrets.

LOVEL

Why do you question me, who know my habits?

JOHN

I think you are no sot,
No tavern-troubler, worshipper of the grape;
But all men drink sometimes,
And veriest saints at festivals relax,
The marriage of a friend, or a wife's birth-day.

LOVEL

How much, sir, may a man with safety drink? (*Smiling*.)

JOHN

Sir, three half pints a day is reasonable;
I care not if you never exceed that quantity.

LOVEL

I shall observe it;
On holidays two quarts.

JOHN

Or stay; you keep no wench?

LOVEL

Ha!

JOHN

No painted mistress for your private hours?
You keep no whore, sir?

LOVEL

What does he mean?

JOHN

Who for a close embrace, a toy of sin,
And amorous praising of your worship's breath,
In rosy junction of four melting lips,
Can kiss out secrets from you?

LOVEL

How strange this passionate behaviour shews in you!
Sure you think me some weak one.

JOHN

Pray pardon me some fears.
You have now the pledge of a dear father's life.
I am a son—would fain be thought a loving one;
You may allow me some fears: do not despise me,
If, in a posture foreign to my spirit,
And by our well-knit friendship I conjure you,
Touch not Sir Walter's life. (*Kneels.*)
You see these tears. My father's an old man.
Pray let him live.

LOVEL

I must be bold to tell you, these new freedoms
Shew most unhandsome in you.

JOHN (*rising*)

Ha! do you say so?
Sure, you are not grown proud upon my secret!
Ah! now I see it plain. He would be babbling.
No doubt a garrulous and hard-fac'd traitor—
But I'll not give you leave. (*Draws.*)

LOVEL
What does this madman mean?

JOHN
Come, sir; here is no subterfuge.
You must kill me, or I kill you.

LOVEL (*drawing*)
Then self-defence plead my excuse.
Have at you, sir.   (*They fight.*)

JOHN
Stay, sir.
I hope you have made your will.
If not, 'tis no great matter.
A broken cavalier has seldom much
He can bequeath: an old worn peruke,
A snuff-box with a picture of Prince Rupert,
A rusty sword he'll swear was used at Naseby,
Though it ne'er came within ten miles of the place;
And, if he's very rich,
A cheap edition of the *Icon Basilike*,
Is mostly all the wealth he dies possest of.
You say few prayers, I fancy;—
So to it again.   (*They fight again. Lovel is disarmed.*)

LOVEL
You had best now take my life. I guess you mean it.

JOHN (*musing*)
No:—Men will say I fear'd him, if I kill'd him.
Live still, and be a traitor in thy wish,
But never act thy thought, being a coward.
That vengeance, which thy soul shall nightly thirst for,
And this disgrace I've done you cry aloud for,
Still have the will without the power to execute.
So now I leave you,
Feeling a sweet security. No doubt
My secret shall remain a virgin for you!—
                       (*Goes out, smiling in scorn.*)

LOVEL (*rising*)
For once you are mistaken in your man.
The deed you wot of shall forthwith be done.
A bird let loose, a secret out of hand,
Returns not back. Why, then 'tis baby policy

To menace him who hath it in his keeping.
I will go look for Gray;
Then, northward ho! such tricks as we shall play
Have not been seen, I think, in merry Sherwood,
Since the days of Robin Hood, that archer good.

ACT THE FOURTH

Scene.—*An Apartment in Woodvil Hall.*

JOHN WOODVIL (*alone*)

A weight of wine lies heavy on my head,
The unconcocted follies of last night.
Now all those jovial fancies, and bright hopes,
Children of wine, go off like dreams.
This sick vertigo here
Preacheth of temperance, no sermon better.
These black thoughts, and dull melancholy,
That stick like burrs to the brain, will they ne'er leave me?
Some men are full of choler, when they are drunk;
Some brawl of matter foreign to themselves;
And some, the most resolved fools of all,
Have told their dearest secrets in their cups.

Scene.—*The Forest.*
SIR WALTER. SIMON. LOVEL. GRAY

LOVEL
Sir, we are sorry we cannot return your *French* salutation.

GRAY
Nor otherwise consider this garb you trust to than as a poor disguise.

LOVEL
Nor use much ceremony with a traitor.

GRAY
Therefore, without much induction of superfluous words, I attach you, Sir Walter Woodvil, of High Treason, in the King's name.

LOVEL
And of taking part in the great Rebellion against our late lawful Sovereign, Charles the First.

SIMON
John has betrayed us, father.

LOVEL
Come, Sir, you had best surrender fairly. We know you, Sir.

SIMON
Hang ye, villains, ye are two better known than trusted. I have seen those faces before. Are ye not two beggarly retainers, trencher-parasites, to John? I think ye rank above his footmen. A sort of bed and board worms—locusts that infest our house; a leprosy that long has hung upon its walls and princely apartments, reaching to fill all the corners of my brother's once noble heart.

GRAY
We are his friends.

SIMON
Fie, Sir, do not weep. How these rogues will triumph! Shall I whip off their heads, father? *(Draws.)*

LOVEL
Come, Sir, though this shew handsome in you, being his son, yet the law must have its course.

SIMON
And if I tell you the law shall not have its course, cannot ye be content? Courage, father; shall such things as these apprehend a man? Which of ye will venture upon me?—Will you, Mr. Constable self-elect? or you, Sir, with a pimple on your nose, got at Oxford by hard drinking, your only badge of loyalty?

GRAY
'Tis a brave youth—I cannot strike at him.

SIMON
Father, why do you cover your face with your hands? Why do you fetch your breath so hard? See, villains, his heart is burst! O villains, he cannot speak. One of you run for some water: quickly, ye knaves; will ye have your throats cut?
(They both slink off.)
How is it with you, Sir Walter? Look up, Sir, the villains are gone. He hears me not, and this deep disgrace of treachery in his son hath touched him even to the death. O most distuned, and distempered world, where sons talk their aged fathers into their graves! Garrulous and diseased world, and still empty, rotten and

hollow *talking* world, where good men decay, states turn round in an endless mutability, and still for the worse, nothing is at a stay, nothing abides but vanity, chaotic vanity.—Brother, adieu!

There lies the parent stock which gave us life,
Which I will see consign'd with tears to earth.
Leave thou the solemn funeral rites to me,
Grief and a true remorse abide with thee. (*Bears in the body.*)

SCENE.—*Another Part of the Forest.*

MARGARET (*alone*)

It was an error merely, and no crime,
An unsuspecting openness in youth,
That from his lips the fatal secret drew,
Which should have slept like one of nature's mysteries,
Unveil'd by any man.
Well, he is dead!
And what should Margaret do in the forest?
O ill-starr'd John!
O Woodvil, man enfeoffed to despair!
Take thy farewell of peace.
O never look again to see good days,
Or close thy lids in comfortable nights,
Or ever think a happy thought again,
If what I have heard be true.—
Forsaken of the world must Woodvil live,
If he did tell these men.
No tongue must speak to him, no tongue of man
Salute him, when he wakes up in a morning;
Or bid "good-night" to John. Who seeks to live
In amity with thee, must for thy sake
Abide the world's reproach. What then?
Shall Margaret join the clamours of the world
Against her friend? O undiscerning world,
That cannot from misfortune separate guilt,
No, not in thought! O never, never, John.
Prepar'd to share the fortunes of her friend
For better or for worse thy Margaret comes,
To pour into thy wounds a healing love,
And wake the memory of an ancient friendship.
And pardon me, thou spirit of Sir Walter,
Who, in compassion to the wretched living,
Have but few tears to waste upon the dead.

SCENE.—*Woodvil Hall.*

SANDFORD. MARGARET
(*As from a Journey.*)

SANDFORD

The violence of the sudden mischance hath so wrought in him, who by nature is allied to nothing *less* than a self-debasing humour of dejection, that I have never seen any thing more changed and spirit-broken. He hath, with a peremptory resolution, dismissed the partners of his riots and late hours, denied his house and person to their most earnest solicitings, and will be seen by none. He keeps ever alone, and his grief (which is solitary) does not so much seem to possess and govern in him, as it is by him, with a wilfulness of most manifest affection, entertained and cherished.

MARGARET

How bears he up against the common rumour?

SANDFORD

With a strange indifference, which whosoever dives not into the niceness of his sorrow might mistake for obdurate and insensate. Yet are the wings of his pride for ever clipt; and yet a virtuous predominance of filial grief is so ever uppermost, that you may discover his thoughts less troubled with conjecturing what living opinions will say, and judge of his deeds, than absorbed and buried with the dead, whom his indiscretion made so.

MARGARET

I knew a greatness ever to be resident in him, to which the admiring eyes of men should look up even in the declining and bankrupt state of his pride. Fain would I see him, fain talk with him; but that a sense of respect, which is violated, when without deliberation we press into the society of the unhappy, checks and holds me back. How, think you, he would bear my presence?

SANDFORD

As of an assured friend, whom in the forgetfulness of his fortunes he past by. See him you must; but not to-night. The newness of the sight shall move the bitterest compunction and the truest remorse; but afterwards, trust me, dear lady, the happiest effects of a returning peace, and a gracious comfort, to him, to you, and all of us.

MARGARET

I think he would not deny me. He hath ere this received farewell letters from his brother, who hath taken a resolution to estrange himself, for a time, from country, friends, and kindred, and to seek occupation for his sad thoughts in travelling in foreign places, where sights remote and extern to himself may draw from him kindly and not painful ruminations.

SANDFORD

I was present at the receipt of the letter. The contents seemed to affect him, for a moment, with a more lively passion of grief than he has at any time outwardly shewn. He wept with many tears (which I had not before noted in him) and appeared to be touched with a sense as of some unkindness; but the cause of their sad separation and divorce quickly recurring, he presently returned to his former inwardness of suffering.

MARGARET

The reproach of his brother's presence at this hour should have been a weight more than could be sustained by his already oppressed and sinking spirit.—Meditating upon these intricate and wide-spread sorrows, hath brought a heaviness upon me, as of sleep. How goes the night?

SANDFORD

An hour past sun-set. You shall first refresh your limbs (tired with travel) with meats and some cordial wine, and then betake your no less wearied mind to repose.

MARGARET

A good rest to us all.

SANDFORD

Thanks, lady.

ACT THE FIFTH

JOHN WOODVIL (*dressing*)

JOHN

How beautiful, (*handling his mourning*)
And comely do these mourning garments shew!
Sure Grief hath set his sacred impress here,
To claim the world's respect! they note so feelingly
By outward types the serious man within.—
Alas! what part or portion can I claim
In all the decencies of virtuous sorrow,
Which other mourners use? as namely,
This black attire, abstraction from society,

Good thoughts, and frequent sighs, and seldom smiles,
A cleaving sadness native to the brow,
All sweet condolements of like-grieved friends,
(That steal away the sense of loss almost)
Men's pity, and good offices
Which enemies themselves do for us then,
Putting their hostile disposition off,
As we put off our high thoughts and proud looks.
(Pauses, and observes the pictures.)
These pictures must be taken down:
The portraitures of our most antient family
For nigh three hundred years! How have I listen'd,
To hear Sir Walter, with an old man's pride,
Holding me in his arms, a prating boy,
And pointing to the pictures where they hung,
Repeat by course their worthy histories,
(As Hugh de Widville, Walter, first of the name,
And Anne the handsome, Stephen, and famous John:
Telling me, I must be his famous John.)
But that was in old times.
Now, no more
Must I grow proud upon our house's pride.
I rather, I, by most unheard of crimes,
Have backward tainted all their noble blood,
Rased out the memory of an ancient family,
And quite revers'd the honors of our house.
Who now shall sit and tell us anecdotes?
The secret history of his own times,
And fashions of the world when he was young:
How England slept out three and twenty years,
While Carr and Villiers rul'd the baby king:
The costly fancies of the pedant's reign,
Balls, feastings, huntings, shows in allegory,
And Beauties of the court of James the First.

Margaret enters.

JOHN

Comes Margaret here to witness my disgrace?
O, lady, I have suffer'd loss,
And diminution of my honor's brightness.
You bring some images of old times, Margaret,
That should be now forgotten.

MARGARET

Old times should never be forgotten, John.
I came to talk about them with my friend.

JOHN

I did refuse you, Margaret, in my pride.

MARGARET

If John rejected Margaret in his pride,
(As who does not, being splenetic, refuse
Sometimes old play-fellows,) the spleen being gone,
The offence no longer lives.
O Woodvil, those were happy days,
When we two first began to love. When first,
Under pretence of visiting my father,
(Being then a stripling nigh upon my age)
You came a wooing to his daughter, John.
Do you remember,
With what a coy reserve and seldom speech,
(Young maidens must be chary of their speech,)
I kept the honors of my maiden pride?
I was your favourite then.

JOHN

O Margaret, Margaret!
These your submissions to my low estate,
And cleavings to the fates of sunken Woodvil,
Write bitter things 'gainst my unworthiness.
Thou perfect pattern of thy slander'd sex,
Whom miseries of mine could never alienate,
Nor change of fortune shake; whom injuries,
And slights (the worst of injuries) which moved
Thy nature to return scorn with like scorn,
Then when you left in virtuous pride this house,
Could not so separate, but now in this
My day of shame, when all the world forsake me,
You only visit me, love, and forgive me.

MARGARET

Dost yet remember the green arbour, John,
In the south gardens of my father's house,
Where we have seen the summer sun go down,
Exchanging true love's vows without restraint?
And that old wood, you call'd your wilderness,
And vow'd in sport to build a chapel in it,
There dwell

        " Like hermit poor
        " In pensive place obscure,

And tell your Ave Maries by the curls
(Dropping like golden beads) of Margaret's hair;
And make confession seven times a day
Of every thought that stray'd from love and Margaret;
And I your saint the penance should appoint—
Believe me, sir, I will not now be laid
Aside, like an old fashion.

JOHN

O lady, poor and abject are my thoughts,
My pride is cured, my hopes are under clouds,
I have no part in any good man's love,
In all earth's pleasures portion have I none,
I fade and wither in my own esteem,
This earth holds not alive so poor a thing as I am.
I was not always thus. (*Weeps.*)

MARGARET

Thou noble nature,
Which lion-like didst awe the inferior creatures,
Now trampled on by beasts of basest quality,
My dear heart's lord, life's pride, soul-honor'd John,
Upon her knees (regard her poor request)
Your favourite, once-beloved Margaret, kneels.

JOHN

What would'st thou, lady, ever-honor'd Margaret?

MARGARET

That John would think more nobly of himself,
More worthily of high heaven;
And not for one misfortune, child of chance,
No crime, but unforeseen, and sent to punish
The less offence with image of the greater,
Thereby to work the soul's humility,
(Which end hath happily not been frustrate quite,)
O not for one offence mistrust heaven's mercy,
Nor quit thy hope of happy days to come—
John yet has many happy days to live;
To live and make atonement.

JOHN

Excellent lady,
Whose suit hath drawn this softness from my eyes,
Not the world's scorn, nor falling off of friends
Could ever do. Will you go with me, Margaret?

MARGARET (*rising*)

Go whither, John?

JOHN

Go in with me,
And pray for the peace of our unquiet minds?

MARGARET

That I will, John.—

(*Exeunt.*)

Scene.—*An inner Apartment.*

(*John is discovered kneeling.—Margaret standing over him.*)

JOHN (*rises*)

I cannot bear
To see you waste that youth and excellent beauty,
('Tis now the golden time of the day with you,)
In tending such a broken wretch as I am.

MARGARET

John will break Margaret's heart, if he speak so.
O sir, sir, sir, you are too melancholy,
And I must call it caprice. I am somewhat bold
Perhaps in this. But you are now my patient,
(You know you gave me leave to call you so,)
And I must chide these pestilent humours from you.

JOHN

They are gone.—
Mark, love, how cheerfully I speak!
I can smile too, and I almost begin
To understand what kind of creature Hope is.

MARGARET

Now this is better, this mirth becomes you, John.

JOHN

Yet tell me, if I over-act my mirth.
(Being but a novice, I may fall into that error,)
That were a sad indecency, you know.

MARGARET

Nay, never fear.
I will be mistress of your humours,
And you shall frown or smile by the book.

And herein I shall be most peremptory,
Cry, " this shews well, but that inclines to levity,
"This frown has too much of the Woodvil in it,
"But that fine sunshine has redeem'd it quite."

JOHN

How sweetly Margaret robs me of myself!

MARGARET

To give you in your stead a better self!
Such as you were, when these eyes first beheld
You mounted on your sprightly steed, White **Margery**,
Sir Rowland my father's gift,
And all my maidens gave my heart for lost.
I was a young thing then, being newly come
Home from my convent education, where
Seven years I had wasted in the bosom of France:
Returning home true protestant, you call'd me
Your little heretic nun. How timid-bashful
Did John salute his love, being newly seen.
Sir Rowland term'd it a rare modesty,
And prais'd it in a youth.

JOHN

Now Margaret weeps herself.

(A noise of bells heard.)

MARGARET

Hark the bells, John.

JOHN

Those are the church bells of St. Mary Ottery.

MARGARET

I know it.

JOHN

Saint Mary Ottery, my native village
In the sweet shire of Devon.
Those are the bells.

MARGARET

Wilt go to church, John?

JOHN

I have been there already.

MARGARET

How canst say thou hast been there already? The bells are only now ringing for morning service, and hast thou been at church already?

JOHN

I left my bed betimes, I could not sleep,
And when I rose, I look'd (as my custom is)
From my chamber window, where I can see the sun rise;
And the first object I discern'd
Was the glistering spire of St. Mary Ottery.

MARGARET

Well, John.

JOHN

Then I remember'd 'twas the sabbath-day.
Immediately a wish arose in my mind,
To go to church and pray with Christian people.
And then I check'd myself, and said to myself,
"Thou hast been a heathen, John, these two years past,
"(Not having been at church in all that time,)
"And is it fit, that now for the first time
"Thou should'st offend the eyes of Christian people
"With a murderer's presence in the house of prayer?
"Thou would'st but discompose their pious thoughts,
"And do thyself no good: for how could'st thou pray,
"With unwash'd hands, and lips unus'd to the offices?"
And then I at my own presumption smiled;
And then I wept that I should smile at all,
Having such cause of grief! I wept outright;
Tears like a river flooded all my face,
And I began to pray, and found I could pray;
And still I yearn'd to say my prayers in the church.
"Doubtless (said I) one might find comfort in it."
So stealing down the stairs, like one that fear'd detection,
Or was about to act unlawful business
At that dead time of dawn,
I flew to the church, and found the doors wide open,
(Whether by negligence I knew not,
Or some peculiar grace to me vouchsaf'd,
For all things felt like mystery).

MARGARET

Yes.

JOHN

So entering in, not without fear,
I past into the family pew,
And covering up my eyes for shame,
And deep perception of unworthiness,
Upon the little hassock knelt me down,
Where I so oft had kneel'd,
A docile infant by Sir Walter's side;
And, thinking so, I wept a second flood
More poignant than the first;
But afterwards was greatly comforted.
It seem'd, the guilt of blood was passing from me
Even in the act and agony of tears,
And all my sins forgiven.

THE WITCH

A Dramatic Sketch of the Seventeenth Century

(1798)

CHARACTERS

Old Servant in the Family of Sir Francis Fairford.   *Stranger.*

SERVANT

ONE summer night Sir Francis, as it chanced,
    Was pacing to and fro in the avenue
That westward fronts our house,
Among those aged oaks, said to have been planted
Three hundred years ago
By a neighb'ring prior of the Fairford name.
Being o'er-task'd in thought, he heeded not
The importunate suit of one who stood by the gate,
And begged an alms.
Some say he shoved her rudely from the gate
With angry chiding; but I can never think
(Our master's nature hath a sweetness in it)
That he could use a woman, an old woman,
With such discourtesy: but he refused her—
And better had he met a lion in his path
Than that old woman that night;
For she was one who practised the black arts,
And served the devil, being since burnt for witchcraft.
She looked at him as one that meant to blast him,
And with a frightful noise,
('Twas partly like a woman's voice,
And partly like the hissing of a snake,)
She nothing said but this:—
(Sir Francis told the words)

> *A mischief, mischief, mischief,*
> *And a nine-times-killing curse,*
> *By day and by night, to the caitiff wight,*
> *Who shakes the poor like snakes from his door,*
> *And shuts up the womb of his purse.*

And still she cried

> *A mischief,*
> *And a nine-fold-withering curse:*
> *For that shall come to thee that will undo thee,*
> *Both all that thou fearest and worse.*

So saying, she departed,
Leaving Sir Francis like a man, beneath
Whose feet a scaffolding was suddenly falling;
So he described it.

STRANGER

A terrible curse! What followed?

SERVANT

Nothing immediate, but some two months after
Young Philip Fairford suddenly fell sick,
And none could tell what ailed him; for he lay,
And pined, and pined, till all his hair fell off,
And he, that was full-fleshed, became as thin
As a two-months' babe that has been starved in the nursing.
And sure I think
He bore his death-wound like a little child;
With such rare sweetness of dumb melancholy
He strove to clothe his agony in smiles,
Which he would force up in his poor pale cheeks,
Like ill-timed guests that had no proper dwelling there;
And, when they asked him his complaint, he laid
His hand upon his heart to shew the place,
Where Susan came to him a-nights, he said,
And prick'd him with a pin.—
And thereupon Sir Francis called to mind
The beggar-witch that stood by the gateway
And begged an alms.

STRANGER

But did the witch confess?

SERVANT

All this and more at her death.

THE WITCH

STRANGER

I do not love to credit tales of magic.
Heaven's music, which is Order, seems unstrung,
And this brave world
(The mystery of God) unbeautified,
Disorder'd, marr'd, where such strange things are acted.

MR. H——

A Farce in Two Acts

As it was performed at Drury Lane Theatre, *December*, 1806

"MR. H——, thou wert DAMNED. Bright shone the morning on the play-bills that announced thy appearance, and the streets were filled with the buzz of persons asking one another if they would go to see Mr. H——, and answering that they would certainly; but before night the gaiety, not of the author, but of his friends and the town, was eclipsed, for thou wert DAMNED! Hadst thou been anonymous, thou haply mightst have lived. But thou didst come to an untimely end for thy tricks, and for want of a better name to pass them off——."

—Theatrical Examiner.

CHARACTERS

MR. H——	*Mr. Elliston.*
BELVIL	*Mr. Bartley.*
LANDLORD PRY	*Mr. Wewitzer.*
MELESINDA	*Miss Mellon.*
Maid to Melesinda	*Mrs. Harlowe.*

Gentlemen, Ladies, Waiters, Servants, &c.

SCENE.—*Bath*

PROLOGUE

Spoken by Mr. Elliston

If we have sinn'd in paring down a name,
All civil well-bred authors do the same.
Survey the columns of our daily writers—
You'll find that some Initials are great fighters.
How fierce the shock, how fatal is the jar,
When Ensign W. meets Lieutenant R.
With two stout seconds, just of their own gizard,
Cross Captain X. and rough old General Izzard!
Letter to Letter spreads the dire alarms,
Till half the Alphabet is up in arms.

Nor with less lustre have Initials shone,
To grace the gentler annals of Crim. Con.
Where the dispensers of the public lash
Soft penance give; a letter and a dash——
Where vice reduced in size shrinks to a failing,
And loses half her grossness by curtailing.
Faux pas are told in such a modest way,—
The affair of Colonel B—— with Mrs. A——
You must forgive them—for what is there, say,
Which such a pliant Vowel must not grant
To such a very pressing Consonant?
Or who poetic justice dares dispute,
When, mildly melting at a lover's suit,
The wife's a Liquid, her good man a Mute?
Even in the homelier scenes of honest life,
The coarse-spun intercourse of man and wife,
Initials I am told have taken place
Of Deary, Spouse, and that old-fashioned race;
And Cabbage, ask'd by Brother Snip to tea,
Replies, "I'll come—but it don't rest with me—
I always leaves them things to Mrs. C."
O should this mincing fashion ever spread
From names of living heroes to the dead,
How would Ambition sigh, and hang the head,
As each lov'd syllable should melt away—
Her Alexander turned into Great A—
A single C. her Cæsar to express—
Her Scipio shrunk into a Roman S—
And nick'd and dock'd to these new modes of speech,
Great Hannibal himself a Mr. H——.

MR. H——

A Farce in Two Acts

ACT I

Scene.—*A Public Room in an Inn—Landlord, Waiters, Gentlemen, &c.*

Enter Mr. H.

MR. H.

Landlord, has the man brought home my boots?

LANDLORD
Yes, Sir.

MR. H.
You have paid him?

LANDLORD
There is the receipt, Sir, only not quite filled up, no name, only blank—"Blank, Dr. to Zekiel Spanish for one pair of best hessians." Now, Sir, he wishes to know what name he shall put in, who he shall say "Dr."

MR. H.
Why, Mr. H. to be sure.

LANDLORD
So I told him, Sir; but Zekiel has some qualms about it. He says, he thinks that Mr. H. only would not stand good in law.

MR. H.
Rot his impertinence, bid him put in Nebuchadnezzar, and not trouble me with his scruples.

LANDLORD
I shall, Sir. [*Exit.*

Enter a Waiter.

WAITER
Sir, Squire Level's man is below, with a hare and a brace of pheasants for Mr. H.

MR. H.
Give the man half-a-crown, and bid him return my best respects to his master. Presents it seems will find me out, with any name, or no name.

Enter Second Waiter.

SECOND WAITER
Sir, the man that makes up the Directory is at the door.

MR. H.
Give him a shilling, that is what these fellows come for.

SECOND WAITER
He has sent up to know by what name your Honour will please to be inserted.

MR. H——

MR. H.

Zounds, fellow, I give him a shilling for leaving out my name, not for putting it in. This is one of the plaguy comforts of going anonymous. [*Exit Second Waiter.*

Enter Third Waiter.

THIRD WAITER

Two letters for Mr. H. [*Exit.*

MR. H.

From ladies (*opens them*). This from Melesinda, to remind me of the morning call I promised; the pretty creature positively languishes to be made Mrs. H. I believe I must indulge her (*affectedly*). This from her cousin, to bespeak me to some party, I suppose (*opening it*)—Oh, "this evening"—"Tea and cards"—(*surveying himself with complacency*). Dear H., thou art certainly a pretty fellow. I wonder what makes thee such a favourite among the ladies: I wish it may not be owing to the concealment of thy unfortunate———pshaw!

Enter Fourth Waiter.

FOURTH WAITER

Sir, one Mr. Printagain is enquiring for you.

MR. H.

Oh, I remember, the poet; he is publishing by subscription. Give him a guinea, and tell him he may put me down.

FOURTH WAITER

What name shall I tell him, Sir?

MR. H.

Zounds, he is a poet; let him fancy a name. [*Exit Fourth Waiter.*

Enter Fifth Waiter.

FIFTH WAITER

Sir, Bartlemy the lame beggar, that you sent a private donation to last Monday, has by some accident discovered his benefactor, and is at the door waiting to return thanks.

MR. H.

Oh, poor fellow, who could put it into his head? Now I shall be teazed by all his tribe, when once this is known. Well, tell him I am glad I could be of any service to him, and send him away.

FIFTH WAITER

I would have done so, Sir; but the object of his call now, he says, is only to know who he is obliged to.

MR. H.

Why, me.

FIFTH WAITER

Yes, Sir.

MR. H.

Me, me, me, who else, to be sure?

FIFTH WAITER

Yes, Sir; but he is anxious to know the name of his benefactor.

MR. H.

Here is a pampered rogue of a beggar, that cannot be obliged to a gentleman in the way of his profession, but he must know the name, birth, parentage, and education of his benefactor. I warrant you, next he will require a certificate of one's good behaviour, and a magistrate's licence in one's pocket, lawfully empowering so and so to——give an alms. Any thing more?

FIFTH WAITER

Yes, Sir: here has been Mr. Patriot, with the county petition to sign; and Mr. Failtime, that owes so much money, has sent to remind you of your promise to bail him.

MR. H.

Neither of which I can do, while I have no name. Here is more of the plaguy comforts of going anonymous, that one can neither serve one's friend nor one's country. Damn it, a man had better be without a nose, than without a name. I will not live long in this mutilated, dismembered state; I will to Melesinda this instant, and try to forget these vexations. Melesinda! there is music in the name; but then, hang it, there is none in mine to answer to it.
[*Exit.*

(*While Mr. H. has been speaking, two Gentlemen have been observing him curiously.*)

FIRST GENTLEMAN

Who the devil is this extraordinary personage?

SECOND GENTLEMAN

Who? why 'tis Mr. H.

FIRST GENTLEMAN
Has he no more name?

SECOND GENTLEMAN
None that has yet transpired. No more! why that single letter has been enough to inflame the imaginations of all the ladies in Bath. He has been here but a fortnight, and is already received into all the first families.

FIRST GENTLEMAN
Wonderful! yet nobody knows who he is, or where he comes from!

SECOND GENTLEMAN
He is vastly rich, gives away money as if he had infinity; dresses well, as you see; and for address, the mothers are all dying for fear the daughters should get him; and for the daughters, he may command them as absolutely as——. Melesinda, the rich heiress, 'tis thought, will carry him.

FIRST GENTLEMAN
And is it possible that a mere anonymous——

SECOND GENTLEMAN
Phoo! that is the charm, Who is he? and What is he? and What is his name?——The man with the great nose on his face never excited more of the gaping passion of wonderment in the dames of Strasburg, than this new-comer with the single letter to his name, has lighted up among the wives and maids of Bath; his simply having lodgings here, draws more visitors to the house than an election. Come with me to the parade, and I will shew you more of him. [*Exeunt.*

SCENE.—*In the Street.*

(MR. H. *walking*, BELVIL *meeting him.*)

BELVIL
My old Jamaica school-fellow, that I have not seen for so many years? it must, it can be no other than Jack (*going up to him*). My dear Ho——

MR. H. (*Stopping his mouth.*)
Ho——! the devil, hush.

BELVIL
Why sure it is—

MR. H.

It is, it is your old friend Jack, that shall be nameless.

BELVIL

My dear Ho——

MR. H. (*Stopping him.*)

Don't name it.

BELVIL

Name what?

MR. H.

My curst, unfortunate name. I have reasons to conceal it for a time.

BELVIL

I understand you—Creditors, Jack?

MR. H.

No, I assure you.

BELVIL

Snapp'd up a ward, peradventure, and the whole Chancery at your heels?

MR. H.

I don't use to travel with such cumbersome luggage.

BELVIL

You ha'n't taken a purse?

MR. H.

To relieve you at once from all disgraceful conjectures, you must know, 'tis nothing but the sound of my name.

BELVIL

Ridiculous! 'tis true your's is none of the most romantic, but what can that signify in a man?

MR. H.

You must understand that I am in some credit with the ladies.

BELVIL

With the ladies!

MR. H.

And truly I think not without some pretensions. My fortune—

BELVIL

Sufficiently splendid, if I may judge from your appearance.

MR. H.

My figure—

BELVIL

Airy, gay, and imposing.

MR. H.

My parts—

BELVIL

Bright.

MR. H.

My conversation—

BELVIL

Equally remote from flippancy and taciturnity.

MR. H.

But then my name—damn my name.

BELVIL

Childish!

MR. H.

Not so. Oh, Belvil, you are blest with one which sighing virgins may repeat without a blush, and for it change the paternal. But what virgin of any delicacy (and I require some in a wife) would endure to be called Mrs.——?

BELVIL

Ha! ha! ha! most absurd. Did not Clementina Falconbridge, the romantic Clementina Falconbridge, fancy Tommy Potts? and Rosabella Sweetlips sacrifice her mellifluous appellative to Jack Deady? Matilda her cousin married a Gubbins, and her sister Amelia a Clutterbuck.

MR. H.

Potts is tolerable, Deady is sufferable, Gubbins is bearable, and Clutterbuck is endurable, but Ho—

BELVIL

Hush, Jack, don't betray yourself. But you are really ashamed of the family name?

MR. H.

Aye, and of my father that begot me, and my father's father, and all their forefathers that have borne it since the conquest.

BELVIL

But how do you know the women are so squeamish?

MR. H.

I have tried them. I tell you there is neither maiden of sixteen nor widow of sixty but would turn up their noses at it. I have been refused by nineteen virgins, twenty-nine relicts, and two old maids.

BELVIL

That was hard indeed, Jack.

MR. H.

Parsons have stuck at publishing the banns, because they averred it was a heathenish name; parents have lingered their consent, because they suspected it was a fictitious name; and rivals have declined my challenges, because they pretended it was an ungentlemanly name.

BELVIL

Ha, ha, ha, but what course do you mean to pursue?

MR. H.

To engage the affections of some generous girl, who will be content to take me as Mr. H.

BELVIL

Mr. H.?

MR. H.

Yes, that is the name I go by here; you know one likes to be as near the truth as possible.

BELVIL

Certainly. But what then? to get her to consent—

MR. H.

To accompany me to the altar without a name——in short to suspend her curiosity (that is all) till the moment the priest shall pronounce the irrevocable charm, which makes two names one.

BELVIL

And that name———and then she must be pleased, ha, Jack?

MR. H.

Exactly such a girl it has been my fortune to meet with, heark'e (*whispers*)———(*musing*) yet hang it, 'tis cruel to betray her confidence.

BELVIL

But the family name, Jack?

MR. H.

As you say, the family name must be perpetuated.

BELVIL

Though it be but a homely one.

MR. H.

True, but come, I will shew you the house where dwells this credulous melting fair.

BELVIL

Ha, ha, my old friend dwindled down to one letter. [*Exeunt.*

SCENE.—*An Apartment in* MELESINDA'S *House.*
MELESINDA *sola, as if musing*

MELESINDA

H. H. H. Sure it must be something precious by its being concealed. It can't be Homer, that is a Heathen's name; nor Horatio, that is no surname; what if it be Hamlet? the Lord Hamlet—pretty, and I his poor distracted Ophelia! No, 'tis none of these; 'tis Harcourt or Hargrave, or some such sounding name, or Howard, high born Howard, that would do; may be it is Harley, methinks my H. resembles Harley, the feeling Harley. But I hear him, and from his own lips I will once for ever be resolved.

Enter MR. H.

MR. H.

My dear Melesinda.

MELESINDA

My dear H. that is all you give me power to swear allegiance to,—to be enamoured of inarticulate sounds, and call with sighs upon an empty letter. But I will know.

MR. H.

My dear Melesinda, press me no more for the disclosure of that, which in the face of day so soon must be revealed. Call it whim, humour, caprice, in me. Suppose I have sworn an oath, never, till the ceremony of our marriage is over, to disclose my true name.

MELESINDA

Oh! H. H. H. I cherish here a fire of restless curiosity which consumes me. 'Tis appetite, passion, call it whim, caprice, in me. Suppose I have sworn I must and will know it this very night.

MR. H.

Ungenerous Melesinda! I implore you to give me this one proof of your confidence. The holy vow once past, your H. shall not have a secret to withhold.

MELESINDA

My H. has overcome: his Melesinda shall pine away and die, before she dare express a saucy inclination; but what shall I call you till we are married?

MR. H.

Call me? call me any thing, call me Love, Love! aye, Love, Love will do very well.

MELESINDA

How many syllables is it, Love?

MR. H.

How many? ud, that is coming to the question with a vengeance. One, two, three, four,—what does it signify how many syllables?

MELESINDA

How many syllables, Love?

MR. H.

My Melesinda's mind, I had hoped, was superior to this childish curiosity.

MELESINDA

How many letters are there in it?

[*Exit* MR. H. *followed by* MELESINDA *repeating the question.*]

SCENE.—*A Room in the Inn.* (*Two Waiters disputing.*)

FIRST WAITER

Sir Harbottle Hammond, you may depend upon it.

SECOND WAITER

Sir Hardy Hardcastle, I tell you.

FIRST WAITER

The Hammonds of Huntingdonshire.

SECOND WAITER

The Hardcastles of Hertfordshire.

MR. H——

FIRST WAITER

The Hammonds.

SECOND WAITER

Don't tell me: does not Hardcastle begin with an H?

FIRST WAITER

So does Hammond for that matter.

SECOND WAITER

Faith, so it does if you go to spell it. I did not think of that. I begin to be of your opinion; he is certainly a Hammond.

FIRST WAITER

Here comes Susan Chambermaid, may be she can tell.

Enter Susan.

BOTH

Well, Susan, have you heard any thing who the strange gentleman is?

SUSAN

Haven't you heard? it's all come out; Mrs. Guesswell, the parson's widow, has been here about it. I overheard her talking in confidence to Mrs. Setter and Mrs. Pointer, and she says, they were holding a sort of *cummitty* about it.

BOTH

What? What?

SUSAN

There can't be a doubt of it, she says, what from his *figger* and the appearance he cuts, and his *sumpshous* way of living, and above all from the remarkable circumstance that his surname should begin with an H., that he must be—

BOTH

Well, well—

SUSAN

Neither more nor less than the Prince.

BOTH

Prince!

SUSAN

The Prince of Hessy-Cassel in disguise.

BOTH

Very likely, very likely.

SUSAN

Oh, there can't be a doubt on it. Mrs. Guesswell says she knows it.

FIRST WAITER

Now if we could be sure that the Prince of Hessy what-do-you-call-him was in England on his travels.

SECOND WAITER

Get a newspaper. Look in the newspapers.

SUSAN

Fiddle of the newspapers, who else can it be?

BOTH

That is very true (*gravely*).

Enter Landlord.

LANDLORD

Here, Susan, James, Philip, where are you all? The London coach is come in, and there is Mr. Fillaside, the fat passenger, has been bawling for somebody to help him off with his boots. (*The Chambermaid and Waiters slip out.*)

(*Solus.*) The house is turned upside down since the strange gentleman came into it. Nothing but guessing and speculating, and speculating and guessing; waiters and chambermaids getting into corners and speculating, ostlers and stable-boys speculating in the yard, I believe the very horses in the stable are speculating too, for there they stand in a musing posture, nothing for them to eat, and not seeming to care whether they have any thing or no; and after all what does it signify? I hate such curious——odso, I must take this box up into his bed-room——he charged me to see to it myself——I hate such inquisitive——I wonder what is in it, it feels heavy (*Reads*) "Leases, title deeds, wills." Here now a man might satisfy his curiosity at once. Deeds must have names to them, so must leases and wills. But I wouldn't——no I wouldn't ——it is a pretty box too——prettily dovetailed——I admire the fashion of it much. But I'd cut my fingers off, before I'd do such a

MR. H——

dirty—what have I to do—curse the keys, how they rattle—rattle in one's pockets—the keys and the halfpence (*takes out a bunch and plays with them*). I wonder if any of these would fit; one might just try them, but I wouldn't lift up the lid if they did. Oh no, what should I be the richer for knowing? (*All this time he tries the keys one by one*). What's his name to me? a thousand names begin with an H. I hate people that are always prying, poking and prying into things,—thrusting their finger into one place—a mighty little hole this—and their keys into another. Oh Lord! little rusty fits it! but what is that to me? I wouldn't go to—no no—but it is odd little rusty should just happen. (*While he is turning up the lid of the box*, MR. H. *enters behind him unperceived.*)

MR. H.

What are you about, you dog?

LANDLORD

Oh Lord, Sir! pardon; no thief as I hope to be saved. Little Pry was always honest.

MR. H.

What else could move you to open that box!

LANDLORD

Sir, don't kill me, and I will confess the whole truth. This box happened to be lying—that is, I happened to be carrying this box, and I happened to have my keys out, and so—little rusty happened to fit——

MR. H.

So little rusty happened to fit!—and would not a rope fit that rogue's neck? I see the papers have not been moved: all is safe, but it was as well to frighten him a little (*aside*). Come, Landlord, as I think you honest, and suspect you only intended to gratify a little foolish curiosity——

LANDLORD

That was all, Sir, upon my veracity.

MR. H.

For this time I will pass it over. Your name is Pry, I think.

LANDLORD

Yes, Sir, Jeremiah Pry, at your service.

MR. H.

An apt name, you have a prying temper. I mean, some little curiosity, a sort of inquisitiveness about you.

VOL. V.—13

LANDLORD

A natural thirst after knowledge you may call it, Sir. When a boy I was never easy, but when I was thrusting up the lids of some of my school-fellows' boxes,—not to steal any thing, upon my honour, Sir,—only to see what was in them; have had pens stuck in my eyes for peeping through key-holes after knowledge; could never see a cold pie with the legs dangling out at top, but my fingers were for lifting up the crust,—just to try if it were pigeon or partridge,—for no other reason in the world. Surely I think my passion for nuts was owing to the pleasure of cracking the shell to get at something concealed, more than to any delight I took in eating the kernel. In short, Sir, this appetite has grown with my growth.

MR. H.

You will certainly be hanged some day for peeping into some bureau or other, just to see what is in it.

LANDLORD

That is my fear, Sir. The thumps and kicks I have had for peering into parcels, and turning of letters inside out,—just for curiosity. The blankets I have been made to dance in for searching parish-registers for old ladies' ages,—just for curiosity! Once I was dragged through a horse-pond, only for peeping into a closet that had glass doors to it, while my Lady Bluegarters was undressing,—just for curiosity!

MR. H.

A very harmless piece of curiosity, truly; and now, Mr. Pry, first have the goodness to leave that box with me, and then do me the favour to carry your curiosity so far, as to enquire if my servants are within.

LANDLORD

I shall, Sir. Here, David, Jonathan,—I think I hear them coming,—shall make bold to leave you, Sir. [*Exit.*

MR. H.

Another tolerable specimen of the comforts of going anonymous!

Enter two Footmen.

FIRST FOOTMAN

You speak first.

SECOND FOOTMAN

No, you had better speak.

FIRST FOOTMAN
You promised to begin.

MR. H.
They have something to say to me. The rascals want their wages raised, I suppose; there is always a favour to be asked when they come smiling. Well, poor rogues, service is but a hard bargain at the best. I think I must not be close with them. Well, David—well, Jonathan.

FIRST FOOTMAN
We have served your honour faithfully——

SECOND FOOTMAN
Hope your honour won't take offence——

MR. H.
The old story, I suppose—wages?

FIRST FOOTMAN
That's not it, your honour.

SECOND FOOTMAN
You speak.

FIRST FOOTMAN
But if your honour would just be pleased to——

SECOND FOOTMAN
Only be pleased to——

MR. H.
Be quick with what you have to say, for I am in haste.

FIRST FOOTMAN
Just to——

SECOND FOOTMAN
Let us know who it is——

FIRST FOOTMAN
Who it is we have the honour to serve.

MR. H.
Why me, me, me; you serve me.

SECOND FOOTMAN
Yes, Sir; but we do not know who you are.

MR. H.

Childish curiosity! do not you serve a rich master, a gay master, an indulgent master?

FIRST FOOTMAN

Ah, Sir! the figure you make is to us, your poor servants, the principal mortification.

SECOND FOOTMAN

When we get over a pot at the public-house, or in a gentleman's kitchen, or elsewhere, as poor servants must have their pleasures—when the question goes round, who is your master? and who do you serve? and one says, I serve Lord So-and-so, and another, I am Squire Such-a-one's footman——

FIRST FOOTMAN

We have nothing to say for it, but that we serve Mr. H.

SECOND FOOTMAN

Or Squire H.

MR. H.

Really you are a couple of pretty modest, reasonable personages; but I hope you will take it as no offence, gentlemen, if, upon a dispassionate review of all that you have said, I think fit not to tell you any more of my name, than I have chosen for especial purposes to communicate to the rest of the world.

FIRST FOOTMAN

Why then, Sir, you may suit yourself.

SECOND FOOTMAN

We tell you plainly, we cannot stay.

FIRST FOOTMAN

We don't chuse to serve Mr. H.

SECOND FOOTMAN

Nor any Mr. or Squire in the alphabet——

FIRST FOOTMAN

That lives in Chris-cross Row.

MR. H.

Go, for a couple of ungrateful, inquisitive, senseless rascals! Go hang, starve, or drown!— Rogues, to speak thus irreverently of the alphabet—I shall live to see you glad to serve old Q—to curl the wig of great S—adjust the dot of little i—stand behind the chair of X, Y, Z—wear the livery of Et-cætera—and ride behind the sulky of And-by-itself-and! [*Exit in a rage.*

ACT II.

SCENE.—*A handsome Apartment well lighted, Tea, Cards, &c.— A large party of Ladies and Gentlemen, among them* MELESINDA.

FIRST LADY
I wonder when the charming man will be here.

SECOND LADY
He is a delightful creature! Such a polish——

THIRD LADY
Such an air in all that he does or says——

FOURTH LADY
Yet gifted with a strong understanding——

FIFTH LADY
But has your ladyship the remotest idea of what his true name is?

FIRST LADY
They say, his very servants do not know it. His French valet, that has lived with him these two years——

SECOND LADY
There, Madam, I must beg leave to set you right: my coachman——

FIRST LADY
I have it from the very best authority: my footman——

SECOND LADY
Then, Madam, you have set your servants on——

FIRST LADY
No, Madam, I would scorn any such little mean ways of coming at a secret. For my part, I don't think any secret of that consequence.

SECOND LADY
That's just like me; I make a rule of troubling my head with nobody's business but my own.

MELESINDA

But then, she takes care to make everybody's business her own, and so to justify herself that way——(*aside*).

FIRST LADY

My dear Melesinda, you look thoughtful.

MELESINDA

Nothing.

SECOND LADY

Give it a name.

MELESINDA

Perhaps it is nameless.

FIRST LADY

As the object——Come, never blush, nor deny it, child. Bless me, what great ugly thing is that, that dangles at your bosom?

MELESINDA

This? it is a cross: how do you like it?

SECOND LADY

A cross! Well, to me it looks for all the world like a great staring H. (*Here a general laugh.*)

MELESINDA

Malicious creatures! Believe me it is a cross, and nothing but a cross.

FIRST LADY

A cross, I believe, you would willingly hang at.

MELESINDA

Intolerable spite! (MR. H. *is announced.*)

(*Enter* MR. H.)

FIRST LADY

O, Mr. H. we are so glad——

SECOND LADY

We have been so dull——

THIRD LADY

So perfectly lifeless——You owe it to us, to be more than commonly entertaining.

MR. H.
Ladies, this is so obliging——

FOURTH LADY
O, Mr. H. those ranunculas you said were dying, pretty things, they have got up——

FIFTH LADY
I have worked that sprig you commended—I want you to come——

MR. H.
Ladies——

SIXTH LADY
I have sent for that piece of music from London.

MR. H.
The Mozart—(*seeing Melesinda*)—Melesinda!

SEVERAL LADIES AT ONCE
Nay positively, Melesinda, you shan't engross him all to yourself.

(*While the Ladies are pressing about* MR. H. *the Gentlemen shew signs of displeasure.*)

FIRST GENTLEMAN
We shan't be able to edge in a word, now this coxcomb is come.

SECOND GENTLEMAN
Damn him, I will affront him.

FIRST GENTLEMAN
Sir, with your leave, I have a word to say to one of these ladies.

SECOND GENTLEMAN
If we could be heard——

(*The ladies pay no attention but to* MR. H.)

MR. H.
You see, gentlemen, how the matter stands. (*Hums an air.*) I am not my own master: positively I exist and breathe but to be agreeable to these——Did you speak?

FIRST GENTLEMAN
And affects absence of mind, Puppy!

MR. H.

Who spoke of absence of mind, did you, Madam? How do you do, Lady Wearwell—how do? I did not see your ladyship before —what was I about to say—O—absence of mind. I am the most unhappy dog in that way, sometimes spurt out the strangest things —the most mal-a-propos—without meaning to give the least offence, upon my honour—sheer absence of mind—things I would have given the world not to have said.

FIRST GENTLEMAN

Do you hear the coxcomb?

FIRST LADY

Great wits, they say——

SECOND LADY

Your fine geniuses are most given——

THIRD LADY

Men of bright parts are commonly too vivacious——

MR. H.

But you shall hear. I was to dine the other day at a great nabob's, that must be nameless, who, between ourselves, is strongly suspected of—being very rich, that's all. John, my valet, who knows my foible, cautioned me, while he was dressing me, as he usually does where he thinks there's a danger of my committing a *lapsus*, to take care in my conversation how I made any allusion direct or indirect to presents—you understand me? I set out double charged with my fellow's consideration and my own, and, to do myself justice, behaved with tolerable circumspection for the first half hour or so—till at last a gentleman in company, who was indulging a free vein of raillery at the expense of the ladies, stumbled upon that expression of the poet, which calls them "fair defects."

FIRST LADY

It is Pope, I believe, who says it.

MR. H.

No, Madam; Milton. Where was I? O, "fair defects." This gave occasion to a critic in company, to deliver his opinion on the phrase—that led to an enumeration of all the various words which might have been used instead of "defect," as want, absence, poverty, deficiency, lack. This moment I, who had not been attending to the progress of the argument (as the denouement will shew) starting suddenly up out of one of my reveries, by some unfortunate connexion of ideas, which the last fatal word had excited, the devil put it into my head to turn round to the Nabob, who was sitting next me, and in a very marked manner (as it seemed to the company) to put the question to him, Pray, Sir, what may be the exact value of a lack of rupees? You may guess the confusion which followed.

FIRST LADY
What a distressing circumstance!

SECOND LADY
To a delicate mind——

THIRD LADY
How embarrassing——

FOURTH LADY
I declare I quite pity you.

FIRST GENTLEMAN
Puppy!

MR. H.
A Baronet at the table, seeing my dilemma, jogged my elbow; and a good-natured Duchess, who does every thing with a grace peculiar to herself, trod on my toes at that instant: this brought me to myself, and—covered with blushes, and pitied by all the ladies—I withdrew.

FIRST LADY
How charmingly he tells a story.

SECOND LADY
But how distressing!

MR. H.
Lord Squandercounsel, who is my particular friend, was pleased to rally me in his inimitable way upon it next day. I shall never forget a sensible thing he said on the occasion—speaking of absence of mind, my foible—says he, my dear Hogs——

SEVERAL LADIES
Hogs——what—ha—

MR. H.
My dear Hogsflesh—my name—(*here an universal scream*)— O my cursed unfortunate tongue!—H. I mean—Where was I?

FIRST LADY
Filthy—abominable!

SECOND LADY
Unutterable!
THIRD LADY
Hogs——foh!
FOURTH LADY
Disgusting!
FIFTH LADY
Vile!
SIXTH LADY
Shocking!
FIRST LADY
Odious!
SECOND LADY
Hogs——pah!
THIRD LADY
A smelling bottle—look to Miss Melesinda. Poor thing! it is no wonder. You had better keep off from her, Mr. Hogsflesh, and not be pressing about her in her circumstances.
FIRST GENTLEMAN
Good time of day to you, Mr. Hogsflesh.
SECOND GENTLEMAN
The compliments of the season to you, Mr. Hogsflesh.
MR. H.
This is too much—flesh and blood cannot endure it.
FIRST GENTLEMAN
What flesh?—hog's-flesh?
SECOND GENTLEMAN
How he sets up his bristles!
MR. H.
Bristles!
FIRST GENTLEMAN
He looks as fierce as a hog in armour.
MR. H.
A hog!——Madam!——(*here he severally accosts the ladies, who by turns repel him*).
FIRST LADY
Extremely obliged to you for your attentions; but don't want a partner.

SECOND LADY

Greatly flattered by your preference; but believe I shall remain single.

THIRD LADY

Shall always acknowledge your politeness; but have no thoughts of altering my condition.

FOURTH LADY

Always be happy to respect you as a friend; but you must not look for any thing further.

FIFTH LADY

No doubt of your ability to make any woman happy; but have no thoughts of changing my name.

SIXTH LADY

Must tell you, Sir, that if by your insinuations, you think to prevail with me, you have got the wrong sow by the ear. Does he think any lady would go to pig with him?

OLD LADY

Must beg you to be less particular in your addresses to me. Does he take me for a Jew, to long after forbidden meats?

MR. H.

I shall go mad!—to be refused by old Mother Damnable—she that's so old, nobody knows whether she was ever married or no, but passes for a maid by courtesy; her juvenile exploits being beyond the farthest stretch of tradition!—old Mother Damnable!

[*Exeunt all, either pitying or seeming to avoid him.*]

Scene.—*The Street.* BELVIL *and another Gentleman.*

BELVIL

Poor Jack, I am really sorry for him. The account which you give me of his mortifying change of reception at the assembly, would be highly diverting, if it gave me less pain to hear it. With all his amusing absurdities, and amongst them not the least, a predominant desire to be thought well of by the fair sex, he has an abundant share of good nature, and is a man of honour. Notwithstanding all that has happened, Melesinda may do worse than take him yet. But did the women resent it so deeply as you say?

GENTLEMAN

O intolerably—they fled him as fearfully when 'twas once blown, as a man would be avoided, who was suddenly discovered to have marks of the plague, and as fast; when before they had been ready to devour the foolishest thing he could say.

BELVIL

Ha! ha! so frail is the tenure by which these women's favourites commonly hold their envied pre-eminence. Well, I must go find him out and comfort him. I suppose, I shall find him at the inn.

GENTLEMAN

Either there or at Melesinda's.—Adieu. [*Exeunt.*

SCENE.—MR. H———'S *Apartment.*

MR. H. (*solus*)

Was ever any thing so mortifying? to be refused by old Mother Damnable!—with such parts and address,—and the little squeamish devils, to dislike me for a name, a sound.—O my cursed name! that it was something I could be revenged on! if it were alive, that I might tread upon it, or crush it, or pummel it, or kick it, or spit it out—for it sticks in my throat and will choak me.

My plaguy ancestors! if they had left me but a Van or a Mac, or an Irish O', it had been something to qualify it.—Mynheer Van Hogsflesh—or Sawney MacHogsflesh,—or Sir Phelim O'Hogsflesh,—but downright blunt———. If it had been any other name in the world, I could have borne it. If it had been the name of a beast, as Bull, Fox, Kid, Lamb, Wolf, Lion; or of a bird, as Sparrow, Hawk, Buzzard, Daw, Finch, Nightingale; or of a fish, as Sprat, Herring, Salmon; or the name of a thing, as Ginger, Hay, Wood; or of a colour, as Black, Grey, White, Green; or of a sound, as Bray; or the name of a month, as March, May; or of a place, as Barnet, Baldock, Hitchin; or the name of a coin, as Farthing, Penny, Twopenny; or of a profession, as Butcher, Baker, Carpenter, Piper, Fisher, Fletcher, Fowler, Glover; or a Jew's name, as Solomons, Isaacs, Jacobs; or a personal name, as Foot, Leg, Crookshanks, Heaviside, Sidebottom, Longbottom, Ramsbottom, Winterbottom; or a long name, as Blanchenhagen, or Blanchenhausen; or a short name, as Crib, Crisp, Crips, Tag, Trot, Tub, Phips, Padge, Papps, or Prig, or Wig, or Pip, or Trip; Trip had been something, but Ho———.

(*Walks about in great agitation,—recovering his calmness a little, sits down.*)

Farewell the most distant thoughts of marriage; the finger-circling ring, the purity-figuring glove, the envy-pining bridemaids, the wishing parson, and the simpering clerk. Farewell, the ambiguous blush-raising joke, the titter-provoking pun, the morning-stirring drum.—No son of mine shall exist, to bear my ill-fated name. No nurse come chuckling, to tell me it is a boy. No midwife, leering at me from under the lids of professional gravity. I dreamed of caudle. (*sings in a melancholy tone*) Lullaby, Lullaby,—hush-a-by-baby—how like its papa it is!— (*makes motions as if he was nursing*). And then, when grown up, "Is this your son, Sir?" "Yes, Sir, a poor copy of me,—a sad young dog,—just what his father was at his age,—I have four more at home." Oh! oh! oh!

Enter Landlord

MR. H.

Landlord, I must pack up to-night; you will see all my things got ready.

LANDLORD

Hope your Honor does not intend to quit the Blue Boar,—sorry any thing has happened.

MR. H.

He has heard it all.

LANDLORD

Your Honour has had some mortification, to be sure, as a man may say; you have brought your pigs to a fine market.

MR. H.

Pigs!

LANDLORD

What then? take old Pry's advice, and never mind it. Don't scorch your crackling for 'em, Sir.

MR. H.

Scorch my crackling! a queer phrase; but I suppose he don't mean to affront me.

LANDLORD

What is done can't be undone; you can't make a silken purse out of a sow's ear.

MR. H.

As you say, Landlord, thinking of a thing does but augment it.

LANDLORD

Does but *hogment* it, indeed, Sir.

MR. H.

Hogment it! damn it, I said, augment it.

LANDLORD

Lord, Sir, 'tis not every body has such gift of fine phrases as your Honour, that can lard his discourse.

MR. H.

Lard!

LANDLORD

Suppose they do smoke you—

MR. H.

Smoke me?

LANDLORD

One of my phrases; never mind my words, Sir, my meaning is good. We all mean the same thing, only you express yourself one way, and I another, that's all. The meaning's the same; it is all pork.

MR. H.

That's another of your phrases, I presume. (*Bell rings, and the Landlord called for.*)

LANDLORD

Anon, anon.

MR. H.

O, I wish I were anonymous. [*Exeunt several ways.*

Scene.—*Melesinda's Apartment.*

(MELESINDA *and* Maid.)

MAID

Lord, Madam! before I'd take on as you do about a foolish—what signifies a name? Hogs—Hogs—what is it—is just as good as any other for what I see.

MELESINDA

Ignorant creature! yet she is perhaps blest in the absence of those ideas, which, while they add a zest to the few pleasures which fall to the lot of superior natures to enjoy, doubly edge the—

MAID

Superior natures! a fig! If he's hog by name, he's not hog by nature, that don't follow—his name don't make him any thing, does it? He don't grunt the more for it, nor squeak, that ever I hear; he likes his victuals out of a plate, as other Christians do, you never see him go to the trough—

MELESINDA
Unfeeling wretch! yet possibly her intentions—

MAID
For instance, Madam, my name is Finch—Betty Finch. I don't whistle the more for that, nor long after canary-seed while I can get good wholesome mutton—no, nor you can't catch me by throwing salt on my tail. If you come to that, hadn't I a young man used to come after me, they said courted me—his name was Lion—Francis Lion, a tailor; but though he was fond enough of me, for all that, he never offered to eat me.

MELESINDA
How fortunate that the discovery has been made before it was too late. Had I listened to his deceits, and, as the perfidious man had almost persuaded me, precipitated myself into an inextricable engagement, before—

MAID
No great harm, if you had. You'd only have bought a pig in a poke—and what then? Oh, here he comes creeping—

Enter MR. H. *abject.*

Go to her, Mr. Hogs—Hogs—Hogsbristles—what's your name? Don't be afraid, man—don't give it up—she's not crying—only *summat* has made her eyes red—she has got a sty in her eye, I believe—(*going.*)

MELESINDA
You are not going, Betty?

MAID
O, Madam, never mind me—I shall be back in the twinkling of a pig's whisker, as they say. [*Exit.*

MR. H.
Melesinda, you behold before you a wretch who would have betrayed your confidence, but it was love that prompted him; who would have tricked you by an unworthy concealment into a participation of that disgrace which a superficial world has agreed to attach to a name—but with it you would have shared a fortune not contemptible, and a heart—but 'tis over now. That name he is content to bear alone—to go where the persecuted syllables shall be no more heard, or excite no meaning—some spot where his native tongue has never penetrated, nor any of his countrymen have landed, to plant their unfeeling satire, their brutal wit, and national ill manners—where no Englishman—(*Here Melesinda,*

who has been pouting during this speech, fetches a deep sigh.) Some yet undiscovered Otaheite, where witless, unapprehensive savages shall innocently pronounce the ill-fated sounds, and think them not inharmonious.

MELESINDA
Oh!

MR. H.
Who knows but among the female natives might be found—

MELESINDA
Sir! (*raising her head*).

MR. H.
One who would be more kind than—some Oberea—Queen Oberea.

MELESINDA
Oh!

MR. H.
Or what if I were to seek for proofs of reciprocal esteem among unprejudiced African maids, in Monomotapa.

Enter Servant.

SERVANT
Mr. Belvil. [*Exit.*

Enter BELVIL.

MR. H.
In Monomotapa (*musing.*)

BELVIL
Heyday, Jack! what means this mortified face? nothing has happened, I hope, between this lady and you? I beg pardon, Madam, but understanding my friend was with you, I took the liberty of seeking him here. Some little difference possibly which a third person can adjust—not a word—will you, Madam, as this gentleman's friend, suffer me to be the arbitrator—strange—hark'e, Jack, nothing has come out, has there? you understand me. Oh I guess how it is—somebody has got at your secret, you hav'n't blabbed it yourself, have you? ha! ha! ha! I could find in my heart—Jack, what would you give me if I should relieve you—

MR. H.
No power of man can relieve me (*sighs*) but it must lie at the root, gnawing at the root—here it will lie.

BELVIL

No power of man? not a common man, I grant you; for instance, a subject—it's out of the power of any subject.

MR. H.

Gnawing at the root—there it will lie.

BELVIL

Such a thing has been known as a name to be changed; but not by a subject—(*shews a Gazette*).

MR. H.

Gnawing at the root (*suddenly snatches the paper out of Belvil's hand*); ha! pish! nonsense! give it me—what! (*reads*) promotions, bankrupts—a great many bankrupts this week—there it will lie (*lays it down, takes it up again, and reads*) "The King has been graciously pleased"—gnawing at the root—"graciously pleased to grant unto John Hogsflesh"—the devil—"Hogsflesh, Esq., of Sty Hall, in the county of Hants, his royal licence and authority"—O Lord! O Lord!—"that he and his issue"—me and my issue—"may take and use the surname and arms of Bacon"—Bacon, the surname and arms of Bacon—"in pursuance of an injunction contained in the last will and testament of Nicholas Bacon, Esq. his late uncle, as well as out of grateful respect to his memory:"—grateful respect! poor old soul——here's more—"and that such arms may be first duly exemplified"—they shall, I will take care of that—"according to the laws of arms, and recorded in the Herald's Office."

BELVIL

Come, Madam, give me leave to put my own interpretation upon your silence, and to plead for my friend, that now that only obstacle which seemed to stand in the way of your union is removed, you will suffer me to complete the happiness which my news seems to have brought him, by introducing him with a new claim to your favour, by the name of Mr. Bacon. (*Takes their hands and joins them, which Melesinda seems to give consent to with a smile.*)

MR. H.

Generous Melesinda!—my dear friend—"he and his issue," me and my issue—O Lord!—

BELVIL

I wish you joy, Jack, with all my heart.

MR. H.

Bacon, Bacon, Bacon—how odd it sounds. I could never be tired of hearing it. There was Lord Chancellor Bacon. Methinks

I have some of the Verulam blood in me already—methinks I could look through Nature—there was Friar Bacon, a conjurer—I feel as if I could conjure too——

Enter a Servant.

SERVANT

Two young ladies and an old lady are at the door, enquiring if you see company, Madam.

MR. H.

"Surname and arms"—

MELESINDA

Shew them up.—My dear Mr. Bacon, moderate your joy.

Enter three Ladies, being part of those who were at the Assembly.

FIRST LADY

My dear Melesinda, how do you do?

SECOND LADY

How do you do? We have been so concerned for you—

OLD LADY

We have been so concerned—(*seeing him*)—Mr. Hogsflesh—

MR. H.

There's no such person—nor there never was—nor 'tis not fit there should be—"surname and arms"—

BELVIL

It is true what my friend would express; we have been all in a mistake, ladies. Very true, the name of this gentleman was what you call it, but it is so no longer. The succession to the long-contested Bacon estate is at length decided, and with it my friend succeeds to the name of his deceased relative.

MR. H.

"His Majesty has been graciously pleased"—

FIRST LADY

I am sure we all join in hearty congratulation—(*sighs*).

SECOND LADY

And wish you joy with all our hearts—(*heigh ho!*)

OLD LADY

And hope you will enjoy the name and estate many years—(*cries*).

BELVIL

Ha! ha! ha! mortify them a little, Jack.

FIRST LADY

Hope you intend to stay—

SECOND LADY

With us some time—

OLD LADY

In these parts—

MR. H.

Ladies, for your congratulations I thank you; for the favours you have lavished on me, and in particular for this lady's (*turning to the old Lady*) good opinion, I rest your debtor. As to any future favours—(*accosts them severally in the order in which he was refused by them at the assembly*)—Madam, shall always acknowledge your politeness; but at present, you see, I am engaged with a partner. Always be happy to respect you as a friend, but you must not look for any thing further. Must beg of you to be less particular in your addresses to me. Ladies all, with this piece of advice, of Bath and you

Your ever grateful servant takes his leave.
Lay your plans surer when you plot to grieve;
See, while you kindly mean to mortify
Another, the wild arrow do not fly,
And gall yourself. For once you've been mistaken;
Your shafts have miss'd their aim—Hogsflesh has saved his Bacon.

THE PAWNBROKER'S DAUGHTER

A Farce

(1825)

CHARACTERS

FLINT, *a Pawnbroker.*
DAVENPORT, *in love with Marian.*
PENDULOUS, *a Reprieved Gentleman.*
CUTLET, *a Sentimental Butcher.*
GOLDING, *a Magistrate.*
WILLIAM, *Apprentice to Flint.*
BEN, *Cutlet's Boy.*
MISS FLYN.
BETTY, *her Maid.*
MARIAN, *Daughter to Flint.*
LUCY, *her Maid.*

ACT I.—SCENE I.—*An Apartment at Flint's house.*

FLINT, WILLIAM

FLINT

Carry those umbrellas, cottons, and wearing-apparel, up stairs. You may send that chest of tools to Robins's.

WILLIAM

That which you lent six pounds upon to the journeyman carpenter that had the sick wife?

FLINT

The same.

WILLIAM

The man says, if you can give him till Thursday——

FLINT

Not a minute longer. His time was out yesterday. These improvident fools!

WILLIAM

The finical gentleman has been here about the seal that was his grandfather's.

FLINT

He cannot have it. Truly, our trade would be brought to a fine pass, if we were bound to humour the fancies of our customers. This man would be taking a liking to a snuff-box that he had inherited; and that gentlewoman might conceit a favourite chemise that had descended to her.

WILLIAM

The lady in the carriage has been here crying about those jewels. She says, if you cannot let her have them at the advance she offers, her husband will come to know that she has pledged them.

FLINT

I have uses for those jewels. Send Marian to me. (*Exit William.*) I know no other trade that is expected to depart from its fair advantages but ours. I do not see the baker, the butcher, the shoemaker, or, to go higher, the lawyer, the physician, the divine, give up any of their legitimate gains, even when the pretences of their art had failed; yet *we* are to be branded with an odious name, stigmatized, discountenanced even by the administrators of those laws which acknowledge us; scowled at by the lower sort of people, whose needs we serve!

Enter Marian.

Come hither, Marian. Come, kiss your father. The report runs that he is full of spotted crime. What is your belief, child?

MARIAN

That never good report went with our calling, father. I have heard you say, the poor look only to the advantages which we derive from them, and overlook the accommodations which they receive from us. But the poor *are* the poor, father, and have little leisure to make distinctions. I wish we could give up this business.

FLINT

You have not seen that idle fellow, Davenport?

MARIAN

No, indeed, father, since your injunction.

FLINT
I take but my lawful profit. The law is not over favourable to us.

MARIAN
Marian is no judge of these things.

FLINT
They call me oppressive, grinding.—I know not what——

MARIAN
Alas!

FLINT
Usurer, extortioner. Am I these things?

MARIAN
You are Marian's kind and careful father. That is enough for a child to know.

FLINT
Here, girl, is a little box of jewels, which the necessities of a foolish woman of quality have transferred into our true and lawful possession. Go, place them with the trinkets that were your mother's. They are all yours, Marian, if you do not cross me in your marriage. No gentry shall match into this house, to flout their wife hereafter with her parentage. I will hold this business with convulsive grasp to my dying day. I will plague these *poor*, whom you speak so tenderly of.

MARIAN
You frighten me, father. Do not frighten Marian.

FLINT
I have heard them say, There goes Flint—Flint, the cruel pawnbroker!

MARIAN
Stay at home with Marian. You shall hear no ugly words to vex you.

FLINT
You shall ride in a gilded chariot upon the necks of these *poor*, Marian. Their tears shall drop pearls for my girl. Their sighs shall be good wind for us. They shall blow good for my girl. Put up the jewels, Marian. [*Exit.*

Enter Lucy.

THE PAWNBROKER'S DAUGHTER

LUCY

Miss, miss, your father has taken his hat, and is stept out, and Mr. Davenport is on the stairs; and I came to tell you——

MARIAN

Alas! who let him in?

Enter Davenport.

DAVENPORT

My dearest girl——

MARIAN

My father will kill me, if he finds you have been here!

DAVENPORT

There is no time for explanations. I have positive information that your father means, in less than a week, to dispose of you to that ugly Saunders. The wretch has bragged of it to his acquaintance, and already calls you *his*.

MARIAN

O heavens!

DAVENPORT

Your resolution must be summary, as the time which calls for it. Mine or his you must be, without delay. There is no safety for you under this roof.

MARIAN

My father——

DAVENPORT

Is no father, if he would sacrifice you.

MARIAN

But he is unhappy. Do not speak hard words of my father.

DAVENPORT

Marian must exert her good sense.

LUCY

(*As if watching at the window.*) O, miss, your father has suddenly returned. I see him with Mr. Saunders, coming down the street. Mr. Saunders, ma'am!

MARIAN

Begone, begone, if you love me, Davenport.

DAVENPORT

You must go with me then, else here I am fixed.

LUCY

Aye, miss, you must go, as Mr. Davenport says. Here is your cloak, miss, and your hat, and your gloves. Your father, ma'am——

MARIAN

O, where, where? Whither do you hurry me, Davenport?

DAVENPORT

Quickly, quickly, Marian. At the back door.—
[*Exit Marian with Davenport, reluctantly; in her flight still holding the jewels.*

LUCY

Away—away. What a lucky thought of mine to say her father was coming! he would never have got her off, else. Lord, Lord, I do love to help lovers. [*Exit, following them.*

SCENE II.—*A Butcher's Shop.*

CUTLET. BEN.

CUTLET

Reach me down that book off the shelf, where the shoulder of veal hangs.

BEN

Is this it?

CUTLET

No—this is "Flowers of Sentiment"—the other—aye, this is a good book. "An Argument against the Use of Animal Food. By J. R." *That* means Joseph Ritson. I will open it anywhere, and read just as it happens. One cannot dip amiss in such books as these. The motto, I see, is from Pope. I dare say, very much to the purpose. (*Reads.*)

> "The lamb thy riot dooms to bleed to-day,
>   Had he thy reason, would he sport and play?
>   Pleas'd to the last, he crops his flowery food,
>   And licks the hand"——

Bless us, is that saddle of mutton gone home to Mrs. Simpson's? It should have gone an hour ago.

BEN

I was just going with it.

CUTLET

Well go. Where was I? Oh!
> "And licks the hand just raised to shed its blood."

THE PAWNBROKER'S DAUGHTER

What an affecting picture! (*turns over the leaves, and reads*). "It is probable that the long lives which are recorded of the people before the flood, were owing to their being confined to a vegetable diet."

BEN

The young gentleman in Pullen's Row, Islington, that has got the consumption, has sent to know if you can let him have a sweetbread.

CUTLET

Take two,—take all that are in the shop. What a disagreeable interruption! (*reads again*). "Those fierce and angry passions, which impel man to wage destructive war with man, may be traced to the ferment in the blood produced by an animal diet."

BEN

The two pound of rump-steaks must go home to Mr. Molyneux's. He is in training to fight Cribb.

CUTLET

Well, take them; go along, and do not trouble me with your disgusting details. [*Exit Ben.*

CUTLET

(*Throwing down the book.*) Why was I bred to this detestable business? Was it not plain, that this trembling sensibility, which has marked my character from earliest infancy, must for ever disqualify me for a profession which—what do ye want? what do ye buy? O, it is only somebody going past. I thought it had been a customer.—Why was not I bred a glover, like my cousin Langston? to see him poke his two little sticks into a delicate pair of real Woodstock——"A very little stretching ma'am, and they will fit exactly"——Or a haberdasher, like my next-door neighbour—"not a better bit of lace in all town, my lady— Mrs. Breakstock took the last of it last Friday, all but this bit, which I can afford to let your ladyship have a bargain—reach down that drawer on your left hand, Miss Fisher."

(*Enter in haste, Davenport, Marian, and Lucy.*)

LUCY

This is the house I saw a bill up at, ma'am; and a droll creature the landlord is.

DAVENPORT

We have no time for nicety.

CUTLET

What do ye want? what do ye buy? O, it is only you, Mrs. Lucy.

Lucy whispers Cutlet.

CUTLET

I have a set of apartments at the end of my garden. They are quite detached from the shop. A single lady at present occupies the ground floor.

MARIAN

Aye, aye, any where.

DAVENPORT

In, in.—

CUTLET

Pretty lamb,—she seems agitated.

Davenport and Marian go in with Cutlet.

LUCY

I am mistaken if my young lady does not find an agreeable companion in these apartments. Almost a namesake. Only the difference of Flyn, and Flint. I have some errands to do, or I would stop and have some fun with this droll butcher.

Cutlet returns.

CUTLET

Why, how odd this is! *Your* young lady knows *my* young lady. They are as thick as flies.

LUCY

You may thank me for your new lodger, Mr. Cutlet.—But bless me, you do not look well?

CUTLET

To tell you the truth, I am rather heavy about the eyes. Want of sleep, I believe.

LUCY

Late hours, perhaps. Raking last night.

CUTLET

No, that is not it, Mrs. Lucy. My repose was disturbed by a very different cause from what you may imagine. It proceeded from too much thinking.

LUCY

The deuce it did! and what, if I may be so bold, might be the subject of your Night Thoughts?

CUTLET

The distresses of my fellow creatures. I never lay my head down on my pillow, but I fall a thinking, how many at this very instant are perishing. Some with cold——

LUCY

What, in the midst of summer?

CUTLET

Aye. Not here, but in countries abroad, where the climate is different from ours. Our summers are their winters, and *vice versâ*, you know. Some with cold——

LUCY

What a canting rogue it is! I should like to trump up some fine story to plague him. [*Aside.*

CUTLET

Others with hunger—some a prey to the rage of wild beasts—

LUCY

He has got this by rote, out of some book.

CUTLET

Some drowning, crossing crazy bridges in the dark—some by the violence of the devouring flame——

LUCY

I have it.—For that matter, you need not send your humanity a travelling, Mr. Cutlet. For instance, last night——

CUTLET

Some by fevers, some by gun-shot wounds——

LUCY

Only two streets off——

CUTLET

Some in drunken quarrels——

LUCY

(*Aloud.*) The butcher's shop at the corner.

CUTLET

What were you saying about poor Cleaver?

LUCY

He has found his ears at last. (*Aside.*) That he has had his house burnt down.

CUTLET

Bless me!

LUCY

I saw four small children taken in at the green grocer's.

CUTLET

Do you know if he is insured?

LUCY

Some say he is, but not to the full amount.

CUTLET

Not to the full amount—how shocking! He killed more meat than any of the trade between here and Carnaby market—and the poor babes—four of them you say—what a melting sight!—he served some good customers about Marybone—I always think more of the children in these cases than of the fathers and mothers—Lady Lovebrown liked his veal better than any man's in the market—I wonder whether her ladyship is engaged—I must go and comfort poor Cleaver, however.— [*Exit.*

LUCY

Now is this pretender to humanity gone to avail himself of a neighbour's supposed ruin to inveigle his customers from him. Fine feelings!—pshaw! [*Exit.*

(*Re-enter Cutlet.*)

CUTLET

What a deceitful young hussey! there is not a word of truth in her. There has been no fire. How can people play with one's feelings so!—(*sings*)—" For tenderness formed "—No, I'll try the air I made upon myself. The words may compose me—(*sings*).

> A weeping Londoner I am,
> A washer-woman was my dam;
> She bred me up in a cock-loft,
> And fed my mind with sorrows soft:
>
> For when she wrung with elbows stout
> From linen wet the water out,—
> The drops so like to tears did drip,
> They gave my infant nerves the hyp.

Scarce three clean muckingers a week
Would dry the brine that dew'd my cheek:
So, while I gave my sorrows scope,
I almost ruin'd her in soap.

My parish learning I did win
In ward of Farringdon-Within;
Where, after school, I did pursue
My sports, as little boys will do.

Cockchafers—none like me was found
To set them spinning round and round.
O, how my tender heart would melt,
To think what those poor varmin felt!

I never tied tin-kettle, clog,
Or salt-box to the tail of dog,
Without a pang more keen at heart,
Than he felt at his outward part.

And when the poor thing clattered off,
To all the unfeeling mob a scoff,
Thought I, "What that dumb creature feels,
With half the parish at his heels!"

Arrived, you see, to man's estate,
The butcher's calling is my fate;
Yet still I keep my feeling ways,
And leave the town on slaughtering days.

At Kentish Town, or Highgate Hill,
I sit, retired, beside some rill;
And tears bedew my glistening eye,
To think my playful lambs must die!

But when they're dead I sell their meat,
On shambles kept both clean and neat;
Sweet-breads also I guard full well,
And keep them from the blue-bottle.

Envy, with breath sharp as my steel,
Has ne'er yet blown upon my veal;
And mouths of dames, and daintiest fops,
Do water at my nice lamb-chops.

[*Exit, half laughing, half crying.*

Scene III.—*A Street.*

(*Davenport, solus.*)

DAVENPORT

Thus far have I secured my charming prize. I can appretiate, while I lament, the delicacy which makes her refuse the protection of my sister's roof. But who comes here?

(*Enter Pendulous, agitated.*)

It must be he. That fretful animal motion—that face working up and down with uneasy sensibility, like new yeast. Jack—Jack Pendulous!

PENDULOUS

It is your old friend, and very miserable.

DAVENPORT

Vapours, Jack. I have not known you fifteen years to have to guess at your complaint. Why, they troubled you at school. Do you remember when you had to speak the speech of Buckingham, where he is going to execution?

PENDULOUS

Execution!—he has certainly heard it. (*Aside.*)

DAVENPORT

What a pucker you were in overnight!

PENDULOUS

May be so, may be so, Mr. Davenport. That was an imaginary scene. I have had real troubles since.

DAVENPORT

Pshaw! so you call every common accident.

PENDULOUS

Do you call my case so common, then?

DAVENPORT

What case?

PENDULOUS

You have not heard, then?

DAVENPORT

Positively not a word.

PENDULOUS

You must know I have been—(*whispers*)—tried for a felony since then.

DAVENPORT

Nonsense!

PENDULOUS

No subject for mirth, Mr. Davenport. A confounded short-sighted fellow swore that I stopt him, and robbed him, on the York race-ground at nine on a fine moonlight evening, when I was two hundred miles off in Dorsetshire. These hands have been held up at a common bar.

DAVENPORT

Ridiculous! it could not have gone so far.

PENDULOUS

A great deal farther, I assure you, Mr. Davenport. I am ashamed to say how far it went. You must know, that in the first shock and surprise of the accusation, shame—you know I was always susceptible—shame put me upon disguising my *name*, that, at all events, it might bring no disgrace upon my family. I called myself *James Thomson*.

DAVENPORT

For heaven's sake, compose yourself.

PENDULOUS

I will. An old family ours, Mr. Davenport—never had a blot upon it till now—a family famous for the jealousy of its honour for many generations—think of that, Mr. Davenport—that felt a stain like a wound—

DAVENPORT

Be calm, my dear friend.

PENDULOUS

This served the purpose of a temporary concealment well enough; but when it came to the—*alibi*—I think they call it—excuse these technical terms, they are hardly fit for the mouth of a gentleman, the *witnesses*—that is another term—that I had sent for up from Melcombe Regis, and relied upon for clearing up my character, by disclosing my real name, *John Pendulous*—so discredited the cause which they came to serve, that it had quite a contrary effect to what was intended. In short, the usual forms passed, and you behold me here the miserablest of mankind.

DAVENPORT

(*Aside*). He must be light-headed.

PENDULOUS

Not at all, Mr. Davenport. I hear what you say, though you speak it all on one side, as they do at the playhouse.

DAVENPORT

The sentence could never have been carried into—pshaw!—you are joking—the truth must have come out at last.

PENDULOUS

So it did, Mr. Davenport—just two minutes and a second too late by the Sheriff's stop-watch. Time enough to save my life—my wretched life—but an age too late for my honour. Pray, change the subject—the detail must be as offensive to you.

DAVENPORT

With all my heart, to a more pleasing theme. The lovely Maria Flyn—are you friends in that quarter, still? Have the old folks relented?

PENDULOUS

They are dead, and have left her mistress of her inclinations. But it requires great strength of mind to—

DAVENPORT

To what?

PENDULOUS

To stand up against the sneers of the world. It is not every young lady that feels herself confident against the shafts of ridicule, though aimed by the hand of prejudice. Not but in her heart, I believe, she prefers me to all mankind. But think what the world would say, if, in defiance of the opinions of mankind, she should take to her arms a—reprieved man!

DAVENPORT

Whims! You might turn the laugh of the world upon itself in a fortnight. These things are but nine days' wonders.

PENDULOUS

Do you think so, Mr. Davenport?

DAVENPORT

Where does she live?

PENDULOUS

She has lodgings in the next street, in a sort of garden-house, that belongs to one Cutlet. I have not seen her since the affair. I was going there at her request.

DAVENPORT

Ha, ha, ha!

PENDULOUS

Why do you laugh?

DAVENPORT

The oddest fellow! I will tell you——But here he comes.

THE PAWNBROKER'S DAUGHTER

Enter Cutlet.

CUTLET

(*To Davenport.*) Sir, the young lady at my house is desirous you should return immediately. She has heard something from home.

PENDULOUS

What do I hear?

DAVENPORT

'Tis her fears, I dare say. My dear Pendulous, you will excuse me?—I must not tell him our situation at present, though it cost him a fit of jealousy. We shall have fifty opportunities for explanation. [*Exit.*

PENDULOUS

Does that gentleman visit the lady at your lodgings?

CUTLET

He is quite familiar there, I assure you. He is all in all with her, as they say.

PENDULOUS

It is but too plain. Fool that I have been, not to suspect that, while she pretended scruples, some rival was at the root of her infidelity!

CUTLET

You seem distressed, Sir. Bless me!

PENDULOUS

I am, friend, above the reach of comfort.

CUTLET

Consolation, then, can be to no purpose?

PENDULOUS

None.

CUTLET

I am so happy to have met with him!

PENDULOUS

Wretch, wretch, wretch!

CUTLET

There he goes! How he walks about biting his nails! I would not exchange this luxury of unavailing pity for worlds.

PENDULOUS

Stigmatized by the world——

CUTLET

My case exactly. Let us compare notes.

PENDULOUS

For an accident which——

CUTLET

For a profession which——

PENDULOUS

In the eye of reason has nothing in it——

CUTLET

Absolutely nothing in it——

PENDULOUS

Brought up at a public bar——

CUTLET

Brought up to an odious trade——

PENDULOUS

With nerves like mine——

CUTLET

With nerves like mine——

PENDULOUS

Arraigned, condemned——

CUTLET

By a foolish world——

PENDULOUS

By a judge and jury——

CUTLET

By an invidious exclusion disqualified for sitting upon a jury at all——

PENDULOUS

Tried, cast, and——

CUTLET

What?

PENDULOUS

HANGED, Sir, HANGED by the neck, till I was——

CUTLET
Bless me!

PENDULOUS
Why should not I publish it to the whole world, since she, whose prejudice alone I wished to overcome, deserts me?

CUTLET
Lord have mercy upon us! not so bad as that comes to, I hope?

PENDULOUS
When she joins in the judgment of an illiberal world against me——

CUTLET
You said HANGED, Sir—that is, I mean, perhaps I mistook you. How ghastly he looks!

PENDULOUS
Fear me not, my friend. I am no ghost—though I heartily wish I were one.

CUTLET
Why, then, ten to one you were——

PENDULOUS
Cut down. The odious word shall out, though it choak me.

CUTLET
Your case must have some things in it very curious. I daresay you kept a journal of your sensations.

PENDULOUS
Sensations!

CUTLET
Aye, while you were being—you know what I mean. They say persons in your situation have lights dancing before their eyes—blueish. But then the worst of all is coming to one's self again.

PENDULOUS
Plagues, furies, tormentors! I shall go mad! [*Exit.*

CUTLET
There, he says he shall go mad. Well, my head has not been very right of late. It goes with a whirl and a buz somehow. I believe I must not think so deeply. Common people that don't reason know nothing of these aberrations.

Great wits go mad, and small ones only dull;
Distracting cares vex not the empty skull:
They seize on heads that think, and hearts that feel,
As flies attack the—better sort of veal.   [*Exit.*

ACT II

Scene.—*At Flint's.*

FLINT. WILLIAM.

FLINT

I have overwalked myself, and am quite exhausted. Tell Marian to come and play to me.

WILLIAM

I shall, Sir.   [*Exit.*

FLINT

I have been troubled with an evil spirit of late; I think an evil spirit. It goes and comes, as my daughter is with or from me. It cannot stand before her gentle look, when, to please her father, she takes down her music-book.

Enter William.

WILLIAM

Miss Marian went out soon after you, and is not returned.

FLINT

That is a pity—That is a pity. Where can the foolish girl be gadding?

WILLIAM

The shopmen say she went out with Mr. Davenport.

FLINT

Davenport? Impossible.

WILLIAM

They say they are sure it was he, by the same token that they saw her slip into his hand, when she was past the door, the casket which you gave her.

FLINT

Gave her, William! I only intrusted it to her. She has robbed me. Marian is a thief. You must go to the Justice, William, and get out a warrant against her immediately. Do you help them in the description. Put in "Marian Flint," in plain words—no remonstrances, William—" daughter of Reuben Flint,"—no remonstrances, but do it——

WILLIAM

Nay, sir——

FLINT

I am rock, absolute rock, to all that you can say—A piece of solid rock.—What is it that makes my legs to fail, and my whole frame to totter thus? It has been my over walking. I am very faint. Support me in, William. [*Exeunt.*

Scene.—*The Apartment of Miss Flyn.*

MISS FLYN. BETTY.

MISS FLYN

'Tis past eleven. Every minute I expect Mr. Pendulous here. What a meeting do I anticipate!

BETTY

Anticipate, truly! what other than a joyful meeting can it be between two agreed lovers who have been parted these four months?

MISS FLYN

But in that cruel space what accidents have happened!—(*aside*) As yet I perceive she is ignorant of this unfortunate affair.

BETTY

Lord, madam, what accidents? He has not had a fall or a tumble, has he? He is not coming upon crutches?

MISS FLYN

Not exactly a fall—(*aside*)—I wish I had courage to admit her to my confidence.

BETTY

If his neck is whole, his heart is so too, I warrant it.

MISS FLYN

His neck!—(*aside*)—She certainly mistrusts something. He writes me word that this must be his last interview.

BETTY

Then I guess the whole business. The wretch is unfaithful. Some creature or other has got him into a noose.

MISS FLYN

A noose!

BETTY
And I shall never more see him hang——

MISS FLYN
Hang, did you say, Betty?

BETTY
About that dear, fond neck, I was going to add, madam, but you interrupted me.

MISS FLYN
I can no longer labour with a secret which oppresses me thus. Can you be trusty?

BETTY
Who, I, madam?—(*aside*)—Lord, I am so glad. Now I shall know all.

MISS FLYN
This letter discloses the reason of his unaccountable long absence from me. Peruse it, and say if we have not reason to be unhappy.

(*Betty retires to the window to read the letter, Mr. Pendulous enters.*)

MISS FLYN
My dear Pendulous!

PENDULOUS
Maria!—nay, shun the embraces of a disgraced man, who comes but to tell you that you must renounce his society for ever.

MISS FLYN
Nay, Pendulous, avoid me not.

PENDULOUS
(*Aside.*) That was tender. I may be mistaken. Whilst I stood on honourable terms, Maria might have met my caresses without a blush.

(*Betty, who has not attended to the entrance of Pendulous, through her eagerness to read the letter, comes forward.*)

BETTY
Ha! ha! ha! What a funny story, madam; and is this all you make such a fuss about? I should not care if twenty of my lovers had been——(*seeing Pendulous*)—Lord, Sir, I ask pardon.

PENDULOUS
Are we not alone, then?

MISS FLYN

'Tis only Betty—my old servant. You remember Betty?

PENDULOUS

What letter is that?

MISS FLYN

O! something from her sweetheart, I suppose.

BETTY

Yes, ma'am, that is all. I shall die of laughing.

PENDULOUS

You have not surely been shewing her——

MISS FLYN

I must be ingenuous. You must know, then, that I was just giving Betty a hint—as you came in.

PENDULOUS

A hint!

MISS FLYN

Yes, of our unfortunate embarrassment.

PENDULOUS

My letter!

MISS FLYN

I thought it as well that she should know it at first.

PENDULOUS

'Tis mighty well, madam. 'Tis as it should be. I was ordained to be a wretched laughing-stock to all the world; and it is fit that our drabs and our servant wenches should have their share of the amusement.

BETTY

Marry come up! Drabs and servant wenches! and this from a person in his circumstances!

(*Betty flings herself out of the room, muttering.*)

MISS FLYN

I understand not this language. I was prepared to give my Pendulous a tender meeting. To assure him, that however, in the eyes of the superficial and the censorious, he may have incurred a partial degradation, in the esteem of one, at least, he stood as high as ever. That it was not in the power of a ridiculous *accident*, involving no guilt, no shadow of imputation, to separate two hearts, cemented by holiest vows, as ours have been. This untimely repulse to my affections may awaken scruples in me, which hitherto, in tenderness to you, I have suppressed.

PENDULOUS

I very well understand what you call tenderness, madam; but in some situations, pity—pity—is the greatest insult.

MISS FLYN

I can endure no longer. When you are in a calmer mood, you will be sorry that you have wrung my heart so. [*Exit.*

PENDULOUS

Maria! She is gone—in tears. Yet it seems she has had her scruples. She said she had tried to smother them. Her maid Betty intimated as much.

Re-enter Betty.

BETTY

Never mind Betty, sir; depend upon it she will never 'peach.

PENDULOUS

'Peach!

BETTY

Lord, sir, these scruples will blow over. Go to her again, when she is in a better humour. You know we must stand off a little at first, to save appearances.

PENDULOUS

Appearances! *we!*

BETTY

It will be decent to let some time elapse.

PENDULOUS

Time elapse!

> Lost, wretched Pendulous! to scorn betrayed,
> The scoff alike of mistress and of maid!
> What now remains for thee, forsaken man,
> But to complete thy fate's abortive plan,
> And finish what the feeble law began? [*Exeunt.*

Re-enter Miss Flyn, with Marian.

MISS FLYN

Now both our lovers are gone, I hope my friend will have less reserve. You must consider this apartment as yours while you stay here. 'Tis larger and more commodious than your own.

MARIAN

You are kind, Maria. My sad story I have troubled you with. I have some jewels here, which I unintentionally brought away. I have only to beg, that you will take the trouble to restore them to my father; and, without disclosing my present situation, to tell him, that my next step—with or without the concurrence of Mr. Davenport—shall be to throw myself at his feet, and beg to be forgiven. I dare not see him till you have explored the way for me. I am convinced I was tricked into this elopement.

MISS FLYN

Your commands shall be obeyed implicitly.

MARIAN

You are good (*agitated*).

MISS FLYN

Moderate your apprehensions, my sweet friend. I too have known my sorrows—(*smiling*).—You have heard of the ridiculous affair.

MARIAN

Between Mr. Pendulous and you? Davenport informed me of it, and we both took the liberty of blaming the over-niceness of your scruples.

MISS FLYN

You mistake. The refinement is entirely on the part of my lover. He thinks me not nice enough. I am obliged to feign a little reluctance, that he may not take quite a distaste to me. Will you believe it, that he turns my very constancy into a reproach, and declares, that a woman must be devoid of all delicacy, that, after a thing of that sort, could endure the sight of her husband in——

MARIAN

In what?

MISS FLYN

The sight of a man at all in——

MARIAN

I comprehend you not.

MISS FLYN

In—in a—(*whispers*)—night cap, my dear; and now the mischief is out.

MARIAN
Is there no way to cure him?

MISS FLYN
None, unless I were to try the experiment, by placing myself in the hands of justice for a little while, how far an equality in misfortune might breed a sympathy in sentiment. Our reputations would be both upon a level then, you know. What think you of a little innocent shop-lifting, in sport?

MARIAN
And by that contrivance to be taken before a magistrate? the project sounds oddly.

MISS FLYN
And yet I am more than half persuaded it is feasible.

Enter Betty.

BETTY
Mr. Davenport is below, ma'am, and desires to speak with you.

MARIAN
You will excuse me—(*going—turning back.*)—You will remember the casket? [*Exit.*

MISS FLYN
Depend on me.

BETTY
And a strange man desires to see you, ma'am. I do not half like his looks.

MISS FLYN
Shew him in.

(*Exit Betty, and returns with a Police Officer. Betty goes out.*)

OFFICER
Your servant, ma'am. Your name is——

MISS FLYN
Flyn, sir. Your business with me?

OFFICER
(*Alternately surveying the lady and his paper of instructions.*) Marian Flint.

MISS FLYN
Maria Flyn.

OFFICER

Aye, aye, Flyn or Flint. 'Tis all one. Some write plain Mary, and some put ann after it. I come about a casket.

MISS FLYN

I guess the whole business. He takes me for my friend. Something may come out of this. I will humour him.

OFFICER

(*Aside*)—Answers the description to a tittle. "Soft, grey eyes, pale complexion,"——

MISS FLYN

Yet I have been told by flatterers that my eyes were blue—(*takes out a pocket-glass*)—I hope I look pretty tolerably to-day.

OFFICER

Blue!—they are a sort of blueish-gray, now I look better; and as for colour, that comes and goes. Blushing is often a sign of a hardened offender. Do you know any thing of a casket?

MISS FLYN

Here is one which a friend has just delivered to my keeping.

OFFICER

And which I must beg leave to secure, together with your ladyship's person. "Garnets, pearls, diamond-bracelet,"—here they are, sure enough.

MISS FLYN

Indeed, I am innocent.

OFFICER

Every man is presumed so till he is found otherwise.

MISS FLYN

Police wit! Have you a warrant?

OFFICER

Tolerably cool that! Here it is, signed by Justice Golding, at the requisition of Reuben Flint, who deposes that you have robbed him.

MISS FLYN

How lucky this turns out! (*aside.*)—Can I be indulged with a coach?

OFFICER

To Marlborough Street? certainly—an old offender—(*aside*.) The thing shall be conducted with as much delicacy as is consistent with security.

MISS FLYN

Police manners! I will trust myself to your protection then.

[*Exeunt.*

Scene.—*Police-Office.*
JUSTICE, FLINT, OFFICERS, &c.

JUSTICE

Before we proceed to extremities, Mr. Flint, let me entreat you to consider the consequences. What will the world say to your exposing your own child?

FLINT

The world is not my friend. I belong to a profession which has long brought me acquainted with its injustice. I return scorn for scorn, and desire its censure above its plaudits.

JUSTICE

But in this case delicacy must make you pause.

FLINT

Delicacy—ha! ha!—pawnbroker—how fitly these words suit. Delicate pawnbroker—delicate devil—let the law take its course.

JUSTICE

Consider, the jewels are found.

FLINT

'Tis not the silly baubles I regard. Are you a man? are you a father? and think you I could stoop so low, vile as I stand here, as to make money—filthy money—of the stuff which a daughter's touch has desecrated? Deep in some pit first I would bury them.

JUSTICE

Yet pause a little. Consider. An only child.

FLINT

Only, only,—there, it is that stings me, makes me mad. She was the only thing I had to love me—to bear me up against the nipping injuries of the world. I prate when I should act. Bring in your prisoner.

(*The Justice makes signs to an Officer, who goes out, and returns with Miss Flyn.*)

FLINT
What mockery of my sight is here? This is no daughter.

OFFICER
Daughter, or no daughter, she has confessed to this casket.

FLINT
(*Handling it.*) The very same. Was it in the power of these pale splendours to dazzle the sight of honesty—to put out the regardful eye of piety and daughter-love? Why, a poor glow-worm shews more brightly. Bear witness how I valued them—(*tramples on them*).—Fair lady, know you aught of my child?

MISS FLYN
I shall here answer no questions.

JUSTICE
You must explain how you came by the jewels, madam.

MISS FLYN
(*Aside.*) Now confidence assist me!——A gentleman in the neighbourhood will answer for me——

JUSTICE
His name——

MISS FLYN
Pendulous——

JUSTICE
That lives in the next street?

MISS FLYN
The same——now I have him sure.

JUSTICE
Let him be sent for. I believe the gentleman to be respectable, and will accept his security.

FLINT
Why do I waste my time, where I have no business? None—I have none any more in the world—none.

Enter Pendulous.

PENDULOUS
What is the meaning of this extraordinary summons?—Maria here?

FLINT
Know you any thing of my daughter, Sir?

PENDULOUS
Sir, I neither know her nor yourself, nor why I am brought hither; but for this lady, if you have any thing against her, I will answer it with my life and fortunes.

JUSTICE
Make out the bail-bond.

OFFICER
(*Surveying Pendulous.*) Please, your worship, before you take that gentleman's bond, may I have leave to put in a word?

PENDULOUS
(*Agitated.*) I guess what is coming.

OFFICER
I have seen that gentleman hold up his hand at a criminal bar.

JUSTICE
Ha!

MISS FLYN
(*Aside.*) Better and better.

OFFICER
My eyes cannot deceive me. His lips quivered about, while he was being tried, just as they do now. His name is not Pendulous.

MISS FLYN
Excellent!

OFFICER
He pleaded to the name of Thomson at York assizes.

JUSTICE
Can this be true?

MISS FLYN
I could kiss the fellow!

OFFICER
He was had up for a footpad.

MISS FLYN
A dainty fellow!

PENDULOUS
My iniquitous fate pursues me everywhere.

THE PAWNBROKER'S DAUGHTER

JUSTICE

You confess, then.

PENDULOUS

I am steeped in infamy.

MISS FLYN

I am as deep in the mire as yourself.

PENDULOUS

My reproach can never be washed out.

MISS FLYN

Nor mine.

PENDULOUS

I am doomed to everlasting shame.

MISS FLYN

We are both in a predicament.

JUSTICE

I am in a maze where all this will end.

MISS FLYN

But here comes one who, if I mistake not, will guide us out of all our difficulties.

Enter Marian and Davenport.

MARIAN

(*Kneeling.*) My dear father!

FLINT

Do I dream?

MARIAN

I am your Marian.

JUSTICE

Wonders thicken!

FLINT

The casket—

MISS FLYN

Let me clear up the rest.

FLINT

The casket—

MISS FLYN

Was inadvertently in your daughter's hand, when, by an artifice of her maid Lucy,—set on, as she confesses, by this gentleman here,—

DAVENPORT

I plead guilty.

MISS FLYN

She was persuaded, that you were in a hurry going to marry her to an object of her dislike; nay, that he was actually in the house for the purpose. The speed of her flight admitted not of her depositing the jewels; but to me, who have been her inseparable companion since she quitted your roof, she intrusted the return of them; which the precipitate measures of this gentleman (*pointing to the Officer*) alone prevented. Mr. Cutlet, whom I see coming, can witness this to be true.

Enter Cutlet, in haste.

CUTLET

Aye, poor lamb! poor lamb! I can witness. I have run in such a haste, hearing how affairs stood, that I have left my shambles without a protector. If your worship had seen how she cried (*pointing to Marian*), and trembled, and insisted upon being brought to her father. Mr. Davenport here could not stay her.

FLINT

I can forbear no longer. Marian, will you play once again, to please your old father?

MARIAN

I have a good mind to make you buy me a new grand piano for your naughty suspicions of me.

DAVENPORT

What is to become of me?

FLINT

I will do more than that. The poor lady shall have her jewels again.

MARIAN

Shall she?

FLINT

Upon reasonable terms (*smiling*). And now, I suppose, the court may adjourn.

DAVENPORT

Marian!

FLINT

I guess what is passing in your mind, Mr. Davenport; but you have behaved upon the whole so like a man of honour, that it will give me pleasure, if you will visit at my house for the future; but (*smiling*) not clandestinely, Marian.

MARIAN

Hush, father.

FLINT

I own I had prejudices against gentry. But I have met with so much candour and kindness among my betters this day—from this gentleman in particular—(*turning to the Justice*)—that I begin to think of leaving off business, and setting up for a gentleman myself.

JUSTICE

You have the feelings of one.

FLINT

Marian will not object to it.

JUSTICE

But (*turning to Miss Flyn*) what motive could induce this lady to take so much disgrace upon herself, when a word's explanation might have relieved her?

MISS FLYN

This gentleman (*turning to Pendulous*) can explain.

PENDULOUS

The devil!

MISS FLYN

This gentleman, I repeat it, whose backwardness in concluding a long and honourable suit from a mistaken delicacy—

PENDULOUS

How!

MISS FLYN

Drove me upon the expedient of involving myself in the same disagreeable embarrassments with himself, in the hope that a more perfect sympathy might subsist between us for the future.

PENDULOUS

I see it—I see it all.

VOL. V.—16

JUSTICE

(*To Pendulous.*)   You were then tried at York?

PENDULOUS

I was——cast—

JUSTICE

Condemned—

PENDULOUS

Executed.

JUSTICE

How?

PENDULOUS

Cut down and came to life again. False delicacy, adieu! The true sort, which this lady has manifested—by an expedient which at first sight might seem a little unpromising, has cured me of the other. We are now on even terms.

MISS FLYN

And may—

PENDULOUS

Marry,—I know it was your word.

MISS FLYN

And make a very quiet—

PENDULOUS

Exemplary—

MISS FLYN

Agreeing pair of—

PENDULOUS

Acquitted Felons.

FLINT

And let the prejudiced against our profession acknowledge, that a money-lender may have the heart of a father; and that in the casket, whose loss grieved him so sorely, he valued nothing so dear as (*turning to Marian*) one poor domestic jewel.

THE WIFE'S TRIAL; OR, THE INTRUDING WIDOW

A Dramatic Poem

Founded on Mr. Crabbe's Tale of " The Confidant."

(1827)

CHARACTERS

Mr. Selby, *a Wiltshire Gentleman.*
Katherine, *Wife to Selby.*
Lucy, *Sister to Selby.*
Mrs. Frampton, *a Widow.*
Servants.
Scene.—*At Mr. Selby's house, or in the grounds adjacent.*

Scene—*A Library.*

MR. SELBY. KATHERINE.

SELBY

Do not too far mistake me, gentlest wife;
   I meant to chide your virtues, not yourself,
And those too with allowance. I have not
Been blest by thy fair side with five white years
Of smooth and even wedlock, now to touch
With any strain of harshness on a string
Hath yielded me such music. 'Twas the quality
Of a too grateful nature in my Katherine,
That to the lame performance of some vows,
And common courtesies of man to wife,
Attributing too much, hath sometimes seem'd
To esteem in favours, what in that blest union
Are but reciprocal and trivial dues,
As fairly yours as mine: 'twas this I thought
Gently to reprehend.

KATHERINE
                    In friendship's barter
The riches we exchange should hold some level,
And corresponding worth. Jewels for toys
Demand some thanks thrown in. You took me, sir,
To that blest haven of my peace, your bosom,
An orphan founder'd in the world's black storm.
Poor, you have made me rich; from lonely maiden,
Your cherish'd and your full-accompanied wife.

SELBY
But to divert the subject: Kate too fond,
I would not wrest your meanings; else that word
Accompanied, and full-accompanied too,
Might raise a doubt in some men, that their wives
Haply did think their company too long;
And over-company, we know by proof,
Is worse than no attendance.

KATHERINE
                        I must guess,
You speak this of the Widow—

SELBY
                            'Twas a bolt
At random shot; but if it hit, believe me,
I am most sorry to have wounded you
Through a friend's side. I know not how we have swerved
From our first talk. I was to caution you
Against this fault of a too grateful nature:
Which, for some girlish obligations past,
In that relenting season of the heart,
When slightest favours pass for benefits
Of endless binding, would entail upon you
An iron slavery of obsequious duty
To the proud will of an imperious woman.

KATHERINE
The favours are not slight to her I owe.

SELBY
Slight or not slight, the tribute she exacts
Cancels all dues—   [*A voice within.*
         even now I hear her call you
In such a tone, as lordliest mistresses
Expect a slave's attendance. Prithee, Kate,

Let her expect a brace of minutes or so.
Say, you are busy. Use her by degrees
To some less hard exactions.

     KATHERINE
       I conjure you,
Detain me not. I will return—

     SELBY
      Sweet wife
Use thy own pleasure—   *[Exit Katherine.*
      but it troubles me.
A visit of three days, as was pretended,
Spun to ten tedious weeks, and no hint given
When she will go! I would this buxom Widow
Were a thought handsomer! I'd fairly try
My Katherine's constancy; make desperate love
In seeming earnest; and raise up such broils,
That she, not I, should be the first to warn
The insidious guest depart.

    Re-enter Katherine.

      So soon return'd!
What was our Widow's will?

     KATHERINE
      A trifle, Sir.

     SELBY
Some toilet service—to adjust her head,
Or help to stick a pin in the right place—

     KATHERINE
Indeed 'twas none of these.

     SELBY
      or new vamp up
The tarnish'd cloak she came in. I have seen her
Demand such service from thee, as her maid,
Twice told to do it, would blush angry-red,
And pack her few clothes up. Poor fool! fond slave!
And yet my dearest Kate!—This day at least
(It is our wedding-day) we spend in freedom,
And will forget our Widow.—Philip, our coach—
Why weeps my wife? You know, I promised you
An airing o'er the pleasant Hampshire downs

To the blest cottage on the green hill side,
Where first I told my love. I wonder much,
If the crimson parlour hath exchanged its hue
For colours not so welcome. Faded though it be,
It will not shew less lovely than the tinge
Of this faint red, contending with the pale,
Where once the full-flush'd health gave to this cheek
An apt resemblance to the fruit's warm side,
That bears my Katherine's name.—
                                    Our carriage, Philip.

Enter a Servant.

Now, Robin, what make you here?

SERVANT

May it please you,
The coachman has driven out with Mrs. Frampton.

SELBY

He had no orders—

SERVANT

                    None, Sir, that I know of,
But from the lady, who expects some letter
At the next Post Town.

SELBY

        Go, Robin.   [*Exit Servant.*
            How is this?

KATHERINE

I came to tell you so, but fear'd your anger—

SELBY

It was ill done though of this Mistress Frampton,
This forward Widow. But a ride's poor loss
Imports not much. In to your chamber, love,
Where you with music may beguile the hour,
While I am tossing over dusty tomes,
Till our most reasonable friend returns.

KATHERINE

I am all obedience.   [*Exit Katherine.*

SELBY

            Too obedient, Kate,
And to too many masters. I can hardly

On such a day as this refrain to speak
My sense of this injurious friend, this pest,
This household evil, this close-clinging fiend,
In rough terms to my wife. 'Death! my own servants
Controll'd above me! orders countermanded!
What next? [*Servant enters and announces the Sister.*

Enter Lucy.

Sister! I know you are come to welcome
This day's return. 'Twas well done.

LUCY
               You seem ruffled.
In years gone by this day was used to be
The smoothest of the year. Your honey turn'd
So soon to gall?

SELBY
            Gall'd am I, and with cause,
And rid to death, yet cannot get a riddance,
Nay, scarce a ride, by this proud Widow's leave.

LUCY
Something you wrote me of a Mistress Frampton.

SELBY
She came at first a meek admitted guest,
Pretending a short stay; her whole deportment
Seem'd as of one obliged. A slender trunk,
The wardrobe of her scant and ancient clothing,
Bespoke no more. But in a few days her dress,
Her looks, were proudly changed. And now she flaunts it
In jewels stolen or borrow'd from my wife;
Who owes her some strange service, of what nature
I must be kept in ignorance. Katherine's meek
And gentle spirit cowers beneath her eye,
As spell-bound by some witch.

LUCY
            Some mystery hangs on it.
How bears she in her carriage towards yourself?

SELBY
As one who fears, and yet not greatly cares
For my displeasure. Sometimes I have thought,
A secret glance would tell me she could love,
If I but gave encouragement. Before me

She keeps some moderation; but is never
Closeted with my wife, but in the end
I find my Katherine in briny tears.
From the small chamber, where she first was lodged,
The gradual fiend by specious wriggling arts
Has now ensconced herself in the best part
Of this large mansion; calls the left wing her own;
Commands my servants, equipage.—I hear
Her hated tread.   What makes she back so soon?

Enter Mrs. Frampton.

MRS. FRAMPTON

O, I am jolter'd, bruised, and shook to death,
With your vile Wiltshire roads.   The villain Philip
Chose, on my conscience, the perversest tracks,
And stoniest hard lanes in all the county,
Till I was fain get out, and so walk back,
My errand unperform'd at Andover.

LUCY

And I shall love the knave for ever after.   [*Aside.*

MRS. FRAMPTON

A friend with you!

SELBY

My eldest sister, Lucy,
Come to congratulate this returning morn.—
Sister, my wife's friend, Mistress Frampton.

MRS. FRAMPTON

Pray
Be seated.   For your brother's sake, you are welcome.
I had thought this day to have spent in homely fashion
With the good couple, to whose hospitality
I stand so far indebted.   But your coming
Makes it a feast.

LUCY

She does the honours naturally—   [*Aside.*

SELBY

As if she were the mistress of the house—   [*Aside.*

MRS. FRAMPTON

I love to be at home with loving friends.
To stand on ceremony with obligations,

Is to restrain the obliger. That old coach, though,
Of yours jumbles one strangely.

SELBY
                I shall order
An equipage soon, more easy to you, madam—

LUCY
To drive her and her pride to Lucifer,
I hope he means.   [*Aside.*

MRS. FRAMPTON
I must go trim myself; this humbled garb
Would shame a wedding feast. I have your leave
For a short absence?—and your Katherine—

SELBY
You'll find her in her closet—

MRS. FRAMPTON
            Fare you well, then.   [*Exit.*

SELBY
How like you her assurance?

LUCY
              Even so well,
That if this Widow were my guest, not yours,
She should have coach enough, and scope to ride.
My merry groom should in a trice convey her
To Sarum Plain, and set her down at Stonehenge,
To pick her path through those antiques at leisure;
She should take sample of our Wiltshire flints.
O, be not lightly jealous! nor surmise,
That to a wanton bold-faced thing like this
Your modest shrinking Katherine could impart
Secrets of any worth, especially
Secrets that touch'd your peace. If there be aught,
My life upon 't, 'tis but some girlish story
Of a First Love; which even the boldest wife
Might modestly deny to a husband's ear,
Much more your timid and too sensitive Katherine.

SELBY
I think it is no more; and will dismiss
My further fears, if ever I have had such.

LUCY
Shall we go walk? I'd see your gardens, brother;
And how the new trees thrive, I recommended.
Your Katherine is engaged now—

SELBY
      I'll attend you. [*Exeunt.*

SCENE.—*Servants' Hall.*

HOUSEKEEPER, PHILIP, *and* OTHERS, *laughing.*

HOUSEKEEPER
Our Lady's guest, since her short ride, seems ruffled,
And somewhat in disorder. Philip, Philip,
I do suspect some roguery. Your mad tricks
Will some day cost you a good place, I warrant.

PHILIP
Good Mistress Jane, our serious housekeeper,
And sage Duenna to the maids and scullions,
We must have leave to laugh; our brains are younger,
And undisturb'd with care of keys and pantries.
We are wild things.

BUTLER
   Good Philip, tell us all.

ALL
Ay, as you live, tell, tell—

PHILIP
Mad fellows, you shall have it.
The Widow's bell rang lustily and loud—

BUTLER
I think that no one can mistake her ringing.

WAITING-MAID
Our Lady's ring is soft sweet music to it,
More of entreaty hath it than command.

PHILIP
I lose my story, if you interrupt me thus.
The bell, I say, rang fiercely; and a voice,
More shrill than bell, call'd out for "Coachman Philip."

THE WIFE'S TRIAL

I straight obey'd, as 'tis my name and office.
"Drive me," quoth she, "to the next market town,
Where I have hope of letters." I made haste.
Put to the horses, saw her safely coach'd,
And drove her—

WAITING-MAID

—By the straight high-road to Andover,
I guess—

PHILIP

Pray, warrant things within your knowledge,
Good Mistress Abigail; look to your dressings,
And leave the skill in horses to the coachman.

BUTLER

He'll have his humour; best not interrupt him.

PHILIP

'Tis market-day, thought I; and the poor beasts,
Meeting such droves of cattle and of people,
May take a fright; so down the lane I trundled,
Where Goodman Dobson's crazy mare was founder'd,
And where the flints were biggest, and ruts widest,
By ups and downs, and such bone-cracking motions,
We flounder'd on a furlong, till my madam,
In policy, to save the few joints left her,
Betook her to her feet, and there we parted.

ALL

Ha! ha! ha!

BUTLER

Hang her! 'tis pity such as she should ride.

WAITING-MAID

I think she is a witch; I have tired myself out
With sticking pins in her pillow; still she 'scapes them—

BUTLER

And I with helping her to mum for claret,
But never yet could cheat her dainty palate.

HOUSEKEEPER

Well, well, she is the guest of our good Mistress,
And so should be respected. Though I think
Our Master cares not for her company,

He would ill brook we should express so much,
By rude discourtesies, and short attendance,
Being but servants. (*A bell rings furiously.*) 'Tis her bell speaks now;
Good, good, bestir yourselves: who knows who's wanted?

BUTLER

But 'twas a merry trick of Philip coachman.   [*Exeunt.*

Scene.—*Mrs. Selby's Chamber.*

MRS. FRAMPTON, KATHERINE, *working.*

MRS. FRAMPTON

I am thinking, child, how contrary our fates
Have traced our lots through life. Another needle,
This works untowardly. An heiress born
To splendid prospects, at our common school
I was as one above you all, not of you;
Had my distinct prerogatives; my freedoms,
Denied to you. Pray, listen—

KATHERINE

          I must hear
What you are pleased to speak!—How my heart sinks here!
                                   [*Aside.*

MRS. FRAMPTON

My chamber to myself, my separate maid,
My coach, and so forth.—Not that needle, simple one,
With the great staring eye fit for a Cyclops!
Mine own are not so blinded with their griefs
But I could make a shift to thread a smaller.
A cable or a camel might go through this,
And never strain for the passage.

KATHERINE

           I will fit you.—
Intolerable tyranny!   [*Aside.*

MRS. FRAMPTON

        Quick, quick;
You were not once so slack.—As I was saying,
Not a young thing among ye, but observed me
Above the mistress. Who but I was sought to

In all your dangers, all your little difficulties,
Your girlish scrapes? I was the scape-goat still,
To fetch you off; kept all your secrets, some,
Perhaps, since then—

KATHERINE
No more of that, for mercy,
If you'd not have me, sinking at your feet,
Cleave the cold earth for comfort. [*Kneels.*

MRS. FRAMPTON
This to me?
This posture to your friend had better suited
The orphan Katherine in her humble school-days
To the *then* rich heiress, than the wife of Selby,
Of wealthy Mr. Selby,
To the poor widow Frampton, sunk as she is.
Come, come,
'Twas something, or 'twas nothing, that I said;
I did not mean to fright you, sweetest bed-fellow!
You once were so, but Selby now engrosses you.
I'll make him give you up a night or so;
In faith I will: that we may lie, and talk
Old tricks of school-days over.

KATHERINE
Hear me, madam—

MRS. FRAMPTON
Not by that name. Your friend—

KATHERINE
My truest friend,
And saviour of my honour!

MRS. FRAMPTON
This sounds better;
You still shall find me such.

KATHERINE
That you have graced
Our poor house with your presence hitherto,
Has been my greatest comfort, the sole solace
Of my forlorn and hardly guess'd estate.
You have been pleased
To accept some trivial hospitalities,
In part of payment of a long arrear
I owe to you, no less than for my life.

MRS. FRAMPTON
You speak my services too large.

KATHERINE
      Nay, less;
For what an abject thing were life to me
Without your silence on my dreadful secret!
And I would wish the league we have renew'd
Might be perpetual—

MRS. FRAMPTON
    Have a care, fine madam! [*Aside.*

KATHERINE
That one house still might hold us. But my husband
Has shown himself of late—

MRS. FRAMPTON
     How Mistress Selby?

KATHERINE
Not, not impatient. You misconstrue him.
He honours, and he loves, nay, he must love
The friend of his wife's youth. But there are moods
In which—

MRS. FRAMPTON
   I understand you;—in which husbands,
And wifes that love, may wish to be alone,
To nurse the tender fits of new-born dalliance,
After a five years' wedlock.

KATHERINE
     Was that well
Or charitably put? do these pale cheeks
Proclaim a wanton blood? this wasting form
Seem a fit theatre for Levity
To play his love-tricks on; and act such follies,
As even in Affection's first bland Moon
Have less of grace than pardon in best wedlocks?
I was about to say, that there are times,
When the most frank and sociable man
May surfeit on most loved society,
Preferring loneness rather—

MRS. FRAMPTON
     To my company—

KATHERINE

Ay, your's, or mine, or any one's. Nay, take
Not this unto yourself. Even in the newness
Of our first married loves 'twas sometimes so.
For solitude, I have heard my Selby say,
Is to the mind as rest to the corporal functions;
And he would call it oft, the *day's soft sleep.*

MRS. FRAMPTON

What is your drift? and whereto tends this speech,
Rhetorically labour'd?

KATHERINE

    That you would
Abstain but from our house a month, a week;
I make request but for a single day.

MRS. FRAMPTON

A month, a week, a day! A single hour
In every week, and month, and the long year,
And all the years to come! My footing here,
Slipt once, recovers never. From the state
Of gilded roofs, attendance, luxuries,
Parks, gardens, sauntering walks, or wholesome rides,
To the bare cottage on the withering moor,
Where I myself am servant to myself,
Or only waited on by blackest thoughts—
I sink, if this be so. No; here I sit.

KATHERINE

Then I am lost for ever!
    [*Sinks at her feet—curtain drops.*

Scene.—*An Apartment, contiguous to the last.*

  SELBY, *as if listening.*

SELBY

The sounds have died away. What am I changed to?
What do I here, list'ning like to an abject,
Or heartless wittol, that must hear no good,
If he hear aught? "This shall to the ear of your husband."
It was the Widow's word. I guess'd some mystery,
And the solution with a vengeance comes.
What can my wife have left untold to me,

That must be told by proxy? I begin
To call in doubt the course of her life past
Under my very eyes. She hath not been good,
Not virtuous, not discreet; she hath not outrun
My wishes still with prompt and meek observance.
Perhaps she is not fair, sweet-voiced; her eyes
Not like the dove's; all this as well may be,
As that she should entreasure up a secret
In the peculiar closet of her breast,
And grudge it to my ear. It is my right
To claim the halves in any truth she owns,
As much as in the babe I have by her;
Upon whose face henceforth I fear to look,
Lest I should fancy in its innocent brow
Some strange shame written.

Enter Lucy.

Sister, an anxious word with you.
From out the chamber, where my wife but now
Held talk with her encroaching friend, I heard
(Not of set purpose heark'ning, but by chance)
A voice of chiding, answer'd by a tone
Of replication, such as the meek dove
Makes, when the kite has clutch'd her. The high Widow
Was loud and stormy. I distinctly heard
One threat pronounced—" Your husband shall know all."
I am no listener, sister; and I hold
A secret, got by such unmanly shift,
The pitiful'st of thefts; but what mine ear,
I not intending it, receives perforce,
I count my lawful prize. Some subtle meaning
Lurks in this fiend's behaviour; which, by force;
Or fraud, I must make mine.

LUCY

                    The gentlest means
Are still the wisest. What, if you should press
Your wife to a disclosure?

SELBY

                  I have tried
All gentler means; thrown out low hints, which, though
Merely suggestions still, have never fail'd
To blanch her cheek with fears. Roughlier to insist,
Would be to kill, where I but meant to heal.

LUCY

Your own description gave that Widow out
As one not much precise, nor over coy,
And nice to listen to a suit of love.
What if you feign'd a courtship, putting on,
(To work the secret from her easy faith,)
For honest ends, a most dishonest seeming?

SELBY

I see your drift, and partly meet your counsel.
But must it not in me appear prodigious,
To say the least, unnatural, and suspicious,
To move hot love, where I have shewn cool scorn,
And undissembled looks of blank aversion?

LUCY

Vain woman is the dupe of her own charms,
And easily credits the resistless power,
That in besieging Beauty lies, to cast down
The slight-built fortress of a casual hate.

SELBY

I am resolved—

LUCY

    Success attend your wooing!

SELBY

And I'll about it roundly, my wise sister.   [*Exeunt.*

Scene.—*The Library.*

MR. SELBY. MRS. FRAMPTON.

SELBY

A fortunate encounter, Mistress Frampton.
My purpose was, if you could spare so much
From your sweet leisure, a few words in private.

MRS. FRAMPTON

What mean his alter'd tones? These looks to me,
Whose glances yet he has repell'd with coolness?
Is the wind changed? I'll veer about with it,
And meet him in all fashions.   [*Aside.*
             All my leisure,
Feebly bestow'd upon my kind friends here,

VOL. V.—17

Would not express a tithe of the obligements
I every hour incur.

SELBY
No more of that.—
I know not why, my wife hath lost of late
Much of her cheerful spirits.

MRS. FRAMPTON
It was my topic
To-day; and every day, and all day long,
I still am chiding with her. "Child," I said,
And said it pretty roundly—it may be
I was too peremptory—we elder school-fellows,
Presuming on the advantage of a year
Or two, which, in that tender time, seem'd much,
In after years, much like to elder sisters,
Are prone to keep the authoritative style,
When time has made the difference most ridiculous—

SELBY
The observation's shrewd.

MRS. FRAMPTON
"Child," I was saying,
"If some wives had obtained a lot like yours,"
And then perhaps I sigh'd, "they would not sit
In corners moping, like to sullen moppets
That want their will, but dry their eyes, and look
Their cheerful husbands in the face," perhaps
I said, their Selby's, "with proportion'd looks
Of honest joy."

SELBY
You do suspect no jealousy?

MRS. FRAMPTON
What is his import?   Whereto tends his speech?   [*Aside.*
Of whom, of what, should she be jealous, sir?

SELBY
I do not know, but women have their fancies;
And underneath a cold indifference,
Or show of some distaste, husbands have mask'd
A growing fondness for a female friend,
Which the wife's eye was sharp enough to see
Before the friend had wit to find it out.
You do not quit us soon?

MRS. FRAMPTON
'Tis as I find
Your Katherine profits by my lessons, sir.—
Means this man honest? Is there no deceit?   [*Aside.*

SELBY
She cannot chuse.—Well, well, I have been thinking,
And if the matter were to do again—

MRS. FRAMPTON
What matter, sir?

SELBY
This idle bond of wedlock;
These sour-sweet briars, fetters of harsh silk;
I might have made, I do not say a better,
But a more fit choice in a wife.

MRS. FRAMPTON
The parch'd ground,
In hottest Julys, drinks not in the showers
More greedily than I his words!   [*Aside.*

SELBY
My humour
Is to be frank and jovial; and that man
Affects me best, who most reflects me in
My most free temper.

MRS. FRAMPTON
Were you free to chuse,
As jestingly I'll put the supposition,
Without a thought reflecting on your Katherine,
What sort of woman would you make your choice?

SELBY
I like your humour, and will meet your jest.
She should be one about my Katherine's age;
But not so old, by some ten years, in gravity.
One that would meet my mirth, sometimes outrun it;
No puling, pining moppet, as you said,
Nor moping maid, that I must still be teaching
The freedoms of a wife all her life after:
But one, that, having worn the chain before,
(And worn it lightly, as report gave out,)
Enfranchised from it by her poor fool's death,
Took it not so to heart that I need dread

To die myself, for fear a second time
To wet a widow's eye.

MRS. FRAMPTON

                Some widows, sir,
Hearing you talk so wildly, would be apt
To put strange misconstruction on your words,
As aiming at a Turkish liberty,
Where the free husband hath his several mates,
His Penseroso, his Allegro wife,
To suit his sober, or his frolic fit.

SELBY

How judge you of that latitude?

MRS. FRAMPTON

                    As one,
In European customs bred, must judge. Had I
Been born a native of the liberal East,
I might have thought as they do. Yet I knew
A married man that took a second wife,
And (the man's circumstances duly weigh'd,
With all their bearings) the considerate world
Nor much approved, nor much condemn'd the deed.

SELBY

You move my wonder strangely. Pray, proceed.

MRS. FRAMPTON

An eye of wanton liking he had placed
Upon a Widow, who liked him again,
But stood on terms of honourable love,
And scrupled wronging his most virtuous wife—
When to their ears a lucky rumour ran,
That this demure and saintly-seeming wife
Had a first husband living; with the which
Being question'd, she but faintly could deny.
" A priest indeed there was ; some words had passed,
But scarce amounting to a marriage rite.
Her friend was absent ; she supposed him dead ;
And, seven years parted, both were free to chuse."

SELBY

What did the indignant husband? Did he not
With violent handlings stigmatize the cheek
Of the deceiving wife, who had entail'd
Shame on their innocent babe?

MRS. FRAMPTON
                    He neither tore
His wife's locks nor his own; but wisely weighing
His own offence with her's in equal poise,
And woman's weakness 'gainst the strength of man,
Came to a calm and witty compromise.
He coolly took his gay-faced widow home,
Made her his second wife; and still the first
Lost few or none of her prerogatives.
The servants call'd her mistress still; she kept
The keys, and had the total ordering
Of the house affairs; and, some slight toys excepted,
Was all a moderate wife would wish to be.

SELBY
A tale full of dramatic incident!—
And if a man should put it in a play,
How should he name the parties?

MRS. FRAMPTON
                    The man's name
Through time I have forgot—the widow's too;—
But his first wife's first name, her maiden one,
Was—not unlike to *that* your Katherine bore,
Before she took the honour'd style of Selby.

SELBY
A dangerous meaning in your riddle lurks.
One knot is yet unsolved; that told, this strange
And most mysterious drama ends. The name
Of that first husband—

          Enter Lucy.

MRS. FRAMPTON
                Sir, your pardon—
The allegory fits your private ear.
Some half hour hence, in the garden's secret walk,
We shall have leisure.   [*Exit.*

SELBY
          Sister, whence come you?

LUCY
From your poor Katherine's chamber, where she droops
In sad presageful thoughts, and sighs, and weeps,
And seems to pray by turns. At times she looks

As she would pour her secret in my bosom—
Then starts, as I have seen her, at the mention
Of some immodest act. At her request
I left her on her knees.

SELBY

              The fittest posture;
For great has been her fault to Heaven and me.
She married me, with a first husband living,
Or not known not to be so, which, in the judgment
Of any but indifferent honesty,
Must be esteem'd the same. The shallow Widow,
Caught by my art, under a riddling veil
Too thin to hide her meaning, hath confess'd all.
Your coming in broke off the conference,
When she was ripe to tell the fatal *name*,
That seals my wedded doom.

LUCY

              Was she so forward
To pour her hateful meanings in your ear
At the first hint?

SELBY

           Her newly flatter'd hopes
Array'd themselves at first in forms of doubt;
And with a female caution she stood off
Awhile, to read the meaning of my suit,
Which with such honest seeming I enforced,
That her cold scruples soon gave way; and now
She rests prepared, as mistress, or as wife,
To seize the place of her betrayed friend—
My much offending, but more suffering, Katherine.

LUCY

Into what labyrinth of fearful shapes
My simple project has conducted you—
Were but my wit as skilful to invent
A clue to lead you forth!—I call to mind
A letter, which your wife received from the Cape,
Soon after you were married, with some circumstances
Of mystery too.

SELBY

         I well remember it.
That letter did confirm the truth (she said)
Of a friend's death, which she had long fear'd true,

But knew not for a fact. A youth of promise
She gave him out—a hot adventurous spirit—
That had set sail in quest of golden dreams,
And cities in the heart of Central Afric;
But named no names, nor did I care to press
My question further, in the passionate grief
She shew'd at the receipt. Might this be he?

LUCY

Tears were not all. When that first shower was past,
With clasped hands she raised her eyes to Heav'n,
As if in thankfulness for some escape,
Or strange deliverance, in the news implied,
Which sweeten'd that sad news.

SELBY
      Something of that
I noted also—

LUCY
    In her closet once,
Seeking some other trifle, I espied
A ring, in mournful characters deciphering
The death of "Robert Halford, aged two
And twenty." Brother, I am not given
To the confident use of wagers, which I hold
Unseemly in a woman's argument;
But I am strangely tempted now to risk
A thousand pounds out of my patrimony,
(And let my future husband look to it
If it be lost,) that this immodest Widow
Shall name the name that tallies with that ring.

SELBY

That wager lost, I should be rich indeed—
Rich in my rescued Kate—rich in my honour,
Which now was bankrupt. Sister, I accept
Your merry wager, with an aching heart
For very fear of winning. 'Tis the hour
That I should meet my Widow in the walk,
The south side of the garden. On some pretence
Lure forth my Wife that way, that she may witness
Our seeming courtship. Keep us still in sight,
Yourselves unseen; and by some sign I'll give,
(A finger held up, or a kerchief waved,)
You'll know your wager won—then break upon us,
As if by chance.

LUCY

I apprehend your meaning—

SELBY

And may you prove a true Cassandra here,
Though my poor acres smart for 't, wagering sister.

[*Exeunt.*

Scene.—*Mrs. Selby's Chamber.*

MRS. FRAMPTON, KATHERINE

MRS. FRAMPTON

Did I express myself in terms so strong?

KATHERINE

As nothing could have more affrighted me.

MRS. FRAMPTON

Think it a hurt friend's jest, in retribution
Of a suspected cooling hospitality.
And, for my staying here, or going hence,
(Now I remember something of our argument,)
Selby and I can settle that between us.
You look amazed. What if your husband, child,
Himself has courted me to stay?

KATHERINE

You move
My wonder and my pleasure equally.

MRS. FRAMPTON

Yes, courted me to stay, waiv'd all objections.
Made it a favour to yourselves; not me,
His troublesome guest, as you surmised. Child, child!
When I recall his flattering welcome, I
Begin to think the burden of my presence
Was—

KATHERINE

What, for Heaven—

MRS. FRAMPTON

A little, little spice
Of jealousy—that's all—an honest pretext,
No wife need blush for. Say that you should see
(As oftentimes we widows take such freedoms,

Yet still on this side virtue,) in a jest
Your husband pat me on the cheek, or steal
A kiss, while you were by,—not else, for virtue's sake.

KATHERINE

I could endure all this, thinking my husband
Meant it in sport—

MRS. FRAMPTON

     But if in downright earnest
(Putting myself out of the question here)
Your Selby, as I partly do suspect,
Own'd a divided heart—

KATHERINE

     My own would break—

MRS. FRAMPTON

Why, what a blind and witless fool it is,
That will not see its gains, its infinite gains—

KATHERINE

Gain in a loss,
   Or mirth in utter desolation!

MRS. FRAMPTON

He doting on a face—suppose it mine,
Or any other's tolerably fair—
What need you care about a senseless secret?

KATHERINE

Perplex'd and fearful woman! I in part
Fathom your dangerous meaning. You have broke
The worse than iron band, fretting the soul,
By which you held me captive. Whether my husband
Is what you gave him out, or your fool'd fancy
But dreams he is so, either way I am free.

MRS. FRAMPTON

It talks it bravely, blazons out its shame;
A very heroine while on its knees;
Rowe's Penitent, an absolute Calista!

KATHERINE

Not to thy wretched self these tears are falling;
But to my husband, and offended heaven,
Some drops are due—and then I sleep in peace,
Reliev'd from frightful dreams, my dreams though sad.
            [*Exit.*

MRS. FRAMPTON

I have gone too far. Who knows but in this mood
She may forestall my story, win on Selby
By a frank confession?—and the time draws on
For our appointed meeting. The game's desperate,
For which I play. A moment's difference
May make it hers or mine. I fly to meet him. [*Exit.*

Scene.—*A Garden.*

MR. SELBY, MRS. FRAMPTON

SELBY

I am not so ill a guesser, Mrs. Frampton,
Not to conjecture, that some passages
In your unfinished story, rightly interpreted,
Glanced at my bosom's peace;
      You knew my wife?

MRS. FRAMPTON

Even from her earliest school-days.—What of that?
Or how is she concerned in my fine riddles,
Framed for the hour's amusement?

SELBY

      By my *hopes*
Of my new interest conceived in you,
And by the honest passion of my heart,
Which not obliquely I to you did hint;
Come from the clouds of misty allegory,
And in plain language let me hear the worst.
Stand I disgraced or no?

MRS. FRAMPTON

    Then, by *my* hopes
Of my new interest conceiv'd in you,
And by the kindling passion in *my* breast,
Which through my riddles you had almost read,
Adjured so strongly, I will tell you all.
In her school years, then bordering on fifteen,
Or haply not much past, she loved a youth—

SELBY

My most ingenuous Widow—

MRS. FRAMPTON
                Met him oft
By stealth, where I still of the party was—

SELBY
Prime confidant to all the school, I warrant,
And general go-between—   [*Aside.*

MRS. FRAMPTON
                One morn he came
In breathless haste. "The ship was under sail,
Or in few hours would be, that must convey
Him and his destinies to barbarous shores,
Where, should he perish by inglorious hands,
It would be consolation in his death
To have call'd his Katherine *his*."

SELBY
              Thus far the story
Tallies with what I hoped.   [*Aside.*

MRS. FRAMPTON
                Wavering between
The doubt of doing wrong, and losing him;
And my dissuasions not o'er hotly urged,
Whom he had flatter'd with the bride-maid's part;—

SELBY
I owe my subtle Widow, then, for this.   [*Aside.*

MRS. FRAMPTON
Briefly, we went to church. The ceremony
Scarcely was huddled over, and the ring
Yet cold upon her finger, when they parted—
He to his ship; and we to school got back,
Scarce miss'd, before the dinner-bell could ring.

SELBY
And from that hour—

MRS. FRAMPTON
            Nor sight, nor news of him,
For aught that I could hear, she e'er obtain'd.

SELBY
Like to a man that hovers in suspense
Over a letter just receiv'd, on which

The black seal hath impress'd its ominous token,
Whether to open it or no, so I
Suspended stand, whether to press my fate
Further, or check ill curiosity
That tempts me to more loss.—The name, the name
Of this fine youth?

MRS. FRAMPTON

What boots it, if 'twere told?

SELBY

                      Now, by our loves,
And by my hopes of happier wedlocks, some day
To be accomplish'd, give me his name!

MRS. FRAMPTON

'Tis no such serious matter. It was—Huntingdon.

SELBY

How have three little syllables pluck'd from me
A world of countless hopes!—   [*Aside.*
                 Evasive Widow.

MRS. FRAMPTON

How, Sir! I like not this.   [*Aside.*

SELBY

                No, no, I meant
Nothing but good to thee. That other woman,
How shall I call her but evasive, false,
And treacherous?—by the trust I place in thee,
Tell me, and tell me truly, was the name
As you pronounced it?

MRS. FRAMPTON

               Huntingdon—the name,
Which his paternal grandfather assumed,
Together with the estates, of a remote
Kinsman: but our high-spirited youth—

SELBY

Yes—

MRS. FRAMPTON

               Disdaining
For sordid pelf to truck the family honours,
At risk of the lost estates, resumed the old style,
And answer'd only to the name of—

SELBY
What?
MRS. FRAMPTON
Of Halford—

SELBY
A Huntingdon to Halford changed so soon!
Why, then I see, a witch hath her good spells,
As well as bad, and can by a backward charm
Unruffle the foul storm she has just been raising.   [*Aside.*
                              [*He makes the signal.*
My frank, fair spoken Widow! let this kiss,
Which yet aspires no higher, speak my thanks,
Till I can think on greater.

Enter LUCY *and* KATHERINE.
MRS. FRAMPTON
Interrupted!
SELBY
My sister here! and see, where with her comes
My serpent gliding in an angel's form,
To taint the new-born Eden of our joys.
Why should we fear them?   We'll not stir a foot,
Nor coy it for their pleasures.   [*He courts the Widow.*

LUCY (*to Katherine.*)
               This your free,
And sweet ingenuous confession, binds me
For ever to you; and it shall go hard,
But it shall fetch you back your husband's heart,
That now seems blindly straying; or at worst,
In me you have still a sister.—Some wives, brother,
Would think it strange to catch their husbands thus
Alone with a trim widow; but your Katherine
Is arm'd, I think, with patience.

KATHERINE
                I am fortified
With knowledge of self-faults to endure worse wrongs,
If they be wrongs, than he can lay upon me;
Even to look on, and see him sue in earnest,
As now I think he does it but in seeming,
To that ill woman.

SELBY

     Good words, gentle Kate,
And not a thought irreverent of our Widow.
Why, 'twere unmannerly at any time,
But most uncourteous on our wedding day,
When we should shew most hospitable.—Some wine.
             [Wine is brought.
I am for sports. And now I do remember,
The old Egyptians at their banquets placed
A charnel sight of dead men's skulls before them,
With images of cold mortality,
To temper their fierce joys when they grew rampant.
I like the custom well: and ere we crown
With freer mirth the day, I shall propose,
In calmest recollection of our spirits,
We drink the solemn " Memory of the dead."

MRS. FRAMPTON

Or the supposed dead.   *[Aside to him.*

SELBY

     Pledge me, good wife. *[She fills.*
Nay, higher yet, till the brimm'd cup swell o'er.

KATHERINE

I catch the awful import of your words;
And, though I could accuse you of unkindness,
Yet as your lawful and obedient wife,
While that name lasts (as I perceive it fading,
Nor I much longer may have leave to use it)
I calmly take the office you impose;
And on my knees, imploring their forgiveness,
Whom I in heav'n or earth may have offended,
Exempt from starting tears, and woman's weakness,
I pledge you, Sir—the Memory of the Dead!
          [She drinks kneeling.

SELBY

'Tis gently and discreetly said, and like
My former loving Kate.

MRS. FRAMPTON

Does he relent?   *[Aside.*

SELBY

That ceremony past, we give the day
To unabated sport.   And, in requital
Of certain stories, and quaint allegories,
Which my rare Widow hath been telling to me
To raise my morning mirth, if she will lend
Her patient hearing, I will here recite
A Parable; and, the more to suit her taste,
The scene is laid in the East.

MRS. FRAMPTON
     I long to hear it.
Some tale, to fit his wife.   [*Aside.*

KATHERINE
    Now, comes my TRIAL.

LUCY

The hour of your deliverance is at hand,
If I presage right.   Bear up, gentlest sister.

SELBY

"The Sultan Haroun"—Stay—O now I have it—
"The Caliph Haroun in his orchards had
A fruit-tree, bearing such delicious fruits,
That he reserved them for his proper gust;
And through the Palace it was Death proclaim'd
To any one that should purloin the same."

MRS. FRAMPTON

A heavy penance for so light a fault—

SELBY

Pray you, be silent, else you put me out.
"A crafty page, that for advantage watch'd,
Detected in the act a brother page,
Of his own years, that was his bosom friend;
And thenceforth he became that other's lord,
And like a tyrant he demean'd himself,
Laid forced exactions on his fellow's purse;
And when that poor means fail'd, held o'er his head
Threats of impending death in hideous forms;
Till the small culprit on his nightly couch
Dream'd of strange pains, and felt his body writhe
In tortuous pangs around the impaling stake."

MRS. FRAMPTON

I like not this beginning—

SELBY

      Pray you, attend.
"The Secret, like a night-hag, rid his sleeps,
And took the youthful pleasures from his days,
And chased the youthful smoothness from his brow,
That from a rose-cheek'd boy he waned and waned
To a pale skeleton of what he was;
And would have died, but for one lucky chance."

KATHERINE

Oh!

MRS. FRAMPTON

Your wife—she faints—some cordial—smell to this.

SELBY

Stand off. My sister best will do that office.

MRS. FRAMPTON

Are all his tempting speeches come to this? [*Aside.*

SELBY

What ail'd my wife?

KATHERINE

     A warning faintness, sir,
Seized on my spirits, when you came to where
You said "a lucky chance." I am better now,
Please you go on.

SELBY

    The sequel shall be brief.

KATHERINE

But brief or long, I feel my fate hangs on it. [*Aside.*

SELBY

"One morn the Caliph, in a covert hid,
Close by an arbour where the two boys talk'd
(As oft, we read, that Eastern sovereigns
Would play the eaves-dropper, to learn the truth,
Imperfectly received from mouths of slaves,)
O'erheard their dialogue; and heard enough
To judge aright the cause, and know his cue.
The following day a Cadi was dispatched

To summon both before the judgment-seat:
The lickerish culprit, almost dead with fear,
And the informing friend, who readily,
Fired with fair promises of large reward,
And Caliph's love, the hateful truth disclosed."

MRS. FRAMPTON

What did the Caliph to the offending boy,
That had so grossly err'd?

SELBY

                His sceptred hand
He forth in token of forgiveness stretch'd,
And clapp'd his cheeks, and courted him with gifts,
And he became once more his favourite page.

MRS. FRAMPTON

But for that other—

SELBY

                He dismiss'd him straight,
From dreams of grandeur and of Caliph's love,
To the bare cottage on the withering moor,
Where friends, turn'd fiends, and hollow confidants,
And widows, hide, who, in a husband's ear,
Pour baneful truths, but tell not all the truth;
And told him not that Robert Halford died
Some moons before *his* marriage-bells were rung.
Too near dishonour hast thou trod, dear wife,
And on a dangerous cast our fates were set;
But Heav'n, that will'd our wedlock to be blest,
Hath interposed to save it gracious too.
Your penance is—to dress your cheek in smiles,
And to be once again my merry Kate.—
Sister, your hand.
Your wager won makes me a happy man,
Though poorer, Heav'n knows, by a thousand pounds.
The sky clears up after a dubious day.
Widow, your hand. I read a penitence
In this dejected brow; and in this shame
Your fault is buried. You shall in with us,
And, if it please you, taste our nuptial fare:
For, till this moment, I can joyful say,
Was never truly Selby's Wedding Day.

FINIS

NOTES

Page 1. Dedication to S. T. Coleridge, Esq.

In 1818, when Lamb wrote these words, he was forty-three and Coleridge forty-six. The *Works*, in the first volume of which this dedication appeared, were divided into two volumes, the second, containing prose, being dedicated to Martin Burney, in the sonnet which I have placed on page 42. The publishers of the *Works* were Charles and James Ollier, who, starting business about 1816, had already published for Leigh Hunt, Keats and Shelley.

For the allusion to the threefold cord, in the second paragraph, see the note on page 282.

The ********** Inn was the Salutation and Cat, in Newgate Street, since rebuilt, where Coleridge used to stay on his London visits when he was at Cambridge, and where the landlord is said to have asked him to continue as a free guest—if only he would talk and talk. Writing to Coleridge in 1796 Lamb recalls "the little smoky room at the Salutation and Cat, where we have sat together through the winter nights, beguiling the cares of life with Poesy;" and again, "I have been drinking egg-hot and smoking Oronooko (associated circumstances, which ever forcibly recall to my mind our evenings and nights at the Salutation)." Later he added to these concomitants of a Salutation evening, "Egg-hot, Welsh-rabbit, and metaphysics," and gave as his highest idea of heaven, listening to Coleridge "repeating one of Bowles's sweetest sonnets, in your sweet manner, while we two were indulging sympathy, a solitary luxury, by the fireside at the Salutation."

Two at least of Lamb's quotations are drawn from favourite authors of his. The line—

> Of summer days and of delightful years

I have not succeeded in tracing.

> What words have I heard
> Spoke at the Mermaid!

from Francis Beaumont's "Letter to Ben Jonson written before he and Master Fletcher came to London with two of the precedent comedies, then not finished, which deferred their merry meetings at the Mermaid." The lines run:—

(275)

> What things have we seen
> Done at the Mermaid! heard words that have been
> So nimble and so full of subtle flame
> As if that every one from whence they came
> Had meant to put his whole wit in a jest
> And had resolv'd to live a fool the rest
> Of his dull life.

The third quotation, at the close of the fifth paragraph, is a recollection of Shakespeare's 116th sonnet :—

> Love is not love
> Which alters when it alteration finds,
> Or bends with the remover to remove.

Page 3.   POEMS IN COLERIDGE'S "POEMS ON VARIOUS SUBJECTS."
This book was published by Cottle, of Bristol, in 1796. Lamb contributed four poems, which were thus referred to by Coleridge in the Preface : " The Effusions signed C. L. were written by Mr. CHARLES LAMB, of the India House—independently of the signature their superior merit would have sufficiently distinguished them." Lamb reprinted the first only once, in 1797, in the second edition of Coleridge's *Poems*, the remaining three again in his *Works* in 1818. I have followed in the body of this volume the text of these later appearances, the original form of the sonnets being relegated to the notes.

Page 3.   *As when a child on some long winter's night.*
Some mystery attaches to the authorship of this sonnet. On December 1, 1794, Coleridge wrote to the editor of the *Morning Chronicle* saying that he proposed to send a series of sonnets (" as it is the fashion to call them ") addressed to eminent contemporaries ; and he enclosed one to Mr. Erskine. The editor, with almost Chinese politeness, inserted beneath the sonnet this note : " Our elegant Correspondent will highly gratify every reader of taste by the continuance of his exquisitely beautiful productions." The series continued with Burke, Priestley, Lafayette, Kosciusko, Chatham, Bowles, and, on December 29, 1794, Mrs. Siddons—the sonnet here printed—all signed S. T. C.

But the next appearance of the sonnet was as an effusion by Lamb in Coleridge's *Poems on Various Subjects*, 1796, signed C. L. ; and its next in the *Poems*, 1797, among Lamb's contributions. In 1803, however, we find it in Coleridge's *Poems*, third edition, with no reference to Lamb whatever. This probably means that Lamb and Coleridge had written it together, that Coleridge's original share had been the greater, and that Lamb and he had come to an arrangement by which Coleridge was to be considered the sole author ; for Lamb did not reprint it in 1818 with his other early verse. Writing in 1796 to Coleridge concerning his treatment of other of Lamb's sonnets, Lamb says : " That to Mrs. Siddons, now, you were welcome to improve, if it had been worth it ; but I say unto you again, Coleridge, spare my ewe lambs." Such a distinction drawn between the sonnet to Mrs. Siddons and the others supports the belief that Lamb had not for it a wholly parental feeling.

POEMS

ON

VARIOUS SUBJECTS,

BY

S. T. COLERIDGE,

LATE OF JESUS COLLEGE, CAMBRIDGE.

Felix curarum, cui non Heliconia cordi
Serta, nec imbelles Parnaffi e vertice laurus!
Sed viget ingenium, et magnos accinctus in ufus
Fert animus quafcunque vices.—— Nos triftia vitæ
Solamur cantu.
      Stat. Silv. Lib. iv. 4.

LONDON:

PRINTED FOR G. G. AND J. ROBINSONS, AND

J. COTTLE, BOOKSELLER, BRISTOL.

1796.

NOTES

This was not the only occasion on which Lamb and Coleridge wrote a sonnet in partnership. Writing to Southey in December, 1794, Coleridge says: "Of the following sonnet, the four *last* lines were written by Lamb, a man of uncommon genius. ...."

SONNET

O gentle look, that didst my soul beguile,
Why hast thou left me? Still in some fond dream
Revisit my sad heart, auspicious smile!
As falls on closing flowers the lunar beam;
What time in sickly mood, at parting day
I lay me down and think of happier years;
Of joys, that glimmered in Hope's twilight ray,
Then left me darkling in a vale of tears.
O pleasant days of Hope—for ever flown!
Could I recall one!—But that thought is vain,
Availeth not Persuasion's sweetest tone
To lure the fleet-winged travellers back again:
Anon, they haste to everlasting night,
Nor can a giant's arm arrest them in their flight.

Subsequently Coleridge rewrote the final couplet.

The same letter to Southey informs us that the sonnet to Mrs. Siddons was not Lamb's earliest poem, although it stands first in his poetical works; for Coleridge remarks: "Have you seen his [Lamb's] divine sonnet, 'O! I could laugh to hear the winter wind'?" (see page 4).

A phrase in the ninth line of the present sonnet has an Elizabethan parentage, as have so many of Lamb's phrases. Romeo says to Juliet, "Romeo and Juliet," Act III., Scene 5, line 59: "Dry sorrow drinks our blood."

Lamb printed the sonnet to Mrs. Siddons twice—in 1796 and 1797.

Page 3. *Was it some sweet device of Faery.*

This sonnet passed through various vicissitudes. Lamb had sent it to Coleridge for his *Poems on Various Subjects* in 1796, and Coleridge proceeded to re-model it more in accordance with his own views. The following version, representing his modifications, was the one that found its way into print as Lamb's:—

Was it some sweet device of faery land
That mock'd my steps with many a lonely glade,
And fancied wand'rings with a fair-hair'd maid?
Have these things been? Or did the wizard wand
Of Merlin wave, impregning vacant air,
And kindle up the vision of a smile
In those blue eyes, that seem'd to speak the while
Such tender things, as might enforce Despair
To drop the murth'ring knife, and let go by
His fell resolve? Ah me! the lonely glade
Still courts the footsteps of the fair-hair'd maid,
Among whose locks the west-winds love to sigh:
But I forlorn do wander, reckless where,
And mid my wand'rings find no ANNA there!
                                             C. L.

Lamb naturally protested when the result came under his eyes. "I love my own feelings: they are dear to memory," he says in a letter in 1796, "though they now and then wake a sigh or a tear. 'Thinking on divers things foredone,' I charge you, Coleridge, spare my ewe lambs." Later, when Coleridge's second edition was in preparation, Lamb wrote again (January 10, 1797): "I need not repeat my wishes to have my little sonnets printed *verbatim* my last way. In particular, I fear lest you should prefer printing my first sonnet [this one] as you have done more than once, 'Did the wand of Merlin wave?' It looks so like *Mr.* Merlin, the ingenious successor of the immortal Merlin, now living in good health and spirits, and flourishing in magical reputation in Oxford Street." The phrase "more than once" in the foregoing passage needs explanation. It refers to the little pamphlet of sonnets, entitled *Sonnets from Various Authors*, which Coleridge issued privately in 1796, and of which only one copy is now known to exist—that preserved in the Dyce and Forster collection at South Kensington. The little pamphlet contains twenty-eight sonnets in all, of which three are by Bowles, four by Southey, four by Charles Lloyd, four by Coleridge, four by Lamb, and others by various writers: all of which were chosen for their suitability to be bound up with the sonnets of Bowles. Lamb's sonnets were: "We were two pretty babes" (see page 8), "Was it some sweet device" (printed with Coleridge's alterations), "When last I roved" (see page 7), and "O! I could laugh" (see page 4).

The present sonnet belongs to the series of four love sonnets which is completed by the one that follows, "Methinks, how dainty sweet it were," and those on page 7 beginning, "When last I roved" and "A timid grace." Anna is believed to have been Ann Simmons, who lived at Blenheims, a group of cottages near Blakesware, the house where Mrs. Field, Lamb's grandmother, was housekeeper. Mrs. Field died in 1792, after which time Lamb's long visits to that part of the country probably ceased. He was then seventeen. Nothing is known of Lamb's attachment beyond these sonnets, the fact that when he lost his reason for a short time in 1795-1796 he attributed the cause to some person unmentioned who is conjectured to have been Anna, and the occasional references in the *Elia* essays to "Alice W——" and to his old passion for her (see "Dream Children" in particular, Vol. II., page 100). The death of Mrs. Lamb in September, 1796, and the duty of caring for and nursing his sister Mary, which then devolved upon Charles, put an end to any dreams of private happiness that he may have been indulging; and his little romance was over. How deep his passion was we are not likely ever to know; but Lamb thenceforward made very light of it, except in the pensive recollections in the essays twenty-five years later. In November, 1796, when sending Coleridge poems for his second edition, he says: "Do not entitle any of my *things* Love Sonnets, as I told you to call 'em; 'twill only make me look little in my own eyes; for it is a passion of which I retain nothing. . . . Thank God, the folly has left me for ever. Not even a review of my love verses renews one wayward wish in me. . . ." Again, in November, 1796, in another letter to Coleridge, about his poems in the 1797 edition, Lamb says: "Oh, my friend! I think sometimes, could I recall the days that are past, which among them should I choose?

not those 'merrier days,' not the 'pleasant days of hope,' not 'those wanderings with a fair-hair'd maid,' which I have so often and so feelingly regretted, but the days, Coleridge, of a *mother's* fondness for her *school-boy.*" We have no evidence that Lamb ever thought again of marrying until many years after when he asked Miss Kelly to be his wife (see note on page 302).

In the 1797 edition of the Poems "device," in the first line of this sonnet, was "Delight." Lamb probably took "impregning," line 5, from Milton:—

> And in her ears the sound
> Yet rung of his persuasive words, impregn'd
> With reason.
> *Paradise Lost*, IX., 736-738.

Lamb printed this sonnet three times—in 1796, 1797 and 1818.

Page 4. *Methinks how dainty sweet it were, reclin'd.*

When this sonnet was printed by Coleridge in 1796 the sestet was made to run thus :—

> But ah! sweet scenes of fancied bliss, adieu!
> On rose-leaf beds amid your faery bowers
> I all too long have lost the dreamy hours!
> Beseems it now the sterner Muse to woo,
> If haply she her golden meed impart,
> To realise the vision of the heart.

Lamb remonstrated: "I had rather have seen what I wrote myself, though they bear no comparison with your exquisite lines—

> "On rose-leaf'd beds, amid your faery bowers, etc.

I love my sonnets because they are the reflected images of my own feelings at different times." When the sonnet was reprinted by Lamb in 1797, in the second edition of Coleridge's *Poems*, it ran as now printed (from the *Works*, 1818), except that, in line 7, "all a summer's day" was "the long summer day;" "losing the time," in line 8, was "cheating the time;" and "friend forgot," line 11, was "friends forgot." In 1796 and 1797 "out-stretching," in line 2, was "o'er-shadowing."

One of Lamb's many Miltonic recollections is to be noticed in lines 6, 7 and 8:—

> To sport with Amaryllis in the shade,
> Or with the tangles of Neæra's hair.
> *Lycidas*, 68, 69.

"Dainty sweet," in the first line, is probably from Fletcher's song in "Nice Valour": "Nothing so dainty-sweet as melancholy."

This sonnet was printed by Lamb three times—in 1796, 1797 and 1798.

Page 4. *O! I could laugh to hear the midnight wind.*

This sonnet, written probably at Margate, was entitled, in 1796, "Written at Midnight, by the Seaside, after a Voyage." The fourth line then ran:—

> Ev'n as a child! For now to my rapt mind

the sixth line :—

> And her dread visions give a rude delight!

and the last three lines :—

> And almost wish'd it were no crime to die!
> How Reason reel'd! What gloomy transports rose!
> Till the rude dashings rock'd them to repose.

The couplet was Coleridge's, and Lamb protested (June 10, 1796), describing them as good lines, but adding that they "must spoil the whole with me who know it is only a fiction of yours and that the rude dashings did in fact not rock me to repose."

When reprinted in 1797, line 6 ran :—

> And her rude visions give a dread delight,

and the final couplet was omitted, asterisks standing instead. Lamb may have borrowed "unbonnetted" from "Lear"—"Unbonneted he runs," Act III., Scene 1, line 14. The present sonnet was probably the earliest of Lamb's printed poems. In the *Elia* essay "The Old Margate Hoy" (Vol. II., page 177) Lamb states that the first time he saw the sea was on a visit to Margate as a boy, by water—probably the voyage that suggested this sonnet. See the letter from Coleridge to Southey, quoted above, when Lamb was nineteen.

Lamb printed the sonnet three times—in 1796, 1797 and 1818.

Page 5. LLOYD'S "POEMS ON THE DEATH OF PRISCILLA FARMER."

Charles Lloyd (1775-1839), the son of Charles Lloyd, of Birmingham (a cultured and philanthropical Quaker banker), joined Coleridge at Bristol late in 1796 as his private pupil, and moved with the family to Nether Stowey. Priscilla Farmer was Lloyd's maternal grandmother, to whom he was much attached, and on her death he composed the sonnets that form this costly quarto, published for Lloyd by Coleridge's friend, Joseph Cottle, of Bristol, in the winter of 1796.

Page 5. *The Grandame.*

Lamb sent these lines in their first state to Coleridge in June, 1796, at which time they were, I conjecture, part of a long blank-verse poem which he was then meditating, and of which "Childhood," "Fancy Employed on Divine Subjects," and "The Sabbath Bells" (see pages 8 and 9) were probably other portions. The poem was never finished. On June 13, 1796, he writes to Coleridge :—

"Of the blank verses I spoke of, the following lines are the only tolerably complete ones I have writ out of not more than one hundred and fifty. That I get on so slowly you may fairly impute to want of practice in composition, when I declare to you that (the few verses which you have seen excepted) I have not writ fifty lines since I left school. It may not be amiss to remark that my grandmother (on whom the verses are written) lived housekeeper in a family the fifty or sixty last years of her life—that she was a woman of exemplary piety and goodness—and for many years before her death was terribly afflicted

POEMS

ON

The Death

OF

PRISCILLA FARMER,

BY HER GRANDSON

CHARLES LLOYD.

DEATH! THOU HAST VISITED THAT PLEASANT PLACE,
WHERE IN THIS HARD WORLD I HAVE HAPPIEST BEEN.

BOWLES.

BRISTOL:

PRINTED BY N. BIGGS,
And Sold by JAMES PHILLIPS, George-Yard, Lombard-Street, LONDON.

1796.

with a cancer in her breast, which she bore with true Christian patience. You may think that I have not kept enough apart the ideas of her heavenly and her earthly master; but recollect I have designedly given into her own way of feeling; and if she had a failing 'twas that she respected her master's family too much, not reverenced her Maker too little. The lines begin imperfectly, as I may probably connect 'em if I finish at all: and if I do, Biggs shall print 'em (in a more economical way than you yours), for, Sonnets and all, they won't make a thousand lines as I propose completing 'em, and the substance must be wire-drawn."

When Charles Lloyd joined Coleridge later in the year, and was preparing his *Poems in Memory of Priscilla Farmer*, Coleridge obtained Lamb's permission for "The Grandam" to be included with them. The lines were introduced by Lloyd in these words: "The following beautiful fragment was written by CHARLES LAMB, of the India-House. —Its subject being the same with that of my Poems, I was solicitous to have it printed with them: and I am indebted to a Friend of the Author's for the permission."

The poem differed then very slightly from its present form: line 1 had "hill top green;" line 2 "humble roof;" line 3 "In nought distinguished." These were the principal alterations. There were also changes of pronoun made by Coleridge or Lloyd. When the book was sent to Lamb he remarked (in December, 1796) on "the odd coincidence of two young men, in one age, carolling their grandmothers. . . . I cannot but smile to see my Granny so gayly deck'd forth [the book was expensively produced by Lloyd], tho', I think, whoever altered 'thy' praises to 'her' praises—'thy' honoured memory to 'her' honoured memory [lines 27 and 28], did wrong—they best express my feelings. There is a pensive state of recollection, in which the mind is disposed to apostrophise the departed objects of its attachment; and, breaking loose from grammatical precision, changes from the 1st to the 3rd, and from the 3rd to the 1st person, just as the random fancy or feeling directs."

Mrs. Mary Field, *née* Bruton, Lamb's maternal grandmother, was housekeeper at Blakesware house, near Widford, the seat of the Plumer family for very many years, during the latter part of her life being left in sole charge, for William Plumer had moved to his other seat, Gilston, a few miles distant (see "Blakesmoor in H——shire," and notes, Vol. II., page 153). Lamb and his brother and sister visited their grandmother at Blakesware as though in her own house. Mrs. Field died of cancer in the breast, July 31, 1792, aged seventy-nine, and was buried in Widford churchyard.

Approached from the east the churchyard seems to be anything but on the hilltop, for one descends to it; but it stands on a ridge, and seen from the north, or, as at the old Blakesware house, from the west, it appears to crown an eminence. The present spire, though slender and tapering, is not that which Lamb used to see. Mrs. Field's plain stone, whose legibility was not long since threatened by overhanging branches, has now been saved from danger and may still be read. It merely records the name "Mary Feild" (a mistake of the stone-cutter) and the bare dates.

This poem was printed by Lamb three times—in 1796 (in Lloyd's book), in 1797 (with Coleridge) and in 1818.

Page 7. COLERIDGE'S "POEMS," 1797.

Coleridge's *Poems on Various Subjects*, 1796, went into a second edition in 1797 under the title, *Poems by S. T. Coleridge, Second Edition, to which are now added Poems by Charles Lamb and Charles Lloyd*. Coleridge invented a motto from Groscollius for the title-page, bearing upon this poetical partnership: "Duplex nobis vinculum, et amicitiæ et similium junctarumque Camœnarum; quod utinam neque mors solvat, neque temporis longinquitas!" "Double is the bond which binds us—friendship, and a kindred taste in poetry. Would that neither death nor lapse of time could dissolve it!"

Lamb's contributions were thus referred to by Coleridge in the Preface: "There were inserted in my former Edition, a few Sonnets of my Friend and old School-fellow, CHARLES LAMB. He has now communicated to me a complete Collection of all his Poems; quæ qui non prorsus amet, illum omnes et Virtutes et Veneres odore." (Which things, whoever is not unreservedly in love with, is detested by all the Virtues and the Graces.) Lamb's poems came last in the book, an arrangement insisted upon in a letter from him to Coleridge in November, 1796:—

"Do you publish with Lloyd, or without him? In either case my little portion may come last; and after the fashion of orders to a country correspondent, I will give directions how I should like to have 'em done. The title-page to stand thus:—

POEMS
BY
CHARLES LAMB, OF THE INDIA HOUSE

Under this leaf the following motto, which, for want of room, I put over leaf, I desire you to insert, whether you like it or no. May not a gentleman choose what arms, mottoes, or armorial bearings the Herald will give him leave, without consulting his republican friend, who might advise none? May not a publican put up the sign of the *Saracen's Head*, even though his undiscerning neighbour should prefer, as more genteel, the *Cat and Gridiron*?

"[MOTTO]
"This Beauty, in the blossom of my Youth,
When my first fire knew no adulterate incense,
Nor I no way to flatter but my fondness,
In the best language my true tongue could tell me,
And all the broken sighs my sick heart lend me,
I sued and served. Long did I love this Lady.

"Massinger." [1]

---

[1] [This is from Massinger's "A Very Woman," Act IV., Scene 3. The passage enshrining it was included by Lamb in his *Specimens* in 1808.]

POEMS,

BY

S. T. COLERIDGE,

SECOND EDITION.

TO WHICH ARE NOW ADDED

POEMS

By *CHARLES LAMB,*

AND

CHARLES LLOYD.

Duplex nobis vinculum, et amicitiæ et similium junctarumque Camœnarum; quod utinam neque mors solvat, neque temporis longinquitas!
Groscoll. Epist. ad Car. Utenhov. et Ptol. Lux.Tast.

PRINTED BY N. BIGGS,
FOR J. COTTLE, BRISTOL, AND MESSRS.
ROBINSONS, LONDON.
1797.

NOTES

"THE DEDICATION

THE FEW FOLLOWING POEMS,
CREATURES OF THE FANCY AND THE FEELING
IN LIFE'S MORE *VACANT* HOURS,
PRODUCED, FOR THE MOST PART, BY
LOVE IN IDLENESS;
ARE,
WITH ALL A BROTHER'S FONDNESS,
INSCRIBED TO
MARY ANN LAMB,
THE AUTHOR'S BEST FRIEND AND SISTER"

The dedication was printed as Lamb wished, in the form I have followed above, and the book appeared. Lamb's poems were these—the page after each signifying the place where it may be found in the present volume:—

SONNETS	Page	FRAGMENTS	Page
* Was it some sweet device	3	Childhood	8
* Methinks how dainty	4	The Grandame	5
When last I roved	7	The Sabbath Bells	9
A timid grace	7	Fancy Employed on Divine Subjects	9
* O! I could laugh	4	The Tomb of Douglas	9
If from my lips	8	To Charles Lloyd (*In the Supplement*)	11
We were two pretty	8	A Vision of Repentance	12
* As when a child	3		

Of these only the sonnet "As when a child" and "The Tomb of Douglas" were not reprinted by Lamb. Those with asterisks had been included in Coleridge's 1796 volume.

Page 7. *When last I roved these winding wood-walks green.*

This was sent to Coleridge on June 1, 1796, in a letter containing also the sonnets, "The Lord of Life," page 14; "A timid grace," page 7; and "We were two pretty babes," page 8. It was written, said Lamb, "on revisiting a spot, where the scene was laid of my 1st sonnet"—"Was it some sweet device," page 3 (see also note on page 278).

Lamb printed this sonnet twice—in 1797 and 1818.

Page 7. *A timid grace sits trembling in her eye.*

This, the last of the four love sonnets (see note on page 278), seems to be a survival of a discarded effort, for Lamb tells Coleridge, in the letter referred to in the preceding note, that it "retains a few lines from a sonnet of mine, which you once remarked had no 'body of thought' in it." In 1797 the seventh line ran, "faith, and meek quietness."

Lamb printed this sonnet twice—in 1797 and 1818.

Page 8. *If from my lips some angry accents fell.*

Lamb sent this sonnet, which is addressed to his sister, to Coleridge in May, 1796. " The Sonnet I send you has small merit as poetry but you will be curious to read it when I tell you it was written in my prison-house [an asylum] in one of my lucid Intervals." It is dated 1795 in Coleridge's *Poems*.

Lamb printed the sonnet twice—in 1797 and 1818.

Page 8. *We were two pretty babes, the youngest she.*

First printed in the *Monthly Magazine*, July, 1796, where line 5 ran, " we two had wept t' have been;" line 6, "with show of seeming good ;" and line 11, " Hiding in deepest shades." "The next and last [wrote Lamb in the letter to Coleridge referred to in the notes on page 283] I value most of all. 'Twas composed close upon the heels of the last ['A timid grace,' page 7], in that very wood I had in mind when I wrote 'Methinks how dainty sweet' [page 4]." It is dated 1795 in Coleridge's *Poems*. In the same letter Lamb adds :—

" Since writing it, I have found in a poem by Hamilton of Bangour [William Hamilton, 1704-1754, the Scotch poet, of Bangour, Linlithgowshire] these 2 lines to happiness :—

" Nun sober and devout, where art thou fled,
To hide in shades thy meek contented head.

Lines eminently beautiful, but I do not remember having re'd 'em previously, for the credit of my 10th and 11th lines. Parnell [Thomas Parnell, 1679-1718] has 2 lines (which probably suggested the *above*) to Contentment

" Whither ah whither art Thou fled,
To hide thy meek contented head.

"Cowley's exquisite Elegy on the death of his friend Harvey suggested the phrase of 'we two'

" Was there a tree [about] that did not know
The love betwixt us two ?———"

When Coleridge printed the sonnet in the pamphlet described on page 278, he appended to the eleventh line the following note :—

Innocence, which, while we possess it, is playful as a babe, becomes AWFUL when it has departed from us. This is the sentiment of the line—a fine sentiment and nobly expressed.

Lamb printed this sonnet twice—in 1797 and 1818. The 1797 form differed somewhat in punctuation.

Page 8. *Childhood.*

See note to "The Grandame," page 280. The "turf-clad slope" in line 4 was probably at Blakesware. It is difficult to re-create the scene, for the new house stands a quarter of a mile west of the old one, the site of which is hidden by grass and trees. Where once were gardens is now meadow land.

Lamb printed this poem twice—in 1797 and 1818.

NOTES

Page 9. *The Sabbath Bells.*

Lamb printed this poem twice—in 1797 and 1818. Church bells seem always to have had charms for him (see the reference in *John Woodvil*, page 174, and in Susan Yates' story in *Mrs. Leicester's School*, Vol. III.). See note to "The Grandame."

Page 9. *Fancy Employed on Divine Subjects.*

In the letter of December 5, 1796, quoted below and on page 290, Lamb remarks concerning this poem: "I beg you to alter the words 'pain and want,' to 'pain and grief' (line 10), this last being a more familiar and ear-satisfying combination. Do it, I beg of you." But the alteration either was not made, or was cancelled later. The reference in lines 6, 7 and 8 is to Revelation xxii. 1, 2. See note to "The Grandame."

Lamb printed this poem twice—in 1797 and 1818.

Page 9. *The Tomb of Douglas.*

The play on which this poem was founded was the tragedy of "Douglas" by John Home (1722-1808), produced in 1756. Young Norval, or Douglas, the hero, after killing the false Glenalvon, is slain by his stepfather, Lord Randolph, unknowing who he is. On hearing of Norval's death his mother, Lady Randolph, throws herself from a precipice. In the letter to Coleridge of December 5, 1796, quoted above, Lamb also copied out "The Tomb of Douglas," prefixing these remarks:—

"I would also wish to retain the following if only to perpetuate the memory of so exquisite a pleasure as I have often received at the performance of the tragedy of Douglas, when Mrs. Siddons has been the Lady Randolph. . . . To understand the following, if you are not acquainted with the play, you should know that on the death of Douglas his mother threw herself down a rock; and that at that time Scotland was busy in repelling the Danes."

This was how "The Tomb of Douglas" ended in the original draft:—

> Bending, warrior, o'er thy grave,
> Young light of Scotland early spent!
> Thy country thee shall long lament,
> *Douglas "Beautiful and Brave"!*
> And oft to after times shall tell,
> *In Hope's sweet prime my Hero fell.*
>
> Thane or Lordling, think no scorn
> Of the poor and lowly-born.
> In brake obscure or lonely dell
> The simple flowret prospers well:
> The *gentler* virtues cottage-bred
> Thrive best beneath the humble shed.
>
> Low-born Hinds, opprest, obscure,
> Ye who patiently endure
> To bend the knee and bow the head,
> And thankful eat *another's bread*,
> Well may ye mourn your best friend dead.
> Till Life with Grief together end:
> He would have been the poor man's friend.

> Bending, warrior, o'er thy grave,
> Young light of Scotland early spent!
> Thy country thee shall long lament,
> Douglas, *Beautiful and Brave!*
> And oft to after times shall tell,
> *In Life's young prime my Hero fell.*

Coleridge told Southey that Lamb during his derangement at the end of 1795 and beginning of 1796 believed himself at one time to be Young Norval.

Lamb printed this poem, which differs curiously in character from all his other poetical works, only once—in 1797.

Page 11. *To Charles Lloyd.*

Lamb copied these lines in a letter to Coleridge on January 18, 1797, remarking :—

"You have learned by this time, with surprise, no doubt, that Lloyd is with me in town. The emotions I felt on his coming so unlooked for are not ill expressed in what follows, and what if you do not object to them as too personal, and to the world obscure, or otherwise wanting in worth I should wish to make a part of our little volume."

It must be remembered, in reading the poem, that Lamb was still in the shadow of the tragedy in which he lost his mother, and, for a while, his sister, and which had ruined his home. For other lines to Charles Lloyd see page 19.

This poem was printed by Lamb twice—in 1797 and 1818.

Page 12. *A Vision of Repentance.*

Writing to Coleridge on June 13, 1797, Lamb says of this Spenserian exercise :—

"You speak slightingly. Surely the longer stanzas were pretty tolerable; at least there was one good line in it [line 5]:

> "Thick-shaded trees, with dark green leaf rich clad.

To adopt your own expression, I call this a 'rich' line, a fine full line. And some others I thought even beautiful."

When the poem was printed in 1797 it was placed in the Supplement as one of the poems which the author regarded as of inferior merit.

In the first stanza on page 13 we have a Shakespearian echo: the stag in "As You Like It" stood at the extremest verge of a still brook augmenting it with his tears (see Act II., Scene 1, line 42).

Lamb printed the poem twice—in 1797 and 1818.

Page 14. POEMS WRITTEN IN THE YEARS 1795-1798 AND NOT REPRINTED BY LAMB FROM PERIODICALS.

Page 14. *Sonnet : The Lord of Life shakes off his drowsihed.*

The *Monthly Magazine*, December, 1797. Signed Charles Lamb.

Lamb sent the first draft of this sonnet to Coleridge in 1796, saying that it was composed "during a walk down into Hertfordshire early in last Summer." "The last line," he adds, "is a copy of Bowles's 'to the green hamlet in the peaceful plain.' Your ears are not so very fastidious—many people would not like words so prosaic and familiar in a sonnet as Islington and Hertfordshire." We must take Lamb's word for it; but Mr. W. J. Craig has found for the last line a nearer parallel than Bowles'. In William Vallans' "Tale of the Two Swannes" (1590), which is quoted in Leland's *Itinerary*, Hearne's edition, is the phrase: "The fruitful fields of pleasant Hertfordshire." Lamb quotes his own line in the *Elia* essay "My Relations."

The sonnet copied in Lamb's letter to Coleridge differed so considerably from that in the *Monthly Magazine* that it is given here:—

> The lord of light shakes off his drowsyhed.
>   Fresh from his couch up springs the lusty sun,
>   And girds himself his mighty race to run.
> Meantime, by truant love of rambling led,
>   I turn my back on thy detested walls.
> Proud City, and thy sons I leave behind,
> A selfish, sordid, money-getting kind,
>   Who shut their ears when holy Freedom calls.
> I pass not thee so lightly, humble spire,
>   Thou mindest me of many a pleasure gone,
>   Of merriest days, of love and Islington,
> Kindling anew the flames of past desire;
>   And I shall muse on thee, slow journeying on,
> To the green plains of pleasant Hertfordshire.

Line 1. *The Lord of Life shakes off his drowsihed.* Of the last word Lamb wrote: "Drowsyhed I have met with I think in Spencer. 'Tis an old thing, but it rhymes with led, and rhyming covers a multitude of licences." Lamb was probably remembering the line:—

> The royal virgin shook off drowsy-hed.
> *The Faerie Queen*, I., Canto 2, Stanza 7.

This sonnet is perhaps the only occasion on which Lamb, even in play, wrote anything against his beloved city.

It may be noted here that this was Lamb's last contribution to the *Monthly Magazine*, which had printed in the preceding number, November, 1797, Coleridge's satirical sonnets, signed Nehemiah Higginbottom, in which Lamb and Lloyd were ridiculed, and which had perhaps some bearing on the coolness that for a while was to subsist between Coleridge and Lamb (see *Charles Lamb and the Lloyds*, 1898, pages 44-47).

Page 14. *To the Poet Cowper.*
The *Monthly Magazine*, December, 1796. Signed C. Lamb.
Lamb wrote these lines certainly as early as July, 1796, for he sends them to Coleridge on the 6th of that month, adding:—

"I fear you will not accord entirely with my sentiments of Cowper, as *exprest* above, (perhaps scarcely just), but the poor Gentleman has just recovered from his Lunacies, and that begets pity, and pity love, and love admiration, and then it goes hard with People but they lie!"

Lamb admired Cowper greatly in those days—particularly his "Crazy Kate" ("Task," Book I., 534-556). "I have been reading 'The Task' with fresh delight," he says on December 5, 1796. "I am glad you love Cowper. I could forgive a man for not enjoying Milton, but I would not call that man my friend, who should be offended with the 'divine chit-chat of Cowper.'" And again a little later, "I do so love him."

In the verses as sent to Coleridge were certain differences. In line 4 "the worthy head" was "thy worthy head;" in line 13 "enticed forth" was "elicited;" and line 15 ran :—

<blockquote>Of Sidney and his peerless Maiden Queen.</blockquote>

Page 15. *Lines addressed, from London, to Sara and S. T. C. at Bristol, in the Summer of* 1796.

The *Monthly Magazine,* January, 1797. Signed Charles Lamb.

Lamb sent the lines in their original state to Coleridge in the letter of July 5, 1796, immediately before the words "*Let us prose,*" at the head of that document as it is now preserved. By the kindness of Mrs. Alfred Morrison I have been permitted to copy the letter afresh and thus to recapture certain allusions to this poem. The original verses having been cut off, they cannot be given; but at the end of the letter, which was finished two days after it was begun, Lamb added certain revised readings. Thus :—

" Let 'em run thus :—

<blockquote>
" I may not come a pilgrim, to the Banks
Of *Avon, lucid stream*, to taste the wave [1]
Which Shakespeare drank, our British Helicon ;
Or with mine eye, &c., &c.,
To muse in tears, on that mysterious youth,[2] &c.
</blockquote>

Then the last paragraph alter thus :—

<blockquote>
" Complaint, begone, begone, unkind reproof,[3]
Take up, my song, take up a merrier strain,
For yet again, and lo ! from Avon's vales,
Another Minstrel cometh ! Youth *endeared*,
God and Good Angels, &c., as before."
</blockquote>

"[1] 'Inspiring wave' was too commonplace." "[2] Better than 'drop a tear.'"

"[3] Better refer to my own 'complaint' solely than half to that and half to Chatterton, as in your copy, which creates confusion—' ominous fears,' &c."

Although Lamb appended the reference to Coleridge's "Monody on Chatterton" to the words "another minstrel," that description applies to Coleridge. Chatterton is the mysterious youth of line 16. Thomas Chatterton (1752-1770) was baptised at St. Mary Redcliffe, Bristol; he was the nephew of the sexton ; he brooded for many hours a day in the church ; he copied his antique writing from the parchment in its muniment room ; one of his later dreams was to be able to build a new spire ; and a cenotaph to his memory was erected by public subscription in 1840 near the north-east angle of the churchyard. Chatterton went to London on April 24, 1770, aged seventeen and a half, and died there by his own hand on August 25 of the same year.

The Clifton Avon and the Warwickshire Avon, it has been pointed out, are different streams, a fact of which Lamb was unaware. In the *Monthly Magazine* version of the lines the confusion, however, was removed. Another error was also there remedied—the slip by which the Avon was called the British Helicon. As Mr. Dykes Campbell remarked in his letter to *The Athenæum* on this subject (September 8, 1894), Byron—by a curious chance also when writing of Bristol—made the same mistake. He spoke in *English Bards and Scotch Reviewers* of the "lines forty thousand, cantos twenty-five" of Cottle's epic, "fresh fish from Helicon". In the annotation to the 1816 edition he exclaimed: "'Fresh fish from Helicon!'—Helicon is a mountain, and not a fish-pond. It should have been 'Hippocrene'."

The poem originated in an invitation to Lamb from the Coleridges at Bristol, which he hoped to be able to accept; but to his request for the necessary holiday from the India House came refusal. Lamb went to Nether Stowey, however, in the following summer and met Wordsworth there.

Lamb at one time wished these lines to be included among his poems in the second edition of Coleridge's *Poems*, 1797. Writing on January 18, 1797, Lamb says: "I shall be sorry if that volume comes out, as it necessarily must do, unless you print those very school boyish verses I sent you on not getting leave to come down to Bristol last Summer." At the end of the letter he adds: "Yet I should feel ashamed that to you I wrote nothing better. But they are too personal, almost trifling and obscure withal."

In the fourth line is a Biblical echo (see Matt. xx., 12).

Page 16. *Sonnet to a Friend.*
The *Monthly Magazine*, October, 1797. Signed Charles Lamb.

Lamb sent this sonnet to Coleridge on January 2, 1797, remarking: "If the fraternal sentiment conveyed in the following lines will atone for the total want of any thing like merit or genius in it, I desire you will print it next after my other Sonnet to my Sister." The other sonnet was, "If from my lips some peevish accents fall," printed with Coleridge's *Poems* in 1797 (see page 8), concerning which book Lamb was writing in the above letter. Coleridge apparently decided against the present sonnet, for it was not printed in that book. After copying the sonnet (dated 1797, which shows it to have been fresh from his pen), Lamb adds: "If you think the epithet 'sooth' quaint, substitute 'blest messenger.' I hope you are printing my sonnets as I directed you, and particularly the 2nd, 'Methinks,' &c. [see page 4 and note], with my last added 6 lines at ye end; and all of 'em as I last made 'em."

Writing to Coleridge again a week later concerning the present poem Lamb said:—

"I am aware of the unpoetical caste of the 6 last lines of my last sonnet, and think myself unwarranted in smuggling so tame a thing into the book; only the sentiments of those 6 lines are thoroughly congenial to me in my state of mind, and I wish to accumulate perpetuating tokens of my affection to poor Mary."

It has to be borne in mind that only three months had elapsed since the death of Mrs. Lamb, and Mary was still in confinement.

NOTES

Page 16. *To a Young Lady.* Signed C. L.

Monthly Magazine, March, 1797, afterwards copied into the *Poetical Register* for 1803, signed C. L. in both cases. We know these to be Lamb's from a letter to Coleridge of December 5, 1796, now in Mrs. Alfred Morrison's collection, of which only a portion has been published, wherein he copied the poem, adding: "Coleridge, the above has some few decent lines [in] it, and in the paucity of my portion of your volume may as well be inserted." The verses in the letter, entitled "To a Young Lady, going out to India," differ in many places from those printed in the *Monthly Magazine,* the most interesting change being in the third couplet, which originally ran :—

> To her loved native land, and early home,
> In search of peace thro' "stranger climes to roam." [1]

The identity of the young lady is not now known.

Page 17. *Living without God in the World.*
The *Annual Anthology,* Vol. I., 1799.

Vol. I. of the *Annual Anthology,* edited by Southey for Joseph Cottle, was issued in September, 1799; and that was, I believe, this poem's first appearance as a whole. Early in 1799, however, Charles Lloyd had issued a pamphlet entitled *Lines suggested by the Fast appointed on Wednesday, February* 27, 1799 (Birmingham, 1799), in which, in a note, he quotes a passage from Lamb's poem, beginning, "some braver spirits" (line 23), and ending, "prey on carcases" (line 36), with the prefatory remark : "I am happy in the opportunity afforded me of introducing the following striking extract from some lines, intended as a satire on the Godwinian jargon."

Writing to Southey concerning this poem Lamb says :—

"I can have no objection to you printing 'Mystery of God' [afterwards called 'Living without God in the World'] with my name, and all due acknowledgments for the honour and favour of the communication: indeed, 'tis a poem that can dishonour no name. Now, that is in the true strain of modern modesto vanitas."

Line 44. *"Loose about."*

> Nor do I name of men the common rout,
> That wand'ring loose about,
> Grow up and perish, as the summer-fly.
> *Samson Agonistes,* 674-676.

Line 48. *"Like an armed man."* I cannot find exactly these words. The Bible has several phrases that are closely akin to it, and it was probably, I think, one of these that Lamb was remembering.

Page 19. "BLANK VERSE." BY CHARLES LLOYD AND CHARLES LAMB. 1798.

Charles Lloyd (see note on page 280) left Coleridge early in 1797, and was in the winter 1797-1798 living in London, sharing lodg-

---

[1] Bowles.

BLANK VERSE,

BY

CHARLES LLOYD

AND

CHARLES LAMB.

LONDON:
PRINTED BY T. BENSLEY;
FOR JOHN AND ARTHUR ARCH, N° 23, GRACE-
CHURCH STREET.

1798.

NOTES 291

ings with James White (Lamb's friend and the author of *Original Letters, etc., of Sir John Falstaff*, 1796). It was then that the joint production of this volume was entered upon. Of the seven poems contributed by Lamb only "The Old Familiar Faces" (shorn of one stanza) and the lines "Composed at Midnight" were reprinted by him: on account, it may be assumed, of his wish not to revive in his sister, who would naturally read all that he published, any painful recollections. Not that she refused in after years to speak of her mother, but Lamb was, I think, sensitive for her and for himself and the family too. As a matter of fact the circumstances of Mrs. Lamb's death were known only to a very few of the Lambs' friends until after Charles' death. When *Blank Verse* was originally published, in 1798, it must be remembered that Mary Lamb was still living apart, nor was it known that she would ever be herself again.

It was this little volume which gave Gillray an opportunity for introducing Lamb and Lloyd into his cartoon "The New Morality," published in the first number of *The Anti-Jacobin Review and Magazine* (which succeeded Canning's *Anti-Jacobin*), August 1, 1798. Canning's lines, "The New Morality," had been published in *The Anti-Jacobin* on July 9, 1798, containing the couplets :—

> And ye five other wandering Bards that move
> In sweet accord of harmony and love,
> C——dge and S——th—y, L——d, and L——be and Co.,
> Tune all your mystic harps to praise Lepaux !

In the picture Gillray introduced "Coleridge" as a donkey offering a volume of "Dactylics," and Southey as another donkey, flourishing a volume of "Saphics." Behind them, seated side by side, poring over a manuscript entitled "Blank Verse, by Toad and Frog," are a toad and frog which the Key states to be Lloyd and Lamb. It was in reference to this picture that Godwin, on first meeting Lamb, asked him, " Pray, Mr. Lamb, are you toad or frog ?"

Page 19. *To Charles Lloyd.*

The *Monthly Magazine*, October, 1797. Signed.

Lamb sent these lines to Coleridge in September, 1797, remarking : "The following I wrote when I had returned from Charles Lloyd, leaving him behind at Burton, with Southey. To understand some of it you must remember that at that time he was very much perplexed in mind." Lloyd throughout his life was given to religious speculations which now and then disturbed his mind to an alarming extent, affecting him not unlike the gloomy forebodings and fears that beset Cowper. On this particular occasion he was in difficulty also as to his engagement with Sophia Pemberton, with whom he was meditating elopement and a Scotch marriage. This poem, when printed in the *Monthly Magazine*, differed slightly from its present form. Lloyd's name was omitted from the body of the poem, and it was entitled "To a Friend ;" line 4, "well-known voice," was "pleasant voice ;" line 8, "again," was "once more ;" line 15, "tender thou my heart," was "soften thou my heart." The punctuation also differed.

Page 19. *Written on the Day of my Aunt's Funeral.*
"This afternoon," Lamb wrote to Coleridge on February 13, 1797, "I attend the funeral of my poor old aunt, who died on Thursday. I own I am thankful that the good creature has ended all her days of suffering and infirmity. She was to me the 'cherisher of infancy.' ..." Lamb's Aunt Hetty was his father's sister. Her real name was Sarah Lamb. All that we know of her is found in this poem, in the *Letters*, in the passages in "Christ's Hospital Five and Thirty Years Ago," and "My Relations" (see pages 13 and 70 of Vol. II.); in the story of "The Witch Aunt," in *Mrs. Leicester's School* (Vol. III.), and in a reference in one of Mary Lamb's letters to Sarah Stoddart (see Hazlitt's *Mary and Charles Lamb,* 1874, page 24), where, writing of her aunt and her mother,—"the best creatures in the world,"—she speaks of Miss Lamb as being "as unlike a gentlewoman as you can possibly imagine a good old woman to be;" contrasting her with Mrs. Lamb, "a perfect gentlewoman." The description in "The Witch Aunt" bears out Mary Lamb's letter.

After the tragedy of September, 1796, Aunt Hetty was taken into the house of a rich relative. This lady, however, seems to have been of too selfish and jealous a disposition (see Lamb's letter to Coleridge, December 9, 1796) to exert any real effort to make her guest comfortable or happy. Hence Aunt Hetty returned to her nephew.

"My poor old aunt [Lamb wrote to Coleridge on January 5, 1797], whom you have seen, the kindest, goodest creature to me when I was at school; who used to toddle there to bring me fag [food], when I, school-boy like, only despised her for it, and used to be ashamed to see her come and sit herself down on the old coal-hole steps as you went into the old grammar-school, opend her apron, and bring out her bason with some nice thing she had caused to be saved for me—the good old creature is now lying on her death bed. ... She says, poor thing, she is glad to come home to die with me. I was always her favourite."

Line 24. *One parent yet is left.* John Lamb, who is described as he was in his prime, as Lovel, in the *Elia* essay on "The Old Benchers of the Inner Temple" (see Vol. II., page 87), died in 1799.

Line 27. *A semblance most forlorn of what he was.* Lamb uses this line as a quotation, slightly altered, in his account of Lovel.

Page 20. *Written a Year after the Events.*
Lamb sent this poem to Coleridge in September, 1797, entitling it "Written a Twelvemonth after the Events," and adding, " Friday next, Coleridge, is the day on which my Mother died." Mrs. Lamb's death, at the hands of her daughter in a moment of frenzy, occurred on September 22, 1796. Lamb added that he wrote the poem at the office with "unusual celerity." "I expect you to like it better than anything of mine; Lloyd does, and I do myself." The version sent to Coleridge differs only in minor and unimportant points from that in *Blank Verse.*

The second paragraph of the poem is very similar to a passage which Lamb had written in a letter to Coleridge on November 14, 1796:—

"Oh, my friend! I think sometimes, could I recall the days that are past, which among them should I choose? not those 'merrier days,' not the 'pleasant days of hope,' not 'those wanderings with a fair-hair'd maid,' which I have so often and so feelingly regretted, but the days, Coleridge, of a *mother's* fondness for her *school-boy*. What would I give to call her back to earth for *one* day!—on my knees to ask her pardon for all those little asperities of temper which, from time to time, have given her gentle spirit pain!—and the day, my friend, I trust, will come. There will be 'time enough' for kind offices of love, if 'Heaven's eternal year' be ours. Hereafter, her meek spirit shall not reproach me."

In the last paragraph of the poem is a hint of "The Old Familiar Faces," that was to follow it in the course of a few months.

Line 34. *Wanderings with a fair-hair'd maid.* In the version sent to Coleridge these words were between quotation marks, the quotation being from Lamb's own sonnet, "Was it some sweet device," on page 3, line 11.

Lines 52, 53. *And one, above the rest.* Probably Coleridge is meant.

Page 22. *Written soon after the Preceding Poem.*

The poem is addressed to Lamb's mother. Lamb seems to have sent a copy to Southey, although the letter containing it has not been preserved, for we find Southey passing it on to his friend C. W. W. Wynn on November 29, 1797, with a commendation: "I know that our tastes differ much in poetry, and yet I think you must like these lines by Charles Lamb."

The following passage in *Rosamund Gray*, which Lamb was writing at this time, is curiously like these poems in tone. It occurs in one of the letters from Elinor Clare to her friend—letters in which Lamb seems to describe sometimes his own feelings, and sometimes those of his sister, on their great sorrow:—

"Maria! shall not the meeting of blessed spirits, think you, be something like this?—I think, I could even now behold my mother without dread—I would ask pardon of her for all my past omissions of duty, for all the little asperities in my temper, which have so often grieved her gentle spirit when living. Maria! I think she would not turn away from me.

"Oftentimes a feeling, more vivid than memory, brings her before me—I see her sit in her old elbow chair—her arms folded upon her lap—a tear upon her cheek, that seems to upbraid her unkind daughter for some inattention—I wipe it away and kiss her honored lips.

"Maria! when I have been fancying all this, Allan will come in, with his poor eyes red with weeping, and taking me by the hand, destroy the vision in a moment.

"I am prating to you, my sweet cousin, but it is the prattle of the heart, which Maria loves. Besides, whom have I to talk to of these things but you—you have been my counsellor in times past, my companion, and sweet familiar friend. Bear with me a little—I mourn the 'cherishers of my infancy.'"

Page 22. *Written on Christmas Day,* 1797.

Mary Lamb, to whom these lines were addressed, after seeming to be on the road to perfect recovery, had suddenly had a relapse necessitating a return to confinement from the lodging in which her brother had placed her.

Page 23. *The Old Familiar Faces.*

This, the best known of all Lamb's poems, was written in January, 1798, following, it is suggested, upon a fit of resentment against Charles Lloyd. Writing to Coleridge in that month Lamb tells of that little difference, adding, "but he has forgiven me." Mr. J. A. Rutter, who through Canon Ainger enunciated this theory, thinks that Lloyd may be the "friend" of the fourth stanza, and Coleridge the "friend" of the sixth. The old—but untenable—supposition was that it was Coleridge whom Lamb had left abruptly. On the other hand it might possibly have been James White, especially as he was of a resolutely high-spirited disposition.

In its 1798 form the poem began with this stanza :—

> Where are they gone, the old familiar faces?
> I had a mother, but she died, and left me,
> Died prematurely in a day of horrors—
> All, all are gone, the old familiar faces.

And the last stanza began with the word "For," and italicised the words

> *And some are taken from me.*

I am inclined to think from this italicisation that it was Mary Lamb's new seizure that was the real impulse of the poem.

The poem was dated January, 1798. Lamb printed it twice—in 1798 and 1818.

Page 24. *Composed at Midnight.*

In its original form, in *Blank Verse*, 1798, the fiftieth line had "The measures of his judgments are not fixed," and the fifty-fourth "So" for "Such." On the appearance of Lamb's *Works*, 1818, Leigh Hunt printed in *The Examiner* (February 7 and 8, 1819) the passage beginning with line 32, entitling it "A HINT to the GREATER CRIMINALS who are so fond of declaiming against the crimes of the poor and uneducated, and in favour of the torments of prisons and prisonships in this world, and worse in the next. Such a one, says the poet,

> 'on his couch
> Lolling, &c.'"

JOHN WOODVIL

A TRAGEDY.

BY

C. LAMB.

TO WHICH ARE ADDED,

FRAGMENTS OF BURTON,

THE AUTHOR OF

THE ANATOMY OF MELANCHOLY.

London:

PRINTED BY T. PLUMMER, SEETHING-LANE;
FOR G. AND J. ROBINSON, PATERNOSTER-ROW.

1802.

NOTES

Page 26. POEMS AT THE END OF "JOHN WOODVIL," 1802.

The volume containing *John Woodvil*, 1802, which is placed in the present edition among Lamb's plays, on page 131, included also the "Fragments of Burton" (see Vol. I., page 31 and notes) and two lyrics.

Page 26. *Helen.*

Lamb sent this poem to Coleridge on August 26, 1800, remarking :—
" How do you like this little epigram ? It is not my writing, nor had I any finger in it. If you concur with me in thinking it very elegant and very original, I shall be tempted to name the author to you. I will just hint that it is almost or quite a first attempt."

The author was, of course, Mary Lamb. In his *Elia* essay "Blakesmoor in H——shire" (see Vol. II., page 408), on its first appearance in the *London Magazine*, September, 1824, Lamb quoted the poem, stating that "Bridget took the hint" of her "pretty whimsical lines" from a portrait of one of the Plumers' ancestors. The portrait was the cool pastoral beauty with a lamb, and it was partly to make fun of her brother's passion for the picture that Mary wrote the lines.

The poem was reprinted in the *Works*, 1818.

Page 27. *Ballad from the German.*

This poem was written for Coleridge's translation of "The Piccolimini," the first part of Schiller's "Wallenstein," in 1800—Coleridge supplying a prose paraphrase (for Lamb knew no German) for the purpose. The original is Thekla's song in Act II., Scene 6 :—

> Der Eichwald brauset, die Wolken ziehn,
> Das Mägdlein wandelt an Ufers Grün,
> Es bricht sich die Welle mit Macht, mit Macht,
> Und sie singt hinaus in die finstre Nacht,
>   Das Auge von Weinen getrübet :
> Das Herz ist gestorben, die Welt ist leer,
> Und weiter giebt sie dem Wunsche nichts mehr.
> Du Heilige, rufe dein Kind zurück,
> Ich habe genossen das irdische Glück,
>   Ich habe gelebt und geliebet.

Coleridge, in his edition of Schiller's play, introduced Lamb's version (probably touched up by himself) with these words : "I cannot but add here an imitation of this song, with which the author of *The Tale of Rosamund Gray and Blind Margaret* has favoured me, and which appears to me to have caught the happiest manner of our old ballads."

The version then followed ; thus :—

THEKLA'S SONG

> The clouds are black'ning, the storms threat'ning,
>   The cavern doth mutter, the greenwood moan ;
> Billows are breaking, the damsel's heart aching,
>   Thus in the dark night she singeth alone,
>   Her eye upward roving :
> The world is empty, the heart is dead surely,
>   In this world plainly all seemeth amiss ;
> To thy heaven, Holy One, take home thy little one,
>   I have partaken of all earth's bliss,
>   Both living and loving.

Lamb, it will be seen on comparing this version with that on page 27, made several changes; or put back, as he had done in the case of his early sonnets, his original text in place of Coleridge's imposed improvements.

Coleridge's own translation of Thekla's song, which was printed alone in later editions of the play, ran thus:—

> The cloud doth gather, the greenwood roar,
> The damsel paces along the shore;
> The billows they tumble with might, with might;
> And she flings out her voice to the darksome night;
> Her bosom is swelling with sorrow;
> The world it is empty, the heart will die,
> There's nothing to wish for beneath the sky:
> Thou Holy One, call thy child away!
> I've lived and loved, and that was to-day—
> Make ready my grave-clothes to-morrow.

Barry Cornwall, in his memoir of Lamb, says: "Lamb used to boast that he supplied one line to his friend in the fourth scene [Act IV., Scene 1] of that tragedy, where the description of the Pagan deities occurs. In speaking of Saturn, he is figured as 'an old man melancholy'. 'That was my line,' Lamb would say, exultingly". The line did not reach print in this form.

Lamb printed his translation twice—in 1802 and 1818.

Page 27. *Hypochondriacus.*
Page 28. *A Ballad Noting the Difference of Rich and Poor.*

These two poems formed, in the *John Woodvil* volume, 1802, portions of the "Fragments of Burton," which will be found in Vol. I., page 31. Lamb afterwards took out these poems and printed them separately in the *Works*, 1818, in the form here given. Originally "Hypochondriacus" formed Extract III. of the "Fragments," under the title "A Conceipt of Diabolical Possession." The body of the verses differed very slightly from the present state; but at the end the prayer ran: "*Jesu Mariæ! libera nos ab his tentationibus, orat, implorat, R. B. Peccator*"—R. B. standing for Robert Burton, the anatomist of melancholy, the professed author of the poem.

In one of Lamb's Commonplace Books preserved in the Rowfant collection, which Mr. Godfrey Locker-Lampson has permitted me to examine, Lamb has copied these verses, attributing them without any qualification to the author of the *Anatomy*.

At the end of the last of the "Curious Fragments" in the 1802 volume came a few words, which Lamb never reprinted, introducing the "Ballad Noting the Difference of Rich and Poor." They run thus, following upon the sentence (see Vol. I., page 36), "*These follies are enough to give crying Heraclitus a fit of the spleene*":—

"The fruit, issue, *children,* of these my morning meditations, have been certain crude, impolite, incomposite, *hirsute,* (what shall I say?) *verses,* noting the difference of *rich* and *poor,* in the ways of a rich noble's palace and a poor workhouse.

"*Sequuntur.*

THE WORKS

OF

CHARLES LAMB.

IN TWO VOLUMES.

VOL. I.

LONDON:
PRINTED FOR C. AND J. OLLIER,
VERE-STREET, BOND-STREET.

1818.

NOTES

"THE ARGUMENT.

"*In a costly palace Youth meets respect:
In a wretched workhouse Age finds neglect*

"EVINCED THUS:

"In a costly palace Youth goes clad in gold;
In a wretched workhouse Age's limbs are cold:
There they sit, the old men, by a shivering fire,
Still close and closer cowering, warmth is their desire.

"In a costly palace, when the brave gallants dine,
They have store of good venison, with old Canary wine,
With singing and musick to heighten the cheer;
Coarse bits, with grudging, are the pauper's best fare.

"In a costly palace Youth is still carest,
By a train of attendants, which laugh at my young Lord's jeste;
In a wretched workhouse the contrary prevails,
Does Age begin to prattle? No man heark'neth to his tales.

"In a costly palace, if the child, with a pin,
Do but chance to prick a finger, strait the Doctor is call'd in;
In a wretched workhouse men are left to perish
For want of proper cordials, which their old age might cherish.

"In a costly palace Youth enjoys his lust;
In a wretched workhouse Age, in corners thrust,
Thinks upon the former days, when he was well to do,
Had children to stand by him, both friends and kinsmen too.

"In a costly palace Youth his temples hides
With a new devised peruke, that reaches to his sides;
In a wretched workhouse Age's crown is bare,
With a few thin locks just to fence out the cold air.

"In peace, as in war, 'tis our young gallants' pride,
To walk, each one i' the streets, with a rapier at his side,
That none to do them injury may have pretence;
Wretched Age, in poverty, must brook offence.

"THE CONSEQUENCE.

"Wanton Youth is oft times haught and swelling found,
When Age for very shame goes stooping to the ground.

"THE CONCLUSION—*Dura Paupertas!*"

By referring to page 28 the difference between this poem, in its original and revised forms, will be manifest. Writing to Coleridge on August 6, 1800, Lamb says: "If I could but stretch out the circumstances to twelve more verses, *i.e.*, if I had as much genius as the writer of that old song ['The Old and Young Courtier'] I think it would be excellent." And "in its feature of taking the extremes of two situations for just parallel, it resembles the old poetry exactly." "The Old and Young Courtier" may be found in the *Percy Reliques*. Lamb copied it into one of his Commonplace Books. In the first stanza on page 29 is a Shakespearian echo: "Age, in corners thrust," surely is derived from

And unregarded age in corners thrown.
"As You Like It," Act II., Scene 3, line 42.

Page 30. The "Works" of Charles Lamb, 1818.

This book, in two volumes, was published by C. & J. Ollier in 1818 : the first volume containing the dedication to Coleridge that is here printed on page 1, all of Lamb's poetry that he then wished to preserve, "John Woodvil," "The Witch," the "Fragments of Burton," "Rosamund Gray" and "Recollections of Christ's Hospital;" the second volume, dedicated to Martin Charles Burney in the sonnet on page 42, containing criticisms, essays and "Mr. H."

The scheme of the present volume, under which the plays are put at the end and the poems arranged in the chronological order of the publication of the books that first contained them, makes it impossible to keep together the poetical portion of Lamb's *Works;* since many of the poems there appearing were reprinted by him from previous volumes. In order, however, to present clearly to the reader Lamb's mature selection, in 1818, of the poetry by which he wished to be known, I have indicated in this volume the position in his *Works* of those poems that have already been printed on earlier pages.

Page 30. *Hester.*

Lamb sent this poem to Manning in March 1803—

"I send you some verses I have made on the death of a young Quaker you may have heard me speak of as being in love with for some years while I lived at Pentonville, though I had never spoken to her in my life. She died about a month since."

Hester Savory was the daughter of Joseph Savory, a goldsmith in the Strand. She was born in 1777 and was thus by two years Lamb's junior. She married, in July, 1802, Charles Stoke Dudley, a merchant, and she died in February of the following year, and was buried at Bunhill Fields. The portrait of Hester Savory, on the opposite page, is from an old miniature, now in the possession of Mrs. Braithwaite, of Kendal. Lamb was living in Pentonville from the end of 1796 until 1799.

Page 31. *Dialogue between a Mother and Child.* By Mary Lamb.

Charles Lamb, writing to Dorothy Wordsworth on June 2, 1804, in a letter that has not yet been published, says : "I send you two little copies of verses by Mary L—b." Then follow this "Dialogue" and the "Lady Blanch" verses on page 38. Lamb adds at the end: "I wish they may please you : we in these parts are not a little proud of them." Beyond the substitution of "glad" for "gay" in the eleventh line, and some changes of punctuation, the "Dialogue" was not altered.

Page 32. *A Farewell to Tobacco.*

First printed in *The Reflector*, No. IV., 1811.

Lamb had begun to think poetically of tobacco as early as 1803. Writing to Coleridge in April 13 of that year, he says :—

"What do you think of smoking? I want your sober, *average, noon opinion* of it. I generally am eating my dinner about the time I should determine it.

"Morning is a girl, and can't smoke—she's no evidence one way or

HESTER SAVORY

From the miniature in the possession of Mrs. Braithwaite of Kendal

the other; and Night is so [? evidently] *bought over*, that he can't be a very upright judge. May be the truth is, that *one* pipe is wholesome; *two* pipes toothsome; *three* pipes noisome; *four* pipes fulsome; *five* pipes quarrelsome; and that's the *sum* on't. But that is deciding rather upon rhyme than reason."

Writing to William and Dorothy Wordsworth on September 28, 1805, Lamb remarked regarding his literary plans :—

"Sometimes I think of a farce—but hitherto all schemes have gone off,—an idle brag or two of an evening vaporing out of a pipe, and going off in the morning—but now I have bid farewell to my 'Sweet Enemy' Tobacco, as you will see in my next page, I perhaps shall set soberly to work. Hang work!"

On the next page Lamb copied the "Farewell to Tobacco," adding :—

"I wish you may think this a handsome farewell to my 'Friendly Traitress.' Tobacco has been my evening comfort and my morning curse for these five years: and you know how difficult it is from refraining to pick one's lips even when it has become a habit. This Poem is the only one which I have finished since so long as when I wrote 'Hester Savory' [in March, 1803]. . . . The 'Tobacco,' being a little in the way of Withers (whom Southey so much likes), perhaps you will somehow convey it to him with my kind remembrances."

Mr. Bertram Dobell has a MS. copy of the poem, in Lamb's hand, inscribed thus: "To his *quondam* Brethren of the Pipe, Capt. B[urney], and J[ohn] R[ickman], Esq., the Author dedicates this his last Farewell to Tobacco." At the end is a rude drawing of a pipe broken—"My Emblem."

It is perhaps hardly needful to say that Lamb's farewell was not final. He did not give up smoking for many years. When asked (Talfourd's version of the story says by Dr. Parr) how he was able to emit such volumes of smoke, he replied, "I toiled after it, sir, as some men toil after virtue;" and Macready records having heard Lamb express the wish to draw his last breath through a pipe and exhale it in a pun. Talfourd says that in late life Lamb ceased to smoke except very occasionally. But the late Mrs. Coe, who knew Lamb at Widford when she was a child, told me that she remembered Lamb's black pipe and his devotion to it, about 1830.

In his character sketch of the late Elia (see Vol. II., page 153), written in 1822, Lamb describes the effect of tobacco upon himself. "He took it, he would say, as a solvent of speech. Marry—as the friendly vapour ascended, how his prattle would curl up sometimes with it! the ligaments, which tongue-tied him, were loosened, and the stammerer proceeded a statist!"

When printed in *The Reflector*, No. IV., 1811, the fourth couplet of the poem ran :—

(Still the phrase is wide an acre)
To take leave of thee, Tobacco,

a piece of loose rhyming that was greatly admired (for its licentiousness) by Leigh Hunt, *The Reflector's* editor. Hazlitt, including this poem with several others of Lamb's in his *Select British Poets*, 1824, remarked that it is "rarely surpassed in quaint wit."

Line 1. *The Babylonish curse.* See Genesis xi. 1 to 9.

Lines 43, 44. *Cerberus, Geryon . . . Ixion.* Cerberus, the many-headed dog, guarding the entrance to Hades. Geryon, the three-headed King of Hesperia. Ixion, the lover of Hera, whom Jupiter transformed to a cloud.

Lines 77, 78. *Stinking'st of the stinking kind . . .* An adaptation of the couplet—

> Offspring of a heavenly kind,
> Frost of the mouth and thaw of the mind,

from *The Invocation to Silence*, by Richard Flecknoe, which Lamb afterwards used as the motto for his *Elia* essay "A Quaker's Meeting."

Line 133. *Katherine of Spain.* Referring to Katharine of Arragon, who after being divorced by Henry VIII. adhered to the title of queen.

Last line. *An unconquered Canaanite.* The reference is to the Israelites' fruitless attempts to drive the Canaanites out of their borders (see Josh. xvii. and Jud. i.).

Page 35. *To T. L. H.*

First printed in *The Examiner*, January 1, 1815.

The lines are to Thornton Leigh Hunt, Leigh Hunt's little boy, who was born in 1810, and, during his father's imprisonment for a libel on the Regent from February, 1813, to February, 1815, was much in the Surrey gaol. Lamb, who was among Hunt's constant visitors, probably first saw him there. Lamb mentions him again in his *Elia* essay "Witches and other Night Fears" (see Vol. II., page 68, and see also note to the "Letter to Southey," Vol. I., pages 483, 484). Thornton Leigh Hunt became a journalist, and held an important post on the *Daily Telegraph*. He died in 1873.

When printed in Leigh Hunt's *Examiner*, signed C. L., the poem had these prefatory words by the editor:—

> The following piece perhaps we had some personal reasons for not admitting, but we found more for the contrary; and could not resist the pleasure of contemplating together the author and the object of his address,—to one of whom the Editor is owing for some of the lightest hours of his captivity, and to the other for a main part of its continual solace.

Lines 31, 32. *Birds shall sing . . .* Adapted from the couplet—

> The shepherd swains shall dance and sing
> For thy delight each May morning,

in Marlowe's "Passionate Shepherd to his Love."

Page 36. *Salome.* By Mary Lamb.

Hone quoted this poem in his *Year Book*, 1831, with Charles Lamb's name attached in mistake.

Page 38. *Lines Suggested by a Picture of Two Females by Lionardo da Vinci.* By Mary Lamb.

This was the second poem which Lamb sent to Dorothy Wordsworth

MODESTY AND VANITY

After the picture by Leonardo da Vinci

in the letter of June 2, 1804 (quoted on page 298). There it was entitled "Suggested by a Print of 2 Females, after Lionardo da Vinci, called Prudence and Beauty, which hangs up in our room." This print, the usual title of which is "Modesty and Vanity," is reproduced on the opposite page. In the *Elia* essay "Old China" (Vol. II., page 249) Bridget Elia recalls its purchase:—

"When you came home with twenty apologies for laying out a less number of shillings upon that print after Lionardo, which we christened the 'Lady Blanch;' when you looked at the purchase, and thought of the money—and thought of the money, and looked again at the picture—was there no pleasure in being a poor man?"

Page 38. *Lines on the Same Picture being Removed to make Place for a Portrait of a Lady by Titian.* By Mary Lamb.

Writing to Dorothy Wordsworth on June 14, 1805, Lamb says: "You had her [Mary's] Lines about the 'Lady Blanch.' You have not had some which she wrote upon a copy of a girl from Titian, which I had hung up where that print of Blanch and the Abbess (as she beautifully interpreted two female figures from L. da Vinci) had hung, in our room. 'Tis light and pretty." It is not possible, I fear, now to identify the Titian.

Page 39. *Lines on the Celebrated Picture by Lionardo da Vinci, called The Virgin of the Rocks.*

This was the picture, one version of which hangs in the National Gallery, that was known to Lamb's friends as his "Beauty," and which led to the Scotchman's mistake in the *Elia* essay "Imperfect Sympathies" (see Vol. II., page 60). The engraving was given to Miss Lamb by Crabb Robinson on July 13, 1816 (see his *Diary*). A reproduction will be found opposite page 302.

Page 39. *On the Same.* By Mary Lamb.

In the letter to Dorothy Wordsworth of June 14, 1805, quoted just above, Lamb says: "I cannot resist transcribing three or four Lines which poor Mary [she was at this time away from home in one of her enforced absences] made upon a Picture (a Holy Family) which we saw at an Auction only one week before she left home. . . . They are sweet Lines, and upon a sweet Picture."

Mary Lamb wrote little verse besides the *Poetry for Children* (see Vol. III. of this edition). To the pieces that are printed in the present volume I would add the lines suggested by the death of Captain John Wordsworth, the poet's brother, in the foundering of the *Abergavenny* in February, 1805, when Coleridge was in Malta, which were sent by Mary Lamb to Dorothy Wordsworth, May 7, 1805:—

> Why is he wandering on the sea?
> Coleridge should now with Wordsworth be.
> By slow degrees he'd steal away
> Their woe, and gently bring a ray
> (So happily he'd time relief)
> Of comfort from their very grief.

He'd tell them that their brother dead,
When years have passed o'er their head,
Will be remember'd with such holy,
True, and perfect melancholy,
That ever this lost brother John
Will be their hearts' companion.
His voice they'll always hear, his face they'll always see;
There's nought in life so sweet as such a memory.

SONNETS

Page 40. *To Miss Kelly.*

Frances Maria Kelly (1790-1882)—or Fanny Kelly, as she was usually called—was Lamb's favourite actress of his middle and later life and a personal friend of himself and his sister: so close indeed that we have Miss Kelly's authority for the statement that Lamb seriously proposed marriage to her—in, I think, the Enfield days. See Lamb's criticisms of Miss Kelly's acting in Vol. I., pages 184 to 191, and notes; see also " Barbara S――," Vol. II., page 202, and note. Another sonnet addressed by Lamb to Miss Kelly will be found on page 55 of the present volume.

Page 40. *On the Sight of Swans in Kensington Garden.*

This is, I think, Lamb's only poem the inspiration of which was drawn from nature.

Lines 6 and 7. *Helen of Troy*, the daughter of Jupiter and Leda, sprang from a swan's egg.

Page 41. *The Family Name.*

John Lamb, Charles's father, came from Lincoln. A recollection of his boyhood there is given in the *Elia* essay " Poor Relations " (Vol. II., page 162). The " stream " seems completely to have ended with Charles Lamb and his sister Mary: at least, research has yielded no descendants. See the letter on page, 343, where a distant cousin is mentioned as living in 1872.

Crabb Robinson visited Goethe in the summer of 1829. The *Diary* has this entry: " I inquired whether he knew the name of Lamb. ' Oh, yes! Did he not write a pretty sonnet on his own name? ' Charles Lamb, though he always affected contempt for Goethe, yet was manifestly pleased that his name was known to him."

In the little memoir of Lamb prefixed by M. Amédée Pichot to a French edition of the *Tales from Shakespeare* in 1842 the following translation of this sonnet is given:—

MON NOM DE FAMILLE

Dis-moi, d'où nous viens-tu, nom pacifique et doux,
Nom transmis sans reproche? . . . A qui te devons-nous,
Nom qui meurs avec moi? mon glason de poëte
A l'aïeul de mon père obscurément s'arrête.
—Peut-être nous viens-tu d'un timide pasteur,
Doux comme ses agneaux, raillé pour sa douceur.
Mais peut-être qu'aussi, moins commune origine,
Nous viens-tu d'un héros, d'un pieux paladin,

THE VIRGIN OF THE ROCKS

By Leonardo da Vinci. 1452-1519

Qui croyant honorer ainsi l'Agneau divin,
Te prit en revenant des champs de Palestine.
Mais qu'importe après tout . . . qu'il soit illustre ou non,
Je ne ferai jamais une tache à ce nom.

Page 41. *To John Lamb, Esq.*

John Lamb, Charles's brother, was born in 1763 and was thus by twelve years his senior. At the time this poem appeared, in 1818, he was accountant of the South-Sea House. He died on October 26, 1821 (see the *Elia* essays "My Relations" and "Dream Children," Vol. II., pages 71 and 102).

Page 42. *To Martin Charles Burney, Esq.*

Lamb prefixed this sonnet to Vol. II. of his *Works*, 1818. In Vol. I. he had placed the dedication to Coleridge which we have already seen. Martin Charles Burney was the son of Rear-Admiral James Burney, Lamb's old friend, and nephew of Madame d'Arblay. He was a barrister by profession; dabbled a little in authorship; was very quaint in some of his ways and given to curiously intense and sudden enthusiasms; and was devoted to Mary Lamb and her brother. When these two were at work on their *Tales from Shakespear* Martin Burney would sit with them and attempt to write for children too. Lamb's letter of May 24, 1830, to Sarah Hazlitt has some amusing stories of his friend, at whom (like George Dyer) he could laugh as well as love. Lamb speaks of him on one occasion as on the top round of his ladder of friendship. Writing to Sarah Hazlitt Lamb says:—

"Martin Burney is as good, and as odd as ever. We had a dispute about the word 'heir,' which I contended was pronounced like 'air'; he said that might be in common parlance; or that we might so use it, speaking of the 'Heir at Law,' a comedy; but that in the law courts it was necessary to give it a full aspiration, and to say *hayer*; he thought it might even vitiate a cause, if a counsel pronounced it otherwise. In conclusion, he 'would consult Serjeant Wilde,' who gave it against him. Sometimes he falleth into the water; sometimes into the fire. He came down here, and insisted on reading Virgil's 'Eneid' all through with me (which he did), because a Counsel must know Latin. Another time he read out all the Gospel of St. John, because Biblical quotations are very emphatic in a Court of Justice. A third time, he would carve a fowl, which he did very ill-favouredly, because 'we did not know how indispensable it was for a barrister to do all those sort of things well? Those little things were of more consequence than we supposed.' So he goes on, harassing about the way to prosperity, and losing it. With a long head, but somewhat a wrong one —— harum-scarum. Why does not his guardian angel look to him? He deserves one: may be, he has tired him out."

Martin Burney, of whom another glimpse is caught in the *Elia* essay "Detached Thoughts on Books and Reading" (Vol. II., page 176), died in 1860. At Mary Lamb's funeral he was inconsolable.

Page 43. CHARLES LAMB'S "ALBUM VERSES," 1830.

The publication of this volume, in 1830, was due more to Lamb's kindness of heart than to any desire to come before the world again as a poet. But Edward Moxon, Lamb's young friend, was just starting his publishing business, with Samuel Rogers as a financial patron; and Lamb, who had long been his chief literary adviser, could not well refuse the request to help him with a new book. *Album Verses* became thus the first of the many notable books of poetry which Moxon was to issue between 1830 and 1858, the year of his death. Among them Tennyson's *Poems*, 1833 and 1842; *The Princess*, 1847; *In Memoriam*, 1850; *Maud*, 1855; and Browning's *Sordello*, 1840, and *Bells and Pomegranates*, 1843-1846.

The dedication of *Album Verses* tells the story of its being:—

"DEDICATION

"TO THE PUBLISHER

"DEAR MOXON,

"I do not know to whom a Dedication of these Trifles is more properly due than to yourself. You suggested the printing of them. You were desirous of exhibiting a specimen of the *manner* in which Publications, entrusted to your future care, would appear. With more propriety, perhaps, the 'Christmas,' or some other of your own simple, unpretending Compositions, might have served this purpose. But I forget—you have bid a long adieu to the Muses. I had on my hands sundry Copies of Verses written for *Albums*—

> "Those Books kept by modern young Ladies for show,
> Of which their plain grandmothers nothing did know—

or otherwise floating about in Periodicals; which you have chosen in this manner to embody. I feel little interest in their publication. They are simply—*Advertisement Verses.*

"It is not for me, nor you, to allude in public to the kindness of our honoured Friend, under whose auspices you are become a Bookseller. May that fine-minded Veteran in Verse enjoy life long enough to see his patronage justified! I venture to predict that your habits of industry, and your cheerful spirit, will carry you through the world.

"I am, Dear Moxon,
"Your Friend and sincere Well-wisher,
"CHARLES LAMB.

"ENFIELD, 1st June, 1830."

The reference to "Christmas" is to Moxon's poem of that name, published in 1829, and dedicated to Lamb.—The couplet concerning Albums is from one of Lamb's own pieces (see page 91).—The Veteran in Verse was Samuel Rogers, who, then sixty-seven, lived yet another twenty-five years. Moxon published the superb editions of his *Italy* and his *Poems* illustrated by Turner and Stothard.

Lamb's motives in issuing *Album Verses* were cruelly misunderstood by the *Literary Gazette* (edited by William Jerdan). In the number

ALBUM VERSES,

WITH A FEW OTHERS,

BY CHARLES LAMB.

LONDON:
EDWARD MOXON, 64, NEW BOND STREET.
1830.

for July 10, 1830, was printed a contemptuous review beginning with this passage :—

> If any thing could prevent our laughing at the present collection of absurdities, it would be a lamentable conviction of the blinding and engrossing nature of vanity. We could forgive the folly of the original composition, but cannot but marvel at the egotism which has preserved, and the conceit which has published.

Lamb himself probably was not much disturbed by Jerdan's venom, but Southey took it much to heart, and a few weeks later sent to *The Times* (of August 6, 1830) the following lines in praise of his friend :—

TO CHARLES LAMB

On the Reviewal of his *Album Verses* in the *Literary Gazette*

> Charles Lamb, to those who know thee justly dear,
> For rarest genius, and for sterling worth,
> Unchanging friendship, warmth of heart sincere,
> And wit that never gave an ill thought birth,
> Nor ever in its sport infix'd a sting ;
> To us who have admired and loved thee long,
> It is a proud as well as pleasant thing
> To hear thy good report, now borne along
> Upon the honest breath of public praise :
> We know that with the elder sons of song,
> In honouring whom thou hast delighted still,
> Thy name shall keep its course to after days.
> The empty pertness, and the vulgar wrong,
> The flippant folly, the malicious will,
> Which have assailed thee, now, or heretofore,
> Find, soon or late, their proper meed of shame ;
> The more thy triumph, and our pride the more,
> When witling critics to the world proclaim,
> In lead, their own dolt incapacity.
> Matter it is of mirthful memory
> To think, when thou wert early in the field,
> How doughtily small Jeffrey ran at thee
> A-tilt, and broke a bulrush on thy shield.
> And now, a veteran in the lists of fame,
> I ween, old Friend ! thou art not worse bested
> When with a maudlin eye and drunken aim,
> Dulness hath thrown *a jerdan* at thy head.
>   SOUTHEY.

This was, I think, Southey's first public utterance concerning Lamb since Lamb's famous open letter to him of October, 1823 (see Vol. I., page 226, and notes). Lamb wrote to Bernard Barton in the same month : " How noble . . . in R. S. to come forward for an old friend who had treated him so unworthily." For the critics, Lamb said in the same letter, he did not care, the " five hundred thousandth part of a half-farthing ; " and we can believe him. On page 109 will be found, however, an epigram on the *Literary Gazette*, which may have been written after the occurrence.

The design in the title-page of *Album Verses* is from a figure by Canova representing "Writing." A companion piece represented "Reading."

ALBUM VERSES

Page 43. *In the Album of a Clergyman's Lady.*
This lady was probably Mrs. Williams, of Fornham, in Suffolk, in whose house Lamb's adopted daughter, Emma Isola, lived as a governess in 1829-1830. The epitaph on page 60 and the acrostic on pages 94-95 were written for the same lady.

Page 43. *In the Autograph Book of Mrs. Sergeant W——.*
Mrs. Sergeant Wilde, *née* Wileman, was the first wife of Thomas Wilde, afterwards Lord Truro (1782-1855), for whose election at Newark in 1831 Lamb is said to have written facetious verses (see page 341). The Wildes were Lamb's neighbours at Enfield.

Page 44. *In the Album of Lucy Barton.*
These lines were sent by Lamb to Lucy Barton's father, Bernard Barton, the Quaker poet, in the letter of September 30, 1824. Lucy Barton, who afterwards became the wife of Edward FitzGerald, the translator of Omar Khayyam, lived until November 27, 1898. She retained her faculties almost to the end, and in 1892 kindly wrote out for me her memory of a visit paid with her father to the Lambs at Colebrook Row about 1825—a little reminiscence first printed in *Bernard Barton and His Friends*, 1893.

Page 44. *In the Album of Miss ——.*
This poem was first printed in *Blackwood's Magazine*, May, 1829, entitled "For a Young Lady's Album." The identity of the young lady is not now discoverable.

Page 45. *In the Album of a very young Lady.*
Josepha was a daughter of Mrs. Williams, of Fornham.
Lines 8, 9. *Bees at their sweet labour sing.* Milton writes, in *Il Penseroso*, line 143, of the bee:—

That at her flowry work doth sing.

Line 11. "*Deep unto Deep doth call.*" See Psalm xlii., 7.

Page 45. *In the Album of a French Teacher.*
First printed in *Blackwood's Magazine*, June, 1829, entitled "For the Album of Miss ——, French Teacher at Mrs. Gisborn's School, Enfield." In line 5, "choice collection" originally ran "curious volume" (see note to "The Christening," page 307).

Page 46. *In the Album of Miss Daubeny.*
Miss Daubeny was a schoolfellow of Emma Isola's, at Dulwich.

Page 47. *In the Album of Mrs. Jane Towers.*
Charles Clarke—in line 7—was Charles Cowden Clarke (1787-1877), a friend of the Lambs not only for his own sake, but for that of his wife, Mary Victoria Novello, whom he married in 1828 and who died as recently as 1898. Their *Recollections of Writers*, 1878, have many interesting reminiscences of Charles and Mary Lamb. Writing to Cowden Clarke on February 25, 1828, Lamb says:—

"I had a pleasant letter from your sister, greatly over acknowledging my poor sonnet. . . . Alas for sonnetting, 'tis as the nerves are; all the summer I was dawdling among green lanes, and verses came as thick as fancies. I am sunk winterly below prose and zero."

Mrs. Towers lived at Standerwick, in Somersetshire, and was fairly well known in her day as a writer of books for children, *The Children's Fireside*, etc.

Page 47. *In my own Album.*

This poem was first printed in *The Bijou*, 1828, edited by William Fraser, under the title "Verses for an Album."

Line 6. Have "*written strange defeatures*" there.

> Ægeon. O, grief hath changed me since you saw me last,
> And careful hours with time's deformed hand
> Have written strange defeatures in my face.
> "Comedy of Errors," Act V., Scene 1, lines 297-9.

MISCELLANEOUS

Page 48. *Angel Help.*

This poem was first printed in the *New Monthly Magazine*, 1827, with trifling differences, and the addition, at the end, of this couplet:—

> Virtuous Poor Ones, sleep, sleep on,
> And, waking, find your labours done.

I am sorry to be unable to trace the picture and reproduce it. I am afraid that the "Nonsense Verses" on page 109 represent an attempt to make fun of this beautiful poem.

Aders' house in Euston Square was hung with engravings principally of the German school (see the poem on page 85 addressed to him).

Page 49. *The Christening.*

These lines were first printed in *Blackwood's Magazine*, May, 1829, with certain slight changes: as, for example, in line 8, "Sacred water" for "Cleansing Water;" line 26, "easy conscience" for "quiet conscience;" and, last line, "All that my Sponsors kind renounced for me." In *Mary and Charles Lamb*, 1874, Mr. W. C. Hazlitt states

> Copies of these verses are still preserved at Enfield. They were written by Lamb to celebrate the christening of the son of Charles and Mary Gisburne May there, March 25, 1829; when Miss Lamb and her brother stood sponsors. Mr. Tuff, the historian of Enfield, writes: "I knew both the families (the Mays and Gisburnes). The head of the first was Dr. May, who conducted a first-class school for nearly half a century. He occupied the 'Old Palace,' hence it was called *The Palace School.* The Doctor had a brother, Charles May, who married Miss Gisburne, mistress of a ladies' school here for many years. The child of Charles and Mary May, for whom Lamb and his sister stood sponsors, was the issue of this marriage. There is nothing in the parish book, beyond the signatures of Charles May and his wife."

Page 49. *On an Infant Dying as soon as Born.*

This poem was first printed in *The Gem*, 1829. *The Gem* was then edited by Thomas Hood, whose child—his firstborn—it was that inspired the poem. Lamb sent the verses to Hood in May, 1827. Mr. W. C. Hazlitt prints in *The Lambs*, 1897, a note from Lamb to Hood written at the time of his little child's death:—

308 NOTES

"DEAREST HOOD,

"Your news has spoil'd us a merry meeting. Miss Kelly and we were coming, but your note elicited a flood of tears from Mary, and I saw she was not fit for a party. God bless you and the mother (or should be mother) of your sweet girl that should have been. I have won sexpence of Moxon by the *sex* of the dear gone one.—Yours most truly and hers, C. L."

This is, I think, in some ways Lamb's most remarkable poem.

Hood's own poem on the same event, printed in *Memorials of Thomas Hood*, by his daughter, 1860, has some of the grace and tenderness of the Greek Anthology :—

> Little eyes that scarce did see,
> Little lips that never smiled;
> Alas! my little dear dead child,
> Death is thy father, and not me,
> I but embraced thee, soon as he!

Page 51. *To Bernard Barton.*

These lines were sent to Barton in 1827, together with the picture, a reproduction of which in its frame is given on the opposite page by kind permission of Mrs. Edmund Lyons, to whom it was left by Mrs. Fitz-Gerald, Bernard Barton's daughter. On June 11, Lamb wrote again :—

"DEAR B. B.,

"One word more of the picture verses, and that for good and all; pray, with a neat pen alter one line—

> "His learning seems to lay small stress on—

to

> "His learning lays no mighty stress on,

to avoid the unseemly recurrence (ungrammatical also) of 'seems' in the next line, besides the nonsense of 'but' there, as it now stands. And I request you, as a personal favor to me, to erase the last line of all, which I should never have written from myself. The fact is, it was a silly joke of Hood's, who gave me the frame, (you judg'd rightly it was not its own,) with the remark that you would like it because it was b——d b——d [the last line in question was 'And broad brimmed, as the owner's calling'] and I lugg'd it in : but I shall be quite hurt if it stands, because tho' you and yours have too good sense to object to it, I would not have a sentence of mine seen that to any foolish ear might sound unrespectful to thee. Let it end at 'appalling.'"

Barton replied with the following poem, published in *New Year's Eve*, 1828, entitled "Fireside Quatrains, to Charles Lamb," afterwards revised. I quote the latest version.

> It is a mild and lovely winter night,
> The breeze without is scarcely heard to sigh;
> The crescent moon and stars of twinkling light
> Are shining calmly in a cloudless sky.

THE PICTURE SENT BY LAMB TO BERNARD BARTON

"A MOTHER TEACHING TO HER CHIT
SOME GOOD BOOK AND EXPLAINING IT"

Within the fire burns clearly : in its rays
  My old oak book-case wears a cheerful smile ;
  Its antique mouldings brighten'd by the blaze
  Might vie with any of more modern style.

That rural sketch—that scene in Norway's land
  Of rocks and pine trees by the torrent's foam—
That landscape traced by Gainsborough's youthful hand,
  Which shows how lovely is a peasant's home—

That Virgin and her Child, with those sweet boys—
  All of the fire-light own the genial gleam ;
And lovelier far than in day's light and noise
  At this still hour to me their beauties seem.

One picture more there is, which should not be
  Unhonoured or unsung, because it bears
In many a lonely hour my thoughts to thee,
  Heightening to fancy every charm it wears—

A quaint familiar group—a mother mild
  And young and fair, who fain would teach to read
That urchin, by her patience unbeguiled,
  The volume open on her lap to heed.

With fingers thrust into his ears he looks
  As much he wished the weary task were done ;
And more, far more, of pastime than of books
  Lurks in that arch, dark eye so full of fun.

Graver, or in the pouts (I know not well
  Which of the twain), his elder sister plies
Her needle so that it is hard to tell
  What the full meaning of her downcast eyes.

Dear Charles, if thou shouldst haply chance to know
  Where such a picture hung in days of yore,
Its highest worth, its deepest charm, to show
  I need not tax my rhymes or fancy more.

It is not womanhood in all its grace,
  And lovely childhood plead to me alone ;
Though these each stranger still delights to trace,
  And with congratulating smile to own ;

No—with all these my feelings fondly blend
  A hidden charm unborrowed from the eye ;
That wakes the memory of my absent friend,
  And chronicles the pleasant hours gone by.

Line 1. *Woodbridge.* Barton lived at Woodbridge, in Suffolk, where he was a clerk in the old Quaker bank of Dykes & Alexander.

Line 15. *Ann Knight.* Ann Knight was a Quaker lady, also resident at Woodbridge, who kept a small school there, and who had visited the Lambs in London and greatly charmed them.

Line 16. *Classic Mitford.* The Rev. John Mitford (1781-1859) was rector of Benhall, in Suffolk, near Woodbridge, and a friend of Barton's, through whom Lamb's acquaintance with him was carried on. Mitford edited many poets, among them Vincent Bourne. He was editor of the *Gentleman's Magazine* from 1834 to 1850.

Footnote. Carrington Bowles. Carington Bowles, 69, St. Paul's Churchyard, was the publisher of this print, which was the work of the elder Morland, and was engraved by Philip Dawe, father of Lamb's George Dawe (see the essay "Recollections of a late Royal Academician," Vol. I., page 331, and note).

Lines 26, 27, 28. *Obstinate . . . Bunyan.* It was not Obstinate, but Christian, who put his fingers in his ears (see the first pages of *The Pilgrim's Progress*). Lamb had the same slip of memory in his paper "On the Custom of Hissing at the Theatre" (Vol I., page 90).

Page 52. *The Young Catechist.*
Lamb sent this poem to Barton in a letter in 1827, wherein he tells the story of its inception:—

"An artist who painted me lately, had painted a Blackamoor praying, and not filling his canvas, stuff'd in his little girl aside of Blacky, gaping at him unmeaningly; and then didn't know what to call it. Now for a picture to be promoted to the Exhibition (Suffolk Street) as HISTORICAL, a subject is requisite. What does me. I but christen it the 'Young Catechist,' and furbishd it with Dialogue following, which dubb'd it an Historical Painting. Nothing to a friend at need. . . . When I'd done it the Artist (who had clapt in Miss merely as a fill-space) swore I exprest his full meaning, and the damsel bridled up into a Missionary's vanity. I like verses to explain Pictures: seldom Pictures to illustrate Poems."

The version sent to Barton is practically identical with that printed.

The artist was Henry Meyer (1782?-1847), one of the foundation members of the Society of British Artists in Suffolk Street, to the exhibition of which in 1826 he sent his portrait of Lamb, now in the India Office and engraved as the frontispiece to Vol. VI. of this edition. I cannot find any trace of the picture for which Lamb wrote this poem.

Page 53. *She is Going.*
I have not been able to discover of whom these lines were written.

Page 53. *To a Young Friend.*
The young friend was Emma Isola, who lived with the Lambs for some years as their adopted daughter. Emma Isola was the daughter of Charles Isola, Esquire Bedell of the University of Cambridge, who died in 1823, leaving her unprovided for. His father, and Emma Isola's grandfather, was Agostino Isola, who settled at Cambridge and taught Italian there. Wordsworth was among his pupils. He edited a collection of *Pieces selected from the Italian Poets*, 1778; also editions of *Gerusalemme Liberata* and *Orlando Furioso*, and a book of *Italian Dialogues*. Emma Isola is first mentioned by Lamb in an unpublished letter written to her aunt, Miss Humphreys, in January, 1821, arranging for the little girl's return to Trumpington Street, Cambridge, from London, where she had been spending her holidays with the Lambs. The Lambs had met her at Cambridge in the summer of 1820. The exact date of her adoption by the Lambs cannot be ascertained now. Emma Isola married Edward Moxon in 1833, and lived until 1891. This poem was written when she was at Fornham (see note on page 306).

NOTES 311

Page 54. *To the Same.*
Writing to Procter in January, 1829, Lamb calls Miss Isola "a silent brown girl," and in his letter of November, 1833, to Mr. and Mrs. Moxon, he says: "I hope you [Moxon] and Emma will have many a quarrel and many a make-up (and she is beautiful in reconciliation!) . . ." See the poem "To a Friend on His Marriage," page 75, for a further description of Emma Isola's character.

SONNETS

Page 54. *Harmony in Unlikeness.*
The two lovely damsels were Mary Lamb and Emma Isola.

Page 55. *Written at Cambridge.*
This sonnet was first printed in *The Examiner*, August 29 and 30, 1819, dated August 15. Part of the same thought is expressed in prose in the *Elia* essay "Oxford in the Vacation" (Vol. II., page 9), written, I fancy, on an impulse gained at Cambridge. Hazlitt in his essay "On the Conversation of Authors" in the *London Magazine* for September, 1820, referred to Lamb's visit to him some years before, and his want of ease among rural surroundings, adding: "But when we crossed the country to Oxford, then he spoke a little. He and the old collegers were hail-fellow-well-met; and in the quadrangle he 'walked gowned.'"

Lines 10 and 14. *Old Ramus . . . that stout Stagirite.* Petrus Ramus (1515-1572), the French logician, whose *Treatise on Logic* attacked the system of Aristotle, the Stagirite.

Page 55. *To a Celebrated Female Performer in the "Blind Boy."*
First printed in the *Morning Chronicle*, 1819. "The Blind Boy," "attributed," says Genest, "to Hewetson," was produced in 1807. It was revived from time to time. Miss Kelly used to play Edmond, the title *rôle*.

This sonnet was sent to Hone's *Table Book* in 1827 by Moxon with the title, "Sonnet to Miss Kelly on her Excellent performance of Blindness, in the revived Opera of 'Arthur and Emmeline'"—the suggestion being that Lamb had just written it. In the next number of the *Table Book* Lamb put the matter right in the following letter:—

"Miss Kelly"
"*To the Editor*"

"Dear Sir,—Somebody has fairly play'd a *hoax* on you (I suspect that pleasant rogue *M-x-n*[1]) in sending the Sonnet in my name, inserted in your last Number. True it is, that I must own to the Verses being mine, but not written on the occasion there pretended, for I have not yet had the pleasure of seeing the Lady in the part of Emmeline; and I have understood, that the force of her acting in it is rather in the expression of new-born sight, than of the previous want of it.—The lines were really written upon her performance in the 'Blind Boy,' and appeared in the Morning Chronicle some years back. I suppose, our

[1] "It was.—ED. [*Table Book*]."

facetious friend thought that they would serve again, like an old coat new turned.　　　　　　　　Yours (and his nevertheless)
"C. LAMB."

Page 55. *Work.*

First printed in *The Examiner*, June 20 and 21, 1819, under the title "Sonnet," when it ran thus :—

> Who first invented *work* and bound the free
> And holiday-rejoicing spirit down
> To the unremitting importunity
> Of business, in the green fields, and the town ;
> To plough, loom, anvil, spade,—and oh ! most sad !
> To this dry drudgery of the desk's dead wood ?
> Who but the Being unblest, alien from good,
> SABBATHLESS SATAN ! he who his unglad
> Task ever plies in rotatory burnings,
> That round and round incalculably reel—
> For wrath divine hath made him like a wheel—
> In that red realm from whence are no returnings ;
> Where, toiling and turmoiling, ever and aye
> His thoughts and he keep pensive worky-day.

Many years earlier we see the germ of this sonnet in Lamb's mind, as indeed we see the germ of so many ideas that were not fully expressed till later : Lamb always kept his thoughts at call. Writing to Wordsworth in September, 1805, he says (in a passage that has never before been printed exactly as it was written) :—

"Hang work ! I wish that all the year were holyday. I am sure that Indolence indefeasible Indolence is the true state of man, and business the invention of the Old Teazer who persuaded Adam's Master to give him an apron and set him a-houghing. Pen and Ink and Clerks, and desks, were the refinements of this old torturer a thousand years after. . . ."

Lamb probably was as fond of this sonnet as of anything he wrote in what might be called his second poetical period. He copied it into his first letter to Bernard Barton, in September, 1822, and he drew attention to it in his *Elia* essay "The Superannuated Man" (see Vol. II., page 428).

Page 56. *Leisure.*

First printed in the *London Magazine* for April, 1821, probably, I think, as a protest against the objection taken by some persons to the opinions expressed by Lamb in his essay on "New Year's Eve" in that magazine for January (see Vol. II., page 27, and note). Lamb had therein said, speaking of death :—

"I am not content to pass away 'like a weaver's shuttle.' Those metaphors solace me not, nor sweeten the unpalatable draught of mortality. I care not to be carried with the tide, that smoothly bears human life to eternity ; and reluct at the inevitable course of destiny. I am in love with this green earth ; the face of town and country ; the unspeakable rural solitudes, and the sweet security of streets. I would set up my tabernacle here. I am content to stand still at the age to which I am arrived ; I, and my friends. To be no younger, no richer, no handsomer. I do not want to be weaned by age; or drop, like mellow fruit, as they say, into the grave."

Such sentiments probably called forth some private as well as public protests; and it was, as I imagine, in a whimsical wish to emphasise the sincerity of his regard for life that Lamb reiterated that devotion in the emphatic words of "Leisure" in the April number. This sonnet was a special favourite with Edward FitzGerald.

It is sad to think that Lamb, when his leisure came, had too much of it. Writing to Barton on July 25, 1829, during one of his sister's illnesses, he says: "I bragg'd formerly that I could not have too much time. I have a surfeit. . . . I am a sanguinary murderer of time, that would kill him inchmeal just now."

Page 56. *To Samuel Rogers, Esq.*

Daniel Rogers, the poet's elder brother, died in 1829. In acknowledging Lamb's sonnet, Samuel Rogers wrote the following letter, which Lamb described to Barton (July 3, 1829) as the prettiest he ever read.

Many, many thanks. The verses are beautiful. I need not say with what feelings they were read. Pray accept the grateful acknowledgments of us all, and believe me when I say that nothing could have been a greater cordial to us in our affliction than such a testimony from such a quarter. He was—for none knew him so well—we were born within a year or two of each other—a man of a very high mind, and with less disguise than perhaps any that ever lived. Whatever he was, *that* we saw. He stood before his fellow beings (if I may be forgiven for saying so) almost as before his Maker: and God grant that we may all bear as severe an examination. He was an admirable scholar. His Dante and his Homer were as familiar to him as his Alphabets: and he had the tenderest heart. When a flock of turkies was stolen from his farm, the indignation of the poor far and wide was great and loud. To me he is the greatest loss, for we were nearly of an age; and there is now no human being alive in whose eyes I have always been young.

Yours most gratefully,
SAMUEL ROGERS.

Another sonnet to Rogers will be found on p. 90.

Page 57. *The Gipsy's Malison.*

First printed in *Blackwood's Magazine*, January, 1829; where, in the eighth line, "tend" was printed "tender," and in the thirteenth, "Beldam," "Sybil." Lamb had sent it to *The Gem*, but, as he told Procter in a letter on January 22, 1829: "The editors declined it, on the plea that it would *shock all mothers;* so they published the 'Widow' [Hood's parody of Lamb] instead. I am born out of time. I have no conjecture about what the present world calls delicacy. I thought *Rosamund Gray* was a pretty modest thing. Hessey assures me that the world would not bear it. I have lived to grow into an indecent character. When my sonnet was rejected, I exclaimed, 'Hang[1] the age, I will write for Antiquity!'"

In another letter to Procter Lamb tells the sonnet's history:—

"*January* 29, 1829.

"When Miss Ouldcroft (who is now Mrs. Beddam [Badams], and Bed-dam'd to her!) was at Enfield, which she was in summer-time, and owed her health to its suns and genial influences, she visited (with young

---
[1] Talfourd. Canon Ainger gives "Damn".

lady-like impertinence) a poor man's cottage that had a pretty baby (O the yearnling !), gave it fine caps and sweetmeats. On a day, broke into the parlour our two maids uproarious. 'O ma'am, who do you think Miss Ouldcroft (they pronounce it Holcroft) has been working a cap for?' 'A child,' answered Mary, in true Shandean female simplicity. ''Tis the man's child as was taken up for sheep-stealing.' Miss Ouldcroft was staggered, and would have cut the connection; but by main force I made her go and take her leave of her protégée. I thought, if she went no more, the Abactor or the Abactor's wife (*vide* Ainsworth) would suppose she had heard something; and I have delicacy for a sheep-stealer. The overseers actually overhauled a mutton pie at the baker's (his first, last, and only hope of mutton pie), which he never came to eat, and thence inferred his guilt. *Per occasionem cujus*, I framed the sonnet; observe its elaborate construction. I was four days about it. [Here came the sonnet.] Barry, study that sonnet. It is curiously and perversely elaborate. 'Tis a choking subject, and therefore the reader is directed to the structure of it. See you? and was this a fourteener to be rejected by a trumpery annual? forsooth, 'twould shock all mothers; and may all mothers, who would so be shocked, be damned! as if mothers were such sort of logicians as to infer the future hanging of *their* child from the theoretical hangibility (or capacity of being hanged, if the judge pleases) of every infant born with a neck on. Oh B. C.! my whole heart is faint, and my whole head is sick (how is it?) at this damned canting unmasculine age!"

Page 57. *To the Author of Poems, published under the name of Barry Cornwall.*

Printed in the *London Magazine*, September, 1820. Signed ****. The sonnet was on the same page as the lines to Sheridan Knowles (see page 58) which were signed C. Lamb: hence probably its four-star disguise.

Barry Cornwall was the pen name of Bryan Waller Procter (not Proctor, as Lamb too often spelled it), 1787-1874, whose impulse to write poetry came largely from Lamb himself. In his *Dramatic Scenes*, 1819, was the beginning of a blank-verse treatment or adaptation of Lamb's "Rosamund Gray" (see Vol. I., page 393). Procter addressed to Lamb some excellent lines "Over a Flask of Sherris," which were printed in the *London Magazine*, 1825, and again in *English Songs*, 1832. His *Marcian Colonna; an Italian Tale*, was published in 1820 and his *Sicilian Story* later in the same year. The "Dream" was printed in *Dramatic Scenes*. Lamb thought very highly of it (see the reference in the *Elia* essay "Witches, and other Night Fears," Vol. II., page 69, and note). Procter in his old age wrote a charming memoir of Lamb.

In the *London Magazine* version the second line ran :—

In riddling *Junius*, or in L——*e's* name,

L——e being Little, the name under which Moore had published his early Anacreontics. Later Lamb met and liked Moore.

Page 58. *To R. S. Knowles, Esq.*
First printed in the *London Magazine*, September, 1820. By a curious oversight the error in Knowles's initials was repeated in the *Album Verses*, 1830, Knowles's first name being, of course, James. James Sheridan Knowles (1784-1862) had been a doctor, a schoolmaster, an actor, and a travelling elocutionist, before he took seriously to writing for the stage. His first really successful play was "Virginius," written for Edmund Kean, transferred to Macready, and produced in 1820. His greatest triumph was "The Hunchback," 1832. Lamb, who met Knowles through William Hazlitt, of Wem, the essayist's father, wrote both the prologue and epilogue for Knowles's play "The Wife," 1833 (see page 129).

Page 58. *Quatrains to the Editor of the "Every-Day Book."*
First printed in the *London Magazine*, May, 1825, and copied by Hone into the *Every-Day Book* for July 9 of the same year. William Hone (see Vol. I., page 506), 1780-1842, was a bookseller, pamphleteer and antiquary, who, before he took to editing his *Every-Day Book* in 1825, had passed through a stormy career on account of his critical outspokenness and want of ordinary political caution ; and Lamb did by no means a fashionable thing when he commended Hone thus publicly. The *Every-Day Book*, begun in 1825, was, when published in 1826, dedicated by Hone to Charles Lamb and his sister. "Your daring to publish me your 'friend,' with your 'proper name' annexed," Hone wrote, "I shall never forget." In reprinting the "Quatrains" from the *London Magazine,* Hone appended a reply, consisting of "Quatorzains" by himself, addressed to Lamb. The second stanza ran thus :—

> I *am* "ingenuous ; " it is all I can
>   Pretend to ; it is all I wish to be ;
> Yet, through obliquity of sight in man,
>   From constant gaze on tortuosity,
> Few people understand me ; still, I am
>   Warmly affection'd to each human being ;
> Loving the right, for right's sake ; and, friend Lamb,
>   Trying to see things as they are ; hence, seeing
> Some "good in ev'ry thing" however bad,
>   Evil in many things that look most fair,
> And pondering on all : this may be madness, but it is my method ; and I dare
> Deductions from a strange diversity
>   Of things, not taught within a University.

In the next stanza was a delicate allusion to Lamb's own sonnet, "I was not train'd in Academic bowers" (see page 55).

Pages 59 to 61. ACROSTICS.
In his more leisurely years, at Islington and Enfield, Lamb wrote a great number of acrostics—many more probably than have been preserved—of which these, printed in *Album Verses*, are all that he cared to see in print. Probably he found his chief impulse in Emma Isola's schoolfellows and friends, who must have been very eager to

obtain in their albums a contribution from so distinguished a gentleman as Elia, and who passed on their requests through his adopted daughter. I have not been able to trace the identity of Caroline Maria Applebee (page 59), or Cecilia Catherine Lawton (page 60)—both were probably, like Miss Daubeny on page 46, Emma Isola's schoolfellows at Dulwich; but the lady who desired her epitaph (page 60) was the Mrs. Williams of pages 43 and 94, in whose house Emma Isola was governess. While there Emma was seriously ill, and Lamb travelled down to Fornham, in Suffolk, in 1830, to bring her home. On returning he wrote Mrs. Williams several letters, in one of which, dated Good Friday, he said :—

"I beg you to have inserted in your county paper something like this advertisement; 'To the nobility, gentry, and others, about Bury.—C. Lamb respectfully informs his friends and the public in general, that he is leaving off business in the acrostic line, as he is going into an entirely new line. Rebuses and Charades done as usual, and upon the old terms. Also, Epitaphs to suit the memory of any person deceased.'"

Mrs. Williams probably then suggested that Lamb should write her epitaph, for in his next letter he says :—

"I have ventured upon some lines, which combine my old acrostic talent (which you first found out) with my new profession of epitaph-monger. As you did not please to say, when you would die, I have left a blank space for the date. May kind heaven be a long time in filling it up."

On page 45 will be found some lines to one of Mrs. Williams' daughters. The acrostic on page 61 is to another. These would both be Emma Isola's pupils. In Emma Isola's Extract Book, which by the kindness of the Misses Moxon, her daughters, I have been permitted to see, are some lines on the rectory at Fornham and her happiness there, accompanied by a sketch of the house. There is also a copy of verses by Mrs. Williams.

Page 61. *Translations from Vincent Bourne.*

Vincent Bourne (1695-1747), the English Latin poet, entered Westminster School on the foundation in 1710, and, on leaving Cambridge, returned to Westminster as a master. He was so indolent a teacher and disciplinarian that Cowper, one of his pupils, says : "He seemed determined, as he was the best, so to be the last, Latin poet of the Westminster line." Bourne's *Poemata* appeared in 1734. It is mainly owing to Cowper's translations (particularly "The Jackdaw") that he is known, except to Latinists. Lamb first read Bourne in 1815. Writing to Wordsworth in April of that year he says :—

"Since I saw you I have had a treat in the reading way which comes not every day. The Latin Poems of V. Bourne which were quite new to me. What a heart that man had, all laid out upon town and scenes, a proper counterpoise to *some people's* rural extravaganzas.

Why I mention him is that your Power of Music reminded me of his poem of the ballad singer in the Seven Dials. Do you remember his epigram on the old woman who taught Newton the A B C, which after all he says he hesitates not to call Newton's *Principia*? I was lately fatiguing myself with going through a volume of fine words by Ld Thurlow, excellent words, and if the heart could live by words alone, it could desire no better regale, but what an aching vacuum of matter— I don't stick at the madness of it, for that is only a consequence of shutting his eyes and thinking he is in the age of the old Elisabeth poets—from thence I turned to V. Bourne—what a sweet unpretending pretty-mannered *matter-ful* creature, sucking from every flower, making a flower of every thing—his diction all Latin, and his thoughts all English. Bless him, Latin wasn't good enough for him— why wasn't he content with the language which Gay and Prior wrote in."

On the publication of *Album Verses*, wherein these nine poems from Vincent Bourne were printed, Lamb reviewed the book in Moxon's *Englishman's Magazine* for September, 1831, under the title "The Latin Poems of Vincent Bourne" (see Vol. I., page 337). There Lamb quotes "The Ballad Singers," and the "Epitaph on an Infant Sleeping"—remarking of Bourne:—

"He is 'so Latin,' and yet 'so English' all the while. In diction worthy of the Augustan age, he presents us with no images that are not familiar to his countrymen. His topics are even closelier drawn; they are not so properly English, as *Londonish*. From the streets, and from the alleys, of his beloved metropolis, he culled his objects, which he has invested with an Hogarthian richness of colouring. No town picture by that artist can go beyond his BALLAD-SINGERS; Gay's TRIVIA alone, in verse, comes up to the life and humour of it."

Bourne's poems were edited, in 1840, by the Rev. John Mitford, Bernard Barton's friend.

Lamb's "Epitaph on the Beggar's Dog" was first printed in *The Indicator*, May 3, 1820, where the ninth line ran:—

His seat by some road side, nigh where the tide.

Lamb quoted it, both Latin and English, in his *Elia* essay on "The Decay of Beggars" (Vol. II., page 117) in the *London Magazine*, June, 1822.

The Latin originals of the poems translated by Lamb bear the titles (1) "In Statuam Sepulchralem Infantis dormientis;" (2) "Certamen Musicum;" (3) "Epitaphium in Canem;" (4) "Cantatrices;" (5) "Ad Davidem Cook Nocturnum Custodem;" (6) "Memoriæ Sacrum Benjamini Ferrers, Pictoris surdi et muti;" (7) "Perveniri ad Summum nisi ex Principiis non potest;" (8) "Limax," and (9) "Schola Rhetorices."

Page 67. *Pindaric Ode to the Tread Mill.*

First printed in *The New Times*, October 24, 1825. The version there given differed considerably from that preserved by Lamb. It had no divisions. At the end of what is now the first strophe came these lines :—

> Now, by Saint Hilary,
> (A Saint I love to swear by,
> Though I should forfeit thereby
> Five ill-spared shillings to your well-warm'd seat,
> Worshipful Justices of Worship-street ;
> Or pay my crown
> At great Sir Richard's still more awful mandate down:)
> They raise my gorge—
> Those Ministers of Ann, or the First George,
> (Which was it ?
> For history is silent, and my closet-
> Reading affords no clue ;
> I have the story, Pope, alone from you ;)
> In such a place, &c.

In the fourth strophe, line 6, read "thine own mighty race," and line 7, " to keep thee countenance ; " in the sixth strophe lines 4 and 5 were :—

> Religious Rump !
> Thou dost not jump.

Lamb offered the Ode to his friend Walter Wilson, for his work on Defoe, to which Lamb contributed prose criticisms (see Vol. I., page 325, and note), but Wilson did not use it. The letter making this offer, together with the poem, differing very slightly in one or two places, is preserved in the Bodleian.

Compare " Reflections in the Pillory " (Vol. I., page 280).

Strophe 1, line 1. *De Foe.* Daniel Defoe was sentenced to the pillory as part of his punishment for writing *The Shortest Way with Dissenters*, 1702. He stood in the pillory on three days in July, 1703 ; but it was not the ordinary ordeal, for the people had decorated the instrument with flowers and they drank his health the while. Defoe afterwards wrote the " Hymn to the Pillory " which suggested Lamb's "Ode to the Treadmill." Compare with strophe 4 the prologue to "Faulkener" on page 123.

Strophe 6, line 2. *Jumping Sect.* The Jumpers were an extreme body of Welsh Calvinistic Methodists.

Strophe 7, line 3. *Cynic Cub.* Diogenes.

Strophe 7, last line. "*Walking Stewart.*" Walking Stewart was the name given to John Stewart (1749-1822), orientalist, eccentric and philosopher, who delivered lectures on the mind and had walked all over Persia, Arabia, Abyssinia and Europe.

Page 70. *Going or Gone.*

First printed in Hone's *Table Book*, 1827, signed Elia, under the title "Gone or Going." It was there longer, after stanza 6 coming the following :—

> Had he mended in right time,
> He need not in night time,
> (That black hour, and fright-time,)
> Till sexton interr'd him,

> Have groan'd in his coffin,
> While demons stood scoffing—
> You'd ha' thought him a-coughing—
>   My own father[1] heard him!
>
> Could gain so importune,
> With occasion opportune,
> That for a poor Fortune,
>   That should have been ours,[2]
> In soul he should venture
> To pierce the dim center,
> Where will-forgers enter
>   Amid the dark Powers?—

And in the *Table Book* the last stanza ended thus :—

> And flaunting Miss Waller—
> *That* soon must befal her,
> Which makes folks seem taller,[3]—
>   Though proud, once, as Juno!

To annotate this curious tale of old friendships, dating back, as I suppose, in some cases to Lamb's earliest memories, both of London and Hertfordshire, is a task that is probably beyond completion. The day is too distant. But a search in the Widford register and churchyard reveals a little information and oral tradition a little more.

Stanza 2. *Rich Kitty Wheatley.* The Rev. Joseph Whately, vicar of Widford in the latter half of the eighteenth century, married Jane Plumer, sister of William Plumer, of Blakesware, the employer of Mrs. Field, Lamb's grandmother. Archbishop Whately was their son. Kitty Wheatley may have been a relative.

Stanza 2. *Polly Perkin.* On June 1, 1770, according to the Widford register, Samuel Perkins married Mary Lanham. This may have been Polly.

Stanza 3. *Carter . . . Lily.* Mrs. Tween, a daughter of Randal Norris, Lamb's friend, and a resident in Widford, told Canon Ainger that Carter and Lily were servants at Blakesware. Lily had noticeably red cheeks. Lamb would have seen them often when he stayed there as a boy. In Cussan's *Hertfordshire* is an entertaining account of William Plumer's widow's adhesion to the old custom of taking the air. She rode out always—from Gilston, only a few miles from Widford and Blakesware—in the family chariot, with outriders and postilion (a successor to Lily), and so vast was the equipage that "turn outs" had to be cut in the hedges (visible to this day), like sidings on a single-line railway, to permit others to pass. The Widford register gives John Lilley, died October 18, 1812, aged 85, and Johanna Lilley, died January 1, 1823, aged 90. It also gives Benjamin Carter's marriage, in 1781, but not his death.

Stanza 4. *Clemitson's widow.* Mrs. Tween told Canon Ainger that Clemitson was the farmer of Blakesware farm. I do not find the name in the Widford register. An Elizabeth Clemenson is there.

Stanza 4. *Good Master Clapton.* There are several Claptons in

---

[1] Who sat up with him.   [2] I have this fact from Parental tradition only.
[3] Death lengthens people to the eye.

Widford churchyard. Thirty years from 1827, the date of the poem, takes us to 1797: the Clapton whose death occurred nearest that time is John Game Clapton, May 5, 1802.

Stanza 5. *Tom Dockwra.* I cannot find definite information either concerning this Dockwra or the William Dockwray, of Ware, of whom Lamb wrote in his "Table Talk" in *The Athenæum,* 1834 (see Vol. I., page 345). There was, however, a Joseph Docwray, of Ware, a Quaker maltster; and the late Mrs. Coe, *née* Hunt, the daughter of the tenant of the water mill at Widford in Lamb's day, where Lamb often spent a night, told me that a poor family named Docwra lived in the neighbourhood.

Stanza 6. *Roger de Coverley.* At first blush this might be taken for another old companion of Lamb's youth; but in the *Table Book* version the meaning is clearer. Thus:—

> (Roger de Coverley
> Not more good man than he),

a parenthesis descriptive of Tom Dockwra.

Stanza 6. *Worral . . . Dorrell.* I find neither Worral nor Dorrell in the Widford archives, but Morrils and Morrells in plenty, and one Horrel. Lamb alludes to old Dorrell again in the *Elia* essay "New Year's Eve" (Vol. II., page 28), where he is accused of swindling the family out of money. Particulars of his fraud have perished with him, but I have no doubt it is the same William Dorrell who witnessed John Lamb's will in 1761. In the *Table Book* this stanza ended thus:—

> With cuckoldy Worral,
> And wicked old Dorrel,
> 'Gainst whom I've a quarrel—
> His end might affright us.

Stanzas 8 and 9. *Fanny Hutton . . . Betsy Chambers . . . Miss Wither . . . Miss Waller.* Fanny Hutton, Betsy Chambers, Miss Wither and Miss Waller elude one altogether. Lamb's schoolmistress, Mrs. Reynolds, was a Miss Chambers.

Page 73. "The Poetical Works of Charles Lamb," 1836.

In 1836 Moxon issued a new edition of Lamb's poems, consisting of those in the *Works,* 1818, and those in *Album Verses*—with a few exceptions and several additions—under the embracive title *The Poetical Works of Charles Lamb.* Whether Moxon himself made up this volume, or whether Mary Lamb or Talfourd assisted, I do not know. The dedication to Coleridge stood at the beginning, and that to Moxon half way through.

Page 73. *In the Album of Edith S——.*

First printed in *The Athenæum,* March 9, 1833, under the title "Christian Names of Women." Edith S—— was Edith May Southey, the poet's daughter, who married the Rev. John Wood Warter.

NOTES

Page 73. *To Dora W——*.
Dora, *i.e.*, Dorothy Wordsworth, the poet's daughter, who married Edward Quillinan and thus became stepmother of Rotha Q—— of the next sonnet.

Page 74. *In the Album of Rotha Q——*.
Rotha Quillinan, younger daughter of Edward Quillinan (1791-1851), Wordsworth's friend and, afterwards, son-in-law. His first wife, a daughter of Sir Samuel Egerton Brydges, was burned to death in 1822 under the most distressing circumstances. Rotha Quillinan, who was Wordsworth's god-daughter, was so called from the Rotha which flows through Rydal, close to Quillinan's house (see page 96 for an acrostic by Lamb upon Miss Quillinan's name).

Page 74. *In the Album of Catherine Orkney*.
I have not been able to trace this lady.

Page 75. *To T. Stothard, Esq.*
First printed in *The Athenæum*, December 21, 1833. In a letter to Rogers in December, 1833, Lamb alludes to his sonnet to the poet (see page 90), adding that for fear it might not altogether please Stothard he has "ventured at an antagonist copy of verses, in *The Athenæum*, to *him*, in which he is as every thing, and you [Rogers] as nothing." Thomas Stothard (1755-1834) was at that time seventy-eight. He had long been the friend of Rogers, having helped in the decoration of his house in 1803 and illustrated the *Pleasures of Memory* as far back as 1793. Lamb's sonnet refers particularly to the edition of Rogers' *Poems* that is dated 1834, which Stothard and Turner embellished. Stothard illustrated very many of the standard novels for Harrison's *Novelists' Magazine* towards the end of the eighteenth century, among these being Richardson's, Fielding's, Smollett's and Sterne's. In Robert Paltock's *Life and Adventures of Peter Wilkins*, 1751, a flying people are described, among whom the males were "Glums" and the females "Gawries."—Titian lived to be ninety-nine.

Page 75. *To a Friend on His Marriage*.
First printed in *The Athenæum*, December 7, 1833. The friend was Edward Moxon, whose marriage to Emma Isola, Lamb's adopted daughter, was solemnised on July 30, 1833. Lamb mentions more than once the absence of any dowry with Miss Isola. His own wedding present to them was the portrait of Milton which his brother, John Lamb, had left to him.
Lines 21 and 22—see note on page 311, where Lamb speaks of Emma Isola as "beautiful in reconciliation."

Page 76. *The Self-Enchanted*.
First printed in *The Athenæum*, January 7, 1832.

Page 76. *To Louisa M——, whom I used to call "Monkey."*
First printed in Hone's *Year Book* for December 30, 1831, under the title "The Change." (See the verses "The Ape," on page 80, the forerunner of the present poem, addressed also to Louisa Martin; see also note on page 323.)

VOL. V.—21

Page 77. *Cheap Gifts : a Sonnet.*
First printed in *The Athenæum*, February 15, 1834.

Page 77. *Free Thoughts on Several Eminent Composers.*
Lamb was very fond of these lines, which he sent to more than one of his friends. The text varies in some of the copies, but I have not thought it necessary to indicate the differences. Its inspiration was attributed by him both to William Ayrton (1777-1858), the musical critic, and to Vincent Novello (1781-1861), the organist, composer and close friend of Lamb. In a letter to Sarah Hazlitt in 1830 Lamb copies the poem, remarking—

"Having read Hawkins and Burney recently, I was enabled to talk [to Ayrton] of Names, and show more knowledge than he had suspected I possessed; and in the end he begg'd me to shape my thoughts upon paper, which I did after he was gone, and sent him."

So Lamb wrote to Mrs. Hazlitt. But to Ayrton, when he sent the verses, he said:—

"[Novello] desiring me to give him my real opinion respecting the distinct grades of excellence in all the eminent Composers of the Italian, German and English schools, I have done it, rather to oblige him than from any overweening opinion I have of my own judgment in that science."

Both these statements are manifestations of what Lamb called his "matter-of-lie" disposition. To Mrs. Hazlitt he thought that Ayrton's name would be more important; to Ayrton, Novello's.

The verses, whatever their origin, were written by Lamb in Novello's Album, with this postscript, signed by Mary Lamb, added:—

> The reason why my brother's so severe,
> Vincentio, is—my brother has no *ear;*
> And Caradori, his mellifluous throat
> Might stretch in vain to make him learn a note.
> Of common tunes he knows not anything,
> Nor " Rule Britannia " from " God save the King."
> He rail at Handel! He the gamut quiz!
> I'd lay my life he knows not what it is.
> His spite at music is a pretty whim—
> He loves not it, because it loves not him.
>   M. LAMB.

MISCELLANEOUS POEMS

Page 79. *Dramatic Fragment.* Signed with three stars.
London Magazine, January, 1822. An excerpt from Lamb's play, " Pride's Cure" (*John Woodvil*). See note on page 360.

Page 80. *Epitaph on a Young Lady, etc.*
Morning Post, February 7, 1804. Signed C. L. Lamb sends the poem both to Wordsworth and Manning in 1803, "sleep" standing for " lie" in the second line. He says to Manning:—

"Did I send you an epitaph I scribbled upon a poor girl who died at nineteen?—a good girl, and a pretty girl, and a clever girl, but strangely neglected by all her friends and kin. . . . Brief, and pretty, and tender, is it not? I send you this, being the only piece of poetry I have *done* since the Muses all went with T. M. [Thomas Manning] to Paris."

In *An Old Man's Diary*, I., 23, by John Payne Collier (privately printed in 1872) is the following version, printed from a manuscript copy :—

EPITAPH FOR MARY DRUITT
Buried at Wimborne, Dorset, Aged 19.

Under this cold marble stone
Sleep the sad remains of one
Who, when alive, by few or none
Was loved, as she might have been,
By lovers many, rich I ween,
If she prosperous days had seen.
Only this funereal stone
Tells the simple grief of one,
That loved her, and her alone.

Collier, who, I believe, copied the verses from an album belonging to Sarah Stoddart (afterwards Sarah Hazlitt), adds a fourth stanza, which, he says, Lamb afterwards expunged :—

Death will prey on flesh and bone,
Hateful to be look'd upon ;
And where then her beauty ?—Gone.

This poem led to some correspondence in *Notes and Queries* in 1892, which revealed the fact that Mary Druitt died of consumption in 1801, and that the verses are not on her tombstone. A hitherto unpublished letter from Lamb to his friend Rickman, from which Canon Ainger quotes, shows that it was for Rickman that the lines were written. Lamb did not know Mary Druitt. Writing to Rickman in February, 1802, Lamb sends another epitaph :—

" Your own prose, or nakedly the letter which you sent me, which was in some sort an epitaph, would do better on her gravestone than the cold lines of a stranger :—

" A Heart which felt unkindness, yet complained not,
A Tongue which spake the simple Truth, and feigned not :
A Soul as white as the pure marble skin
(The beauteous Mansion it was lodgèd in)
Which, unrespected, could itself respect,
On Earth was all the Portion of a Maid
Who in this common Sanctuary laid,
Sleeps unoffended by the World's neglect."

Page 80. *The Ape.*
Printed in the *London Magazine*, October, 1820, where it was preceded by these words :—

"To the Editor

" Mr. Editor,—The riddling lines which I send you, were written upon a young lady, who, from her diverting sportiveness in childhood, was named by her friends The Ape. When the verses were written, L. M. had outgrown the title—but not the memory of it—being in her teens, and consequently past child-tricks. They are an endeavour to express that perplexity, which one feels at any alteration, even supposed for the better, in a beloved object; with a little oblique grudging at TIME, who cannot bestow new graces without taking away some portion of the older ones, which we can ill miss.

"****."

L. M. was Louisa Martin, who is now and then referred to in Lamb's letter as Monkey, and to whom he addressed the lines on page 76, which come as a sequel to the present ones. In a letter to Wordsworth, many years later, dated February 22, 1834, Lamb asks a favour for this lady :—

"The oldest and best friends I have left are in trouble. A branch of them (and they of the best stock of God's creatures, I believe) is establishing a school at Carlisle; Her name is Louisa Martin . . . her qualities . . . are the most amiable, most upright. For thirty years she has been tried by me, and on her behaviour I would stake my soul."

Page 82. *In Tabulam Eximii* . . .
These Latin verses were printed in *The Champion,* May 6 and 7, 1820, signed Carlagnulus, accompanied by this notice : " We insert, with great pleasure, the following beautiful Latin Verses on HAYDON's fine Picture, and shall be obliged to any of our correspondents for a spirited translation for our next." The following week brought one translation—Lamb's own—signed C. L. Both were reprinted in *The Poetical Recreations of "The Champion"* in 1822, and again in Tom Taylor's *Life of Haydon,* 1853, where the title ran: "In tabulam egregii pictoris B. Haydoni, in quâ Judæiante pedes Christi palmas prosternentes mirâ arte depinguntur;" and where there were also slight alterations in the text: "at" for "sed" in the fifth line; and "cinge" for "cingas" in the last.

Benjamin Robert Haydon (1786-1846) was for six years at work upon this picture—"Christ's Entry into Jerusalem"—which was exhibited at the Egyptian Hall in 1820. The story goes that Mrs. Siddons established the picture's reputation in society. While the private-view company were assembled in doubt the great actress entered and walked across the room. "It is completely successful," she was heard to say to Sir George Beaumont; and then, to Haydon, "The paleness of your Christ gives it a supernatural look." A stream of 30,000 persons followed this verdict. The picture, a reproduction of which will be found on the opposite page, is now in Philadelphia. The figure with bent head on the right is Wordsworth, a type of "awful veneration," in contrast to Voltaire, next him, as the "sneerer."

Line 4. *Palma.* There were two Palmas, both painters of the Venetian school. Giacomo Palma the Elder, who is referred to here, was born about 1480. Both painted many scenes in the life of Christ.

Lines 7 and 8.   *Flaccus' sentence.*
>   Valeat res ludicra si me
> Palma negata macrum, donata reducit opimum.
> Horace, *Epist.*, *II.*, 1, 180-181.

(Farewell to performances, if the palm, denied, sends one home lean, but, granted, flourishing.)

Lamb has not quite represented the poet's meaning, which is a profession of independence in regard to popular applause.

Page 82.   *Sonnet to Miss Burney* . . .
First printed in the *Morning Chronicle*, July 13, 1820.

The Burney family began to be famous with Dr. Charles Burney (1726-1814), the musician, the author of the *History of Music*, and the friend of Dr. Johnson and Sir Joshua Reynolds. Among his children were the Rev. Charles Burney (1757-1817), the classical scholar and owner of the Burney Library, now in the British Museum; Rear-Admiral James Burney (1750-1821), who sailed with Cook, wrote the *Chronological History of the Discoveries in the South Sea or Pacific Ocean*, and became a friend of Lamb; Frances Burney, afterwards Madame d'Arblay (1752-1840), the novelist, author of *Evelina*, *Camilla* and *Cecilia;* and Sarah Harriet Burney (1770?-1844), a daughter of Dr. Burney's second wife, also a novelist, and the author, among other stories, of *Geraldine Fauconberg.* "Country Neighbours; or, The Secret," the tale that inspired Lamb's sonnet, formed Vols. II. and III. of Sarah Burney's *Tales of Fancy.* Blanch is the heroine.

The good old man in Madame d'Arblay's *Camilla* is Sir Hugh Tyrold, who adopted the heroine.

Page 83.   *To my Friend The Indicator.*
Printed in *The Indicator*, September 27, 1820, signed ****, preceded by these words by Leigh Hunt, the editor :—

> Every pleasure we could experience in a friend's approbation, we have felt in receiving the following verses. They are from a writer, who of all other men, knows how to extricate a common thing from commonness, and to give it an underlook of pleasant consciousness and wisdom. . . . The receipt of these verses has set us upon thinking of the good-natured countenance, which men of genius, in all ages, have for the most part shewn to contemporary writers.

Line 6.   *The days of Bickerstaff.*   Isaac Bickerstaff was the pseudonym adopted by Steele (borrowed from Swift) when he edited *The Tatler* (1709-1711).

Line 9.   *Old Priscian's head.*   Priscianus Cæsariensis, a famous grammarian of the fifth and sixth centuries. The Latin phrase "Diminuĕre Prisciani caput"—to break Priscian's head—signified to defy the rules of grammar.

Page 83.   *To Emma, Learning Latin, and Desponding.*
First printed in *Blackwood's Magazine*, June, 1829.

Mary Lamb had other pupils in her time, among them Miss Kelly, the actress, Mary Victoria Novello (afterwards Mrs. Cowden Clarke), and William Hazlitt, the essayist's son. Emma was, of course, Emma Isola. Sara Coleridge's translation of Martin Dobrizhoffer's *Historia de*

Abiponibus under the title *Account of the Abipones* was published in 1822, when she was only twenty.

"To think [Lamb wrote to Barton, on February 17, 1823, of Sara Coleridge] that she should have had to toil thro' five octavos of that cursed (I forget I write to a Quaker) Abbey pony History, and then to abridge them to 3, and all for £113. At her years, to be doing stupid Jesuits' Latin into English, when she should be reading or writing Romances."

Sara Coleridge's romance-writing came later, in 1837, when her fairy tale, *Phantasmion*, appeared.

Page 84. *Lines addressed to Lieut. R. W. H. Hardy, R.N.* . . .

First printed in *The Athenæum*, January 10, 1846, contributed by an anonymous correspondent (probably Thomas Westwood the Younger) who sent also "The First Leaf of Spring" (page 91). *Travels in the Interior of Mexico in* 1825 . . . 1828, by Robert William Hale Hardy, was published in 1829. Lamb made an exception in favour of Hardy's book. Writing to Dilke for something to read from *The Athenæum* office, in 1833, he particularly desired that "no natural history or useful learning, such as Pyramids, Catacombs, Giraffes, or Adventures in Southern Africa" might be sent.

Page 84. *Lines for a Monument* . . .

First printed in *The Athenæum*, November 5, 1831, and again in *The Tatler*, Hunt's paper, December 31, 1831. In August 1830 four sons and two daughters of John and Ann Rigg, of York, were drowned in the Ouse. Several literary persons were asked for inscriptions for the monument, erected at York in 1831, and that by James Montgomery, of Sheffield, was chosen. Lamb sent his verses to Vincent Novello, through whom he seems to have been approached in the matter, on November 8, 1830, adding: "Will these lines do? I despair of better. Poor Mary is in a deplorable state here at Enfield."

Page 85. *To C. Aders, Esq.*

First printed in Hone's *Year Book* (March 19), 1831 (see note to "Angel Help," page 307).

Page 85. *Hercules Pacificatus.*

First printed in the *Englishman's Magazine*, August, 1831. The poem is preserved in one of Lamb's albums, where the sixtieth line is altered by him to—

> My Neighbour with such a beam in his eye.

Suidas is supposed to have lived in the tenth or eleventh century, and to have compiled a *Lexicon*—a blend of biographical dictionary. The phrase "white boys," in line 25, is a common term of endearment in the old dramatists.

Page 88. *The Parting Speech of the Celestial Messenger to the Poet.*

First printed in *The Athenæum*, February 25, 1832.

Palingenius was an Italian poet of the sixteenth century, whose real name was Pietro Angelo Mazolli, but who wrote in Latin under the

CHRIST'S ENTRY INTO JERUSALEM
After the painting by B. R. Haydon, now at Philadelphia

name of Marcellus Palingenius Stollatus. His *Zodiacus Vitæ*, a philosophical poem, was published in 1536.

Page 89. *Existence, Considered in itself, no Blessing.*
First printed in The Athenæum, July 7, 1832. Lamb added the Latin in a footnote: "*Zod. Vit.*, Lib. 6, apud finem."

Page 90. *To Samuel Rogers, Esq., on the New Edition of his "Pleasures of Memory."*
First printed in The Times, December 13, 1833. Signed C. Lamb. This is the sonnet mentioned in the letter which is quoted on page 321, in the note to the sonnet to Stothard. The new edition of *Pleasures of Memory* was published by Moxon in 1833, dated 1834.

Page 90. *To Clara N——.*
First printed in The Athenæum, July 26, 1834. Clara N—— was, of course, Clara Anastasia Novello, daughter of Lamb's friend, Vincent Novello (1781-1861), the organist, and herself a fine soprano singer (see also the poem "The Sisters," page 98). Miss Novello, who was born in 1818, became the Countess Gigliucci, and is still living.

Both Crabb Robinson and Barron Field tell us that Lamb was capable of humming tunes. See the "Chapter on Ears," Vol. II., p. 38.

Page 91. *To Margaret W——.*
This poem, believed to be the last that Lamb wrote, was printed in The Athenæum for March 14, 1835. I have not been able to ascertain who Margaret W—— was.

ADDITIONAL ALBUM VERSES AND ACROSTICS

Page 92. *What is an Album?*
These lines were probably written for Emma Isola's Album, which must not be confounded with her Extract Book. The Album was the volume for which Lamb, in his letters, occasionally solicited contributions. It was sold some years ago to Mr. Quaritch, and is now, I believe, in a private collection, although in a mutilated state, several of the poems having been cut out. These particular lines of Lamb's were probably written by him also in other albums, for John Mathew Gutch, his old school-fellow, discovered them on the fly-leaf of a copy of *John Woodvil*, and sent them to Notes and Queries, Oct. 11, 1856. In that version the twenty-first line ran:—

There you have, Madelina, an album complete.

Lamb quoted from the lines in his review of his *Album Verses*, under the title "The Latin Poems of Vincent Bourne," in the *Englishman's Magazine* (see Vol. I., page 337). Two versions of the lines are copied by Lamb into one of his Commonplace Books.

Line 6. *Sweet L. E. L.'s.* L. E. L. was, of course, Letitia Elizabeth Landon, afterwards Mrs. Maclean (1802-1838), famous as an Album- and Annual-poetess. Lamb, if an entry in P. G. Patmore's diary is correct, did not admire her, or indeed any female author. He said, "If she belonged to me I would lock her up and feed her on bread and water till she left off writing poetry".

NOTES

Page 92. *The First Leaf of Spring.*

Printed in *The Athenæum,* January 10, 1846, contributed probably by Thomas Westwood. In a note prefacing the three poems which he was sending, this correspondent stated that "The First Leaf of Spring" had been printed before, but very obscurely. I have not discovered where.

Page 93. *To Mrs. F—— on Her Return from Gibraltar.*

This would probably be Mrs. Jane Field, *née* Carncroft, the wife of Lamb's friend, Barron Field, who inspired the *Elia* essay on "Distant Correspondents" (see Vol. II., page 104, and note). Field held the Chief Justiceship of Gibraltar for some years. For the quotation in the last line see Genesis xxvii. 27.

Page 94. *To M. L—— F——.*

M. L. Field, the second daughter of Henry Field, and Barron Field's sister. This lady, who lived to a great age, gave Canon Ainger the copy of the prologue to "Richard II." written by Lamb for an amateur performance at her home (see page 128 and note).

Page 94. *To Esther Field.*
Another of Barron Field's sisters.

Page 94. [*To Mrs. Williams.*]

See note on page 316. In writing to Mrs. Williams on April 2, 1830, to tell of Emma Isola's safe journey after her illness, Lamb says:—

"How I employed myself between Epping and Enfield the poor verses in the front of my paper may inform you, which you may please to christen an Acrostic in a Cross Road."

Mrs. Williams seems to have replied with an acrostic upon Lamb's name, for he says (Good Friday, 1830):—

"I do assure you that your verses gratified me very much, and my sister is quite *proud* of them. For the first time in my life I congratulated myself upon the shortness and meanness of my name. Had it been Schwartzenberg or Esterhazy it would have put you to some puzzle."

Later in the same letter, referring to the present acrostic, he said, speaking of Harriet Isola, Emma's sister, she "blames my last verses as being more written on *Mr.* Williams than on yourself; but how should I have parted whom a Superior Power has brought together?"

Page 95. *To the Book.*

Written for the Album of Sophia Elizabeth Frend, afterwards the wife of Augustus De Morgan, the mathematician (1806-1871). Her father was William Frend (1757-1841), the reformer and a friend of Crabb Robinson and George Dyer. The lines were printed in Mrs. De Morgan's *Three Score Years and Ten,* as are also those that follow—"To S. F." They are reprinted here by permission of Mr. Augustus De Morgan.

Page 96. *To S. F.*
To Sophia Elizabeth Frend (see preceding note).

NOTES

Page 96. *To R. Q.*

These lines are copied from the Album of Rotha Quillinan by permission of Mr. Gordon Wordsworth, its present owner (see page 74 and note).

Pages 96, 97. *To S. L. . . . To M. L.*

I have not been able to identify the Lockes. The J. F. of the last line might be Jane Field. Copies of these poems are preserved at South Kensington.

Page 97. "*An Acrostic against Acrostics.*"

I have not found anything concerning Edward Hogg. These verses were first printed in *The Lambs* by Mr. W. C. Hazlitt.

Page 97. "*On being Asked to Write in Miss Westwood's Album.*"

Frances Westwood was the daughter of the Westwoods with whom the Lambs were domiciled at Enfield Chase in 1829-1832. See letters to Gillman and Wordsworth (November 30, 1829, and January 22, 1830) for description of the Westwoods. The only son, Thomas Westwood, who died in 1888, and was an authority on the literature of angling, contributed to *Notes and Queries* some very interesting reminiscences of the Lambs in those days. This poem and that which follows it were sent to *Notes and Queries* by Thomas Westwood (June 4, 1870). It had, however, been printed in *The Athenæum*, together with the lines to Lieutenant Hardy (see page 84) and "The First Leaf of Spring" (see page 92) on January 10, 1846, contributed by an anonymous correspondent—probably Thomas Westwood.

It is concerning these lines that Lamb writes to Barton, in 1827 :—

"Adieu to Albums—for a great while—I said when I came here, and had not been fixed two days, but my Landlord's daughter (not at the Pot-house) requested me to write in her female friend's, and in her own. If I go to   thou art there also, O all pervading Album ! All over the Leeward Islands, in Newfoundland, and the Back Settlements, I understand there is no other reading. They haunt me. I die of Albo-phobia !"

Page 98. *The Sisters.*

These verses, printed in Mr. W. C. Hazlitt's *Lamb and Hazlitt*, 1900, were addressed :—

"*For* SAINT CECILIA,
"At Sign^r Vincenzo Novello's
"Music Repository,
"No. 67 Frith Street,
"Soho."

They were signed C. Lamb. One might imagine Emma, the nut-brown maid, to be Emma Isola, as that was a phrase Lamb was fond of applying to her—assuming the title "The Sisters" to be a pleasantry ; but Miss Mary Sabilla Novello assures me that the sisters were herself, Emma Aloysia Novello and Clara Anastasia Novello, now the Countess Gigliucci.

NOTES

POEMS NOW PRINTED FOR THE FIRST TIME

Page 99. *Un Solitaire.*
E. I., who made the drawing in question, would be Emma Isola. The verses were copied by Lamb into his Album, which is now in the possession of Mrs. Alfred Morrison.

Page 99. *To S[arah] T[homas].*
From Lamb's Album. I have not been able to trace this lady. "Terah's faithful son" is from Milton's paraphrase of Psalm cxiv. written when he was fifteen.

Page 100. *To Mrs. Sarah Robinson.*
From the copy preserved among Henry Crabb Robinson's papers at Dr. Williams' Library. Sarah Robinson was the niece of H. C. R., who was the pilgrim in Rome. The stranger to thy land was Emma Isola, Fornham, in Suffolk, where she was living, being near to Bury St. Edmunds, the home of the Robinsons.

Page 100. *To Sarah.*
From the Album of Sarah Apsey.

Page 100. *Acrostic.*
From Lamb's Album. Joseph Vale Asbury was the Lambs' doctor at Enfield. There are extant two amusing letters from Lamb to Asbury.

Page 101. *To D. A.*
From Lamb's Album. Dorothy Asbury, the wife of the doctor.

Page 101. *To Louisa Morgan.*
From Lamb's Album. Louisa Morgan was probably the daughter of Coleridge's friend, John Morgan, of Calne, in Wiltshire, with whom the Lambs stayed in 1817—the same Morgan—"Morgan demigorgon" —who ate walnuts better than any man Lamb knew, and munched cos-lettuce like a rabbit (see letters to Coleridge in August, 1814). Southey and Lamb each allowed John Morgan £10 a year in his old age and adversity, beginning with 1819.

See also page 373.

Page 102. POLITICAL AND OTHER EPIGRAMS.
Lamb was not a politician, but he had strong—almost passionate— prejudices against certain statesmen and higher persons, which impelled him now and then to sarcastic verse. The earliest examples in this vein which can be identified are two quatrains from the *Morning Post* in January, 1802, printed on page 102, and the epigram on Sir James Mackintosh in *The Albion*, printed on the same page, to which Lamb refers in the *Elia* essay on "Newspapers Thirty-five Years Ago" (see Vol. II., page 224, and note). The next belong to the year 1812—in *The Examiner* (see pages 102 and 103)—and we then leap another seven years or so until 1819-1820, Lamb's busiest period as a

THE

POETICAL RECREATIONS

OF

THE CHAMPION,

AND HIS

LITERARY CORRESPONDENTS;

WITH A

SELECTION OF ESSAYS, LITERARY & CRITICAL,

WHICH HAVE APPEARED IN

THE CHAMPION NEWSPAPER.

With some few minds congenial let me stray
Along the Muses' haunts,

LONDON:

PRINTED AT THE CHAMPION PRESS, 271, STRAND, BY AND
FOR JOHN THELWALL; AND SOLD BY SIR R. PHILLIPS,
BRIDGE-STREET; RIDGWAY, PICCADILLY, &c.

1822.

NOTES 331

caustic critic of affairs—in *The Examiner,* possibly the *Morning Chronicle,* and principally in *The Champion.* After 1820, however, he returned to this vein very seldom, and then with less bitterness and depth of feeling. "The Royal Wonders," in *The Times* for August 10, 1830 (see page 108), and "Lines Suggested by a Sight of Waltham Cross," in the *Englishman's Magazine,* September, 1831 (written, however, some years earlier), see page 107, being his latest efforts that we know of. Of course there must be many other similar productions to which we have no clue—the old *Morning Post* days doubtless saw many an epigram that cannot now be definitely claimed for Lamb—but those that are preserved here sufficiently show how feelingly Lamb could hate and how trenchantly he could chastise. Others that seem to me likely to be Lamb's I could have included ; but it is well to dispense as much as possible with the problematic. For example, I suspect Lamb of the authorship of several of the epigrams quoted in *The Examiner* in 1819 and 1820 from the *Morning Chronicle.* He used to send verses to the *Morning Chronicle* at that time (see the sonnet to Sarah Burney on page 82), and Leigh Hunt would be naturally pleased to give anything of his friend's an additional publicity. The following single specimen may be cited as very possibly Lamb's, quoted in *The Examiner* of January 24 and 25, 1819 :—

ON THE CURTAILING THE CARTOONS OF RAPHAEL, TO FIT THE PANNELS IN BUCKINGHAM HOUSE

The Ancients suck'd cruelty e'en to the dregs,
  Their custom for ever accurst is—
When men were too tall, they cut off their legs,
  As witness the bed of *Procrustes.*

But now, the whole world our humanity strikes,
  For, shunning such terrible strictures,
We let the man grow just as tall as he likes,
  Confining *retrenchment* to *Pictures.*

O! happy the nation so wise and so chaste,
  Whose Princes the Graces so nourish ;
With them so abounding in exquisite taste,[1]
  No wonder *our Painting* should flourish!

[1] For what has Visto *painted, built* and *planted ?*
Only to shew *how many tastes* he wanted.
What brought Sir Visto's ill-got wealth to waste ?
Some demon whisper'd—Visto ! *have a taste!*
                                                    Pope, *Epist. IV.*

The majority of the epigrams printed in this section might have remained unidentified were it not that in 1822 John Thelwall, who owned and edited *The Champion* in 1818-1820, issued a little volume entitled *The Poetical Recreations of "The Champion,"* wherein Lamb's contributions were signed R. et R. This signature being appended to certain poems of which we know Lamb to have been the author—as "The Three Graves," which he sent also to the *London Magazine* (in 1825), and which he was in the habit of reading or reciting to his friends—enables us to ascertain the authorship of the others. A note placed by Thelwall above the index of the book states, "it is much to be regretted that, by mere oversight, or rather mistake, several of the printed epigrams of R. et R. have been omitted;" but a search through the piles of *The Champion* has failed to bring to light any others with Lamb's adopted signature.

The origin of the signature R. et R. is unknown. Mr. Percy Fitzgerald suggests that it might stand for Romulus and Remus, but offers no supporting theory. He might have added that so unfamiliar a countenance is in these epigrams shown by their author, that the suggestion of a wolf rather than a Lamb might have been intended.

Lamb's principal political epigrams were drawn from him by his intense contempt for the character of George IV., then Prince of Wales. His treatment of Caroline of Brunswick, as we see, moved Lamb to utterances of almost sulphurous indignation not only for the prince himself, but for all who were on his side, particularly Canning. Lamb, we must suppose, was wholly on the side of the queen, thus differing from Coleridge, who when asked how his sympathies were placed would admit only to being anti-Prince.

Most of the epigrams are here printed from the text of *The Poetical Recreations of "The Champion."* I have not thought it worth while to note all changes.

John Thelwall (1764-1834)—Citizen Thelwall—was one of the most popular and uncompromising of the Radicals of the seventeen-nineties. He belonged to the Society of the Friends of the People and other Jacobin confederacies. In May, 1794, he was even sent to the Tower (with Horne Tooke and Thomas Hardy) for sedition; moved to Newgate in October; and tried and acquitted in December. Lamb first met him, I fancy, in 1797, when Thelwall was intimate with Coleridge. After 1798 Thelwall's political activities were changed for those of a lecturer on more pacific subjects, and later he opened an institution in London where he taught elocution and corrected the effects of malformation of the organs of speech. He bought *The Champion* in 1818, and held it for two or three years, but it did not succeed. Thelwall died in 1834. Among his friends were Coleridge, Haydon, Hazlitt, Southey, Crabb Robinson and Lamb, all of whom, although they laughed at his excesses and excitements as a reformer, saw in him an invincible honesty and sincerity.

Before leaving this subject I should like to quote the following lines from *The Champion* of November 4 and 5, 1820:—

A LADY'S SAPPHIC

Now the calm evening hastily approaches,
Not a sound stirring thro' the gentle woodlands,
Save that soft Zephyr with his downy pinions
    Scatters fresh fragrance.

Now the pale sun-beams in the west declining
Gild the dew rising as the twilight deepens,
Beauty and splendour decorate the landscape;
    Night is approaching.

> By the cool stream's side pensively and sadly
> Sit I, while birds sing on the branches sweetly,
> And my sad thoughts all with their carols soothing,
> Lull to oblivion.
>
> M. L.

A correspondence on English sapphics was carried on in *The Champion* for some weeks at this time, various efforts being printed. On November 4 appeared the "Lady's Sapphic," just quoted, signed M. S. On the following day—for *The Champion*, like *The Examiner*, had a Saturday and Sunday edition—this signature was changed to M. L., and was thus given when the verses were reprinted in *The Poetical Recreations of "The Champion"* in 1822. There is no evidence that Mary Lamb wrote it; but she played with verse, and presumably read *The Champion*, since her brother was writing for it, and the poem might easily be hers. Personally I like to think it is, and that Lamb, on seeing the mistake in the initials in the Saturday edition, hurried down to the office to have it put right in that of Sunday.

Page 102. *To Sir James Mackintosh.*

In a letter to Manning in August, 1801, Lamb quotes this epigram as having been printed in *The Albion* and caused that paper's death the previous week. In his *Elia* essay on "Newspapers" (Vol. II., page 225), written thirty years later, he stated that the epigram was written at the time of Mackintosh's departure for India to reap the fruits of his apostasy; but here Lamb's memory deceived him, for Mackintosh was not appointed Recorder of Bombay until 1803 and did not sail until 1804, whereas there is reason to believe the date of Lamb's letter to Manning of August, 1801, to be accurate. The epigram must then have referred to a rumour of some earlier appointment, for Mackintosh had been hoping for something for several years. I cannot find anywhere a file of *The Albion*, or other epigrams of Lamb's would probably be discovered.

Sir James Mackintosh (1765-1832), the lawyer and philosopher, had in 1791 issued his *Vindiciæ Gallicæ*, a reply to Burke's *Reflections on the French Revolution*. Later, however, he became one of Burke's friends and an opponent of the Revolution, and in 1798 he issued his Introductory Discourse to his lectures on "The Law of Nature and Nations," in which the doctrines of his *Vindiciæ Gallicæ* were repudiated. Hence his "apostasy." Mackintosh applied unsuccessfully for a judgeship in Trinidad, and for the post of Advocate-General in Bengal, and Lord Wellesley had invited him to become the head of a college in Calcutta. Rumour may have credited him with any of these posts and thus have suggested Lamb's epigram. In 1803 he was appointed Recorder of Bombay. Lamb's dislike of Mackintosh may have been due in some measure to Coleridge, between whom and Mackintosh a mild feud subsisted. It had been Mackintosh, however, brother-in-law of Daniel Stuart of the *Morning Post*, who introduced Coleridge to that paper. (See Vol. II., page 220, where further particulars of *The Albion*, edited by Lamb's friend, John Fenwick, will be found.

Lamb may or may not have invented the sarcasm in this epigram; but it was not new. In Mrs. Montagu's letters, some years before, we find something of the kind concerning Charles James Fox: "His rapid journeys to England, on the news of the king's illness, have brought on him a violent complaint in the bowels, which will, it is imagined, prove mortal. However, if it should, it will vindicate his character from the general report that he has no bowels, as has been most strenuously asserted by his creditors."

Page 102. *Twelfth-Night Characters* . . .
Morning Post, January 8, 1802.

These epigrams were identified by the late Mr. Dykes Campbell by means of a letter of Lamb's to John Rickman that has not been printed.

A—— is, of course, Henry Addington (1757-1844), afterwards Viscount Sidmouth. After being Speaker for eleven years, he became suddenly Prime Minister in 1801, at the wish of George III., who was rendered uneasy by Pitt's project for Catholic relief.

C—— and F—— were George Canning (1770-1827) and John Hookham Frere (1769-1846) of *The Anti-Jacobin*, against whom Lamb had a grudge on account of the *Anti-Jacobin's* treatment of himself and Lloyd (see note to *Blank Verse*, page 291). Lamb returned to the attack on Canning again and again, as the epigrams that follow will show.

Lamb's epigrams were only two among many printed in the *Morning Post* for January 7 and 8, 1802. Whether he wrote only those or all the others I do not know, not having seen the letter to Rickman. But here are others which are not inconceivably from Lamb's hand:—

LORD NELSON

Off with BRIAREUS, and his HUNDRED HANDS,
OUR NELSON, with *one arm*, unconquer'd stands!

THE CITY CHAMPION

Don't be afraid, tho' cas'd, SUCH ARMOUR bright in,
There's nothing *further from my thoughts than fighting.*

SIR TOBY FILLPOT

When the nightingale sings in yon harbour so snug,
Pray what is her burthen, but sweet jug, jug, jug?
Your daddle, my hearty, *that chorus* we'll join,
In *jug* after *jug*, of the juice of the vine.

MR. P[IT]T

By crooked arts, and actions sinister,
I came at first to be a Minister;
And now I am no longer Minister,
I still retain my actions sinister.

Page 102. *Two Epigrams.*
The Examiner, March 22, 1812.

These epigrams have no signature, but the second of them was reprinted in *The Poetical Recreations of "The Champion"* (1822) with Lamb's signature, R. et R., appended, and a note saying that it was

written in the last reign, together with an announcement that it had
not appeared in *The Champion*, but was inserted in that collection at
the author's request. By Princeps and the heir-apparent is meant, of
course, the Prince of Wales, afterwards George IV., who had just
entered upon office as Regent. The epigrams refer to his transfer of
confidence, if so it may be called, from the Whig party to the Marquis
Wellesley, Perceval and the Tory party. The circumstance that the
Prince of Wales was also Duke of Cornwall is referred to in the first
epigram. The second of the epigrams is copied into one of Lamb's
Commonplace Books with the title "On the Prince breaking with his
Party."

Page 103. *The Triumph of the Whale.*

The Examiner, March 15, 1812. Reprinted in *The Poetical Recreations of "The Champion,"* signed R. et R., with a note stating that
it had not appeared in *The Champion*, but was collected with the
other pieces by the author's request.

The subject of the verses was, of course, the first gentleman in
Europe. *The Examiner* was never over nice in its treatment of the
prince, and it was in the same year, 1812, that Leigh Hunt, the editor,
and his brother, the printer, of the paper were prosecuted for the article
styling him a "libertine" and the "companion of gamblers and
demireps" (which appeared the week following Lamb's poem), and
were condemned to imprisonment for it. Lamb's lines came very
little short of expressing equally objectionable criticisms; but verse is
often privileged. Thelwall—and Lamb—showed some courage in reprinting the lines in 1822, when the prince had become king. Talfourd
relates that Lamb was in the habit of checking harsh comments on
the prince by others with the smiling remark, "*I love my Regent.*"

In Galignani's 1828 edition of Byron this piece was attributed to his
lordship.

Page 104. *St. Crispin to Mr. Gifford.*

The Examiner, October 3 and 4, 1819. Reprinted in *The Poetical
Recreations of "The Champion,"* 1822.

William Gifford (1756-1826), editor of the *Quarterly Review*, had
been apprenticed to a cobbler. Lamb had an old score against him
on account of his editorial treatment of Lamb's review of Wordsworth's
Excursion, in 1814, and other matters (see note to "Letter to Southey,"
Vol. I., page 476). Writing to the Olliers, on the publication of his
Works, June 18, 1818, Lamb says, in reference to this sonnet: "I meditate an attack upon that Cobler Gifford, which shall appear immediately
after any favourable mention which S. [Southey] may make in the
Quarterly. It can't in decent *gratitude* appear *before*." When the
sonnet was printed in the *Examiner* it purported to have reference to
the *Quarterly's* treatment of Shelley's *Revolt of Islam*, which treatment Leigh Hunt was then exposing in a series of articles.

Page 104. *The Godlike.*

The Champion, March 18 and 19, 1820. Reprinted in *The Poetical
Recreations of "The Champion,"* 1822.

Another contribution to the character of George IV., who had just succeeded to the throne, and was at that moment engaged upon the task of divorcing his wife, Caroline of Brunswick. The eighth line must be read probably with a medical eye. The concluding three lines refer to George III.'s insanity. As a political satirist Lamb disdained half measures.

Page 105. *The Three Graves.*

The Champion, May 13 and 14, 1820. Signed Dante. Reprinted in *The Poetical Recreations of "The Champion,"* 1822, signed Dante and R. et R. Reprinted in the *London Magazine,* May, 1825, unsigned, with the names in the last line printed only with initials and dashes, and the sub-title, "Written during the time, now happily almost forgotten, of the spy system."

Lamb probably found a certain mischievous pleasure in giving these lines the title of one of Coleridge's early poems.

The spy system was a protective movement undertaken by Lord Sidmouth (1757-1844) as Home Secretary in 1817—after the Luddite riots, the general disaffection in the country, Thistlewood's Spa Fields uprising and the break down of the prosecution. Curious reading on the subject is to be found in the memoirs of Richmond the Spy, and Peter Mackenzie's remarks on that book and its author, in *Tait's Magazine.* The spy system culminated with the failure of the Cato Street Conspiracy in 1820, which cost Thistlewood his life. That plot to murder ministers was revealed by George Edwards, one of the spies named by Lamb in the last line of this poem. Castles and Oliver were other government spies mentioned by Richmond.

Line 2. *Bedloe, Oates . . .* William Bedloe (1650-1680) and Titus Oates (1649-1705) were associated as lying informers of the proceedings of the imaginary Popish Plot against Charles II.

Page 105. *Sonnet to Mathew Wood, Esq.*

The Champion, May 13 and 14, 1820. Reprinted in *The Poetical Recreations of "The Champion,"* 1822.

Matthew Wood, afterwards Sir Matthew (1768-1843), was twice Lord Mayor of London, 1815-1817, and M.P. for the city. He was one of the principal friends and advisers of Caroline of Brunswick, George IV.'s repudiated wife. Hence his particular merit in Lamb's eyes. Later he administered the affairs of the Duke of Kent, whose trustee he was, and his baronetcy was the first bestowed by Queen Victoria. The sonnet contains another of Lamb's attacks on Canning. This statesman's mother, after the death of George Canning, her first husband, in 1771, took to the stage, where she remained for thirty years. Canning was at school at Eton, as we have seen on page 102. The course on which Wood was adjured to hold was the defence of Queen Caroline; but Canning's opposition to her cause was not so absolute as Lamb seemed to think. The ministry, of which Canning was a member, had prepared a bill by which the queen was to receive £50,000 annually so long as she remained abroad. The king insisted on divorce or nothing, and it was his own repugnance to this measure that caused Canning to tender his resignation. The king refused it, and Canning went abroad and did not return until it was abandoned.

Line 11. *Pickpocket Peer.* This would be Henry Dundas, Viscount Melville (1742-1811), Pitt's lieutenant, who was impeached for embezzling money as First Lord of the Admiralty. He was acquitted, but that was a circumstance that would hardly concern Lamb when in this mood.

Page 106. *On a Projected Journey.*

The Champion, July 15 and 16, 1820. Reprinted in *The Poetical Recreations of "The Champion,"* 1822. George IV.'s visit to Hanover did not, however, occur till October, 1821. This is entitled in Ayrton's MS. book (see page 338) "Upon the King's embarcation at Ramsgate for Hanover, 1821."

Page 106. *On a Late Empiric of "Balmy" Memory.*

The Champion, July 15 and 16, 1820. Reprinted (twice) in *The Poetical Recreations of "The Champion,"* 1822. The Empiric was Solomon, a notorious quack doctor, author of the *Guide to Health* and the purveyor of a nostrum called Balm of Gilead. One of Southey's letters (October 14, 1801) contains a diverting account of this Empiric. I copy one of Solomon's advertisements from a provincial paper:—

DR. SOLOMON'S
CORDIAL BALM OF GILEAD

To the young it will afford lasting health, strength and spirits, in place of lassitude and debility ; and to the aged and infirm it will assuredly furnish great relief and comfort by gently and safely invigorating the system ; it will not give immortality ; but if it be in the power of medicine to gild the autumn of declining years, and calmly and screnely protract the close of life beyond its narrow span, this restorative is capable of effecting that grand desideratum.

The price was 10s. 6d. a bottle.

The reference to his "namesake" is to King Solomon, whose wisdom (1 Kings iv. 33) included knowledge of trees, "from the cedar tree that is in Lebanon even unto the hyssop that springeth out of the wall."

Page 106. *Song for the C———n.*

The Champion, July 15 and 16, 1820. Reprinted in *The Poetical Recreations of "The Champion,"* 1822.

A song for the Coronation, which was fixed for 1821. Queen Caroline returned to England in June, 1820, staying with Alderman Wood (see page 336) in order to be on the spot against that event. Meanwhile the divorce proceedings began, but were eventually withdrawn. Caroline made a forcible effort to be present at the Coronation, on July 29, 1821, but was repulsed at the Abbey door. She was taken ill the next day and died on August 7. "Roy's Wife of Aldivalloch" is the Scotch song by Anne Grant.

Page 106. *The Unbeloved.*

The Champion, September 23 and 24, 1820. Reprinted in *The*

VOL. V.—22

Poetical Recreations of "The Champion," 1822. In *The Champion* the last line was preceded by

<blockquote>Place-and-heiress-hunting elf,</blockquote>

the reference to heiress-hunting touching upon Canning's marriage to Miss Joan Scott, a sister of the Duchess of Portland, who brought him £100,000.

Line 4. *C——gh.* Robert Stewart, Viscount Castlereagh and second Marquis of Londonderry (1769-1822), Foreign Secretary from 1812 until his death. He committed suicide in a state of unsound mind.

Line 6. *The Doctor.* This was the nickname commonly given to Henry Addington, Viscount Sidmouth.

Line 8. *Their chatty, childish Chancellor.* John Scott, afterwards Earl of Eldon (1751-1838), the Lord Chancellor.

Line 9. *In Liverpool some virtues strike.* Robert Banks Jenkinson, Earl of Liverpool (1770-1828), Prime Minister at the time, and therefore principal scapegoat for the Divorce Bill.

Line 10. *And little Van's beneath dislike.* Nicholas Vansittart, afterwards Baron Bexley (1766-1851), Chancellor of the Exchequer.

Line 12. *H——t.* Thomas Taylour, first Marquis of Headfort (1757-1829), the principal figure in a crim. con. case in 1804 when he was sued by a clergyman named Massey and had to pay £10,000 damages.

Page 107. *On the Arrival in England of Lord Byron's Remains.*
From a MS. book of William Ayrton's. Now first identified as Lamb's. In *The New Times*, October 24, 1825, the verses followed the "Ode to the Treadmill." The epigram, which was unsigned, then ran thus:—

<blockquote>THE POETICAL CASK

With change of climate manners alter not;
Transport a drunkard—he'll return a sot.
So lordly Juan, d——d to endless fame,
Went out a *pickle*—and comes back the same.</blockquote>

Lord Byron's body had been brought home from Greece, for burial at Hucknall Torkard, in 1824, and the cause of the epigram was a paragraph in *The New Times* of October 19, 1825, stating that the tub in which Byron's remains came home was exhibited by the captain of the *Rodney* for 2s. 6d. a head; afterwards sold to a cooper in Whitechapel; resold to a museum; and finally sold again to a cooper in Middle New Street, who was at that time using it as an advertisement.

The third line recalls Pope's line—

<blockquote>See Cromwell damn'd to everlasting fame.
Essay on Man, IV., 284.</blockquote>

Page 107. *Lines Suggested by a Sight of Waltham Cross.*
First printed in the *Englishman's Magazine*, September, 1831.

Lamb sent the epigram to Barton in a letter in November, 1827. This was then its form :—

> A stately Cross each sad spot doth attest,
> Whereat the corpse of Elinor did rest,
> From Herdly fetch'd—her Spouse so honour'd her—
> To sleep with royal dust at Westminster.
> And, if less pompous obsequies were thine,
> Duke Brunswick's daughter, princely Caroline,
> Grudge not, great ghost, nor count thy funeral losses ;
> Thou in thy life-time had'st thy share of crosses.

The body of Caroline of Brunswick, the rejected wife of George IV., was conveyed through London only by force—involving a fatal affray between the people and the Life Guards at Hyde Park corner—on its way to burial at Brunswick.

Page 108. *For the "Table Book."*
This epigram accompanies a note to William Hone. It was marked " For the *Table Book*," but does not seem to have been printed there.

Page 108. *The Royal Wonders.*
The Times, August 10, 1830. Signed Charles Lamb. This poem has not before been reprinted. The epigram refers to the Paris insurrection of July 26, 1830, which cost Charles X. his throne ; and, at home, to William IV.'s extreme fraternal friendliness to his subjects.

Page 108. *Brevis Esse Laboro.* "*One Dip.*"
Page 109. *Suum Cuique.*
These epigrams were written for the sons of James Augustus Hessey, the publisher, two Merchant Taylor boys. In *The Taylorian* for March, 1884, the magazine of the Merchant Taylors' School, the late Archdeacon Hessey, one of the boys in question, told the story of their authorship. It was a custom many years ago for Election Day at Merchant Taylors' School to be marked by the recitation of original epigrams in Greek, Latin and English, which, although the boys themselves were usually the authors, might also be the work of other hands. Archdeacon Hessey and his brother, as the following passage explains, resorted to Charles Lamb for assistance :—

> The subjects for 1830 were *Suum Cuique* and *Brevis esse laboro*. After some three or four exercise nights I confess that I was literally " at my wits' end." But a brilliant idea struck me. I had frequently, boy as I was, seen Charles Lamb (Elia) at my father's house, and once, in 1825 or 1826, I had been taken to have tea with him and his sister, Mary Lamb, at their little house, Colebrook Cottage, a whitish-brown tenement, standing by itself, close to the New River, at Islington. He was very kind, as he always was to young people, and very quaint. I told him that I had devoured his " Roast Pig ;" he congratulated me on possessing a thorough schoolboy's appetite. And he was pleased when I mentioned my having seen the boys at Christ's Hospital at their public suppers, which then took place on the Sunday evenings in Lent. " Could this good-natured and humorous old gentleman be prevailed upon to give me an Epigram ?" "I don't know," said my father, to whom I put the question, " but I will ask him at any rate, and send him the mottoes." In a day or two there arrived from Enfield, to which Lamb had removed some time in 1827, not one, but two epigrams, one on each subject. That on *Suum Cuique* was in Latin, and was suggested by the grim satisfaction which had recently been expressed by the public at the capture and execution of some notorious highwayman. That on *Brevis esse laboro* was in English, and might have represented an adventure

which had befallen Lamb himself, for he stammered frequently, though he was not so grievous a *Balbulus* as his friend George Darley, whom I had also often seen. I need scarcely say that the two Epigrams were highly appreciated, and that my brother and myself, for I gave my brother one of them, were objects of envy to our schoolfellows.

The death of George IV., however, prevented their being recited on the occasion for which they were written.

"*Suum Cuique*," which was signed F. Hessey, was thus translated by its presumptive author :—

> A thief, on dreary Bagshot's heath well known,
> Was fond of making others' goods his own ;
> *Meum* was never thought of, nor was *Tuum*,
> But everything with him was counted *Suum*.
> At length each gets his own, and no one grieves ;
> The rope his neck, Jack Ketch his clothes receives :
> His body to dissecting knife has gone ;
> Himself to Orcus : well—each gets his own.

The English epigram, which was signed J. A. Hessey, was a rhyming version of a story which Lamb was fond of telling. Three, at least, of his friends relate the story in their recollections of him : Mrs. Mathews in her life of her husband ; Leigh Hunt in *The Companion;* and De Quincey in *Fraser's Magazine*. The incident possibly occurred to Lamb when as a boy—or little more—he stayed at Margate about 1790. Lamb must have written Merchant Taylors' epigrams before, for in 1803, in a letter to Godwin about writing to order, he speaks of having undertaken, three or four times, a schoolboy copy of verses for Merchant Taylors' boys at a guinea a copy, and refers to the trouble and vexation the work was to him.

Writing to Southey on May 10, 1830, Lamb said, at the end :—

"Perhaps an epigram (not a very happy-gram) I did for a schoolboy yesterday may amuse. I pray Jove he may not get a flogging for any false quantity ; but 'tis, with one exception, the only Latin verses I have made for forty years, and I did it 'to order.'

"CUIQUE SUUM"

> " Adsciscit sibi divitias et opes alienas
> Fur, rapiens, spolians quod mihi, quod-que tibi,
> Proprium erat, temnens hæc verba, meum-que tuum-que
> Omne suum est : tandem Cui-que Suum tribuit.
> Dat resti collum ; restes, vah ! carnifici dat ;
> Sese Diabolo, sic bene ; Cuique Suum."

Page 109. [*On "The Literary Gazette."*]

This epigram, headed "Rejected Epigrams, 6"—evidently torn from a paper containing a number of verses (the figure 7 is just visible underneath it)—is in the British Museum among the letters left by Vincent Novello. It is inscribed, "In handwriting of Mr. Charles Lamb." The same collection contains a copy, in Mrs. Cowden Clarke's handwriting, of the sonnet to Mrs. Jane Towers (see page 47). *The Literary Gazette* was William Jerdan's paper, a poor thing, which Lamb had reason to dislike for the attack it made upon him when *Album Verses* was published (see note on page 305).

Page 109. *Epigram: On the Fast-Day.*
John Payne Collier, in his privately printed reminiscences, *An Old Man's Diary*, quotes this epigram as being by Charles Lamb. It may have been written for the Fast-Day on October 19, 1803, for that on May 25, 1804, or for a later one. Lamb tells Hazlitt in February, 1806, that he meditates a stroll on the Fast-Day.

Page 109. *Nonsense Verses.*
Mr. W. Carew Hazlitt, in *Mary and Charles Lamb*, 1874, says: " I found these lines—a parody on the popular, or nursery, ditty, ' Lady-bird, lady-bird, fly away home'—officiating as a wrapper to some of Mr. Hazlitt's hair. There is no signature; but the handwriting is unmistakably Lamb's; nor are the lines themselves the worst of his playful effusions." The piece suggests that Lamb, in a wild mood, was turning his own "Angel Help" (see page 48) into ridicule—possibly to satisfy some one who dared him to do it, or vowed that such a feat could not be accomplished.

ELECTION VERSES

In connection with *The Champion* trifles I should like to refer to the election squibs which Lamb is said to have written for Sergeant Wilde, afterwards Lord Truro (1782-1855), for use at the Newark election of 1829. Wilde, who stood in the Blue interest, opposed Michael Thomas Sadler (1780-1835), the reformer, of Leeds, whose most influential supporter was the Duke of Newcastle, the owner of much neighbouring property, acting in the person of his agent, Mr. Tallents. Whether or no Lamb really had a hand in this election I am not able to say with certainty; but it is so stated in Messrs. Ford and Hodson's *History of Enfield*, 1873. We know that the Wildes were Lamb's neighbours at Enfield, while the presence at Newark of Martin Burney as one of the Sergeant's helpers is circumstantial evidence of a kind. It is easy to believe that as the need for squibs arose Burney applied to Lamb as the man to write them. By the kindness of Mr. Cornelius Brown, of Newark, I have seen a complete collection of these squibs, both for the election of 1829 and of 1830, at both of which Wilde was unsuccessful. My impression is that two of the 1829 squibs may have been written by Lamb, but that none of those of 1830 were. Of the verses which I think Lamb may have written, the first is in imitation of "The Beggar's Petition," an old and favourite piece of rhyme that we know him to have been interested in, from his postscript to the *Elia* essay on the "Decay of Beggars" (see Vol. II., page 387):—

THE BEATEN CANDIDATE'S PETITION

Pity the sorrows of a poor LEEDS MAN,
  A flattering Duke has brought him to your door;
His Hopes are dwindled to the shortest span;
  Oh! give one *cheer*, he will not ask for more.

The POLL—the Votes my poverty bespeak;
  Those horrid sounds still more enhance my fears;
And many a furrow in my time-worn cheek
  Will be a channel to a flood of tears.

A pleasant seat in NEWARK's beauteous town,
  With tempting aspect drew me from *my book*,
For my DUKE *there* a residence had found,
  His *Tallents* had a most engaging look.

Hard is the fate of DUKE'S MEN here I find,
  For, as I craved your Int'rest and your Vote,
A fearful WILDE Man, rushing like the wind,
  Has chas'd the Duke, and greatly chang'd my note.

Oh! take me back again to my own Town,
  Keen are your Questions—meet them fair I can't;
Like DUKE'S IDEAS are my answers flown,
  And, like a whipt child, now for home I pant.

Sadler was not, however, beaten. The other piece which Lamb might have written ran thus:—

WILDE!
OR, NOW OR NEVER

Freemen! do not be beguil'd,
One and all go poll for WILDE;
Now's the time to strike the blow,
Lay your daring Tyrants low.

Freedom's Sun has on you smil'd,
Hasten then and vote for WILDE;
He's the Man to set you free—
Up, and gain your Liberty.

Britons look at each dear Child
Praying you to vote for WILDE;
Will you hear them plead in vain?
Will you hug the galling chain?

Do not fear to be revil'd,
Boldly on and vote for WILDE;
Nature's birthright o'er you waves,
Burst your bonds, be no more Slaves.

Act with firm resolve, tho' mild,
Bravely fix your choice on WILDE;
He the DUCAL power has shook,
He will bring your foes to *book*.

Even now the Bill is fil'd,
And your Counsel, SERJEANT WILDE,
He will make the SADLER *sidle*,
Stir him up with *bit* and *bridle*.

If you would be Freemen styl'd,
Go at once and vote for WILDE;
If you'd be a DUCAL Twaddler,
Then turn round and vote for SADLER.

PERSONAL EPIGRAMS

In this connection it may also be of interest to quote the following letter from the *New York Tribune* for February 22, 1879 (preserved in the Alexander Ireland collection in the Manchester Free Library).

The examples therein given of Lamb's humour are not very satisfying; but in appreciating this kind of facetiæ personal knowledge of the author's butts is indispensable; and that we have not.

To the Editor of *The Tribune*.

SIR,—A very few years since I was engaged upon a catalogue of the books of the India Office, London. Among the messengers of the office, whose duty was limited to the conveyance of papers from the secretaries of departments to the council or the clerks, was Fraschini, once the valet of Lord Byron. He had been appointed to the office by Lord Broughton (President of the India Board in 1846), who, as John Cam Hobhouse, was Byron's friend and fellow-traveller. One day Fraschini came to me in the Library, and, remarking that I was occupying the chair which Charles Lamb used when he was a clerk in the old India House, told me there was a small packet of papers among the manuscripts of the library, which had been found in Lamb's desk long after his death. I was curious to look at the packet. It was endorsed "Memoires pour servir," and being opened, disclosed certain *disjecta membra* which had formed the groundwork of some of Elia's sketches and essays. But there were one or two sheets on which Lamb had written some comic epitaphs which he had evidently thrown off at jocular moments for the amusement of fellow-clerks who could bear a little fun at their own expense. Naturally coveting any scraps of it in Lamb's handwriting, I sought the "next of kin," who alone had any right to them, and, after a great deal of trouble, found an elderly lady, the daughter of a cousin of Lamb's. She thought they would be in better keeping at the office than in her or my hands, but she gave me leave to take copies, which I did at once. Seven years have passed, and these queer epitaphs never have left my possession, nor have I shown them to more than one of my friends. Perhaps they would have remained amidst the bundles of MSS. which fill my desk and closets, had not accident lately brought them to my recollection, and the delightful miscellanies of the *Tribune* suggested that they might be acceptable to readers who can appreciate the works and respect the memory of the amiable Charles Lamb. Here they are. The first two epitaphs referred to two clerks in the office whose names I traced as having been in the office sixty years back.

"Here lies the body of Timothy Wagstaff,
Who was once as tall and as straight as a flagstaff;
But now that he's gone to another world,
His staff is broken and his flag is furled."

The second refers to an old invalid officer of the British Infantry, who eked out his miserable half-pay as a copyist in the military department.

"Here lieth the body of Captain Sturms,
Once 'food for powder,' now for worms,
At the battle of Meida he lost his legs,
And stumped about on wooden pegs.
Naught cares he now for such worthless things,
He was borne to heaven on angels' wings."

The following is ingenious and graceful as well as humorous. It was endorsed "On Tom Dix's Mother," and was probably intended as a serious inscription on a "stoned urn."

"*Ci gît* the remains of Margaret Dix,
Who was young in old age I ween,
Though Envy with Malice cried 'seventy-six,'
The Graces declared her 'nineteen.'"

It should be explained that Mrs. Dix was born on February 29 (leap year), and thus had only one birthday every four years. Consequently, by the time she had completed her seventy-sixth year, her nativity had been celebrated only nineteen times.

The last *jeu de mot* was levelled at the medical officer of the establishment, who was not held, professionally, in much respect.

"To the memory of Dr. Onesimus Drake,
Who forced good people his drugs to take—
No wonder his patients were oft on the rack
For this 'duck of a man' was a terrible quack."

My old friend James Kenney, a son of the author of "Raising the Wind" (to whom

I showed the epitaphs), told me of one he had seen of Lamb's on Captain Matthew Day, of the 20th Regiment of Foot. Day was one of the putative sons of George IV.—the mother a handsome lady of Brighton. Kenney repeated the epitaph to me, and I took a copy and added it to my collection. It ran thus :—

> " Beneath this slab lies Matthew Day,
> If his body had not been snatched away
> To be by Science dissected ;
> Should it have gone, one thing is clear :
> His soul the last trump is sure to hear,
> And thus be resurrected."
> * * * *

WASHINGTON, D. C.,
February 17th, 1879.

J. H. SIDDONS.

A fellow clerk of Lamb's named Ogilvie told Mr. Joseph H. Twichell one or two more of Lamb's office rhymes (see *Scribner's Magazine*, March, 1876). The best is this, of a clerk named Wawd :—

> What Wawd knows, God knows ;
> But God knows *what* Wawd knows !

Crabb Robinson in an allusion to Wawd in his diary spells his name Wodd. He once nearly blinded Lamb by jerking a pen full of ink into his eye.

Page 110. SATAN IN SEARCH OF A WIFE, 1831.

This ballad was published by Moxon, anonymously, in 1831, although the authorship was no secret. In its volume form it was illustrated by the quaint woodcuts reproduced opposite the pages 346, 348, 350, 352 and 354, which were the work of George Cruikshank, engraved by G. W. Bonner. Lamb probably did not value his ballad very highly. Writing to Moxon in 1833 he says, "I wish you would omit 'by the Author of Elia' now, in advertising that damn'd 'Devil's Wedding.'"

There is a reference to the poem, in Lamb's letter to Moxon of October 24, 1831, which needs explanation. Moxon's *Englishman's Magazine*, after running under his control for three months, was suddenly abandoned. Lamb, who seems to have been paid in advance for his work, wrote to Moxon on the subject, approving him for getting the weight off his mind and adding :—

"I have one on mine. The cash in hand which as * * * * * * less truly says, burns in my pocket. I feel queer at returning it (who does not ?). You feel awkward at re-taking it (who ought not ?) is there no middle way of adjusting this fine embarrassment. I think I have hit upon a medium to skin the sore place over, if not quite to heal it. You hinted that there might be something under £10 by and by accruing to me *Devil's Money*. You are sanguine—say £7 10s.—that I entirely renounce and abjure all future interest in, I insist upon it, and 'by Him I will not name' I won't touch a penny of it. That will split your loss one half—and leave me conscientious possessor of what I hold. Less than your assent to this, no proposal will I accept of."

Satan in Search of a Wife;

WITH THE WHOLE PROCESS OF

HIS COURTSHIP AND MARRIAGE,

AND WHO DANCED AT THE WEDDING.

BY

AN EYE WITNESS.

London:
EDWARD MOXON, 64, NEW BOND STREET.
M.DCCC.XXXI.

A few months later, writing again to Moxon, he says :—

"I am heartily sorry my Devil does not answer. We must try it a little longer; and, after all, I think I must insist on taking a portion of its loss upon myself. It is too much that you should lose by two adventures."

According to some reminiscences of Lamb by Mr. J. Fuller Russell, printed in *Notes and Queries*, April 1, 1882, Lamb suppressed "Satan in Search of a Wife," for the reason that the Vicar of Enfield, Dr. Cresswell, also had married a tailor's daughter, and might be hurt by the ballad. The correspondence quoted above does not, I think, bear out Mr. Russell's statement. If the book were still being advertised in 1833, we can hardly believe that any consideration for the Vicar of Enfield would cause its suppression. This gentleman had been at Enfield for several years, and Lamb would have either suppressed the book immediately or not at all; but possibly his wish to disassociate the name of Elia from the work was inspired by the coincidence.

The ballad does not call for much annotation. The legend mentioned in the dedication tells how Cecilia, by her music, drew an angel from heaven, who brought her roses of Paradise. The ballad of King Cophetua and the beggar maid may be read in the *Percy Reliques*. Hecate is a triple deity, known as Luna in heaven, Diana on earth, and Proserpine in hell. In the reference to Milton I think Lamb must have been thinking of the lines, *Paradise Lost*, I., 27-28 :—

> Say first, for Heav'n hides nothing from thy view,
> Nor the deep tract of Hell . . .

or, *Paradise Lost*, V., 542 :—

> And so from Heav'n to deepest Hell.

Alecto (Part I, Stanza II.) was one of the Furies.—Old Parr (Stanza IV.) lived to be 152; he died in 1635.—Semiramis (Stanza XVII.) was Queen of Assyria, under whom Babylon became the most wonderful city in the world; Helen was Helen of Troy, the cause of the war between the Greeks and Trojans; Medea was the cruel lover of Jason, who recovered the Golden Fleece.—Clytemnestra (Stanza XVIII.) was the wife and murderer of Agamemnon; Joan of Naples was Giovanna, the wife of Andrea of Hungary, who was accused of assassinating him. Landor wrote a play, "Giovanna of Naples," to "restore her fame" and "requite her wrongs;" Cleopatra was the Queen of Egypt, and lover of Mark Antony; Jocasta married her son Œdipus unknowing who he was.—A tailor's "goose" (Stanza XXII.) is his smoothing-iron, and his "hell" (Stanza XXIII.) the place where he throws his shreds and débris.—Lamb's own "Vision of Horns" (Vol. I., page 254) serves as a commentary on Stanza XXVII.; and in his essay "On the Melancholy of Tailors" (Vol. I., page 172) are further remarks on the connection between tailors and cabbage in Stanza I. of Part II.—The two Miss Crockfords of Stanza XVIII. would be the daughters of William Crockford, of Crockford's Club, who, after succeeding to his father's business of fishmonger, opened the gaming-house which bore his name and amassed a fortune of upwards of a million.—Semele (Stanza XXI.), whose lightest wish Jupiter had sworn to grant, was treacherously induced to express the desire that Jupiter would visit her with the divine pomp in which he approached his lawful wife Juno. He did so, and she was consumed by his lightning and thunderbolts.—The bard of Stanza XXV. is, of course, Virgil.

Page 121. PROLOGUES AND EPILOGUES.

Writing to Sarah Stoddart concerning Godwin's "Faulkener" Mary Lamb remarked: "Prologues and Epilogues will be his [Charles's] death."

Page 121. *Epilogue to "Antonio."*

Had Lamb not sent this epilogue to Manning in the letter of December 13, 1800, we should have no copy of it; for Godwin, by Lamb's advice, did not print it with the play. Writing to Godwin two days before, Lamb remarked:—

"I have been plotting how to abridge the Epilogue. But I cannot see that any lines can be spared, retaining the connection, except these two, which are better out:

"Why should I instance, &c.,
The sick man's purpose, &c.,

and then the following line must run thus,

"The truth by an example best is shown."

See lines 16, 17 and 18.

Godwin's "Antonio," produced at Drury Lane on December 13, 1800, was a failure. Many years afterwards Lamb told the story of the unlucky first night (see "The Old Actors" in Appendix to Vol. II. of this edition, page 292). Godwin, its author, was, of course, William Godwin, the philosopher (1756-1836). Later Lamb wrote the prologue to another of his plays (see page 123 and note).

Lines 35 and 36. *Suett . . . Bannister.* Richard Suett (1755-1805) and Jack Bannister (1760-1836), two famous comedians of that day (see Vol. II., "The Old Actors," again).

Line 62. *"Pizarro."* Sheridan's patriotic melodrama, produced May 24, 1799, at Drury Lane.

Page 123. *Prologue to "Faulkener."*

William Godwin's tragedy "Faulkener" was produced at Drury Lane, December 16, 1807, with some success. Lamb's letters to Godwin of September 9 and 17, 1801, suggest that he had a share in the framing of the plot. Later the play was taken in hand by Thomas Holcroft and made more dramatic.

According to Godwin's preface, 1807, the story was taken from the 1745 edition of Defoe's *Roxana,* which contains the episode of Susannah imagining herself to be Roxana's daughter and throwing herself in her mother's way. Godwin transformed the daughter into a son. Lamb,

SATAN IN SEARCH OF A WIFE
FRONTISPIECE

NOTES

however, seems to have believed this episode to be in the first edition, 1724, and afterwards to have been removed at the entreaty of Southerne, Defoe's friend (see Lamb's letters to Walter Wilson, Defoe's biographer, of December 16, 1822, and February 24, 1823). But it is in reality the first edition which lacks the episode, and Mr. G. A. Aitken, Defoe's latest editor, doubts Southerne's interference altogether and considers Susannah's curiosity an alien interpolation. For Lamb's other remarks on Defoe see also the "Ode to the Tread Mill," page 67 of this volume, and "Estimate of Defoe's Secondary Novels" (Vol. I., page 329 and note). Writing to Walter Wilson on November 15, 1829, on the receipt of his memoirs of Defoe, Lamb exclaims: "De Foe was always my darling."

Page 123. *Epilogue to "Time's a Tell-Tale."*
A play by Henry Siddons (1774-1815), Mrs. Siddons' eldest son. It was produced in 1807 at Drury Lane, with Lamb's prologue, which was, however, received so badly that on the second night another was substituted for it.

Page 125. *Prologue to "Remorse."*
Coleridge's tragedy "Remorse," a recasting of his "Osorio" (written at Sheridan's instigation in 1797), was produced with success on January 23, 1813; and was printed, with the prologue, in the same year. Lamb's prologue, "spoken by Mr. Carr," was also (according to Mr. Dykes Campbell) a recasting of some verses composed for the prize offered by the Drury Lane Committee in the previous year, 1812, in response to their advertisement for a suitable poem to be read at the reopening of the new building after the fire of 1809. It was, of course, this competition which brought forth the *Rejected Addresses* (1812) of the brothers James and Horace Smith. Lamb was not among the writers therein parodied, but Coleridge was. Lamb's turn came later, in 1825, when P. G. Patmore, afterwards his friend and the father of Coventry Patmore, wrote *Rejected Articles*, in which was a very poor imitation of Elia.

Line 9. *Betterton or Booth.* Thomas Betterton, born probably in 1635, acted for the last time in 1710, the year in which he died. Barton Booth (1681-1733) left the stage in 1728. Betterton was much at the Little Theatre in Lincoln's Inn Fields; also at Sir John Vanbrugh's theatre in the Haymarket.

Line 11. *Quin.* James Quin (1693-1766) of Drury Lane and Covent Garden, Garrick's great rival, famous as Falstaff. His last appearance was in 1753.

Line 12. *Garrick.* Garrick's Drury Lane, in which Lamb saw his first play, was that built by Sir Christopher Wren in 1674. It lasted, with certain alterations, including a new face by the brothers Adam, nearly 120 years. The seating capacity of this theatre was modest. In 1794 a new Drury Lane Theatre, the third, was opened— too large for comfortable seeing or hearing. This was burned down in 1809; and the new one, the fourth, and that in which "Remorse" was produced, was opened in 1812. This is the building (with certain additions) that still stands (1903).

Lines 13-16. *Garrick in the shades.* Many years later Lamb used the same idea in connection with Elliston (see "To the Shade of Elliston," Vol. II., page 166).

Line 20. *Ben and Fletcher.* Ben Jonson (1573 ?-1637) and John Fletcher (1579-1625), Beaumont's collaborator. Ben Jonson's "Every Man in His Humour" was produced at the Globe in 1598, Shakspeare being in the caste; but in the main he wrote for Henslowe, who was connected with the Rose and the Swan, on Bankside, and with the theatre in Newington Butts, and who built, with Alleyn, in 1600, the Fortune in Golden Lane, Cripplegate Without. Beaumont and Fletcher's plays went for the most part to Burbage, who owned the Globe at Southwark and the Blackfriars' Theatre. Shakspeare also wrote for Burbage.

Page 126. *Epilogue to "Debtor and Creditor."*

"Debtor and Creditor" was a farce by James Kenney (1780-1849), Lamb's friend, with whom he stayed at Versailles in 1822. The play was produced April 20, 1814.

Gosling's experiences as a dramatic author seem to have been curiously like Lamb's own. See note to "Mr. H." on page 368.

Line 12. *They never bring the Spanish.* Spanish, old slang for money.

Line 40. *Polito's.* Polito at one time kept the menagerie in Exeter Change.

Line 42. *Larry Whack.* Larry Whack is referred to in the play. Says Sampson, on one occasion: "Who be I ? Come, that be capital! Why, ben't I Sampson Miller ? Didn't I bang the Darby Corps at York Races . . . and durst Sir Harry Slang bring me up to town to fight Larry Whack, the Irish ruffian ? . . ."

Page 128. *Epilogue to an Amateur Performance of "Richard II."*

This epilogue, says Canon Ainger, who first printed it, was written for a performance given by the family of Barron Field in 1824. The family of Henry Field, Barron's father, would perhaps be more accurate; for Barron Field was childless. The verses, which I print by permission of Miss Kendall, Miss Field's residuary legatee, were given to Canon Ainger by the late Miss M. L. Field, of Hastings. In his interesting note he adds of this lady (to whom Lamb addressed the verses on page 94), "she told me that she (then a girl of 19) sat by the side of Lamb during the performance. She remembered well, she said, that in course of the play a looking glass was broken, and that Lamb turned to her and whispered 'Sixpence!' She added that before the play began, while the guests were assembling, the butler announced 'Mr. Negus!'—upon which Lamb exclaimed, 'Hand him round!'"

Lamb refers in the opening lines to Edmund Kean and John Philip Kemble. The phrase "sad civility" is from Pope, "Epistle to Dr.

SATAN IN SEARCH OF A WIFE

ILLUSTRATION TO STANZAS VIII AND IX, PART I

NOTES

Arbuthnot," line 37. The reference to Garrick I have not succeeded in tracing.

In this connection it may be interesting to state that Lamb told Patmore that he considered John of Gaunt, time-honoured Lancaster, the grandest name in the world.

Page 129. *Prologue to "The Wife."*
The original form of the prologue to James Sheridan Knowles' comedy, not hitherto collected in any edition of Lamb's writings, is preserved in the Forster collection in the South Kensington Museum. It was sent to Moxon, for Knowles, in April, 1833. Thus:—

> Stern heaven in anger no poor wretch invades
> More sorely than the Man who drives *two trades*,
> Author and Actor! why has wayward fate
> Decreed to oppress me with the double weight?
> Wanting a *Prologue*, I in need applied
> To three Poetic-Friends; was thrice denied.
> One gaped on me with supercilious air,
> And mutter'd "vagabond, rogue, strolling-player."
> A poet once, I found, with looks aghast,
> By turning player, I had lost my *caste*.
> Wanting a *Speaker for my Prologue*, I
> Did to my friends behind the scenes apply
> With like success; each look'd on me askance,
> And scowl'd on me with a suspicious glance.
> The rogues—I dearly like them—but it stung them
> To think—God wot—a bard had got among them!
> Their service in the drama was enough:
> "The poet might rehearse the poet's stuff."
> Driven on myself for speech and prologue too,
> Dear patrons of our art; I turn to you!
> If in these scenes that follow you can trace
> What once has pleased you, an unbidden grace,
> A touch of nature's work, an awkward start,
> Or ebullition of an Irish heart,
> Cry, clap, commend it. If you like it not,
> Your former kindness cannot be forgot.
> Condemn me, damn me, hiss me, to your mind—
> I have a stock of gratitude behind.

In a postscript letter Lamb altered the final couplet to—

> Condemn them, damn them, hiss them—as you will—
> Their author is your grateful servant still.

Lamb added: "Mind I don't care the 100,000th part of a bad sixpence if Knowles gets a prologue more to his mind." Knowles, however, liked it, and it was spoken on the night (April 24, 1833) by Mr. Warde, not by the dramatist. It is curious that the prologue was not attributed to Lamb when the play was printed. Knowles wrote in the preface: "To my early, my trusty and honoured friend, Charles Lamb, I owe my thanks for a delightful Epilogue, composed almost as soon as it was requested. To an equally dear friend, I am equally indebted for my Prologue."

Page 130. *Epilogue to "The Wife."*
This epilogue was spoken by Miss Ellen Tree.

Page 131. JOHN WOODVIL.

First published in 1802 in a slender volume entitled *John Woodvil: a Tragedy. By C. Lamb. To which are added Fragments of Burton, the author of the Anatomy of Melancholy.* The full contents of the book were:—

John Woodvil; Ballad, From the German (see page 27); Helen (see page 26); Curious Fragments, I., II., III., IV.; The Argument; The Consequence (see Vol. I., page 31, and note; also pages 27 and 28 of the present volume and notes).

John Woodvil was reprinted by Lamb in the *Works*, 1818, the text of which is followed here.

If Mr. Fuller Russell was right in his statement in *Notes and Queries*, April 1, 1882, that Lamb told him he "had lost £25 by his best effort, *John Woodvil*," we must suppose that the book was published wholly or partially at his own costs.

The history of the poem which follows is, with an omission and addition here and there, that compiled by the late Mr. Dykes Campbell and contributed by him to *The Athenæum*, October 31 and November 14, 1891. Mr. Campbell had the opportunity of collating the edition of 1802 with a manuscript copy made by Lamb and his sister for Manning. With that patient thoroughness and discrimination which made his work as an editor so valuable, Mr. Campbell minutely examined this copy and put the results on record; and they are now for the first time, by permission of Mrs. Dykes Campbell and the Editor of *The Athenæum*, incorporated in an edition of Lamb's writings. The copy itself, I may add, when it came into the market, was secured by an American collector. Mr. Campbell's words follow, my own interpolations being within square brackets.

Lamb's first allusion to the future *John Woodvil* occurs in a letter to Southey (October 29, 1798), at a time when the two young men were exchanging a good many copies of verses for mutual criticism. "Not having anything of my own," writes Lamb, "to send you in return (though, to tell the truth, I am at work upon something which if I were to cut away and garble, perhaps I might send you an extract or two that might not displease you: but I will not do that; and whether it will come to anything I know not, for I am as slow as a Fleming painter, when I compose anything) I will crave leave to put down a few lines of old Christopher Marlowe's." Lamb must soon have got rid of his objections to cutting away and garbling, for before a month had elapsed he had sent Southey two extracts, first the "Dying Lover" [see "Dramatic Fragment," page 79], and next (November 28) "The Witch" [see page 177], both of which passages were excluded from the printed play. [The letter, which is wrongly dated April 20, 1799, in some editions, concludes (of "The Witch"): "This is the extract I bragged of as superior to that I sent you from Marlowe: perhaps you will smile."]

Charles Lloyd shared with Southey the pains and pleasures of criticising Lamb's verses, for Lamb asks the latter if he agrees with Lloyd in disliking something in "The Witch" [printed on page 178.

SATAN IN SEARCH OF A WIFE

FRONTISPIECE TO PART II

NOTES

Thus: "Lloyd objects to 'shutting up the womb of his purse' in my curse (which, for a Christian witch in a Christian country, is not too mild, I hope). Do you object? I think there is a strangeness in the idea, as well as 'shaking the poor little snakes from his door,' which suits the speaker. Witches illustrate, as fine ladies do, from their own familiar objects, and snakes and the shutting up of wombs are in their way. I don't know that this last charge has been before brought against 'em nor either the sour milk or the mandrake babe; but I affirm these be things a witch would do if she could."]

Lamb proposes also to adopt an emendation of Southey's in the "Dying Lover"—"though I do not feel the objection against 'Silent Prayer,'" and in the event he did very sensibly stick to his own opinion, for in the *London Magazine* the line runs, as first written:—

He put a silent prayer up for the bride.

One wonders what harm Southey can have seen in it. At this time Southey was collecting verses for the first volume of his *Annual Anthology* (provisionally called the *Kalendar*), and inviting contributions from Lamb. In writing before November 28, 1798, "This ['The Witch'] and the 'Dying Lover' I gave you are the only extracts I can give without mutilation," Lamb may have meant that Southey was at liberty to print them in the *Anthology*. A year later, October 31, 1799, when the second volume was in preparation, Lamb wrote:—

"I shall have nothing to communicate, I fear, to the *Anthology*. You shall have some fragments of my play if you desire them; but I think I would rather print it whole."

As a matter of fact, Lamb contributed nothing to the collection except the lines "Living without God in the World," printed in the first volume [see page 17. To *Recreations in Agriculture, Natural History*, etc., 1801, edited by Dr. James Anderson, a friend of George Dyer, Lamb, however, sent "Description of a Forest Life," "The General Lover" (What is it you love?) and the "Dying Lover," called "Fragment in Dialogue." There are slight differences in the text, the chief alteration being in line 3 of the "Description of a Forest Life":—

Bursting the lubbar bonds of sleep that bound him.]

Reverting to the letter of November 28, one learns Lamb's intentions as to the play:—

"My Tragedy will be a medley (as I intend it to be a medley) of laughter and tears, prose and verse, and in some places rhyme, songs, wit, pathos, humour, and, if possible, sublimity; [at least it is not a fault in my intention if it does not comprehend most of these discordant atoms. Heaven send they dance not the 'Dance of Death'!]."

The composition went on slowly and in a very casual way, for on January 21, 1799, he writes again to Southey:—

"I have only one slight passage to send you, scarce worth the sending, which I want to edge in somewhere into my play, which, by the way, hath not received the addition of ten lines, besides, since I saw you."

The "slight passage" is one which, it will be seen, was "edged in" near the end of the second act, but taken out again—that beginning [page 361]:—

> I saw him [John Woodvil] in the day of Worcester fight,
> Whither he came at twice seven years,
> Under the discipline of the Lord Falkland
> (His uncle by the mother's side), etc.

Lamb naïvely asks Southey, "But did Falkland die before the Worcester fight? In that case I must make bold to unclify some other nobleman." I suppose Southey must have answered that Falkland had been killed at Newbury eight years before Worcester fight, for when the passage had been edged into the play, *Naseby* and *Ashley* were substituted for "Worcester" and "Falkland" respectively. This was as bad a shot as the first, for Sir Anthony Cooper, whether at Naseby or no, did not become Lord Ashley until sixteen years after that fight.[1] Had the passage escaped the pruning knife, Lamb's historical research would no doubt have provided a proper battle and a proper uncle for his hero. Again Lloyd appears as a critic, and this time he is obeyed, probably because his objection to "portrayed in his face" was backed by Southey. "I like the line," says Lamb, but he altered it to

> Of Valour's beauty in his youthful face

in the Manning MS. Four months later, on May 20, Lamb sends Southey the charming passage about forest-life on page 153, and defends his blank verse against Southey's censure of the pauses at the end of the lines; he does it on the model of Shakespeare, he says, in his "endeavour after a colloquial ease and spirit." Talfourd printed the passage in full, but some later editors have cut down the twenty-four lines to the six opening ones, to the loss of a point in the letter. Lamb says he "loves to anticipate charges of unoriginality," adding— ["the first line is almost Shakespeare's :—

> "To have my love to bed and to arise.
> "'Midsummer-Night's Dream.'

I think there is a sweetness in the versification not unlike some rhymes in that exquisite play, and] the last line but three is yours." This line describes how the deer, as they came tripping by,

> Then stop and gaze, then turn, they know not why.

Lamb thus gives the line and his reference :—

> —— An eye
> That met the gaze, or turn'd it knew not why.
> "Rosamund's Epistle."

---

[1] Sir Jacob Astley (?), but he too was ennobled *after* Naseby.

SATAN IN SEARCH OF A WIFE
ILLUSTRATION OPPOSITE STANZAS XXII AND XXIII, PART II

But, of course, he misquotes both line and title—though Southey would feel flattered in finding that his friend's memory had done so well. As the editors have not annotated the passage, I will say here that Lamb should have quoted

> The modest eye
> That met the glance, or turn'd, it knew not why.
> "Rosamund to Henry."

The poem is one of those in the now scarce volume which Southey and Lovel published jointly at Bath in 1795, *Poems: containing "The Retrospect."* [It was this forest passage which, as Hazlitt tells us in his *Spirit of the Age*, so puzzled Godwin. After looking in vain through the old dramatists for it, he applied to Lamb himself.]

By the end of October the play had evidently been completed (though not yet named), for on the 31st Southey was asked, "Have you seen it, or shall I lend you a copy? I want your opinion of it." None is recorded here, but more than two years later, when Southey was in London, he gave it to Danvers (*Letters of R. S.*, II., 184): "Lamb and his sister see us often: he is printing his play, which will please you by the exquisite beauty of its poetry, and provoke you by the exquisite silliness of its story."

The play must have been baptised as "Pride's Cure" soon after Hallowe'en, for at Christmas it was submitted under that title to Kemble, and about the same time (December 28, 1799) we find Lamb defending the title (with the vehemence and subtlety of a doubter, as I read) against the adverse criticism of Manning and Mrs. Charles Lloyd. Lamb had lately been on a visit to these friends at Cambridge, and had doubtless taken a copy of his play with him and received their objections there and then—for his defence does not seem to have been provoked by a letter. [In an unpublished letter to Charles Lloyd that has come to light since Mr. Dykes Campbell wrote, belonging to middle December, 1799, Lamb asks for his play to be returned to him, suggesting that Mrs. Lloyd shall despatch it. It was probably in the letter that accompanied the parcel that the criticism of the title was found. Lamb thus defended it:—

"By-the-bye, I think you and Sophia both incorrect with regard to the *title* of the *play*. Allowing your objection (which is not necessary, as pride may be, and is in real life often, cured by misfortunes not directly originating from its own acts, as Jeremy Taylor will tell you a naughty desire is sometimes sent to cure it; I know you read these *practical divines*)—but allowing your objection, does not the betraying of his father's secret directly spring from pride?—from the pride of wine, and a full heart, and a proud over-stepping of the ordinary rules of morality, and contempt of the prejudices of mankind, which are not to bind superior souls—'as *trust* in *the matter* of *secrets* all *ties* of *blood*, etc., etc., keeping of *promises*, the feeble mind's religion, binding our *morning knowledge* to the performance of what *last night's ignorance* spake'—does he not prate, that 'Great Spirits' must do more than die for their friend? Does not the pride of wine incite him to display some evidence of friendship, which its own irregularity shall make great? This I know, that I meant his punishment not alone to be a cure for his daily and habitual *pride,* but the direct consequence and appropriate punishment of a particular act of pride.

"If you do not understand it so, it is my fault in not explaining my meaning."]

Manning seems to have begged for a copy—for reconsideration, perhaps —for Lamb, on February 13, 1800, promised him a copy "of my play and the *Falstaff Letters* in a day or two." There is no trace of the former having been sent, but the latter certainly was, for on March 1 he presses Manning for his opinion of it—hopes he is "prepared to call it a bundle of the sharpest, queerest, profoundest humours," etc., as he was accustomed to hope when that book was in question. The next mention of the play occurs in an undated letter to Coleridge [accompanying a MS. copy of the play for the Wordsworths], dated by Talfourd and other editors "end of 1800," which must have been written in March or April, 1800 [since Coleridge was then staying with Wordsworth, engaged in completing the translation of *Wallenstein,* the last of the MS. being sent to the printer in April]. Talfourd's mistake in dating it perhaps led him to suppose that the copy sent through Coleridge to Wordsworth was a printed copy, and that Lamb had printed *John Woodvil* a year before he published it. If any other proof were needed that Talfourd guessed wrongly, it is supplied by this sentence in the letter to Manning of February 15, 1801 :—

"I lately received from Wordsworth a copy of the second volume [of the *Lyrical Ballads*] accompanied by an acknowledgment of having received from me *many months since* a copy of a certain Tragedy, with excuses for not having made any acknowledgment sooner."

Lamb's reply to Wordsworth (January 30, 1801) is so very dry— "Thank you for Liking my Play!!"—that we may suppose that Wordsworth's expression of "liking" was not very enthusiastic.

Things become clearer when we reach November 3, 1800, on which day he thus addressed Manning (I quote verbatim from the original letter) :—

"At last I have written to Kemble to know the event of my play, which was presented last Christmas. As I suspected, came an answer back that the copy was lost ... with a courteous (reasonable!) request of another copy (if I had one by me), and a promise of a definite answer in a week. I could not resist so facile and moderate demand : so scribbled out another, omitting sundry things, such as the witch story, about half the forest scene (which is too leisurely for *story*), and transposing that damn'd soliloquy about England getting drunk, which like its reciter stupidly stood alone nothing prevenient, or antevenient, and cleared away a good deal besides . . . I sent it last night, and am in weekly expectation of the Tolling Bell and death warrant."

It will be observed that that second copy sent to Kemble must have differed essentially from the one sent to Manning, for the latter

SATAN IN SEARCH OF A WIFE
TAIL-PIECE

NOTES

includes the witch story, and retains in its original place the soliloquy about England getting drunk.

To this copy sent to Manning we now come in chronological order, but the exact date of its despatch must remain uncertain. Clearly it was subsequent, but probably not long subsequent, to Kemble's rejection of the play, which took place soon after All Souls' Day, for Kemble must have made up his mind within half an hour of taking up the manuscript. I venture to assume that the argosy which bore all the treasures recounted in the following bill of lading sailed about Christmas, 1800. It is sad to think that the bill of lading itself and the MS. of " Pride's Cure " are the only salvage.

" I send you all of Coleridge's letters to me which I have preserved ; some of them are upon the subject of my play. I also send you Kemble's two letters, and the prompter's courteous epistle, with a curious critique on 'Pride's Cure' by a young Physician from EDIN-BORO', who modestly suggests quite another kind of plot. These are monuments of my disappointments which I like to preserve. . . . You will carefully keep all (except the Scotch Doctor's, *which burn*) *in statu quo* till I come to claim mine own."

On the reverse of the half-sheet is written: " For Mister Manning | Teacher of the Mathematics | and the Black Arts, | There is another letter in the inside cover of the book opposite the *blank* leaf that *was*."

[This is the other letter, written inside the board cover of the copy of the play, in Charles Lamb's hand :—

" Mind this goes for a letter. (Acknowledge it directly, if only in ten words.)

" DEAR MANNING :

"(I shall want to hear this comes safe.)

" I have scratched out a good deal, as you will see. Generally, what I have rejected was either *false* in *feeling*, or a violation of character, mostly of the first sort. I will here just instance in the concluding few lines of the dying Lover's story, which completely contradicted his character of *violent* and *unreproachful*. I hesitated a good while what copy to send you, and at last resolved to send the *worst*, because you are familiar with it and can make it out ; a stranger would find so much difficulty in doing it, that it would give him more pain than pleasure. This is compounded precisely of the two persons' hands you requested it should be.

" Yours sincerely,

" C. LAMB."

The two persons were undoubtedly Charles Lamb and his sister.]

Before proceeding to the MS. itself, it will be desirable to refer to Lamb's letter to Manning of February 15, 1802, in which he defends himself against Manning's animadversions on the changes found in the printed *John Woodvil*. This letter is addressed to " Mr. Thomas

Manning, Maison Magnan, No. 342 Boulevard Italien, Paris." . . . .
The italics are in the original:—

"*Apropos*, I think you wrong about *my* play. All the omissions are *right*. And the supplementary scene, in which Sandford *narrates* the manner in which his master is affected, is the best in the book. It stands where a hodge-podge of German puerilities used to stand. I insist upon it that you like that scene." . . . .

There is one thing more to add. Its excuse is the best in the world —it is quite new. In that precious letter of February 15, 1801, is a passage [printed in Canon Ainger's *édition de luxe*] which shows that Lamb (probably) tried George Colman the younger with "Pride's Cure." The potentate of the Haymarket was probably less sublimely courteous in his rejection than Kemble.

"Now to my own affairs. I have not taken that thing to Colman, but I have proceeded one step in the business. I have inquired his address and am promised it in a few days."

[The Manning copy of *John Woodvil* is thus described by Mr. Dykes Campbell] :—

It is composed of foolscap sheets stitched into a limp wrapper of marbled paper. The writing is chiefly Mary Lamb's; her brother's portion seems to have been done at various times, for the ink varies in shade, and the handwriting in style.

On the inside of the first cover, as before noted, is written the letter quoted above. Then comes a page with :—

Begun August, 1798, finished May, 1799.
This comes in beginng 2d act.
(Letter)
of Marg. to John

[this being Margaret's "Letter" (page 141 of the present volume).]

On the reverse, Mary has written out the "Characters in 'Pride's Cure,' a Tragedy." In this list Lovel and Gray are described as "two Court spies."

On the next page the play opens, but on the top margin is written :—

"Turn a leaf back for *my* Letter to Manning.

"C. Lamb."

The point of the underlining of "my" is to distinguish Lamb's letter from Margaret's, which chance to face one another in the MS.

Then comes :—

Pride's Cure.
A Tragedy.
Act the First.   Scene the First.
A Servants' apartment in Wodvil [*sic*] Hall.
Servants drinking.
A Song by Daniel.
"When the King enjoys his own again."
Peter. A delicate song upon my verity.
Where didst learn it, fellow?

And so on for some leaves without material difference from print.

NOTES 357

After the speech [page 136] "*All.* Truly a sad consideration" comes this continuation of the dialogue:—

Daniel. You know what he said to you one day in confidence.
Peter. I have reason to remember the words—"'Tis a pity (said he) a traitor should go unpunished."
Francis. Did he say so much?
Peter. As true as I sit here. I told Daniel of it the same day. Did I not, Daniel?
Daniel. Well, I do not know but it may be merrier times with us servants if Sir Walter never comes back.
Francis. But then again, who of us can think of betraying him?
Peter. His son, John Woodvil, is the prince of good masters.
Daniel. Here is his health, and the King's. (*They all drink.*) Well, I cannot see why one of us should not deserve the reward as well as another man.
Martin. Indeed there is something in that.
Sandford enters suddenly.
Sandford. You well-fed and unprofitable grooms.

And so on as printed, until we come to Margaret's reply to Sandford's speech ending [page 138]:—

Since my [" our "] old master quitted all his rights here.

Margaret. Alas! I am sure I find it so.
Ah! Mr. Sandford,
This is no dwelling now for me,
As in Sir Walter's days it was.
I can remember when this house hath been
A sanctuary to a poor orphan girl
From evil tongues and injuries of the world.
Now every day
I must endure fresh insult from the scorn
Of Woodvil's friends, the uncivil jests
And free discourses of the dissolute men
That haunt this mansion, making me their mirth.

Further on in the same dialogue comes the following, after the line in Margaret's speech [page 139, line 27],

His love, which [" that "] long has been upon the wane.

And therefore 'tis men seeing this
Have ta'en their cue and think it now their time
To slur me with their coward disrespects,
Unworthy usages, who, while John lov'd
And while one breath'd
That thought not much to take the orphan's part,
And durst as soon
Hold dalliance with the chafed lion's paw,
Or play with fire, or utter blasphemy,
As think a disrespectful thought of Margaret.
Sandford. I am too mean a man,
Being but a servant in the family,
To be the avenger of a Lady's wrongs,
And such a Lady! but I verily think
That I should cleave the rudesby to the earth
With my good oaken staff, and think no harm,
That offer'd you an insult, I being by.
I warrant you, young Master would forgive,
And thank me for the deed,
Tho' he I struck were one of his dearest friends.
Margaret. O Mr. Sandford, you must think it,
I know, as sad undecency in me
To trouble thus your friendly hearing
With my complaints.
But I have now no female friend

NOTES

> In all this house, adviser none, or friend
> To council with, and when I view your face,
> I call to mind old times,
> And how these things were different once
> When your old friend and master rul'd this house.
> Nay, never weep; why, man, I trust that yet
> Sir Walter shall return one day
> And thank you for these tears,
> And loving services to his poor orphan.
> For me, I am determined what to do.

And so on as printed down to Margaret's line [page 140, line 4]:—

> And cowardice grows enamour'd of rare accidents.

The three lines which follow in print [page 140] are not in the MS. Margaret continues thus:—

> But we must part now.
> I see one coming, that will also observe us.
> Before night comes we will contrive to meet,
> And then I will tell you further. Till when, farewell.
> *Sandford.* My prayers go with you, Lady, and your counsels,
> And heaven so prosper them, as I wish you well.
>   [*They part several ways.*

Here follows:—

> Scene the Second. A Library in Woodvil Hall; John Woodvil alone.
> *John Woodvil* (*alone*). Now universal England getteth drunk.

And so on as printed in Act II. [on pages 145 and 146]. After the last printed line,

> A fishing, hawking, hunting country gentleman,

the MS. has these five lines, but Lamb drew his pen through them:—

> Great spirits ask great play-room; I would be
> The Phaeton, should put the world to a hazard,
> E'er I'd forego the horses of the sun,
> And giddy lustre of my travels' glory
> For tedious common paces.
>   [*Exit.*

Next comes:—

> Scene the Third. An apartment in Woodvil Hall; Margaret. Sandford.
> *Margaret.* I pray you spare me, Mr. Sandford.

And so on as printed as the continuation of the former scene [page 140] to the end of that and of the first act. But in the middle of Sandford's speech comes in the "Witch" story, thus introduced:—

> [*Sandford.*] I know a suit
> Of lovely Lincoln-green, that much shall grace you
> In the wear, being glossy, fresh and worn but seld,
> Young Stephen Woodvil's they were, Sir Walter's eldest son,
> Who died long since in early youth.
> *Margaret.* I have somewhere heard his story. I remember
> Sir Walter Rowland would rebuke me, being a girl,
> When I have asked the manner of his death.
> But I forget it.

NOTES

> *Sandford.* One summer night, Sir Francis, as it chanc'd,
>   Was pacing to and fro in the avenue
>   That westward fronts our house,—
> *Margaret.* Methinks I should learn something of his story
>   Whose garments I am to wear.
> *Sandford.* Among those aged oaks, etc.

And so the witch story goes on, not quite as printed as a separate poem in the *Works* of 1818 [see page 177], but not differing very materially. . . . Then comes "Act the Second. John Woodvil alone. Reading a letter (which stands at the beginning of the book)." The letter is longer in MS. than in print [see page 141], the words in italics having been withdrawn from the middle of the second sentence:—

> "The course I have taken . . . seemed to [me] best *both for the warding off of calumny from myself* (*which should bring dishonor upon the memory of Sir Rowland my father, if a daughter of his could be thought to prefer doubtful ease before virtuous sufferance, softness before reputation*), *and* for the once-for-all releasing of yourself. . . ."

No notable alteration occurs until we come to the second scene, which in the MS. (owing to the transposition of Woodvil's soliloquy) followed immediately on Lovel's reply to Woodvil's speech—

> No, you shall go with me into the gallery—

printed on page 145.

>   Scene the Second.   Sherwood Forest.   Sir Walter Woodvil, Simon, drest as
>   Frenchmen.

Sir Walter's opening speech is long in print [page 146]—in MS. it is but this:—

> *Sir Walter.* How fares my boy, Simon, my youngest born,
>   My hope, my pride, young Woodvil, speak to me;
>   Thinkest thy brother plays thy father false?
>   My life upon his faith and noble heart;
>   Son John could never play thy father false.

There is no further material change to note until we come to the point in the conversation between Sir Walter, Simon and Margaret [page 152], where Simon calls John "a scurvy brother," to whom Margaret responds:—

> *Margaret.* I speak no slander, Simon, of your brother,
>   He is still the first of men.
> *Simon.* I would fain learn that, if you please.
> *Margaret.* Had'st rather hear his praises in the mass
>   Or parcel'd out in each particular?
> *Simon.* So please you, in the detail: general praise
>   We'll leave to his Epitaph-maker.
> *Margaret.* I will begin then—
>   His face is Fancy's tablet, where the witch
>   Paints, in her fine caprice, ever new forms,
>   Making it apt all workings of the soul,
>   All passions and their changes to display;
>   His eye, attention's magnet, draws all hearts.
> *Simon.* Is this all about your son, Sir?
> *Margaret.* Pray let me proceed.   His tongue . . .
> *Simon.* Well skill'd in lying, no doubt—
> *Sir Walter.* Ungracious boy! will you not hear her out?

> *Margaret.* His tongue well skill'd in sweetness to discuss—
> (False tongue that seem'd for love-vows only fram'd)—
> *Simon.* Did I not say so?
> *Margaret.* All knowledge and all topics of converse,
> Ev'n all the infinite stuff of men's debate
> From matter of fact, to the heights of metaphysick,
> How could she think that noble mind
> So furnish'd, so innate in all perfections,
> The manners and the worth
> That go to the making up of a complete Gentleman,
> Could from his proper nature so decline
> And from that starry height of place he mov'd in
> To link his fortune to a lowly Lady
> Who nothing with her brought but her plain heart,
> And truth of love that never swerv'd from Woodvil.
> *Simon.* Wilt please you hear some vices of this brother,
> This all-accomplish'd John?
> *Margaret.* There is no need—
> I grant him all you say and more,
> Vain, ambitious, large of purpose,
> Fantastic, fiery, swift and confident,
> A wayward child of vanity and spleen,
> A hair-brain'd mad-cap, dreamer of gold dreams,
> A daily feaster on high self-conceit,
> With many glorious faults beside,
> Weak minds mistake for virtues.
> *Simon.* Add to these,
> That having gain'd a virtuous maiden's love,
> One fairly priz'd at twenty times his worth,
> He let her wander houseless from his door
> To seek new friends and find elsewhere a home.
> *Sir Walter.* Fie upon't—
> All men are false, I think, etc.

And here we arrive at the "Dying Lover," which was printed anonymously in the *London Magazine* for January, 1822. But before passing from the long passage transcribed above I am bound to say that Lamb drew his pen through it all, marking some bits "bad" and others "very bad." I venture to think that in this he did himself some injustice.

To Sir Walter's sweeping indictment Margaret replies as follows. I keep to the text of the MS., noting some trifling changes made for the *London Magazine* [see page 79]:—

> *Margaret.* All are not false. I knew a youth who died
> For grief, because his Love proved so,
> And married to [1] another.
> I saw him on the wedding day,
> For he was present in the church that day,
> And in his best apparel too,[2]
> As one that came to grace the ceremony.
> I mark'd him when the ring was given,
> His countenance never changed;
> And when the priest pronounced the marriage blessing,
> He put a silent prayer up for the bride,
> [For they stood near who saw his lips move.][3]
> He came invited to the marriage-feast

[1] "With" (*London Magazine*).
[2] "In festive bravery deck'd" (*London Magazine*).
[3] This line erased in MS. and nothing substituted. In the *London Magazine* this took its place:—
   "For so his moving lip interpreted."

NOTES

     With the bride's friends,
     And was the merriest of them all that day;
     But they, who knew him best, call'd it feign'd mirth;
     And others said,
     He wore a smile like death's [1] upon his face.
     His presence dash'd all the beholders' mirth,
     And he went away in tears.
Simon. What followed then?
Margaret. Oh! then
     He did not as neglected suitors use
     Affect a life of solitude in shades,
     But lived,
     In free discourse and sweet society,
     Among his friends who knew his gentle nature best.
     Yet ever when he smiled,
     There was a mystery legible in his face,
     That whoso saw him said he was a man
     Not long for this world.———
     And true it was, for even then
     The silent love was feeding at his heart
     Of which he died:
     Nor ever spake word of reproach,
     Only he wish'd in death that his remains [2]
     Might find a poor grave in some spot, not far
     From his mistress' family vault, "being the place
     Where one day Anna should herself be laid."

      (So far in the *Magazine*.)

  Simon. A melancholy catastrophe. For my part I shall never die for love, being as I am, too general-contemplative for the narrow passion. I am in some sort a general lover.
  Margaret. In the name of the Boy-god who plays at blind man's buff with the Muses, and cares not whom he catches; what is it you love?

And so on until the end of Simon's famous description of the delights of forest life [page 153]. To this

     Margaret (*smiling*). And afterwards them paint in simile.
  (*To Sir Walter*.) I had some foolish questions to put concerning your son, Sir.— Was John so early valiant as hath been reported? I have heard some legends of him.
  Sir Walter. You shall not call them so. Report, in most things superfluous, in many things altogether an inventress, hath been but too modest in the delivery of John's true stories.
  Margaret. Proceed, Sir.
  Sir Walter. I saw him on the day of Naseby Fight—
     To which he came at twice seven years,
     Under the discipline of the Lord Ashley,
     His uncle by the mother's side,
     Who gave his early principles a bent
     Quite from the politics of his father's house.
  Margaret. I have heard so much.
  Sir Walter. There did I see this valiant Lamb of Mars,
     This sprig of honour, this unbearded John,
     This veteran in green years, this sprout, this Woodvil,
     With dreadless ease, guiding a fire-hot steed
     Which seem'd to scorn the manage of a boy,
     Prick forth with such an ease into the field
     To mingle rivalship and deeds of wrath
     Even with the sinewy masters of the art! [3]

---

[1] "Death" (*London Magazine*).
[2] Lamb drew his pen through the four concluding lines, and wrote in the margin "*very bad.*"
[3] Some lines intervene here in the letter to Southey of January 21, 1799, which are not in the MS.

NOTES

    The rough fanatic and blood-practis'd soldiery
    Seeing such hope and virtue in the boy,
    Disclosed their ranks to let him pass unhurt,
    Checking their swords' uncivil injuries
    As loth to mar that curious workmanship
    Of valour's beauty in his youthful face.
 Simon. Mistress Margaret will have need of some refreshment, etc.

Lamb has drawn his pen through this passage, and marked it "bad or dubious."

At the beginning of the fourth act John Woodvil's soliloquy is broken in upon by Sandford. He has just told himself [page 165] that

    Some, the most resolved fools of all,
    Have told their dearest secrets in their cups,

when

    Enter Sandford in haste.

Sandford. O Sir, you have not told them anything?
John. Told whom, Sandford?
Sandford. Mr. Lovel or Mr. Gray, anything concerning your father?
John. Are they not my friends, Sandford?
Sandford. Your friends! Lord help you, they your friends! They were no better than two Court spies set on to get the secret out of you. I have just discovered in time all their practices.
John. But I have told one of them.
Sandford. God forbid, God forbid!
John. How do you know them to be what you said they were?
Sandford. Good God!
John. Tell me, Sandford, my good Sandford, your master begs it of you.
Sandford. I cannot speak to you.

          [*Goes out, John following him.*
    Scene the Second. The forest.

This forest scene has been greatly altered. When Gray has said [page 166], "'Tis a brave youth," etc., there follows:—

Sir Walter. Why should I live any longer? There is my sword (*surrendering*). Son John, 'tis thou hast brought this disgrace upon us all.
Simon. Father, why do you cover your face with your hands? Why do you draw your breath so hard? See, villains, his heart is burst! O villains, he cannot speak! One of you run for some water; quick, ye musty rogues: will ye have your throats cut? [*They both slink off.*] How is it with you, father? Look up, Sir Walter, the villains are gone.

"He hears" [page 166], down to "*Bears in the body*" [page 167], of the print is not in the MS., which goes on thus:—

Sir Walter. Barely a minute's breath is left me now,
    Which must be spent in charity by me,
    And, Simon, as you prize my dying words,
    I charge you with your brother live in peace
    And be my messenger,
    To bear my message to the unhappy boy,
    For certain his intent was short of my death.
Simon. I hope as much, father.
Sir Walter. Tell him I send it with my parting prayer,
    And you must fall upon his neck and weep,
    And teach him pray, and love your brother John,
    For you two now are left in the wide world
    The sole survivors of the Woodvil name.
    Bless you, my sons—
                  [*Dies.*

NOTES

  Simon. My father's soul is fled.
    And now, my trusty servant, my sword,
    One labour yet, my sword, then sleep for ever.
    Drink up the poor dregs left of Woodvil's name
    And fill the measure of our house's crimes.
    How nature sickens,
    To view her customary bands so snapt
    When Love's sweet fires go out in blood of kin,
    And natural regards have left the earth.

    Scene changes to another part of the forest.

  Margaret They are gone to bear the body to the town,
  (*alone*). It was an error merely and no crime.

And so to the end of her long speech as printed [page 167].
  At this point in the MS. comes in "the hodge-podge of German puerilities" (see the letter to Manning, February 15, 1802), the sacrifice of which so discontented Manning, who evidently considered the "supplementary scene" (closing the fourth act, [pages 168 and 169]), as Lamb called it, a poor substitute.

    Scene changes to Woodvil Hall.
   John reading a letter by scraps—A Servant attending.

  "An event beyond the possible reach of foresight. 'Tis thought the deep disgrace of supposed treachery in you o'ercame him. His heart brake. You will acquit yourself of worse crimes than indiscretion. My remorse must end with life.
  "Your quondam companion and penitent for the wrong he has done ye.
                  "GRAY.

  "*Postscript.*—The old man being unhappily removed, the young man's advancement henceforth will find no impediment."

   John. Impediment indeed there now is none:
    For all has happened that my soul presag'd.
    What hinders, but I enter in forthwith
    And take possession of my crowned state?
    For thy advancement, Woodvil, is no less;
    To be a King, a King.
    I hear the shoutings of the under-world,
    I hear the unlawful accents of their mirth,
    The fiends do shout and clap their hands for joy,
    That Woodvil is proclaim'd the Prince of Hell.
    They place a burning crown upon my head,
    I hear it hissing now,   [*Puts his hand to his forehead.*
    And feel the snakes about my mortal brain.
    [*Sinks in a swoon, is caught in the arms of the servant.*

    Scene. A Courtyard before Woodvil Hall.
   Sandford. Margaret (as just arrived from a journey).

  Margaret. Can I see him to-night?
  Sandford. I think ye had better stay till the morning: he will be more calm.
  Margaret. You say he gets no sleep?
  Sandford. He hath not slept since Sir Walter died. I have sat up with him these two nights. Francis takes my place to-night—— O! Mistress Margaret, are not the witch's words come true—"All that we feared and worse"? Go in and change your garments, you have travelled hard and want rest.
  Margaret. I will go to bed. You will promise I shall see him in the morning.
  Sandford. You will sleep in your old chamber?
  Margaret. The Tapestry room: yes. Pray get me a light. A good night to us all.
  Sandford. Amen, say I.   [*They go in.*

     Scene. The Servants' Hall.
     Daniel, Peter and Robert.

  Daniel. Are we all of one mind, fellows? He that lov'd his old master, speak. Shall we quit his son's service for a better? Is it aye, or no?

NOTES

Peter. For my part, I am afraid to go to bed to-night.
Robert. For certain, young Master's indiscretion was that which broke his heart.
Peter. Who sits up with him to-night?
Robert. Francis.
Peter. Lord! what a conscience he must have, that he cannot sleep alone.
Robert. They say he is troubled with the Night-mare.
Daniel. Here he comes, let us go away as fast as we can. [*They run out.*

Enter John Woodvil and Francis.

John. I lay me down to get a little sleep,
And just when I began to close my eyes,
My eyes heavy to sleep, it comes.
Francis. What comes?
John. I can remember when a child the maids [1]
Would place me on their lap, as they undrest me,
As silly women use, and tell me stories
Of Witches—Make me read "Glanvil on Witchcraft,"
And in conclusion show me in the Bible,
The old Family-Bible with the pictures in it,
The 'graving of the Witch raising up Samuel,
Which so possest my fancy, being a child,
That nightly in my dreams an old Hag came
And sat upon my pillow.
I am relapsing into infancy,—
And shortly I shall dote—for would you think it?
The Hag has come again. Spite of my manhood,
The Witch is strong upon me every night.
[*Walks to and fro, then as if recollecting something.*
What said'st thou, Francis, as I stood in the passage?
Something of a Father:
The word is ringing in my ears now—
Francis. I remember, one of the servants, Sir, would pass a few days with his father at Leicester. The poor old man lies on his death-bed, and has exprest a desire to see his son before he dies. But none cared to break the matter to you.
John. Send the man here. [*Francis goes out.*
My very servants shun my company.
I held my purse to a beggar yesterday
Who lay and bask'd his sores in the hot sun,
And the gaunt pauper did refuse my alms.

Francis returns with Robert.

John. Come hither, Robert. What is the poor man ailing?
Robert. Please your honour, I fear he has partly perish'd for want of physic. His means are small, and he kept his illness a secret to me not to put me to expenses.
John. Good son, he weeps for his father.
Go take the swiftest horse in my stables,
Take Lightfoot or Eclipse—no, Eclipse is lame,
Take Lightfoot then, or Princess,[2]
Ride hard all night to Leicester.
And give him money, money, Francis—
The old man must have medicines, cordials.
And broth to keep him warm, and careful nurses.
He must not die for lack of tendance, Robert.
Robert. God bless your honour for your kindness to my poor father.
John. Pray, now make haste. You may chance to come in time.
[*Robert goes out.*
John. Go get some firewood, Francis,
And get my supper ready. [*Francis goes out.*
The night is bitter cold.
They in their graves feel nothing of the cold,
Or if they do, how dull a cold—
All clayey, clayey. Ah God! who waits below?
Come up, come quick. I saw a fearful sight.

[[1] Twice afterwards Lamb returned to this episode—in "The Witch Aunt" story in *Mrs. Leicester's School* (see Vol. III.), and in "Witches and other Night Fears," in *Elia* (Vol. II., page 67).]

[2] Lamb puts his pen through these two lines, and writes across them "miserable bad."

NOTES 365

Francis returns in haste with wood.

John. There are such things as spirits, deny it who may.
  Is it you, Francis? Heap the wood on thick,
  We two shall sup together, sup all night,
  Carouse, drink drunk, and tell the merriest tales—
  Tell for a wager, who tells merriest—
  But I am very weak. O tears, tears, tears,
  I feel your just rebuke. *[Goes out.*

Scene changes to a bed-room. John sitting alone: a lamp burning by him.

"Infinite torments for finite offences." I will never believe it. How divines can reconcile this monstrous tenet with the spirit of their Theology! They have palpably failed in the proof, for to put the question thus :—If he being infinite—have a care, Woodvil, the latitude of doubting suits not with the humility of thy condition. What good men have believed, may be true, and what they profess to find set down clearly in their scriptures, must have probability in its defence.[1] Touching that other question the Casuists with one consent have pronounced the sober man accountable for the deeds by him in a state of drunkenness committed, because tho' the action indeed be such as he, sober, would never have committed, yet the drunkenness being an act of the will, by a moral fiction, the issues are accounted voluntary also. I lose my sleep in attending to these intricacies of the schoolmen. I lay till daybreak the other morning endeavouring to draw a line of distinction between sin of direct malice and sin of malice indirect, or imputable only by the sequence. My brain is overwrought by these labours, and my faculties will shortly decline into impotence. *[Throws himself on a bed.*
  End of the Fourth Act.

In the fifth act of the printed play [page 170] we have simply "Margaret enters." In the MS. Sandford prepares his master for her advent, and announces her thus :—

Sandford. Wilt please you to see company to-day, Sir?
John. Who thinks me worth the visiting?
Sandford. One that travell'd hard last night to see you,
  She waits to know your pleasure.
John. A lady too! pray send her to me—
  Some curiosity, I suppose.
  [Sandford goes out and returns with Margaret.
Margaret. Woodvil![2]
John. Comes Margaret here, etc.

When, a page farther on [page 172], John has declared to Margaret that

  This earth holds not alive so poor a thing as I am—
  I was not always thus,

the MS. went on (but the passage is struck out as "bad") :—

  You must bear with me, Margaret, as a child,
  For I am weak as tender Infancy
  And cannot bear rebuke—
  Would'st think it, Love!
  They hoot and spit upon me as I pass
  In the public streets : one shows me to his neighbour,
  Who shakes his head and turns away with horror—
  I was not always thus—
Margaret. Thou noble nature, etc.

The next scene—the last [page 173]—is much cut about. The long speech of Margaret beginning,

  To give you in your stead a better self,

---
[1] Lamb has crossed out this passage from "Infinite torments," and written at "Touching" "begin here."
[2] "Woodvil!" and some illegible words struck out, and nothing substituted.

NOTES

and John's reply [both printed at page 174], are struck out, and "Nimis" written by Lamb's pen in large characters in the margin; but after that all goes on in harmony with the print, to the end :—

> It seem'd the guilt of blood was passing from me
> Even in the act and agony of tears
> And all my sins forgiven.

At this point in the MS. Simon arrives :—

[A noise is heard as of one without, clamorous to come in.
Margaret. 'Tis your brother Simon, John.
Enter Simon, with his sword in a menacing posture. John staggers towards him and falls at his feet, Margaret standing over him.
Simon. Is this the man I came so far to see—
The perfect Cavalier, the finish'd courtier
Whom Ladies lov'd, the gallant curled Woodvil,
Whom brave men fear'd, the valiant, fighting Woodvil,
The haughty high-ambitioned Parricide—
The same that sold his father's secret in his cups,
And held it but an after-dinner's trick?———
So humble and in tears, a crestfallen penitent,
And crawling at a younger brother's feet!
The sinews of my [*stiff*] revenge grow slack.
My brother, speak to me, my brother John.
(*Aside*) Now this is better than the beastly deed
Which I did meditate.
John (*rising and resuming his old dignity*). You come to take my life, I know it well.
You come to fight with me— [*Laying his hand upon his sword.*
This arm was busy on the day of Naseby :
'Tis paralytic now, and knows no use of weapons.
The luck is yours, Sir. [*Surrenders his sword.*
Simon. My errand is of peace :
A dying father's blessing and last prayers
For his misguided son.
Sir Walter sends it with his parting breath.
He bade me with my brother live in peace,
He bade me fall upon his neck and weep,
(As I now do) and love my brother John ;
For we are only left in the wide world
The poor survivors of the Woodvil name. [*They embrace.*
Simon. And Margaret here shall witness our atonement—
(For Margaret still hath followed all your fortunes).
And she shall dry thy tears and teach thee pray.
So we'll together seek some foreign land,
Where our sad story, John, shall never reach.
End of " *Pride's Cure* " and Charles Lamb's Dramatic Works!!

After all this [Mr. Campbell adds finally] is the reader prepared to think Manning altogether wrong and Lamb altogether right as to what was done in the process of transforming *Pride's Cure* into *John Woodvil*?

The version of 1818 here printed differs practically only in minor matters of typography and punctuation from that of 1802. There are, however, a few alterations which should be noted. On page 155, in John's third speech, "fermentations" was, in 1802, "stimuli." On page 157 at the foot, in the speech of the Third Gentleman, there is a change. In 1802 he said "(*dashing his glass down*) Pshaw, damn these acorn cups, they would not drench a fairy. Who shall pledge," &c. And at the end of Act III. one line is omitted. In 1802 John was made to say, after disarming Lovel (page 164) :—

> Still have the will without the power to execute,
> As unfear'd Eunuchs meditate a rape.

This simile, which one reviewer fell upon with some violence, was not reprinted.

There is little in the text that calls for explanation, but I might point out that the quotation on page 144—

> Ale that will make Grimalkin prate—

is from an old poem, copied by Lamb into one of his Commonplace Books, beginning—

> When as the chill Sirocco blows.

On page 153 Simon's phrase, "thin dancers upon air," may be another of the Elizabethan echoes of which the play is full and of which much might be written. John Ford, in "The Sun's Darling," a masque, has—

> I did but chide thee as a whistling wind
> Playing with leafy dancers.

But there would be no end to the list of such possible derivations if one were to examine *John Woodvil* line for line.

Mr. Thomas Hutchinson, writing in *The Athenæum*, December 28, 1901, remarks : "The truth is that in Lamb's imitations of the elder writers 'anachronistic improprieties' (as Thomas Warton would say) are exceedingly rare. In *John Woodvil* it would not, I think, be easy to discover more than two : *caprice*, which, in the sense of 'a capricious disposition,' seems to belong to the eighteenth century, and *anecdotes* (*i.e.*, 'secret Court history '), which, in its English form at least, probably does not occur much before 1686."

This note is already too long, or I should like to say something of the reception of *John Woodvil*, which was not cordial. The *Annual Review* was particularly severe, and the *Edinburgh* caustic. Hazlitt's criticism, in his *Lectures chiefly on the Dramatic Literature of the Age of Elizabeth*, 1820, may, however, be quoted :—

> Mr. Lamb's *John Woodvil* may be considered as a dramatic fragment, intended for the closet rather than the stage. It would sound oddly in the lobbies of either theatre, amidst the noise and glare and bustle of resort ; but " there where we have treasured up our hearts," in silence and in solitude, it may claim and find a place for itself. It might be read with advantage in the still retreats of Sherwood Forest, where it would throw a new-born light on the green, sunny glades ; the tenderest flower might seem to drink of the poet's spirit, and " the tall deer that paints a dancing shadow of his horns in the swift brook " might seem to do so in mockery of the poet's thought. Mr. Lamb, with a modesty often attendant on fine feeling, has loitered too long in the humbler avenues leading to the temple of ancient genius, instead of marching boldly up to the sanctuary, as many with half his pretensions would have done : " but fools rush in where angels fear to tread." The defective or objectionable parts of this production are imitations of the defects of the old writers : its beauties are his own, though in their manner. The touches of thought and passion are often as pure and delicate as they are profound ; and the character of his heroine Margaret is perhaps the finest and most genuine female character out of Shakespeare. This tragedy was not critic-proof : it had its cracks and flaws and breaches, through which the enemy marched in triumphant. The station which he had chosen was not indeed a walled town, but a straggling village, which the experienced engineers proceeded to lay waste ; and he is pinned down in more than one Review of the day, as an exemplary warning to indiscreet writers, who venture beyond the pale of periodical taste

and conventional criticism. Mr. Lamb was thus hindered by the taste of the polite vulgar from writing as he wished; his own taste would not allow him to write like them : and he (perhaps wisely) turned critic and prose-writer in his own defence. To say that he has written better about Shakespeare, and about Hogarth, than anybody else, is saying little in his praise.

Page 177. "THE WITCH."

In the *Works*, 1818, this dramatic sketch followed *John Woodvil* (see the preceding note, page 358).

Lamb sent "The Witch" to Robert Lloyd in November, 1798 (see *Charles Lamb and the Lloyds*, page 91), in a version differing widely from that of the *Works* here given. The speakers are Sir Walter Woodvil's steward and Margaret. The principal variation is this, after the curse :—

> *Margaret.* A terrible curse !
> *Old Steward.* O Lady ! such bad things are said of that old woman,
>   You would be loth to hear them !
>   Namely, that the milk she gave was sour,
>   And the babe, who suck'd her, shrivell'd like a mandrake,
>   And things besides, with a bigger horror in them,
>   Almost, I think, unlawful to be told !

In the penultimate line "The mystery of God" was "Creation's beauteous workmanship."

Lamb seems also to have shown the poem to Charles Lloyd (see page 351).

Page 180. "MR. H——."

Lamb composed this farce in the winter 1805-1806. Writing to Hazlitt on February 19, 1806, he says : "Have taken a room at 3s. a week to be in between 5 and 8 at night, to avoid my *nocturnal* alias *knock-eternal* visitors. The first-fruits of my retirement has been a farce which goes to manager tomorrow." Mary Lamb, writing to Sarah Stoddart at about the same time, says : "Charles is gone [to the lodging] to finish the farce, and I am to hear it read this night. I am so uneasy between my hopes and fears of how I shall like it, that I do not know what I am doing." The next day or so, February 21, she says that she liked the farce "very much, and cannot help having great hopes of its success"—stating that she has carried it to Mr. Wroughton at Drury Lane.

The reply came on June 11, 1806, saying that the farce was accepted, subject to a few alterations, and would be produced in due course (see Lamb's letter to Wordsworth, written in "wantonness of triumph," of June 26). Mary Lamb, writing to Sarah Stoddart, probably in October, 1806, says that

> Charles took an emendated copy of his farce to Mr. Wroughton, the Manager, yesterday. Mr. Wroughton was very friendly to him, and expressed high approbation of the farce ; but there are two, he tells him, to come out before it. . . . We are pretty well, and in fresh hopes about this farce.

Theatre Royal, Drury-Lane.

This present WEDNESDAY, DECEMBER 10, 1806.

[Their Majesties Servants will act the Operatic Drama of

The TRAVELLERS;

Or, MUSIC's FASCINATION.

With entirely New Music, Scenery, Machinery, Dresses, and Decorations.
The OVERTURE and MUSIC, composed by Mr. CORRI.

ACT I.—CHARACTERS IN CHINA.
Zaphimri, (*Prince of China*) } THE { Mr. DE CAMP,
Koyan, (*his companion*) } { Mr. BRAHAM,
O'Gallagher, } { Mr. JOHNSTONE,
Miadora, (*Mother to Koyan and Celinda*) TRAVELLERS. { Mrs. POWELL,
Celinda, } { Mrs. MOUNTAIN.
Zaphani, Mr. CHATTERLEY, } { Chingtang, Mr. TOKELY,
The Emperor of China, Mr. POWELL,
Mandarins, Mr. MADDOCKS, Mr. SPARKS,
Delvo, (*an old Gardener*) Mr. MATHEWS.
Chorus of Mandarins, Guards, Peasants, &c.

ACT II.—CHARACTERS IN TURKEY.
Mustapha, (*the Grand Vizier*) Mr. BARTLEY,
Chief Aga of the Janizaries, Mr. DIGNUM, Principal Janizary, Mr. COOKE,
Morad, Mr. FISHER, Selim, Mr. EVANS, Centinel, Mr. GIBBON,
Parazade, Mrs. MATHEWS, Safie, Mrs. BLAND.
Chorus of Janizaries, Turkish Ladies, &c.
Principal Dancer, Mrs. SHARP.

ACT III. & IV.—CHARACTERS IN ITALY.
Duke of Pesilepo, Mr. RAYMOND,
Diego, Mr. WEBB, Assassins, Mr. MALE, Mr. MADDOCKS,
The Marchioness Merida, (first time) Mrs. HARLOWE.
Chorus of Lazzaroni, and Trio, by Masters HODSON, MOSS, and WEST.

ACT V.—CHARACTERS IN ENGLAND.
Admiral Lord Hawser, Mr. DOWTON,
Buntline, (*an old Sailor*) Mr. WEWITZER,
Chorus of Sailors, Lads and Lasses.

The Scenes designed by Mr. GREENWOOD,
And executed by him, and under his direction by Mr. BANKS, & Assistants
The Machinery, Dresses, and Decorations, designed by Mr. JOHNSTON,
And executed by him, and under his direction by Mr. UNDERWOOD, & Mr. BANKS.
The Female Dresses, designed and executed by Miss REIN.

After which will be produced (Never Acted) a new Farce, in Two acts, called

Mr. H——

The Characters by
Mr. ELLISTON,
Mr. WEWITZER, Mr. BARTLEY, Mr. PENLEY, Mr. PURSER,
Mr. CARLES, Mr. COOKE, Mr. FISHER, Mr. PLACIDE, Mr. WEBB,
Miss MELLON, Mrs. SPARKS,
Miss TIDSWELL, Mrs. HARLOWE,
Mrs. SCOTT, Mrs. MADDOCKS, Miss SANDERS.
The Prologue to be spoken by Mr. ELLISTON
Places for the Boxes to be taken of Mr. SPRING, at the Box-Office,
in Little Russell-Street.
NO MONEY TO BE RETURNED.

Vivant Rex et Regina! [C. Lowndes, Printer, Marquis Court, Drury Lane.

☞ The new Melo Drama of TEKELI; or, the SIEGE of MONTGA.Z. performed for the fourteenth time last night, continuing to be received with the greatest approbation and applause, will be repeated To-morrow, and Saturday next.
To-morrow, the Comedy of The WEST INDIAN.
Belcour, Mr. ELLISTON, Major O'Flaherty, Mr. JOHNSTONE,
Stockwell, Mr. POWELL.—Miss Rutport, Miss DUNCAN.
On Friday, a COMIC OPERA
On Saturday, (by desire) the Comedy of the WAY to KEEP H.M.
A New COMIC OPERA is in Rehearsal.

REPRODUCTION OF THE PLAY-BILL OF *MR. H*

Lamb tells Manning about it, on December 5, adding after an outline of the plot :—

"That's the idea—how flat it is here—but how whimsical in the farce!" Later he says: "I shall get £200 from the theatre if 'Mr. H——' has a good run, and, I hope, £100 for the copyright. Nothing if it fails; and there never was a more ticklish thing. The whole depends on the manner in which the name is brought out, which I value myself on, as a *chef-d'œuvre.*" And a little later still: "N.B. If my little thing don't succeed, I shall easily survive."

"Mr. H——" was produced on December 10, 1806. The play-bill for the night ran thus :—

Theatre Royal, Drury-Lane
This present Wednesday, December 10, 1806
Their Majesties Servants will act the Operatic Drama of
The Travellers ;
Or, Music's Fascination
[&c. &c.]
After which will be produced (Never Acted) a new Farce, in Two acts, called
Mr. H——
The Characters by
Mr. Elliston
Mr. Wewitzer, Mr. Bartley, Mr. Penley, Mr. Purser
Mr. Carles, Mr. Cooke, Mr. Fisher, Mr. Placide, Mr. Webb
Miss Mellon, Mrs. Sparks
Miss Tidswell, Mrs. Harlowe
Mrs. Scott, Mrs. Maddocks, Miss Sanders
The Prologue to be spoken by Mr. Elliston
[&c., &c.]

According to Mrs. Baron-Wilson's *Memoirs of (Miss Mellon) Harriet, Duchess of St. Albans,* Lamb was allowed to cast "Mr. H——" himself. Miss Mellon played the heroine.

The Lambs sat near the orchestra with Hazlitt and Crabb Robinson, and the house was well salted with friendly clerks from the East India House and the South-Sea House. The prologue went capitally; and all was well with the play until the name of Hogsflesh was pronounced. Then disapproval set in in a storm of hisses, in which, Crabb Robinson tells us, Lamb joined heartily.

In a report of the first night of "Mr. H——" in *Monthly Literary Recreations* for December, 1806, we read that on the secret of the name being made public "all interest vanished, the audience were disgusted, and the farce went on to its very conclusion almost unheard, amidst the contending clamours of 'Silence,' 'Hear! hear!' and 'Off! off! off!'"

Writing to Wordsworth on the next day Lamb told the story :—

"Mr. H—— came out last night and failed. I had many fears; the subject was not substantial enough. John Bull must have solider fare than a *Letter.* We are pretty stout about it, have had plenty of

VOL. V.—24

condoling friends, but after all, we had rather it should have succeeded. You will see the Prologue in most of the Morning Papers. It was received with such shouts as I never witness'd to a Prologue. It was attempted to be encored. How hard! a thing I did merely as a task, because it was wanted—and set no great store by; and Mr. H.!! The quantity of friends we had in the house my brother and I being in Public Offices &c. was astonishing—but they yielded at length to a few hisses—"a hundred hisses—damn the word, I write it like kisses —how different—a hundred hisses outweigh 1000 claps. The former come more directly from the Heart. Well, 'tis withdrawn and there is an end. Better Luck to us."

Writing to Sarah Stoddart, Lamb put the case thus:—

"Mary is a little cut at the ill success of 'Mr. H.,' which came out last night, and *failed*. I know you'll be sorry, but never mind. We are determined not to be cast down. I am going to leave off tobacco, and then we must thrive. A smoking man must write smoky farces." Thereafter Lamb's attitude to "Mr. H——" was always one of humorous resignation.

Lamb should have chosen a better, by which I mean a worse, name than Hogsflesh. As a matter of fact a great number of persons had become quite accustomed to the asperities of Hogsflesh, not only from the famous cricketer of that name, one of the pioneers of the game, but also from the innkeeper at Worthing. Indeed an old rhyme current at the end of the eighteenth century anticipated some of Lamb's humour, for the two principal landlords of Worthing, which was just then beginning to be a fashionable resort, were named Hogsflesh and Bacon, leading to the quatrain:—

> Brighton is a pretty street,
> Worthing is much taken;
> If you can't get any other meat
> There's Hogsflesh and Bacon.

The Drury Lane authorities do not seem to have considered the failure as absolute as did Lamb, for on the next day—December 11— the bills announced:—

* The New Farce of Mr. H——, performed for the first time last night, was received by an overflowing audience with universal applause, and will be repeated for the second time to-morrow.

But the next evening's bill—December 12, 1806—stated that "The New Farce of Mr. H—— is withdrawn at the request of the author."

"Mr. H——" did not then disappear altogether from the stage. A correspondent of *Notes and Queries*, May 26, 1855, remembered seeing it at Philadelphia when he was a boy. The last scene, he says, particularly amused the audience. And in William B. Wood's *Personal Recollections of the Stage*, 1855, it is recorded of the Philadelphia Theatre, of which he was manager, that in 1812 "Charles Lamb's excellent farce of 'Mr. H——' met with extraordinary success, and was played an unusual number of nights." Lamb, however, did not profit thereby.

MR. H.

OR

BEWARE A BAD NAME.

A FARCE IN TWO ACTS:

As performed at the

PHILADELPHIA THEATRE.

PHILADELPHIA:

PUBLISHED BY M. CAREY, 122 MARKET STREET.
A. Fagan, Printer.
1813.

NOTES 371

The little play was published in Philadelphia in 1813 under the title *Mr. H——, or Beware a Bad Name. A farce in two acts, as performed at the Philadelphia Theatre*—Lamb's name not figuring in any way in connection with it.

In England "Mr. H——" was not revived until 1885, when, as a curiosity, it was played by the Dramatic Students' Society. The performance was held at the Gaiety on October 27, 1885, the prologue being spoken by a gentleman made up to resemble Lamb.

In Vol. II. of *The Parterre*, a magazine published in 1835, is a prose version of Lamb's farce with the same title. Melesinda is there called Isabel Hartley, and there is no reconciliation or change of name.

I might add that the Prologue to "Mr. H——" was included in *The Care-Killer*, by Jonathan Jolly, 1807, a collection of anecdotes, epigrams, &c.

The quotation placed by Lamb at the beginning of the play is from Hazlitt's essay "On Great and Little Things." The whole passage runs thus:—

> We often make life unhappy in wishing things to have turned out otherwise than they did, merely because that is possible to the imagination which is impossible in fact. I remember, when Lamb's farce was damned (for damned, it was, that's certain), I used to dream every night for a month after (and then I vowed I would plague myself no more about it) that it was revived at one of the Minor or provincial theatres with great success, that such and such retrenchments and alterations had been made in it, and that it was thought *it might do at the other House*. I had heard, indeed (this was told in confidence to Lamb), that *Gentleman* Lewis was present on the night of its performance, and said, that if he had had it, he would have made it, by a few judicious curtailments, "the most popular little thing that had been brought out for some time." How often did I conjure up in recollection the full diapason of applause at the end of the Prologue, and hear my ingenious friend in the first row of the pit roar with laughter at his own wit! Then I dwelt with forced complacency on some part in which it had been doing well: then we would consider (in concert) whether the long, tedious opera of "The Travellers," which preceded it, had not tired people beforehand, so that they had not spirits left for the quaint and sparkling "wit skirmishes" of the dialogue; and we all agreed it might have gone down after a Tragedy, except Lamb himself, who swore he had no hopes of it from the beginning, and that he knew the name of the hero, when it came to be discovered, could not be got over. "Mr. H——," thou wert damned! Bright shone the morning on the play-bills that announced thy appearance, and the streets were filled with the buzz of persons asking one another if they would go to see "Mr. H——," and answering that they would certainly: but before night the gaiety, not of the author, but of his friends and the town, was eclipsed, for thou wert damned! Hadst thou been anonymous, thou haply mightst have lived. But thou didst come to an untimely end for thy tricks, and for want of a better name to pass them off! In this manner we go back to the critical minutes on which the turn of our fate, or that of any one else in whom we are interested, depended; try them over again with new knowledge and sharpened sensibility; and thus think to alter what is irrevocable, and ease for a moment the pang of lasting regret.

Gentleman Lewis, it might be remarked, was William Thomas Lewis, the actor, who died in 1811.

Page 185. *The man with the great nose.* See Slawkenbergius's tale in *Tristram Shandy*, Vol. IV.

Page 189. *The feeling Harley.* Harley was the hero of Henry Mackenzie's novel, *The Man of Feeling*.

Page 193. *Jeremiah Pry.* John Poole may have taken a hint here for his farce "Paul Pry," produced in September, 1825. Lamb and he knew each other slightly. Lamb analysed the prying nature again in *The New Times* early in 1825, in two papers on "Tom Pry" and "Tom Pry's Wife" which will be found in Vol. I. of this edition.

Page 196. *Old Q——*. William Douglas, fourth Duke of Queensberry (1724-1810), the most notorious libertine of his later days.

Page 200. *John, my valet.* This is a very similar incident to that described in the *Elia* essay on the "Old Benchers," where Lovel (John Lamb) warns Samuel Salt, when dressing him, not to allude, at the party to which he is going, to the unfortunate Miss Blandy.

Page 200. *" Fair defects."*

O, why did God,
Creator wise, that peopl'd highest Heav'n
With spirits masculine, create at last
This novelty on earth, this fair defect
Of Nature. . . .

Paradise Lost, X., lines 888-892.

Page 203, line 21. *Mother Damnable.* There was at Kentish Town a notorious old shrew who bore this nickname in the 17th century.

Page 212. "The Pawnbroker's Daughter."
Printed in *Blackwood*, January, 1830, and not reprinted by Lamb.
This little play was never acted. Lamb refers to it in a letter to Bernard Barton—in July, 1829—as "an old rejected farce"; and Canon Ainger mentions a note of Lamb's to Charles Mathews, in October, 1828, offering the farce for production at the Adelphi. The theme is one that seems always to have interested Lamb (see his essay on the "Inconveniences of Being Hanged," Vol. I., page 56, and note, page 405).

Page 216, line 24. *"An Argument against the Use of Animal Food."* Joseph Ritson, 1752-1803, the antiquarian, was converted to vegetarianism by Mandeville's *Fable of the Bees*. The work from which Cutlet quotes was published in 1802. Pope's motto is from the *Essay on Man*, I., lines 81-84.

Page 217, line 15. *Mr. Molyneux . . . in training to fight Cribb.* Cutlet's rump steak did not avail in either of the great struggles between Tom Cribb and Tom Molineaux. At their first meeting, on December 18, 1810, Molineaux went under at the thirty-third round; and in the return match, on September 28, 1811, Molineaux's jaw was broken at the ninth and he gave in at the eleventh, to the great disappointment of the 20,000 spectators. Mr. Molineaux was a negro.

In a letter to John Pritt Harley, the comedian (1786-1858), printed by Mr. W. C. Hazlitt, Lamb offers him this song to sing at his benefit to the tune of "Billy Lackaday."

Page 222, line 6. *The speech of Buckingham.* In Henry VIII., Act II., Scene 1.

Page 243. "THE WIFE'S TRIAL."
Crabbe's "Confidant," on which Lamb founded this play, is one of the stories in *Tales*, 1813.

The play was first printed in *Blackwood's Magazine*, December, 1828. Writing to Procter in January, 1829, Lamb says: "Blackwood sent me £20 for the drama. Somebody cheated me out of it next day; and my new pair of breeches, just sent home, cracking at first putting on, I exclaimed, in my wrath, 'All tailors are cheats, and all men are tailors.' Then I was better."

"The Wife's Trial" was written in 1827 and was sent to Charles Kemble at Covent Garden in August. Lamb tells Barton of its despatch in the letter of August 28, adding the information that the play's Shakespearian flavour was deliberately striven for: "I made it all ('tis blank verse, and I think, of the true old dramatic cut) or most of it, in the green lanes about Enfield." The play was not accepted.

Crabbe's story is serious. All the comedy of the play belongs to Lamb. In the poem Anna, the wife, was seduced at the age of fifteen. She had a child that died at once. This is the secret known to the widow. At the close of the poem the husband turns the widow out—a more satisfying proceeding than the exercise of clemency in Lamb's stage version.

TWO ADDITIONAL POEMS

The two poems printed below came to hand too late to be arranged in their proper place in the body of this volume. "Love will Come" belongs rightly to the section on page 99 devoted to poems never before printed, and the acrostic to the section on page 92. "Love will Come" was included by Lamb in an unpublished letter (now in the possession of Mr. A. M. S. Methuen) to Miss Fryer, a schoolfellow of Emma Isola. Lamb writes:—

"By desire of Emma I have attempted new words to the old nonsense of Tartar Drum; but *with* the nonsense the sound and spirit of the tune are unaccountably gone, and *we* have agreed to discard the new version altogether. As *you* may be more fastidious in singing mere silliness, and a string of well-sounding images without sense or coherence—Drums of Tartars, who use *none*, and Tulip trees ten foot high, not to mention Spirits in Sunbeams, &c.,—than *we* are, so you are at liberty to sacrifice an enspiriting movement to a little sense, tho' I like LITTLE SENSE less than his vagarying younger sister NO SENSE— so I send them.—The 4th line of 1st stanza is from an old Ballad."

The old ballad is, I imagine, "Waly, Waly," of which Lamb was very fond. See last stanza:—

> But had I wist, before I kist,
>   That love had been sae ill to win;
> I had lockt my heart in a case of gowd
>   And pinn'd it with a siller pin.

NOTES

LOVE WILL COME
Tune—*The Tartar Drum*

I

Guard thy feelings, pretty Vestal,
    From the smooth Intruder free;
Cage thy heart in bars of chrystal,
    Lock it with a golden key:
Thro' the bars demurely stealing,
    Noiseless footstep, accent dumb,
His approach to none revealing—
    Watch, or watch not, LOVE WILL COME.

    His approach to none revealing—
        Watch, or watch not, Love will come—Love,
        Watch, or watch not, Love will come.

II

Scornful Beauty may deny him—
    He hath spells to charm disdain;
Homely Features may defy him—
    Both at length must wear the chain.
Haughty Youth in Courts of Princes—
    Hermit poor with age o'er come—
His soft plea at last convinces;
    Sooner, later, LOVE WILL COME.

    His soft plea at length convinces;
        Sooner, later, Love will come—Love,
        Sooner, later, Love will come.

The other poem is an acrostic, written for Sarah James, Mary Lamb's nurse, and the sister of the Mrs. Parsons with whom she lived during the last years of her life. Miss James was the daughter of the rector of Beguildy, in Shropshire. The verses are reprinted, by permission, from *My Lifetime* by Mr. John Hollingshead, who is the great-nephew of Miss James and Mrs. Parsons, and who can recall an afternoon spent at 41 Alpha Road among Lamb's books in Mary Lamb's sitting-room.

ACROSTIC

S leep hath treasures worth retracing:
A re you not in slumbers pacing
R ound your native spot at times,
A nd seem to hear Beguildy's chimes?
H old the airy vision fast;

Joy is but a dream at last:
And what was so fugitive,
Memory only makes to live.
Even from troubles past we borrow
Some thoughts that may lighten sorrow,

Onwards as we pace through life,
Fainting under care or strife,

By the magic of a thought
Every object back is brought
Gayer than it was when real,
Under influence ideal.
In remembrance as a glass,
Let your happy childhood pass;
Dreaming so in fancy's spells,
You still shall hear those old church bells.

INDEX

A

Acrostics: "In the Album of a very Young Lady," 45, 306.
— "To Caroline Maria Applebee," 59, 316.
— "To Cecilia Catherine Lawton," 60, 316.
— "To a Lady who Desired me to Write Her Epitaph," 60, 316.
— "To Her youngest Daughter," 61, 316.
— "To Mrs. F——, on Her Return from Gibraltar," 93, 328.
— "To Esther Field," 94, 328.
— "To Mrs. Williams," 94, 328.
— "To S. F.," 96, 328.
— "To R. Q.," 96, 329.
— "To S. L.," 96, 329.
— "To M. L.," 97, 329.
— "An Acrostic against Acrostics," 97, 329.
— "To S. T.," 99, 330.
— "To Mrs. Sarah Robinson," 100, 330.
— "To Sarah," 100, 330.
— "Acrostic" (Joseph Vale Asbury), 100, 330.
— "To D. A.," 101, 330.
— "To Sarah James of Beguildy," 374.
Addington, Henry, Lamb's epigram on, 102, 334.
Aders, Charles, Lamb's poem to, 85, 326.
Albion, The, and Lamb, 333.
ALBUM VERSES, 43, 304.
— — "In the Album of a Clergyman's Lady," 43, 306.
— — "In the Autograph Book of Mrs. Sergeant W——," 43, 306.
— — "In the Album of Lucy Barton," 44, 306.
— — "In the Album of Miss ——," 44, 306.
— — "In the Album of a very Young Lady," 45, 306.
— — "In the Album of a French Teacher," 45, 306.

ALBUM VERSES, "In the Album of Mrs. Jane Towers," 47, 306.
— — "In My Own Album," 47, 307.
— — "In the Album of Edith S——," 73, 320.
— — "To Dora W——," 73, 321.
— — "In the Album of Rotha Q——," 74, 321.
— — "In the Album of Catherine Orkney," 74, 321.
— — "What is an Album," 92, 327.
— — "The First Leaf of Spring," 92, 328.
— — "To M. L. F.," 94, 328.
— — "To the Book," 95, 328.
— — "On Being Asked to Write in Miss Westwood's Album," 97, 329.
— — "In Miss Westwood's Album," 98, 329.
— — "The Sisters," 98, 329.
— — "Un Solitaire," 99, 330.

(*See also under the heading of* ACROSTICS.)

"Angel Help," 48, 109, 307, 341.
Ann Simmons (Lamb's "Anna"), 278.
Annual Anthology, Lamb's contribution to, 17, 290.
Anti-Jacobin, The, and Lamb, 291.
"ANTONIO," by Godwin, 121, 346.
"Ape, The," 80, 323.
Athenæum, The, Lamb's contributions to, 73, 75, 76, 77, 84, 88, 90.

B

"Ballad Noting the Difference of Rich and Poor," 28, 296.
" — from the German," 27, 295.
" — Singers, The," 63, 317.
Barton, Bernard, his poem to Lamb, 308.
" — — To," 51, 308.
— Lucy, Lamb's verses to, 44, 306.

(377)

INDEX

Beaumont, Francis, quoted, 2, 275.
Bijou, The, Lamb's contribution to, 47.
Blackwood's Magazine, the Lambs' contributions to, 44, 45, 49, 83, 212, 243.
Blakesware and Widford, 281.
BLANK VERSE, by Lloyd and Lamb, 19, 290.
Bourne, Vincent, 316.
—— — Lamb's translations, 61-67.
Burney, Martin, Lamb's sonnet to, 42, 303.
—— Sarah, Lamb's poem to, 82, 325.
Burton, Lamb's imitation of, 296.
Byron, Lord, Lamb's epigram on, 107, 338.
—— — and Lamb, 289.

C

Campbell, J. Dykes, on Helicon, 289.
—— — on JOHN WOODVIL, 350.
Canning, George, Lamb's epigrams on, 102, 105, 106, 334, 336, 337.
Caroline of Brunswick, Lamb's championship of, 105, 107, 336, 337, 338.
Carter, Ben, of Blakesware, 70, 319.
"Catechist, The Young," 52, 310.
Champion, The, Lamb's contributions to, 82, 104, 105, 106, 330-1.
"Change, The," 76, 321.
Chatterton, Thomas, 288.
"Cheap Gifts," 77, 322.
"Childhood," 8, 284.
"Christening, The," 49, 307.
City champion, epigram on, 334.
Clarkes, the Cowden, 306.
Coleridge, S. T., Lamb's dedication to, 1, 275.
—— — his POEMS ON VARIOUS SUBJECTS, 3, 276.
—— — his POEMS, 7, 282.
—— — and Sara, Lamb's lines to, 15, 288.
—— — his "REMORSE," 125, 347.
—— — his alteration of Lamb's sonnets, 277, 279, 280.
—— — on Lamb's sonnet "We were two pretty babes," 284.
—— — in Gillray's cartoon, 291.
—— — and "The Old Familiar Faces," 294.
—— — his translation of "Thekla's Song," 296.
—— Sara, her Latinity, 83, 325.
"Composed at Midnight," 24, 294.
"Confidant, The," by Crabbe, adapted by Lamb, 243, 373.
"Cook, To David," 64, 317.
Cornwall, Barry. *See* PROCTER, B. W.
Cowley, Abraham, quoted, 284.

"Cowper, To the Poet," 14, 287.
Crabbe, George, Lamb's adaptation of, 243, 373.

D

Da Vinci, Leonardo, poems upon, 38, 39, 300, 301.
Day, Matthew, Lamb's epigram on, 344.
Dedication of Lamb's WORKS to Coleridge, 1, 275.
—— of Lamb's POEMS, 1797, to his sister, 283.
—— of Lamb's ALBUM VERSES to Moxon, 304.
Defoe, Daniel, 67, 318.
"Dialogue between a Mother and Child," 31, 298.
"Divine Subjects, Fancy Employed on," 9, 285.
Dix, Margaret, Lamb's epitaph on, 343.
Dockwra, Tom, of Widford, 71, 320.
Dorrell, William, the swindler, 71, 318, 320.
"Douglas, The Tomb of," 9, 285.
Drake, Onesimus, of the East India House, 343.
"Dramatic Fragment," 79, 322.
Druitt, Mary, Lamb's epitaph upon, 80, 322.
"Dying Lover," 79, 360.

E

East India House epigrams, 342.
Election verses, possibly by Lamb, 341.
Englishman's Magazine, Lamb's contributions to, 85, 107.
Epigrams possibly by Lamb, 331, 334.
Epilogue to Godwin's "ANTONIO," 121, 346.
—— to Siddons' "TIME'S A TELL-TALE," 123, 347.
—— to Kenney's "DEBTOR AND CREDITOR," 126, 348.
—— to an amateur performance of "RICHARD II.," 128, 348.
—— to Knowles' "THE WIFE," 130, 349.
"Epitaph on a Dog," 62, 317.
"—— on a Young Lady," 80, 322.
Examiner, The, Lamb's contributions to, 55, 102, 103, 104.
"Existence, Considered in itself, no Blessing," 89, 327.

F

"Faces, The Old Familiar," 23, 294.
"Family Name, The," 41, 302.

INDEX

"Fancy Employed on Divine Subjects," 9, 285.
"Farewell to Tobacco, A," 32, 298.
FARMER, PRISCILLA, POEMS ON THE DEATH OF, 5, 280.
Fast Day, Lamb's epigrams on, 109, 341.
"FAULKENER," by Godwin, 123, 346.
"Female Orators, The," 67, 317.
Fenwick, John, editor of *The Albion*, 333.
Field, family, the poems to, 93, 94, 328.
— Mrs., Lamb's grandmother, 5, 281.
Flecknoe, Richard, adapted, 300.
"Free Thoughts on Several Eminent Composers," 77, 322.
Frend, Sophia, Lamb's poems to, 95, 96, 328.
Frere, John Hookham, Lamb's epigram on, 102, 334.
"Friend, To a," 16, 289.
Fryer, Miss, Lamb's poem for, 373, 374.

G

George IV., Lamb's epigrams on, 102, 103, 104, 105, 106, 334-338.
Gifford, William, Lamb's sonnet upon, 104, 335.
Gillray, James, his cartoons, 291.
"Gipsy's Malison, The," 57, 313.
Godwin, William, his "ANTONIO," 121, 346.
— — his "FAULKENER," 123, 346.
Goethe on Lamb's "Family Name," 302.
"Going or Gone," 70, 318.
"Grandame, The," 5, 280.
GRAY, ROSAMUND, quoted, 293.

H

Hamilton of Bangor quoted, 284.
Hardy, Lieutenant, Lamb's poem to, 84, 326.
"Harmony in Unlikeness," 54, 311.
Haydon, B. R., Lamb's verses to, 82, 324.
Hazlitt, William, on Lamb in the country, 311.
— — on JOHN WOODVIL, 367.
— — on "MR. H.," 371.
— W. C., quoted, 307.
Helen, 26, 295.
Helicon and Hippocrene confused, 288-9.
"Hercules Pacificatus," 85, 326.
Hessey, Archdeacon, his memories of Lamb, 339.
"Hester," 30, 298.

Hippocrene and Helicon confused, 288-9.
Hogsflesh, a well-known name, 370.
Hone, William, Lamb's poem to, 58, 315.
— — his publications, Lamb's contributions to, 55, 58, 70, 76, 85.
Hood, Thomas, his child's death, 307.
"Housekeeper, The," 66, 317.
Hunt, Leigh, Lamb's poem to, 83, 325.
— — on "Composed at Midnight," 294.
— — and Lamb's poem, "To T. L. H.," 300.
— Thornton, Lamb's poem to, 35, 300.
Hutchinson, Mr. Thomas, on JOHN WOODVIL, 367.
"Hypochondriacus," 27, 296.

I

"In Tabulam Eximii . . ." 82, 324.
Indicator, The, Lamb's contributions to, 62, 83.
Isola, Agostino, 310.
— Emma, Lamb's poems to, 53, 54, 83, 99, 310, 311, 325, 330.

J

Jerdan, William, Lamb's epigram on, 109, 340.
JOHN WOODVIL, 131, 350.
— — volume, 1802, poems in, 26, 295.

K

Kelly, Frances Maria (Fanny), and Lamb, 40, 302, 311.
" — To Miss," 40, 302.
Kenney, James, his "DEBTOR AND CREDITOR," 126, 348.
Knight, Ann, 309.
Knowles, James Sheridan, 58, 315.
— — — his comedy "THE WIFE," 129, 349.

L

"Lady's Sapphic, A," 333.
Lamb, Charles, dedicates his *WORKS* to Coleridge, 1, 275.
— — at the Salutation Inn, 2, 275.
— — his contributions to Coleridge's *POEMS*, 1796, 3.
— — his praise of Mrs. Siddons, 3, 276.
— — his partnership with Coleridge, 3, 276-7.
— — his love poems, 3, 4, 7, 277-280, 283.
— — verses on his grandmother, 5, 280.

380 INDEX

Lamb, Charles, his contributions to Coleridge's *Poems*, 1797, 7, 282.
— — his poems to his sister, 8, 16, 22, 283, 289, 294.
— — his verses to Charles Lloyd, 11, 19, 286, 291.
— — his verses to Cowper, 14, 287.
— — his Bristol holiday refused, 15, 288.
— — his confusion of Helicon and Hippocrene, 15, 288-9.
— — his contributions to *Blank Verse*, 1798, 19, 290.
— — his lines on his aunt, 19, 292.
— — his lines on his father, 19, 292.
— — his grief for his mother's death, 20, 22, 292, 293.
— — his "Old Familiar Faces," 23, 294.
— — Mary Lamb laughs at him in "Helen," 26, 295.
— — his translation from the German, 27, 295.
— — his imitations of Burton, 27, 28, 296.
— — his *Works*, 30, 298.
— — his lines on Hester Savory, 30, 298.
— — his "Farewell to Tobacco," 32, 298.
— — his lines to Thornton Leigh Hunt, 35, 300.
— — his sonnets to Miss Kelly, 40, 55, 302, 311.
— — his sonnet on his name, 41, 302.
— — his sonnet to his brother, 41, 303.
— — his sonnet to Martin Burney, 42, 303.
— — his *Album Verses*, 43, 304.
— — his poem on Hood's child, 49, 307.
— — his verses to Bernard Barton, 51, 308.
— — his verses on Emma Isola, 53, 54, 75, 310, 311, 321.
— — his sonnets on "Work" and "Leisure," 55, 56, 312.
— — his sonnets to Samuel Rogers, 56, 90, 313, 327.
— — his sonnet on the sheep stealer, 57, 313.
— — his sonnet to Barry Cornwall, 57, 314.
— — his lines to Sheridan Knowles, 58, 315.
— — his quatrains to Hone, 58, 315.
— — his skill in acrostics, 59-61, 93-97, 315, 328.
— — his translations from Bourne, 61-67, 316.
— — his "Ode to the Treadmill," 67, 317.
— — his poem on old Widford friends, 70, 318.

Lamb, Charles, his *Poetical Works*, 1836, 73, 320.
— — his sonnet to Stothard, 75, 321.
— — his lines to Moxon on his marriage, 75, 321.
— — his poems on Louisa Martin, 76, 80, 321, 323.
— — his "Free Thoughts on Composers," 77, 322.
— — his epitaph on Mary Druitt, 80, 322.
— — his verses to Haydon, 82, 324.
— — his sonnet to Sarah Burney, 82, 325.
— — his sonnet to Leigh Hunt, 83, 325.
— — his lines to Charles Aders, 85, 326.
— — his translations from Palingenius, 88, 89, 326, 327.
— — his lines to Clara Novello, 90, 327.
— — eight new poems, 99-101, 330, 373, 374.
— — his political epigrams, 102-108, 330-339.
— — and Sir James Mackintosh, 102, 333.
— — his attacks on Canning, 102-106, 291, 334, 336-338.
— — his contempt for George IV., 102-106, 334-338.
— — his attack on Gifford, 104, 335.
— — on the spy system, 105, 336.
— — his defence of Caroline of Brunswick, 105, 106, 107, 336, 337, 338.
— — epigram on Lord Byron, 107, 338.
— — writes for Merchant Taylors' boys, 108, 109, 339.
— — burlesque of "Angel Help," 109, 341.
— — his "Satan in Search of a Wife," 110, 344.
— — as a writer of prologues and epilogues, 121-130, 346-349.
— — as a playwright, 131, 177, 180, 212, 243, 330, 368, 372, 373.
— — and Coleridge's pamphlet of sonnets, 278.
— — his dedication of his verses to Mary Lamb, 283.
— — and *The Anti-Jacobin*, 291.
— — and Coleridge's "Wallenstein," 295.
— — and Dr. Parr, 299.
— — his dedication to Moxon, 304.
— — attacked by *Literary Gazette*, 304.
— — defended by Southey in *The Times*, 305.
— — frames a picture with Hood, 308.
— — and Henry Meyer, 310.
— — and the thought of death, 312.
— — his letter from Samuel Rogers, 313.

INDEX

Lamb, Charles, on "The Gipsy's Malison," 313.
— — and Thomas Moore, 314.
— — Mary Lamb's poem on him, 322.
— — his farewell to albums, 329.
— — Archdeacon Hessey's memories of him, 339.
— — verses for the Newark election, 341.
— — his epigrams on India House clerks, 343.
— — his generosity to Moxon, 344.
— — his history of JOHN WOODVIL, 350.
— — on the title of "Pride's Cure," 353.
— — sends JOHN WOODVIL to Manning, 355.
— — on the plot of "MR. H.," 369.
— — hisses his own play, 369.
— — on nonsense, 373.
— Elizabeth, Lamb's mother, 20, 22, 292, 293, 294.
— John, Lamb's father, 20, 292.
— — Lamb's brother, sonnet to, 41, 303.
— Mary, poems by, 26, 31, 36, 38, 39, 83, 98, 295, 298, 300, 301, 322, 325, 329, 332-3.
— — Lamb's poems to, 8, 16, 22, 283, 289, 294.
— — dedication to, 283.
— — on the death of John Wordsworth, 301.
— — her Latin pupils, 325.
— Sarah (Hetty), Lamb's aunt, 19, 292.
Landon, L. E., Lamb on, 327.
Latin epigram by Lamb, 109, 339.
— verses to Haydon, Lamb's, 82, 324.
"Leisure," 56, 312.
Lewis, "Gentleman," on "MR. H.," 371.
Lilley, John, of Blakesware, 70, 319.
"Lines Addressed . . . to Sara and S. T. C.," 15, 288.
" — Suggested by a Picture of Two Females," 38, 300.
" — on the Same Picture being Removed to Make Place for the Portrait of a Lady by Titian," 38, 301.
" — on Da Vinci's 'Virgin of the Rocks'" (two poems), 39, 301.
" — Addressed to Lieutenant Hardy," 84, 326.
" — for a Monument," 84, 326.
Literary Gazette, Lamb's epigram on, 109, 340.
— — and ALBUM VERSES, 304.
"Living without God in the World," 17, 290.
Lloyd, Charles, POEMS ON THE DEATH OF PRISCILLA FARMER, 5, 280.
— — Lamb's poems to, 11, 19, 286, 291.

Lloyd, Charles, his *BLANK VERSE*, written with Lamb, 19, 290.
— — his "Lines on the Fast," 290.
— — and Sophia Pemberton, 291.
— — and JOHN WOODVIL, 351, 353, 368.
London Magazine, Lamb's contributions to, 56, 57, 58, 79, 80, 105.
"Love will Come," 373, 374.

M

Mackintosh, Sir James, Lamb's verses to, 102, 333.
Manning, Thomas, and JOHN WOODVIL, 353.
Marlowe, Christopher, adapted, 300.
Martin, Louisa, Lamb's poems on, 76, 80, 323.
Massinger, Philip, quoted, 282.
Merchant Taylors' School, epigrams by Lamb, 108, 109, 339.
Meyer, Henry, 310.
Mitford, John, 309.
Molineaux the pugilist, 217, 372.
Monthly Magazine, The, Lamb's contributions to, 8, 14, 15, 16, 19.
Morning Chronicle, Lamb's contributions to, 55, 82.
— Post, Lamb's contributions to, 80, 102, 334.
Moxon, Edward, Lamb's poems to, 75, 321.
— — his career, 304.
— — Lamb's dedication to, 304.
"MR. H.," 180, 368.
— — in America, 371.
Music, Lamb and, 77, 322, 327.

N

Nelson, epigram on, 334.
New Monthly Magazine, Lamb's contribution to, 48.
— Times, Lamb's contribution to, 67, 107, 338.
Newark election, Lamb's connection with, 341.
Newton's *Principia*, 66, 317.
"Nonsense Verses," 109, 341.
Novello, Clara, Lamb's poems to, 90, 98, 327, 329.
— the three sisters, 98, 329.

O

"Old Familiar Faces, The," 23, 294.
"On a Deaf and Dumb Artist," 65, 317.

INDEX

"On a Sepulchral Statue of an Infant Sleeping," 61, 317.
"On an Infant Dying as soon as Born," 49, 307.
"On the Sight of Swans in Kensington Garden," 40, 302.
Orkney, Catherine, Lamb's poem to, 74, 321.

P

Palingenius, Lamb's translations of, 88, 89, 326, 327.
Parr, Dr., and Lamb, 299.
"Parting Speech of the Celestial Messenger," 88, 326.
"Pawnbroker's Daughter, The," 212, 372.
Pemberton, Sophia, and Charles Lloyd, 291.
Pichot, Amédée, his translation of "The Family Name," 302.
"Pindaric Ode to the Tread Mill," 67, 317.
Pitt, William, epigrams on, 334.
Plumer, Mrs., of Gilston, 319.
POEMS ON VARIOUS SUBJECTS, Lamb's contributions to, 3, 276.
Poetical Recreations of "The Champion," 331.
POETICAL WORKS OF CHARLES LAMB, 320.
"Pride's Cure," first name for JOHN WOODVIL, 353.
Procter, B. W. (Barry Cornwall), 57, 296, 314.
Prologue to Godwin's "FAULKENER," 123, 346.
— — Coleridge's "REMORSE," 125, 347.
— — Knowles' "THE WIFE," 129, 349.

Q

"Quatrains to the Editor of the Every-Day Book," 58, 315.
Quillinan, Rotha, Lamb's poems to, 74, 96, 321, 329.

R

Raphael's cartoons at Buckingham House, epigram on, 331.
Reflector, The, Lamb's contribution to, 32, 298.
"Repentance, A Vision of," 12, 286.
"RICHARD II.," Lamb's epilogue for, 128, 348.
Rigg family, the, tragedy of, 326.
"Rival Bells, The," 62, 317.
Rogers, Daniel, Lamb's sonnet on, 56, 313.

Rogers, Samuel, on his brother's death, 313.
"— To Samuel," 56, 313.
ROSAMUND GRAY quoted, 293.
Rutter, Mr. J. A., and "The Old Familiar Faces," 294.

S

"Sabbath Bells, The," 9, 285.
"St. Crispin to Mr. Gifford," 104, 335.
"Salome," 36, 300.
Salutation Inn, 2, 275.
"SATAN IN SEARCH OF A WIFE," 110, 344.
Schiller translated by Lamb, 27, 295.
"Self-Enchanted, The," 76, 321.
"She is Going," 53, 310.
Siddons, Mrs., Lamb's sonnet to, 3, 276.
— J. H., on Lamb, 343.
— Henry, his "TIME'S A TELL-TALE," 123, 347.
Simmons, Ann (Lamb's "Anna"), 278.
"Sir Toby Fillpot"—epigram, 334.
Smoking, Lamb on, 32, 298.
Solomon, Dr., of the Balm of Gilead, 106, 337.
Sonnet: "As when a child," 3, 276.
— "Was it some sweet device," 3, 277.
— "Methinks how dainty sweet," 4, 279.
— "O! I could laugh," 4, 279.
— "When last I roved," 7, 283.
— "A timid grace," 7, 283.
— "If from my lips," 8, 283.
— "We were two pretty," 8, 284.
— "The Lord of Life," 14, 286.
— "To a Friend," 16, 289.
— "To Miss Kelly," 40, 302.
— "On the Sight of Swans in Kensington Garden," 40, 302.
— "The Family Name," 41, 302.
— "To John Lamb, Esq.," 41, 303.
— "To Martin Charles Burney, Esq.," 42, 303.
— "Harmony in Unlikeness," 54, 311.
— "Written at Cambridge," 55, 311.
— "To a Celebrated Female Performer in the 'Blind Boy,'" 55, 311.
— "Work," 55, 312.
— "Leisure," 56, 312.
— "To Samuel Rogers, Esq.," 56, 313.
— "The Gipsy's Malison," 57, 313.
— "To the Author of Poems Published under the Name of Barry Cornwall," 57, 314.
— "In the Album of Edith S——," 73, 320.
— "To Dora W——," 73, 321.

INDEX

Sonnet: "In the Album of Rotha Q——," 74, 321.
— "To T. Stothard, Esq.," 75, 321.
— "O lift with reverent hand," 77, 322.
— "To Miss Burney," 82, 325.
— "To Samuel Rogers, Esq., on the New Edition of his *Pleasures of Memory*," 90, 327.
— "To Louisa Morgan," 101, 330.
— "St. Crispin to Mr. Gifford," 104, 335.
— "To Matthew Wood, Esq.," 105, 336.
— "O gentle look," by Coleridge and Lamb, 277.
Southey, Edith, Lamb's poem to, 73, 320.
— Robert, in Gillray's cartoon, 291.
— — his defence of Lamb, 305.
— — and JOHN WOODVIL, 351.
Spy system, Lamb's verses on, 105, 336.
Stothard, Thomas, Lamb's poem to, 75, 321.
Sturms, Captain, of the East India House, 343.
Suidas, Lamb's adaptation of, 85, 326.

T

"Thekla's Song," by Schiller, 27, 295.
Thelwall, John, and *The Champion*, 332.
"Three Graves, The," 105, 336.
Times, The, Lamb's contributions to, 90, 108.
"To a Young Friend" (two poems), 53, 54, 310, 311.
"To a Young Lady," 16, 290.
"To Bernard Barton," 51, 308.
"To C. Aders, Esq.," 85, 326.
"To Charles Lloyd," 11, 286.
— — — (second poem), 19, 291.
"To Clara N——," 90, 327.
"To David Cook," 64, 317.
"To Emma Learning Latin," 83, 325.
"To John Lamb, Esq.," 41, 303.
"To Margaret W——," 91, 327.
"To Martin Charles Burney, Esq.," 42, 303.
"To Miss Burney," 82, 325.
"To My Friend *The Indicator*," 83, 325.
"To R. S. Knowles, Esq.," 58, 315.
"To Samuel Rogers, Esq.," (two poems), 56, 90, 313, 327.
"To Sir James Mackintosh," 102, 333.
"To T. L. H.," 35, 300.
"To the Author of Poems Published under the Name of Barry Cornwall," 57, 314.
"To the Poet Cowper," 14, 287.
"To T. Stothard, Esq.," 75, 321.
"Tobacco, A Farewell to," 32, 298.
"Tomb of Douglas, The," 9, 285.
Towers, Mrs. Jane, Lamb's verses to, 47, 306.
Treadmill, the, Lamb's ode to, 67, 317.
"Triumph of the Whale, The," 103, 335.
Tween, Mrs., on Lamb, 319.
"Twelfth-Night Characters," 102, 334.

V

"Vision of Repentance, A," 12, 286.

W

Wagstaff, Timothy, of the East India House, 343.
"Wallenstein," ballad from, 27, 295.
Wawd (or Wodd) of the East India House, 344.
Westwood, Frances, the Lambs' poems to, 97, 98, 329.
"Whale, The Triumph of the," 103, 335.
"What is an Album?" 92, 327.
Wheatley, Kitty, 70, 319.
Widford and Blakesware, 70, 281, 318.
"Wife's Trial, The," 243, 373.
Wilde, Sergeant (afterwards Lord Truro), and Lamb, 341.
— — Mrs., Lamb's verses to, 43, 306.
William IV., Lamb's epigram on, 108, 339.
Williams, Mrs., of Fornham, and family, 43, 45, 60, 61, 94, 306, 316, 328.
"Witch, The," 177, 368.
Wood, Matthew, Lamb's sonnet to, 105, 336.
WOODVIL, JOHN, poems in, 26, 295.
Wordsworth, Dora, Lamb's poem to, 73, 321.
— John, lines on his death, 301.
"Work," 55, 312.
WORKS, 1818, dedication of, 1, 275.
— — poems in, 30, 298.
"Written a Year after the Events," 20, 292.
"Written at Cambridge," 55, 311.
"Written on Christmas Day," 22, 294.
"Written on the Day of my Aunt's Funeral," 19, 292.
"Written soon after the Preceding Poem," 22, 293.

Y

"Young Catechist, The," 52, 310.
"Young Friend, To a" (two poems), 53, 54, 310, 311.
"Young Lady, To a," 16, 290.

INDEX OF FIRST LINES

A Heart which felt unkindness, yet complained not, 323.
A passing glance was all I caught of thee, 74.
A stranger, and alone, I past those scenes, 19.
A timid grace sits trembling in her eye, 7.
A tuneful challenge rings from either side, 62.
A weeping Londoner am I, 220.
Adsciscit sibi divitias et opes alienas, 109.
Alas! how am I chang'd! Where be the tears, 20.
All are not false. I knew a youth who died, 79.
All unadvised, and in an evil hour, 104.
Alone, obscure, without a friend, 11.
An Album is a Banquet: from the store, 73.
An Album is a Garden, not for show, 43.
An Ape is but a trivial beast, 80.
An author who has given you all delight, 123.
And hath thy blameless life become, 65.
Array'd—a half-angelic sight, 49.
As when a child on some long winter's night, 3.
At Eton School brought up with dull boys, 102.
Beautiful Infant, who dost keep, 61.
Beneath this slab lies Matthew Day, 344.
Bound for the port of matrimonial bliss, 123.
Bright spirits have arisen to grace the Burney name, 82.
But now time warns (my mission at an end), 88.
By crooked arts and actions sinister, 334.
By Enfield lanes, and Winchmore's verdant hill, 54.
By myself walking, 27.
Canadia! boast no more the toils, 74.
Caroline glides smooth in verse, 59.
Choral service, solemn chanting, 60.

Ci gît the remains of Margaret Dix, 343.
Close by the ever-burning brimstone beds, 105.
Consummate Artist, whose undying name, 75.
Cowper, I thank my God, that thou art heal'd, 14.
Crown me a cheerful goblet, while I pray, 53.
Divided praise, Lady, to you we owe, 101.
Don't be afraid, tho' cas'd, such armour bright in, 334.
Droop not, dear Emma, dry those falling tears, 83.
Envy not the wretched Poet, 97.
Esther, holy name and sweet, 94.
External gifts of fortune, or of face, 54.
False world, 126.
Fine merry franions, 70.
For much good-natured verse received from thee, 64.
For their elder Sister's hair, 53.
Forgive me, Burney, if to thee these late, 42.
Freemen! do not be beguil'd, 342.
Fresh clad from heaven in robes of white, 47.
Friend of my earliest years and childish days, 16.
Friendliest of men, Aders, I never come, 85.
From broken visions of perturbed rest, 24.
Go little Poem, and present, 94.
Grace Joanna here doth lie, 60.
Great Newton's self, to whom the world's in debt, 66.
Guard thy feelings, pretty Vestal, 374.
Had I a power, Lady, to my will, 43.
Hard is the heart that does not melt with ruth, 16.
Here lies the body of Timothy Wagstaff, 343.
Here lieth the body of Captain Sturms, 343.

VOL. V.—25

INDEX OF FIRST LINES

High-born Helen, round your dwelling, 26.
His namesake, born of Jewish breeder, 106.
Hold on thy course uncheck'd, heroic Wood! 105.
How blest is he who in his age, exempt, 101.
How many wasting, many wasted years, 94.
I am a widow'd thing, now thou art gone, 22.
I had a sense in dreams of a beauty rare, 76.
I have had playmates, I have had companions, 23.
I like you, and your book, ingenuous Hone! 58.
I put my night-cap on my head, 102.
I saw a famous fountain, in my dream, 12.
I saw where in the shroud did lurk, 49.
I was not train'd in Academic bowers, 55.
If from my lips some angry accents fell, 8.
If we have sinn'd in paring down a name, 180.
Implored for verse, I send you what I can, 45.
In a costly palace Youth goes clad in gold, 28.
In Christian world Mary the garland wears, 73.
In days of yore, ere early Greece, 85.
In my poor mind it is most sweet to muse, 8.
In one great man we view with odds, 104.
Inspire my spirit, Spirit of De Foe, 67.
Io! Pæan! Io! sing, 103.
Jane, you are welcome from the barren Rock, 93.
John, you were figuring in the gay career, 41.
Joy to unknown Josepha who, I hear, 45.
Judgements are about us thoroughly, 100.
Ladies, ye've seen how Guzman's consort died, 121.
Lady Unknown, who crav'st from me Unknown, 47.
Laura, too partial to her friends' enditing, 108.
Lazy-bones, lazy-bones, wake up, and peep! 109.
Least Daughter, but not least beloved, of Grace, 61.
Let hate, or grosser heats, their foulness mask, 57.
Little Book, surnamed of *white*, 44.

Little Casket! Storehouse rare, 95.
Louisa, serious grown and mild, 76.
Manners, they say, by climate alter not, 107.
Margaret, in happy hour, 91.
Maternal lady with the virgin grace, 39.
May the Babylonish curse, 32.
Methinks how dainty sweet it were, reclin'd, 4.
Model of thy parent dear, 35.
Much speech obscures the sense; the soul of wit, 108.
Must I write with pen unwilling, 97.
My feeble Muse, that fain her best wou'd, 97.
Mystery of God! thou brave and beauteous world, 17.
Nigh London's famous Bridge, a Gate more famed, 67.
Not a woman, child, or man in, 106.
Now the calm evening hastily approaches, 332.
O! I could laugh to hear the midnight wind, 4.
O Lady, lay your costly robes aside, 31.
O lift with reverent hand that tarnish'd flower, 77.
Of all that act, the hardest task is theirs, 128.
Of these sad truths consideration had, 89.
Off with Briareus, and his hundred hands, 334.
On Emma's honest brow we read display'd, 98.
On English ground I calculated once, 109.
On the green hill top, 5.
Once on a charger there was laid, 36.
One summer night Sir Francis, as it chanced, 177.
Pity the sorrows of a poor LEEDS man, 341.
Poor Irus' faithful wolf-dog here I lie, 62.
Princeps his rent from tinneries draws, 102.
Queen-bird that sittest on thy shining nest, 40.
Quid vult iste equitans? et quid oclit ista virorum, 82.
Rare artist! who with half thy tools, or none, 55.
Rogers, of all the men that I have known, 56.
Roi's wife of Brunswick Oëls! 106.
Rotha, how in numbers light, 96.
Sarah, blest wife of "Terah's faithful Son," 99.
Sarah,—your other name I know not, 100.

INDEX OF FIRST LINES

Shall I praise a face unseen, 96.
Sleep hath treasures worth retracing, 374.
Small beauty to your Book my lines can lend, 98.
Solemn Legends we are told, 96.
Solitary man, around thee, 99.
Some cry up Haydn, some Mozart, 77.
Some poets by poetic law, 46.
Soul-breathing verse, thy gentlest guise put on, 100.
Stern heaven in anger no poor wretch invades, 349.
Such goodness in your face doth shine, 44.
"Suck, baby, suck, mother's love grows by giving, 57.
Tears are for lighter griefs. Man weeps the doom, 84.
The Ancients suck'd cruelty e'en to the dregs, 331.
The cheerful sabbath bells, wherever heard, 9.
The clouds are blackening, the storms threatening, 27.
The Devil was sick and queasy of late, 111.
The frugal snail, with fore-cast of repose, 66.
The Gods have made me most unmusical, 90.
The Lady Blanch, regardless of all her lovers' fears, 38.
The Lord of Life shakes off his drowsihed, 14.
The reason why my brother's so severe, 322.
The truant Fancy was a wanderer ever, 9.
There are, I am told, who sharply criticise, 125.
They talk of time, and of time's galling yoke, 56.
This rare tablet doth include, 48.
Thou fragile, filmy, gossamery thing, 92.
Thou should'st have longer liv'd, and to the grave, 22.
Thou too art dead, * * *! very kind, 19.
Though thou'rt like Judas, an apostate black, 102.
Time-mouldering crosses, gemm'd with imagery, 107.

'Tis a Book kept by modern Young Ladies for show, 92.
'Tis pleasant, lolling in our elbow chair, 84.
To gratify his people's wish, 106.
To name a Day for general prayer and fast, 109.
To the memory of Dr. Onesimus Drake, 343.
Twelve years ago I knew thee, Knowles, and then, 58.
Two miracles at once! Compell'd by fate, 108.
Under this cold marble stone, 80.
Untoward fate no luckless wight invades, 129.
Was it so hard a thing? I did but ask, 15.
Was it some sweet device of Faery, 3.
We were two pretty babes, the youngest she, 8.
What makes a happy wedlock? What has fate, 75.
What reason first imposed thee, gentle name, 41.
What rider's that? and who those myriads bringing, 82.
What Wawd knows, God knows, 344.
When first our Bard his simple will express'd, 130.
When her son, her Douglas died, 9.
When last I roved these winding wood-walks green, 7.
When last you left your Woodbridge pretty, 51.
When maidens such as Hester die, 30.
When the nightingale sings in yon harbour so snug, 334.
When thy gay book hath paid its proud devoirs, 90.
Where seven fair Streets to one tall Column draw, 63.
While this tawny Ethiop prayeth, 52.
While young John runs to greet, 39.
Who art thou, fair one, who usurp'st the place, 38.
Who first invented work, and bound the free, 55.
Why is he wandering on the sea? 301.
Ye Politicians, tell me, pray, 103.
You are not, Kelly, of the common strain, 40.
Your easy Essays indicate a flow, 83.